VAGABUNDO

STEVEN-JOHN TAIT

First Published in 2019

Instagram: @vagabundobook @stevenjohn.tait
stevenjohntait@gmail.com
stevenjohntait.com

Typeset by RefineCatch Limited, www.refinecatch.com
Printed and bound in Great Britain by Clays Ltd, Elcograf S.p.A.

VAGABUNDO

VAGABOND, TRAMP, DRIFTER, WANDERER, VAGRANT

It was a distant sound... from childhood... from the orphanage

1

Bruno tied the desert scarf around his face to cover all but his eyes in case they came close enough to look. At the water's edge he removed his sandals and let the lapping tide cool his feet. He'd walked all morning, spotting the strange kites as soon as he got onto the beach. Massive and crescent-shaped, black against the blue sky, they zigzagged on the cross-shore wind, dragging riders across the ocean. Spray rose in arcs from boards strapped to the riders' feet, bursting sunlight into all the colours of the rainbow.

Beyond these kite-surfers, *jangada* fishing boats rocked on the swell. They didn't have engines and their sails were furled around curved masts.

'Hook and line fishermen,' he said to himself as one hauled a shimmering yellowfin aboard. A second clubbed it as it beat itself senseless against the shallow hull. 'Just like the other settlements. Father and son affairs, no doubt about it.' He looked back to the surfers, watched how they manipulated their kites and manoeuvred their boards. The look on their tanned, unburdened faces was of complete control.

He took his Rolleiflex from the perished leather case tied to his neck and snapped a photograph of them, slipped on his sandals and kept walking. A few hundred kilometres further, past the last coastal city and he'd be done with it all.

He'd pick up a vein of the great Amazon River and follow it into the heart of the forest.

Up ahead, the coconut palms that lined the beach came to a stop and a hill dotted with cacti sloped down to a cluster of rocks that reached the water. The sound of reggae music set his heart racing. They only ever played gospel at the other settlements.

The tide was low enough to get around the rocks and he found himself at the opening of a bay, where a few *jangadas* lay beached. Behind the rocks were kiosk-style bars. People were milling around, gathering at tables and relaxing on sunloungers.

'*La puta madre!*' he said, a mixture of exhilaration and terror sweeping through him. 'A holiday resort!'

The voice of Peter Tosh called out from a speaker at the first bar, Natiruts from the next, Trio Mocotó from another. There were masses of people not ten metres from him. Real people, city people, not the simple-minded, end of the road, hallelujah, Jesus Christ people he'd seen at the other settlements. He couldn't help staring. Conversation, laughter, music. How many months had it been since the last *real* town?

Waiters in *abada* trousers and pressed T-shirts moved around lighting cigarettes, serving drinks and collecting bills. An oiled-up beauty, all jelly breasts and backside, rolled onto her stomach. He bit his lip and walked on. The smell of sunscreen, cigarette smoke and fresh cotton lingered.

Bruno smiled under his scarf. People had noticed him and were staring, but not in the way they would have if the scarf was off. It was nice to take them all in without that look of judgement on their faces.

At the final kiosk a barman scalped a coconut, stuck in a straw and handed it to a blonde wearing only a thong. The sight of her tanned, glistening flesh had Bruno reaching for his beard, forgetting the scarf was in the way. He knew he'd never have a woman again; there had only been one for him, but she was long gone, and how could he *not* look at that?

'This could've been you,' he whispered. 'A normal, happy person on holiday.' As soon as he spoke, a voice in his head replied: *Don't stop. You've been through this already and it's time to move on.* He'd turned his back on society long ago, and after what he'd done that night in Santi's apartment, he'd left himself no chance of return.

At the opposite end of the bay a dune rose like a pyramid, dwarfing everything in sight. A 4×4 appeared from behind it, cut across the beach towards him and turned up a street wide enough for four of them abreast.

The street was lined with *caju* trees. Their false fruit hung in bunches under broad, evergreen leaves. He looked down at his arms, following the white lines around the faded ink tattoos, lines he'd drawn using acid from *caju* nut shells. He didn't do that kind of thing any more. There'd be no more self-destruction.

Maybe I can do it this time, he thought. *I could rest here for a bit and take a look around, fill up on water if nothing else.* But he wasn't sure. Their eyes were on him already, standing alone like a fool with a scarf wrapped around his face, a ragged backpack cluttered with knives and bush-tools, and shorts so patched up it was impossible to tell their original material.

This place didn't seem like any other he'd seen since setting off, and nothing like the hellish cities of the south, so why not take a look? Maybe things would be different. There'd be no more chances after this.

The people won't be different though, the voice said. *They never are.* To them he wouldn't be an outdoorsman, an adventurer, a pioneer. Even he couldn't think of himself as such. He was a tramp, a coward and a failure.

He walked the length of Main Street, taking in all it had to offer. The restaurants and bars had wooden patios and facades painted in all colours. Billboards in front of a tourist centre promoted dune buggy tours and donkey rides. There were gift shops, a barbershop and a butcher.

'A bookshop!' he said, stopping under its sign: *A Gata Preta*.

He looked through the window at the stacked shelves until a slender woman with coarse hair sticking out like tobacco strands opened the door and fixed her eyes on him. He stepped back and moved on.

Dune buggies puttered about, shuttling surfers to and from the beach. Down narrow side streets people at cafes sipped from ceramic cups while playing cards or dominoes on the slatted wooden tables. All were fashionably dressed in branded T-shirts, shorts and sandals.

There was no asphalt in sight, only sand. Buildings were never more than three storeys tall, and all the houses had small gardens teeming with tropical flowers and plants. The smell of charred meat, cheese and potatoes emanated from restaurants, drawing saliva from either side of his tongue. He swallowed it down.

How had he not seen this place on the map? He knew a couple of fishing settlements were coming up, but those barely deserved a mark. Compared to them, this place should have had a neon light pointing at it.

A group of male tourists passed, and with an effort that drew sweat from his brow, he forced himself to call out to them. 'What's the name of this place?' he asked in Portuguese, instead of his native Spanish.

Without breaking stride, they exchanged glances with each other. 'Brisas,' one replied, and added in a hushed tone to the others, 'Guy doesn't even know where he is.'

'Neither did you last night!'

'After twenty caipirinhas!' he said, his voice raised above the laughter.

Bruno dropped the bag from his shoulder and pulled out his map. All he could see were those two small dots: Jeri and Jinguba. No sign of a Brisas anywhere. It was an old map, but surely a town like this didn't pop up overnight?

Down an empty side street he found an oversized faucet, filled his bottle with water, and drank as he walked. He arrived at the back of a drystone building and took a look around it, inhaling the lemon scent of the bushes that grew at the base of its walls. From a brass bell fixed to the highest section, a fist-thick frayed rope dangled alongside of a pair of black, salt-eroded doors. Out in front, a driftwood cross cast no shadow under the midday sun. A palm leaf parcel lay at its base. He crouched to look at the cowrie shells, flowers, rice and translucent beads inside it.

A guitar strummed to his right. He turned and saw a crowded camping area. 'Travellers,' he said. Tents were set up in circles around campfires. People in loose, Aztec-print clothing lazed in folding chairs, sat cross-legged on the sand, stood talking. Beyond the campsite was the cacti-covered hill he'd seen from the beach.

He decided to stay for a night. It had been so long since he'd made a real effort with people. Maybe here, before setting off for good, he could try harder. He tore the scarf from his face, deciding to get it over with. The first look was always the hardest to take.

*

At the closest group of tents a woman in a green blouse and hemp trousers spoke to two men. One was dark-skinned and overweight, sitting on a deckchair with a scuff-marked guitar across his knees. The other balanced an infant on his lap and held a skewer of sausages over the fire. He was sickness-pale and junkie-thin, with matted, clumpy hair, lighter in colour than Bruno's and only a little shorter.

'Morning, campers!' Bruno walked through the gap between the tents. Caught off-guard, they were unable to check their expressions. Lips thinned to a knife edge, staring eyes. They loathed him. He didn't blame them, knowing it

5

was his own fault. He smiled at the woman and tried to talk naturally, as out of practice as he was: 'What's the deal with this place? I just arrived. Was thinking of spending a night or two.'

Her eyes fixed on him. They didn't reflect the benevolence he was trying to project. 'The campsite's free, if that's what you mean.'

The man at the fire took the sausages from the flames and blew on them.

'How long you been here?' Bruno asked.

'Two years,' she said. 'Give or take.'

'Long time. How do you live?'

She looked at the men.

'I mean, you don't have to answer,' Bruno stammered. 'It's a personal question, I… I shouldn't have—'

'Sell stuff to the tourists,' said the man by the fire. He broke a sausage in half and fed it to the child. 'Doesn't everyone?'

'Slim pickin's, though,' said the woman. 'And they don't like us here. The locals, I mean. Parasites, that's what they call us.' She turned to the other man. 'Don't they, Golias?'

He nodded. 'Hostile locals like I never saw, and slim pickings ain't the word. Every season's getting worse. What you selling?'

'I'm not here to sell. I was just walking by. Didn't even know this place existed.'

'Walking?' The woman cut in. 'Ain't a city in three hundred kilometres from here!'

'Not in six hundred,' said the man by the fire. Grease from the sausage he was chewing dripped from his chin.

'From where?' she asked.

'Just fancied a stroll,' Bruno said, smiling from one to the other. None of them laughed. 'The South,' he added, clearing his throat.

The woman looked at the men again. Bruno caught Golias mouthing, '*He's not right.*' He ignored it. He tried not to let that kind of thing get to him any more. It was hard enough just to find the courage to talk to people; if he concentrated on their negativity his mouth would never open again. 'Beautiful town though, isn't it?' This wasn't going as he'd hoped. 'I've never seen a place like it.'

'Suppose it's pretty enough,' said the woman.

'Slim pickings, though,' the man with the infant repeated. 'Nasty locals. Best keep moving if you got nothing to sell. You'll get no charity here.'

'You can survive anywhere if you know how. Are there bins?'

'Oh, you can't go looking in the bins!' Golias laughed. 'They'll make you disappear for that. Won't they, Abilio?'

Abilio nodded and set the infant down. It ran to the woman. Bruno couldn't tell if it was a boy or a girl. 'No police here, you know? Local justice. A few travellers been beaten. Isn't that so, Adelina?'

'Some never seen again,' she said.

'Well, I think I'll go tie my hammock up in town anyway. Nice to—'

'In town!' Adelina shook her head. 'Big Mac'll tie *you* up.'

'By the neck!' Abilio yanked at an invisible rope behind his ear.

'Who's Big Mac?'

'*Who's Big Mac?*' Golias mocked. 'Stay in the campsite if you're staying at all.'

It's not as bad as they're making out, Bruno thought. Most likely they didn't want any more competition. The campsite was full of peddlers. All around, people worked at bead jewellery and wooden arts and crafts. Camps were spilling over with stuffed canvas bags. Now he had a better reason to stay. He wanted to find out what this place was all about and see this Big Mac for himself.

'I'll go set up then. See you guys around.'

He had barely taken a step when he heard the woman

whisper, 'Why would you do that to your face? And them all over his arms and legs. Just a bloody mess, they are.'

*

He put some distance between himself and the other tents and decided to get some practice in at building a shelter. He pulled a large tarpaulin sheet from his bag and, with his back to the others, so they couldn't see, he dug a hole in the sand. He dropped his bag into it then covered it over with the tarpaulin and laid some stones on it to keep it flat. Taking a small utility knife and his wallet, containing a few banknotes and an ID card with his face scratched out, he set off to explore again.

He didn't bother to cover his face. They'd have to take him as he was, and he'd have to accept their reactions. Everyone he passed gave him the same look. For the most part the tourists tried to hide it. Some looked away, others pretended not to see. Those he caught staring held eye contact, too polite to drop their eyes, breath held, lips pursed in a half-smile: he was just another normal, everyday guy. The locals, however, stared with open hostility. Their eyes followed him from the restaurants and shops as if he were a stray dog out to steal food from their plates.

He'd tried hard not to let what he'd done get to him. It wasn't even all that bad if he really thought about it. But it was self-inflicted and it was the biggest mistake of his life. Even now, years on, whenever he noticed someone staring, a tremor of regret and anger drove through him. Sometimes it would anchor inside him, and only a dose of calming breaths and thoughts, or the bottle, could stop him from going into a full-blown panic.

He hadn't eaten all day, and although he didn't mind going hungry, it wasn't something he liked to make a habit of. At a bin outside the supermarket, on a street called Beekeeper Close, he reached in amongst the sodden refuse. Flies swarmed as he turned through beer cans, coffee grounds and rotting vegetables, before finding a baguette wrapped in greaseproof paper. He ran it under one of the side street faucets, washed his hands and ate on the move, flicking spots of mould off with his thumbnail, twisting chunks from the stale crust and savouring the fluffy middle.

At the top of a deserted street, near a cavernous old baobab tree, he approached a high-walled, white brick building. It was surrounded by sacred fig trees.

'Some kind of temple,' he said, recognising the trees from a reference book.

The building had a dark wooden door carved with crosses, crescent moons and stars. He traced a hand over its surface, which had been warmed by the sun. Amongst the celestial images were shells, flowers, animals and spears, all carved together in some kind of hieroglyphic scrawl.

A familiar clinking noise, faint but growing louder, sounded from inside. He held his breath, pressed his ear to the door and listened. It was the clinking beat of a tambourine, but without the resonance. He nodded his head to the rhythm, trying to remember where he'd heard it. It was a distant sound… from childhood… from the orphanage, each beat louder than the last, growing louder still. It began to rattle right behind the door. He recognised it! It was a circle of keys, just like the ones the priests used to wear. The door bolt slid and clanked against its stop. He bounded for the corner, dug his heels into the sand and scampered in amongst the trees.

He breathed as quietly as he could, hoping he hadn't been seen or heard. The door closed and was locked again. Whoever was there, as they began to walk away, plucked at a single string instrument he'd become familiar with since entering the country. A *berimbau*. Too frightened to look in case he got caught and confronted, he listened as the scratchy twang of the instrument faded. By the time he did look, the person was gone.

The ground behind the building sloped down towards a mangrove forest. An empty wooden barrow was parked in a clearing from which a trail wound in under the trees. After his heart had slowed, he descended to the forest's edge and cut sections from the straightest mangrove roots to carry back to the campsite.

He ignored the prying eyes of the travellers as he set about building a frame for his shelter. He draped the tarpaulin over it, then with a short rope he'd made from agave leaf, and his machete, he set off over the hill to the coconut palms.

Three townsmen were there with a buggy that had a ladder fixed to its rear. Two men stood at the foot of the ladder, holding a net between them to catch the coconuts, while another man stood at the top, cutting them down. Tanned and shirtless, they wore the same *abada* trousers and espadrilles as the rest of the locals he'd seen.

After they left, Bruno fed his rope around a tree trunk and tied it behind his lower back. With the machete wrapped in his scarf and held between his teeth, he stepped up onto the trunk and dug his back into the rope. He gripped it at either side of his hips and, using it for leverage, shimmied up to the top, where he hacked off some fronds and a couple of coconuts. He repeated this on a few trees to minimise its impact, then headed to the beach to pick fresh seaweed.

In the remaining daylight, he weaved the fronds into mats to cushion the sand within his shelter. At dusk, feeling satisfied with himself, he lay in the shelter with his headlamp on, reading a paperback and chewing on the seaweed.

Bruno woke to the sound of a woman shouting: 'Come on then! Move your arse, time to bring the coin in.'

'If you carried some of this I'd bloody well move faster!' a man replied.

He sat up, catching the book as it fell off his chest. Laying it aside, he took the headlamp off, and drank some coconut water. He looked out of his shelter and watched the sellers hauling their wares into town. He picked up his camera and went to have a look around.

Main Street was lit from top to bottom. People flocked from alleys and side streets. They moved up and down in a throng. After so many months alone in nature, the intensity of all these people, the noise, the music, the electric light, even the smells, made him want to curl up inside himself. He turned back towards the campsite, but hesitated, took a breath, and joined the crowd.

Lightbulbs strung across the street cast a yellow haze on everything underneath. White strings of lights spiralled up the trunks of *caju* trees and out along the branches, under which travellers sat with their bric-a-brac on oversized muslins. Carved cow-bone jewellery, incense burners and sticks, embroidered handbags and purses. They cried out to the tourists, 'Don't be shy, *queridos!* Good price for you!'

Bruno knelt to inspect an incense burner while a ponytailed hawker talked to his neighbour. Without regarding Bruno, the man said, 'Make you a deal on that.' His tone changed when he saw him. 'You're hardly going to buy anything are you? Put it down and off you go.'

'It's dung anyway,' Bruno said. The man lunged at him and laughed as Bruno flinched. He hurried away.

At half-barrel grills in front of crowded restaurant patios, blue-aproned cooks mopped sweat from their brows. Chicken and pork cutlets blackened the sticky grills. Bruno eyed a moist chicken leg as a pair of silver tongs gripped it and turned it over. Fat oozed from the pink-white flesh and sizzled amongst the coals.

'My God.' He pulled at his beard and held his breath against the scent. It had taken a long time to acquire a taste for road-kill and forest trappings. He didn't want to spoil it all for one mouthful of tender, juicy chicken.

Despite the stares and grimaces, the nudging and

whispering he knew was aimed at him, Bruno enjoyed being in the presence of other people again and savoured the sound of conversation and laughter.

'This is what it's all about,' he said. 'This is what I've been missing. Enjoy yourself, but not at the expense of anyone else.' *These are good people*, he thought. *Saving their money and coming here for some fun, some relief from their oppressive bosses, their crooked politicians.* 'There are no bourgeoisie here, are there?' He looked around at no one in particular and let out a bourgeois laugh. He spoke to himself with gentrified enunciation: 'Oh, I can't resist world travel. I plan to visit most countries at some point. Oh, and I must say that I am indeed party to fine foods and the odd quality beer.' He laughed again. People close by slowed their pace and edged away. He didn't mind. 'I understand,' he said, nodding. The habit of talking to himself had formed within a few months of leaving the city. It wasn't healthy to spend long periods of time alone without hearing a voice, even if the only one available was his own.

A three-piece band played at a bar called Zigzag. He stood outside listening to the music while picking out the individual fragrances from incense smouldering in pots on the patio steps. Sandalwood, lavender, patchouli. The scents were infused with the narcotic smell of hydrocarbons. Searching, he traced its source to a circle of people down the street.

In the centre of the crowd a man, dusted with soot and glistening with sweat breathed fire into the night. Bruno inhaled as the heat from the flame and the sweetness of the paraffin hit him. Alongside the man, a girl danced with fire poi, spinning the flaming spheres in rhythmical, hypnotic patterns. Maybe he'd stay longer than just a night. What was the rush to get moving? Wasn't his real test to survive in society, instead of the wilderness?

'Some place, this,' he said to a male tourist standing next to him.

'Sure is,' the man replied, and Before Bruno could say anything else, he moved away.

Bruno thought he heard the call of a familiar name then, and he looked in its direction, but he was wrong. It was a trap, like always. Every thought of *her* was a trap. Before getting caught in it, he hurried further down the street.

At the end of the street, where it opened onto the beach, a pack of tourists drank cocktails between colourful carts. He squeezed through the crowd towards a red cart called Kart de la Revolución.

The young barman picked strawberries from one of the fruit nets hanging from the cart top. He chopped them up, added them to a jug and filled it with spirits from the bottles at his elbow. He shook the mixture over his shoulder as the drunk tourists pushed for space at the cart front. They were skulling their drinks faster than he could make them and trampling their empties into the sand.

How long had it been since he'd had a drink? Surely one wouldn't be a problem. His real drinking days were long behind him. Just one to toast the new town; an accidental discovery, like all the best things. The crowd parted as he approached the counter.

'How much for a vodka?' he asked.

'Want anything in it?' asked the barman as he poured the contents of his jug into a line of cups. He peered out at him over thick acrylic glasses.

Bruno lowered his voice. 'Will that change the price?'

'Seven *contos*, regardless.'

'Lime, then. Put lime in it.'

'One *caipiroska*, coming up.' He slid a cup over from a batch of pre-made drinks and held up seven fingers. Bruno went to hand over the coins, but the barman cleared his throat and tapped the counter. He dropped them onto it and shuffled away.

Against the outside wall of a bar called Ivo's, he watched the tourists as he rolled the sour liquid-lime over his tongue.

He swallowed, enjoying the heat of the vodka as it rose from his stomach. A couple who'd been kissing at the edge of the crowd slipped into the darkness beyond.

Bruno threw his cup into the pile overflowing from the bin and headed over to the kiosk bars. All the chairs, tables and sunloungers had been stacked. The shutters of all the bars were down apart from the last one, where a dark-skinned man buffed a wine glass under a tube-light.

'Hello,' said Bruno, stepping forward before he could stop himself. The vodka had torn off a layer of self-restraint. Insects struck the tube-light and frazzled against a blue bug zapper.

'We're closed,' said the man, talking around a cigar. Lean, with greying stubble, he wore a panama hat cocked so far to the side it looked ready to fall off.

'I thought these bars would be packed like the rest of the place.' Bruno licked the cane sugar from his gums and crunched it between his teeth.

'Only in the daytime. Best go to the *carrinhos*.'

'Those things?' Bruno looked back at the cocktail carts.

The man laid the glass and dishcloth on the counter. He took the cigar from his mouth. 'Yes, son,' he said, raising a finger towards them. His knuckles were covered in scar tissue. 'The locals call them *carrinhos*.'

'You're not a local, then?' Bruno asked, noticing a long-healed bite mark on the man's arm. Maybe he was the one who carried out the beatings Abilio and Adelina had mentioned.

'No, no, no. Been here a few years, though.' When Bruno didn't speak, the man continued. 'I came to get out of the cold, slow down a bit, you know? The simple life.' He looked around and leaned forward, his yellowed eyes peering out from under their coarse black brows. They took on an air of complicity. 'And if I'm honest—' He lowered his voice. 'My ex-wife was a bitch. Tough divorce. Lost a lotta money.' He straightened up and whistled through his teeth.

'A lotta money.' He moved the glass to the shelf with the others. 'You got a name, son?'

Nobody ever asked his name. 'Bruno,' he said. His voice rose at the end as if it were a question. It drew a smile from the man.

'Well, I'm Anderson. What brings you here, Bruno? You don't look much like a tourist.'

Bruno gestured to his face. 'This gave me away?'

Anderson looked him in the eye. 'It is quite a tattoo.' There was no malice in his voice. 'The patchwork shorts and torn vest don't scream holidaymaker either. And what's that leather thing?'

'My camera,' Bruno said, flipping the case open. 'It's old but it takes great photos if you know how to use it.'

'Looks expensive. I'd watch yourself with that if you're staying at the campsite.' He pulled on the cigar and puffed out a cloud of tobacco smoke. 'What you doing here?'

'I'm on my way to the rainforest. Happened to be walking by and I'm thinking I'll stay for a couple of days. Maybe more, who knows?'

Anderson took the cigar from his mouth. 'Walking, you say? Where did you start?'

'Down South. What month is this?'

'It's Saturday, August 20th. Need the year?' He bit the cigar and began buffing another glass.

Bruno tapped the side of his head. 'Got that already. I've been walking for almost two years now.'

The cigar tipped forward, almost dropping from Anderson's mouth. 'Two years! Why?'

Bruno laughed. 'Why not? I've been taking my time, stopping here and there, foraging, trapping, fishing. I've been to a few cities on my way up here, to make money. The film for this thing isn't cheap, but I've managed to sell a few of the photos.'

'So, you're a photographer? Doing some kind of art project?'

'Photography's more of a hobby, really. The main thing is that I want to pit myself against nature, experience its beauty, its ugliness. See how I fare.'

'If you've already been on the move for so long I'd say you've fared quite well. What's the attraction?'

'I don't know.' Bruno looked into Anderson's eyes; he felt at ease talking with him. 'Most people find their niche and have a sense of belonging. I was never going to find that where I was, and I made a—' He motioned to his face. 'An unsound decision. Once I did this there was no turning back. I realised I didn't know who I was, who I was supposed to be. So, I locked the door for a long, long time, read a lot, learned a lot and started to think differently. When I was ready to go out again, I didn't want any part of the past, society, you know? I hated it. I mean, I still do, but maybe all the walking has mellowed me out a bit.'

'You don't get scared being alone in the middle of nowhere? Not afraid of bandits? Don't you get bored?'

'Not really. Sometimes I do wonder what the hell I'm doing. Anyway, I've devoured every book I could find on self-sufficiency, survival, and the Amazon. I might not look the type, but I'm pretty passionate about that forest and the river. The tribes there really know how to respect the planet, but us? Our society does its best to fuck everything up! So, I'll go there and hopefully meet these tribes. See what I can learn from them. Even if I can't make contact, I'll just do my own thing, learn what I can, and who knows? Maybe I'll bring it back someday. How about this town, though? I had no idea it existed. There's something special about it, am I right? What's it like living here?'

Anderson was looking over Bruno's shoulder towards the *carrinhos*. 'Oh, it's special, alright.' He made eye contact again. 'Not thinking about ending your voyage here though, are you?'

'Well, I don't have anything set in mind.'

'It's just that… It's not really a place for people like—' He paused and dragged on his cigar. 'You said you're camping with the others?'

'I'm in the campsite, that's right.'

'Watch yourself up there. I mean, they're not all bad, but… You know…' He lifted an aluminium ashtray from below the counter and tapped the grey off the end of the cigar. 'And it's like I said, keep that thing around your neck if you don't want to lose it. They'll have told you all about the locals, no doubt.'

'About the hostility? Is it that bad?'

'Foreign hands reaching into their pot of gold is how they see it. They would rather keep it all for themselves.' He lowered his voice again. 'Bruno, I don't mean to be curt but I can't sell you anything. My boss might come by here soon and I'd lose my job if I served you. The only place travellers can buy drinks is at the *carrinhos*. Other than that it's the supermarket. You can buy a bottle there and take it back to the campsite.'

'I don't want a drink, Anderson. It's fine.' He had an idea. 'How much do you sell the coconuts for?'

'Four *contos*, but I can't sell you those either.'

'Not a problem. I'll get going before your boss arrives. Thanks for talking to me.'

Anderson put the glass on the shelf. 'Hope you enjoy your time here, and good luck with the trek.'

Bruno watched as Anderson picked up another glass. 'May I take your picture?'

*

'Coconuts!' Bruno shouted as the tourists filed by. 'Cheapest in town. Only two *contos*.' He sat on Main Street with four coconuts on his muslin cloth. He'd torn a page from a paperback, written *2C* on it and set it in front of the coconuts. Adelina sat on his right with the half-asleep toddler gripping her flank. She'd sold two pairs of sandals since he'd arrived. Next to her, Abilio, pale as a tallow candle, had sold

17

a few wooden statuettes. Almost an hour had passed. He was being ignored.

A group of girls were looking at the sandals on Adelina's linen. 'Cheap coconuts here,' he said to them. 'I'll make you a deal.'

The nearest girl, who'd just picked up a pair, handed them back to Adelina and walked on. The rest followed in tow.

'Stop scaring them away!' Adelina slapped the sandals on the ground between her and Bruno.

Nobody trusted him. Ink scorched his eyelids and lips. Jagged marks spider-webbed over the natural lines and contours his face. It blotted the skin of his cheeks, jaw and forehead in shades of blue-grey and black that obscured his expressions and blinded people to his intentions. Once, he'd welcomed their aversion. Any reaction was better than indifference, but he didn't want that any more. He wanted the kind of respect due any stranger.

Why was he even considering staying? Here was the same as everywhere else. He closed his eyes, breathed and visualised his walk. One step in front of the other, over the beach, past the city, finding the river and following it. 'Progression is life,' he repeated on each exhale. 'Stagnation is death.' He calmed down, but sensed someone watching him. A pug-faced man appeared at the edge of his cloth.

'What are you doing?' The man had slicked back, receding hair, and an appearance of athleticism despite the paunch straining his T-shirt. A green bead necklace was slung around his neck.

'I panic sometimes,' Bruno said. 'I do breathing exercises and visualise where I'm going to keep calm.'

'What you prattling on about? I'm asking what you're selling!'

He looked down at the large green fruits in front of him. 'Coconuts,' he said, opening his palms to them. In the corner of his eye he noticed the flashes of delight on Adelina and Abilio's faces.

The man crushed his cigarette between two stubby fingers and dropped it to the sand. 'Fucking parasites!' He looked down the line of travellers then glared at Adelina. Her smile vanished. 'Didn't you tell him how we do business? You're lucky we let you sell anything!' He turned back to Bruno. 'You're taking the fucking piss. Selling them at half the price we sell them! What are you playing at?' Over his shoulder he let out a whistle and beckoned two waiters from a restaurant across the street.

'I'm sorry,' Bruno said. 'I didn't know. I just—'

'He's not one of us, Ivo!' Adelina said. 'He's not one of us!'

'Enough. Arts and crafts, fine, magic tricks, fine.' His cigarette-stained fingers jabbed the air between them. 'Fortune telling, fucking face painting, fine. But never undercut the town. Brothers—' He turned to the waiters. 'Take these coconuts inside.' He glanced at Bruno again. 'Make sure he hasn't tampered with them.'

Death, he'd imagined, would be a release,
an opening into the infinite,
not oppressive and suffocating like this

2

With the tarpaulin billowing in the wind and shards of daylight piercing through its slits, Bruno lay awake in the damp warmth of morning, a threadbare sheet pulled down to his waist. He was thinking about packing up and leaving but could already picture the smug smiles of Adelina and Abilio as they watched him walk away. He imagined Ivo standing on the threshold of his bar, shooing him off: '*That's right, no place for you here, run along.*' Broken. That's what he was. They'd speak about him around their camp fires: '*Remember that guy with the tattooed face? Who? Oh c'mon, you know, Mister Coconut, remember?*'

And what about Anderson. He told him he'd be staying for two nights, if not more. What would he say? '*Gone already? Guess he couldn't handle it. Got into a little trouble, that's what I heard. A little misunderstanding and at the first sign of danger he left like a young boy running from a master. Didn't give a second thought to what great things might happen if he'd stayed and stood up for himself, showed an ounce of courage and beat them at their own game. That's what he should've done, beat them at their own fucking game!*'

Chest tight, teeth clenched, he thought of how easily Adelina had dismissed him. 'Of course I'm not one of you!' he said. 'Wouldn't want to be.' She'd said it as if he wasn't even there, as if he were less significant than the smallest

20

cockroach, to be stepped on without hesitation. How had he got so low that people could cast him aside as if he were sub-human?

He gripped the sheet with both hands and almost ripped it apart as he imagined smashing a coconut over Ivo's head. He pictured himself grabbing handfuls of Adelina's greasy black hair and yelling into her face: '*No I'm not one of you, you stupid little cow. I'll grind you into the dirt until your insides pop out of your arse!*'

He threw the sheet off. What a waste of energy, what pointless aggression. 'Grow up, man!' He got to his knees, tipped his pile of books over and opened one of the three that had been with him from the start. He flicked to a page entitled *Hate* and read aloud in English.

' "...Fear, ignorance, jealousy, anger and disgust. But note that all these emotions, and especially the first three, are about the hater..." '[1]

'About the hater,' he muttered, lying back on the mats. He brought a hand to his forehead and massaged his temples. Was he really afraid, ignorant and jealous? He pushed the idea away and tried to calm down. It could be dealt with later. Right now he didn't want to think. He wanted to disappear. He closed his eyes and focused only on his breathing. It was a long time before he opened them. There was a smile on his face when he did. He'd stay for a week. 'One whole week,' he said. 'I'll show these bastards I can survive anywhere. I don't have to go to the forest if I don't feel like it!' Jewellery was the answer. Everything made from local, sustainable sources, nothing bought or mass manufactured like the travellers' rubbish. It would be far superior. He'd sell it to the tourists, and the money would go straight back into the town. He could function in a society just as well as anyone.

*

1   The Meaning of Things – Prof. A.C. Grayling

On Main Street, 4×4s were arriving from the bay and tipping backpackers onto the sand. With a fresh sense of determination, he crossed to a side street and passed the temple. He slipped in through the door-like hollow in the baobab tree and stripped long fibres from its trunk to use as cordage.

At the beach, hunched over and barefoot, he combed the tideline, picking up shells, sea glass, driftwood and pebbles. After stepping on a torn condom that oozed its warm contents between his toes, he washed his feet in the sea and returned to the campsite.

He sat at his shelter with his whittling tools and the double pinion hand drill he'd almost thrown away and set himself to work as those at the other camps stewed in the heat. He carved the driftwood into spiralling, organic-looking shapes and wove the sea glass and shells into intricate weaves of cordage.

The campsite was full, and although the adults stuck mostly to their own groups, the few kids that were around mingled, chasing each other about. At the nearest group, next to the campsite toilets, Golias strummed his out-of-tune guitar while Abilio and some others joined in to sing some horrific ballad in a grotesque, nasal disharmony. Adelina stirred a pot over the fire, her free hand and haunches pumping the air in time with the music. Bruno struggled to concentrate with them around. *Ignorant, shallow people*, he thought. *Only out for themselves.* 'But who are you to judge?' his inner voice asked. 'What's so wrong about it? Are you any better? You're not.'

He dug a fire pit and lined it with stones then collected fallen fronds and husks from around the coconut palms to use as fuel. He cut down more coconuts, and after quenching his thirst with the water and filling his belly with the flesh, made the shells into bowls.

After dark, next to a cluttered workers' yard, he found a pair of skips. He hauled out a plywood board, a couple

22

of aluminium pots that were beaten out of shape but not cracked, some mendable canvas bags and plastic bottles.

Back at the shelter, he took out his flint and sparked up a fire in the darkness. In the firelight, he enjoyed a hot soup of coconut milk, seaweed and strips of dried meat he'd taken from a dead dog he'd found at the roadside a few weeks earlier. Nobody in the campsite had shown the slightest bit of interest in him the whole day. Even the kids had kept their distance, no doubt obeying their parents' orders.

There was a satisfying ache in his hands as he inspected his work after eating, and he nodded with pride. He'd made many pieces of jewellery, completely different than anything he'd seen in town or anywhere else. With so many strange knots and weaves, each piece looked as if it had grown rather than been made. The sea glass was like florets, the shells like petals, the cordage like vines. With a stone, he hammered rusted nails into the plywood board, bent them over and hooked on the jewellery. As the embers in the fire began to dull, he slipped into his shelter and lay down to sleep, already thinking of how to make the next batch even better.

*

It thrust itself upon him, pinning him down, enveloping him in its dark, malicious matter. Aware of his surroundings, in his shelter, lying on the mats with the sheet twisted around him, he wanted to reach out for something to pull himself up, but he couldn't move.

Its weight compressed his chest, making it harder to breathe. It reached for his neck, his mouth and nose. It was consuming him. He tried to fight it, tried to pull away, but his body wouldn't obey him. It was as if concrete was setting on him. He fought it but could barely open his mouth to breathe. The struggle became too much. He had to accept and submit to it.

Death, he'd imagined, would be a release, an opening into the infinite, not oppressive and suffocating like this.

Unable to breathe, he was hanging from the edge of the void, about to let go and fall. The dark entered his skull and was reaching into his brain when an almost imperceptible strength came to him. Like a tiny, soundless bubble rising from the bottom of the deepest ocean, it amplified in size and force as it rose from the depths. His eyes shot open and he wrenched himself free. Fragile and half-conscious, heaving like a man near drowned, he looked down at his hands, still gripping the twisted, sweat-drenched sheet and exhaled. He let every muscle and tendon in his body relax. He was alive. It had been that same old dream from years before, yet it had never felt more real. He dropped back to the mats, dug two fingers between his ribs and willed his racing heart to slow down.

The wind caught the flap he'd cut in the tarpaulin as he unlatched it and flung it open. He squinted outside, slipped into his sandals and walked up the hill. In the early morning sun the plants cast long shadows down the hillside. Behind a tall cactus he let a trickle of dark, syrupy urine patter on the sand. He stretched his arms out and took every building, with its whitewashed wall and red tiled roof, in his embrace. From here he could see it all, the top of the temple, the dune and, next to the sleeping campsite, the church with its driftwood cross.

He grabbed his towel and walked over the sand and patches of scrub-grass to the campsite toilets. He stepped into a mildewed plastic shower cabinet and turned the valve. A deluge of cold water drenched him, washing the sand and dirt from his body. He worked his fingers into his hair and beard, trying to loosen the clumpy, matted strands. With the edge of a tooth, he scraped the grime from under his nails and spat it into the shower tray.

'Almighty God,' he said in a mock voice, as the water ran down his face, 'who hath regenerated thee by water… anoint thee with the chrism of salvation!' He closed the valve and towelled off. 'Natural jewellery, people!' he said, 'Organic— excuse me, my darling? *How* do I make them you ask?... Years of practise of course... Dedication to the craft... Three, you say? Here, I'll give you a fourth for free. Tell your friends! B.E.J., Bruno Expósito Jewellery. One week only!'

At the day-bars, staff unstacked sunloungers and set chairs around the tables. A dune buggy, filled with crates of beer and bottles of spirits, was being unloaded. The tide was out, and he watched a pair of blondes between the anchored *jangadas* fight with their towels in the wind. The overweight one, pale-skinned in a white one-piece, had the look of a beluga whale. The slim friend wore a string bikini. Both had sunglasses on. Bruno approached the girls, bracing the selling-board on his hip against the gusting wind.

'Just like selling the photos,' he told himself, feeling the sand pricking his legs. 'Fearless. Confident.'

'Good morning,' he said in Portuguese. Neither looked nor replied. They were scooping sand and patting it down on the corners of their towels.

'I can tell you're new arrivals. This part of the beach is constantly swept by the wind. It's why the boats are built like they are. Look inside. No engines. Totally wind dependent. You should go over to the day-bars, where it's sheltered. The sunloungers are empty now, but trust me, they'll fill up soon enough.'

Beluga secured her towel and beached herself on it. She sprayed sunscreen into her cupped hand so the wind couldn't snatch it away. He caught the smell of vanilla and ylang-ylang. The other lay on her back, hands clasped under her head.

He crouched in front of them and propped the board up against his knees so the jewellery caught the sun. He cleared his throat, ignored the look of contempt on their faces and continued his patter, hoping his voice didn't betray his nervousness: 'These are natural pieces of jewellery. All materials gathered from sustainable sources in this very area, and handmade by myself. A true keepsake from Brisas, so no matter how far away you are, you'll always feel near.'

'No thank you,' said the stout girl, in English. She gave up spraying, uncapped the bottle and poured the lotion into her palm.

'Hold on,' he said, switching to English. 'Let me start again. I thought you guys were Brazilian… Allow me to explain. This necklace is—'

'Not interested.'

'These bracelets—'

'No thanks.'

She wobbled onto her side. He continued speaking to her back. 'I made these rings from—'

'Go away.' Her tone had him gritting his teeth.

He stared at the back of her head. She didn't realise how important this was to him. He massaged the bridge of his nose, let out a breath and turned to the slim girl. 'Look, I'm not here to rip you guys off. I worked hard on these. Really hard. Is a couple of *contos* too much to ask for? You can't even buy a drink for that.'

They spoke together in a language he couldn't understand then got up and put their sandals on. He un-hooked two bracelets from his board, tossed one onto each towel and walked away. If other tourists saw his jewellery being worn it might start a trend. He'd only taken a few steps when he heard one of them calling after him. Maybe they'd pay after all.

He turned. Beluga was bounding forward, shouting in the same foreign language. She threw the bracelets at him and marched back to her friend. He picked them up, shook the sand off and put them in his pocket. *Leave*, said the voice in his head as he continued back to Main Street. *Forget this bullshit, get your things and go, you've had enough.*

Restaurants were filling up. Tourists stuffed forkfuls of omelettes and pancakes into their mouths, drained glasses of fruit juice and cups of coffee. Waiters and waitresses sprang at the tourists' calls, filling cups, taking orders, clearing plates.

'Coffee,' he whispered as he caught a whiff of its aroma. After his first sale that's what he'd buy, foil wrapped, medium roast arabica beans. 'Jewellery!' he shouted at tourists trying on sunglasses at souvenir shops. 'Natural handmade jewellery!'

Dune buggies loaded with gear revved past him. Outside the tourist centre, a woman pointed to the pictures on the billboard, and explained the trips to a group of tourists: 'And on this trip,' she said, 'you'll see the lost town of Jinguba, buried after a decade of fighting the sand.'

'Or *won't* see,' said one of the men.

A few steps to her side, a stocky man with hair wound around his head like a bird's nest, held a donkey by its reins. He bit a large chunk from a carrot and fed the remainder to the donkey. 'Roll up, guys,' he called. 'Fastest ass in all of Brisas… Except Honey, of course.'

Bruno swung his board around at a group of passing tourists. 'Natural jewellery!' he cried.

The girl closest to him flinched and ran to the other side of the group.

She's being playful, he thought. Her action had been too exaggerated to be genuine. 'Come on,' he said, chasing after her. 'Take a look! Don't be shy.' He was enjoying himself. Finally, he'd made a connection.

'Get away from me,' she joked, skipping away from him around the group.

'You won't find any better.'

A foot stuck out and tripped him. Angry and confused, he scanned the gawping onlookers dotted about the street. If one had laughed, they all would have.

'What the hell?' He looked back at the group, got to his knees and dusted the sand off his hands. He gathered up the jewellery. 'I was only—'

'Leave her alone,' said a fresh-faced man who couldn't have been more than twenty.

'She was kidding around.'

'No I wasn't, you freak!'

Locals poised at the railings of the restaurants and bars, tourists watched from their tables.

'I just wanted to show you the jewellery.' *Don't embarrass yourself any more, Bruno. It's time to go.* He wouldn't listen, couldn't listen. This was the last chance he'd ever have. Ever. He *had* to succeed. He kept his head down and walked on.

At the top of Main Street he saw the bookshop again. Across from it, meat hung from a pole bridging the butcher's entrance. He imagined it cooking over his fire, could see the salt he'd rub into it dissolving and dripping, could smell it roasting above the flaming embers. He'd slice off little pieces and eat them as it cooked. Just then, a bear of a man appeared in the doorway and Bruno averted his eyes. He sensed the man watching him, staring out from under a battering ram of a forehead. The man wiped a knife on his apron and hung it up behind the entrance. His neck was as broad as a bull's and his hair was short and thick like hide. Bruno had seen many bruisers in his time at the harbour. Men who could clear bars with a single swipe of their fist, who'd steal kegs of beer and crates of whisky and bring them back to their boats without fear of repercussion. Most, he knew, would have lost more than sweat against this one. *This* was the Big Mac Adelina had mentioned.

Aware of the butcher's eyes still on him, Bruno looked in the window of *A Gata Preta*. Taped to the glass was a handwritten sign: *BOOK-SWAP*. He wondered if they'd let him exchange the paperback wearing through his side pocket. Frayed and old, with the front cover peeling from exposure to the sun, it was in poor condition but could still be read. He walked past the shop and back again, unsure what to do.

'Make a decision,' he muttered to himself. 'Go in or go

on, he's still fucking watching you.' With a glance at the butcher, he made for the door.

A chime clanked as he stepped inside. He was met with the smell of coffee, ink and paper. The shop was empty apart from the woman with the coarse black hair at the counter. She turned in his direction as he scanned the room. Under the window was a sofa and a coffee table strewn with magazines; free-standing bookshelves crowded the centre, and along every wall shelves from floor to ceiling were stacked with books. It was perfect. By the woman's elbow a coffee percolator purred and hissed. He turned to greet her, but noticed her bottom lip quivering under a row of glistening, cobbled teeth.

'Out!' she yelled.

'Easy. Keep calm.' With an outstretched hand showing he meant no harm, he reached the other to his pocket and began unbuttoning it. 'I'm only here for the book swap.'

'Out,' she repeated. 'Get out of here.'

'Can't I just change this one?'

'Go!' She pointed at the door. Two women appeared from behind the last bookshelf. Sisters, he noticed as he back-stepped through the doorway, twins.

He closed the door and hurried away, glancing over his shoulder to see if any of them were following. The woman tracked him from the window, her eyes swivelling in their sockets, her nose pressed against the glass. The butcher had stepped onto the sand. Even the barber, scissors in his fist, bald head glossy in the sun, peered from the doorway under his red and white sign. As Bruno walked on, a dog in the street jumped up and barked at him. He cowered and a high-pitched noise escaped his throat.

The butcher laughed. 'Even the dogs can't stand the sight of you.'

Bruno didn't acknowledge him. He felt for the utility knife in his pocket, but it wasn't there. He imagined rounding them all up, everyone who'd ever stared at him, putting them on their knees, and bringing the knife to his forehead. He'd hack the tattoo off and rub the bloody mess into their faces. '*You happy now?*' he'd roar. '*Is this how you wanted it?*'

It was a mistake, stopping in this town. The voice was right. It was time to stop trying to be something he wasn't and let go. Had he not punished himself enough? He just wasn't meant for society.

With sand like hot ash burning the sides of his feet, he arrived at the supermarket. The pressure in his chest and head had risen to a point where it made breathing difficult and thinking nearly impossible. He stood outside and waited, not about to give anyone else the satisfaction of abusing him. The shopkeeper glanced over, a thin, dark-haired man with one eyebrow bleached and the eye underneath it clouded and clotted like a half-fried egg. Bruno dug the remaining coins out of his pocket.

'Can I help you?' the man asked. *LUIS* was etched on his name tag.

'Whisky,' Bruno said, not taking his eyes from the bottle. He had no energy for politeness.

Luis held the coins under his good eye and counted them. He shook his head.

'*Cachaça*, then.'

Luis returned some coins, dropped the others into the till and offered a half-bottle from the shelf behind him.

In a copse of *caju* trees by a corral under the dune, Bruno watched two donkeys eating from pails tied to the fence. The trees blocked out most of the sun and the sand was cool. He kicked off his sandals and threw the selling-board aside. He crushed the bottle's lid between his fingers and gulped the *cachaça* down, gagging by the third swallow. His eyes ran, his stomach and throat burned. He tossed the bottle as his head went light and his stomach rose to his throat. Stumbling against a tree, he gripped his mouth to stop the vomit from shooting out and swallowed it back down before it could all leak out between his fingers. With closed eyes all he saw was the staring faces of the butcher, the bookshop keeper, and the effeminate little barber. He'd made a complete fool of himself again.

'What am I doing wrong?' he asked the feeding donkeys. 'Speak! Say something, you imbeciles! Help me! Lead me!' A rumble of laughter rose from the pit of his stomach. 'You fool! You're a parody, an absolute fucking parody.'

*

When he woke, the sun was low and he was drunk. He got up too fast. Stars dotted his vision. He held his head to stop it spinning and steadied himself against a tree. He picked up his selling-board, gripped the fence of the corral and headed to the dune. There were twelve donkeys now, silent and staring. He ignored them.

The soft sand slipped underfoot as he climbed, and after only a few steps his thighs were burning. The hum of conversation and laughter drifted towards him, or was it just the drink? At the top, he stood in the shadow of two hundred silhouettes. Men carrying cool boxes flitted about selling beer to the tourists. Bottle tops popped off with vacuous *thuuuppps* and cans of slushed lager fizzed over in tourists' hands. Cameras whirred, bottles clinked. '*Salud*,' they said to one another. 'Chin-chin.'

'Chin fucking chin,' Bruno said. His hair flopped from side to side as he dragged one foot past the other.

Down on the beach, surrounded by tourists, a capoeira performance was in session. The noise of the beating drums, clapping hands, and twanging *berimbaus* was faint in the gusting wind. Two *capoeiristas* cartwheeled and flipped in the middle of the *roda*. They stalked each other, attacking and retreating in a dance of beauty and violence.

'Jewellery,' Bruno shouted, his voice hoarse and weak. He weaved amongst the tourists, constantly losing his grip on the board. 'Cheap, natural, fucked-up jewellery.' They

31

pretended he wasn't there. Even if he stood right in front of them, they stared straight through him. Maybe they were right and he wasn't there at all. Maybe all that was left of him was a transparent shell.

'Touch me,' he asked someone in his native Spanish. 'Am I here? Can you see me?'

'Of course I can see you,' the man replied. 'Please move.'

As the sun dipped below the horizon, a chorus of cheers and whistles erupted from the crowd. 'It's only a fucking sunset!' he shouted, but he wondered how many had actually seen a pure one before, just the sun and nature, unpolluted by the concrete, metal and glass, the smog and the noise of their cities.

In a pack, the tourists trudged down the windward side of the dune. Every grain of sand they kicked up seemed to be caught by the wind and driven straight into Bruno's face. He didn't care how pathetic he looked any more. He followed out of spite more than anything else.

'Jewellery,' he shouted at those overtaking him. 'Buy some jewellery, you greedy bastards.'

The *jangadas* anchored in the bay rocked on the incoming tide. The pastel blue of the sky faded to black and the town's electric lights blinked on.

Bruno watched the *capoeiristas* disappear up Main Street in a procession followed by many of the tourists. 'Goodbye,' he said, his tongue thick with the alcohol. 'See you again. Thanks for calling.'

Cart-boys busied themselves hammering ice in dishcloths and cutting fruit. Tourists, windswept and sunburned, ambled around, their towels sodden with sweat and dusted with sand. Some lingered at the carts, sipping their first drinks of the evening. Single travellers, small groups and couples, all standing apart, reluctant to engage each other in conversation.

'Talk,' he shouted. 'What're you waiting for?' Some looked, others turned away. All had expressions of derision on their faces. With the lights on, the musicians tuning up, the cooks tending their grills and the travellers appearing under the *caju* trees, Main Street was assuming its nocturnal persona. To avoid them all, Bruno decided to take the trail behind the day-bars back to the campsite.

'Bruno!' A voice called out as he made for the path. On the corner stool of his bar Anderson snapped a paperback shut and set it on the counter. 'You're a macramé seller now.'

Bruno smiled, watching him through one eye. He didn't have the energy to keep both open. 'You remembered my name.' He threw his arms out to hug him.

Anderson pushed him back. 'A drunk macramé seller.'

'A bad one. Nobody is interested.'

'Well you're supposed to be the sober one selling to drunks, son. That's how it works.' Anderson looked towards Main Street. 'Let's go round the back.' He led Bruno around the kiosk, opened the door and sat on the step. Bruno tried to lower himself to the ground, but his knees gave out and he fell. He punched the scrub grass until the pain in his hip eased. The waves swept over the rocks below, flashing white for an instant before being swallowed up by the night.

'I love the smell of them,' he said, watching Anderson drag on his cigar. 'Don't smoke, though. Never have. Can I...' He hesitated. 'Just one? A beer, I mean. Please?' He squinted up with hopeful eyes for as long as he could then let one close.

'I told you yesterday, Bruno. I can't serve you. Anyway, it looks like you've had enough already.'

Bruno raised a trembling finger. 'No,' he said. 'I've had *cachaça* only. One beer please?'

Anderson shook his head. 'I'd get fired.'

'That guy Ivo... He's the boss? You're scared? Big guy like you!' The humid air drew sweat from his pores. He scratched as it trickled through his beard.

'Ivo's got nothing to do with it. I told you yesterday. Go to the *carrinhos*.'

'Anderson.' Bruno threw his selling-board across the grass. He worked at his pocket, turning it inside out until the coins fell. 'I've had a... a bad day. This—' He scooped the coins up and held them out, '...all I got left. Why can't I... why no respect from anyone?' He took a breath and shouted at the night, 'One... Single... Can... That's all. There's no fucker here!'

The smoking red end of the cigar pointed at Bruno's face. Anderson's calm voice was at odds with his words: 'Keep your voice down, son, or I'll throw you head first onto the rocks. I won't put up with that shit.' He got up to go inside. Bruno eyed the back of his shoulders, saw how he moved. He noticed the size of Anderson's hand as it pushed a cold, wet can into his own. A fighter's hand.

'What's with this place?' he asked.

Smoke snaked from the edge of Anderson's mouth as he spoke. 'Have you heard how this town came to be?'

Bruno shook his head.

'Seen Mac around yet? He runs things here.'

Bruno tapped a finger on the can and thought of all the hostile faces he'd seen that day. 'You're talking about the butcher. Hard to miss that one.'

Anderson smiled. 'No, Bruno. The butcher's called Faka. He's something, I'll give you that. But you'll know Big Mac when you see him.' He whistled through his teeth and smiled. 'You'll know Big Mac alright.'

He brought out an ashtray, laid his cigar in it and cracked his knuckles. 'About thirty years ago this was a small settlement of fishermen and allotment farmers, just like the rest of the towns I'm sure you've seen on your way up here. Back then the people worshipped at that church up by the campsite. The preacher was an old man who didn't get involved in the business side of the town. There *was* no business. He just ran the church services.

'Mac's mother arrived on a fishing boat much bigger than the ones they have here today. A black woman with an ageing white man. You can imagine the gossip. The hull was filled with old wooden trunks carrying all their belongings. They built a small house where the bookshop is now, and as the months passed it became obvious she was pregnant.

'Now think of the chatter that went round when the baby didn't come out *raça mixta*, but dark as the moonless night. This was Big Mac. The family kept to themselves for the most part. The old man would fish and the mother kept the house and grew herbs in pots of soil taken from the forest, but Mac was never isolated from the other kids. He had some friends and taught them the capoeira his mother was teaching him.

'Long after the father died, when Mac was nineteen, he confronted the preacher as he was locking up the church. They said it was so hot that day the paint on the *jangadas* blistered right before your eyes. Mac told the preacher that this church-religion of his was a counterfeit and demanded the keys to the building. The old man was a fisherman himself. They're a tough breed. He wasn't about to hand everything over to a teenage boy, even one like Mac. But Mac took one step forward and the preacher realised how serious he was. His eyes were said to be filled with the fires of hell! And you know those bushes around the church?'

'The small green—' Bruno tried to hide a yawn, 'green leaves... flowers. Lemon scented.'

'Well they burst into flames, one after the other.'

Bruno, who'd been squinting through alternating eyes, opened both and tried not to laugh. He couldn't hold it in.

Anderson straightened up. 'Oh, one minute you're saying, Anderson I've had a bad day, give me a beer. Now you're laughing?'

'I'm sorry,' he said, trying to stop. 'I have had a bad day. I got chased—' He yawned again, 'chased out of the bookshop, ridiculed by the... that fucking butcher. It's good to talk to someone... civilised for once.'

'Well if you want to hear the rest of the story you can

be quiet. You should've known better than to go into the bookshop in the first place. The town's set up for tourists, Bruno; they can't risk letting anyone in anywhere.'

Bruno rattled the ring-pull inside his empty can and raised his eyebrows.

'You're not serious, are you? A fucking joker, you are!' Anderson grabbed the can, went inside and reappeared with two more, opening one for himself.

'So, like I said, I'm telling you how I heard it. They burst into flames and Mac got the keys. The preacher packed his things and took to the streets. He called for the townsfolk to listen. God had spoken and the town wasn't safe. Everyone had to follow him to Jinguba.

'But as devout as they were, the townsfolk didn't want to leave. They'd built their homes here. They were settled. Only a few followed him. Have you heard about Jinguba?'

Bruno mopped the beer from his lips and beard. 'I heard the woman… She mentioned it… outside the tour shop.'

Anderson nodded. 'Silvia. So while the people of Jinguba were building fortifying walls and bailing the sand out of their houses day after day, Mac and his friends were changing things here in Brisas. Can you imagine any of those fishing settlements you've seen growing into a resort like this?'

Bruno shook his head.

'It happened here, though. Mac made links with the city, got his friends the proper training, managed to get everyone behind him. When his mother died, he extended the house and opened the bookshop in her memory – she was never without a book. They say those wooden trunks were filled with books, herbs, seeds and a whole lot more besides. The restaurants and bars sprung up. You know this place was called Jeri before Mac changed the name to Brisas?'

'That explains my map, then.' Bruno dragged the cold can across his forehead.

'For ten years the Jingubans fought to keep the sand out of their houses, but the town was condemned. In that time

Mac had transformed Brisas, and business hasn't slowed since. The Jingubans, along with those who followed the preacher, came back, and Mac allowed them to stay.'

'And the preacher?'

'Wouldn't leave Jinguba. Supposedly smoked and drank himself to death in his house there. Of course, the townsfolk here lost their church. Mac keeps it for his own purposes, but with things happening so fast, people were questioning their own way of life and wondering how to interpret the encounter between him and the preacher. Was the message of the burning bushes, along with what happened in Jinguba, actually confirmation that Mac's was the true religion?'

'He stays in the bookshop?' asked Bruno. He was just about able to keep both eyes open now.

Anderson waved him off and spoke on. 'More and more of the youth wanted to learn his capoeira. They soon converted to his way of thinking. His religion flourished. Brick by brick, they built that temple on the other side of town. Every one of them had a part in it. You know the one? Next to the upside-down tree.'

'Is his religion that much... different? You're a follower?'

Anderson shrugged. 'I don't cast any judgement on it.'

'And how does it affect this place? Everything works well here?'

Anderson dragged on his cigar. 'The elders, most of the Jingubans and others who'd moved in clusters from smaller settlements do most of the fishing and farming. Those who grew up with Mac collect the honey, run the restaurants, bars, hotels and do the kiting.' He nodded. 'It works. It really does. They're hostile to travellers because they see you guys coming in, feeding off the town and giving nothing back. Think about it from their perspective; they can't have the tourists being harassed by you lot all the time. If the tourists stop coming the town's finished.'

'I see... Well, I'm not here to harass anyone... I wanted to give back more than I took. Much more.'

Anderson sipped his beer. 'Are you a Christian, Bruno?'

'I'm nothing. I never got past asking where God came from.'

'But God was always there.'

Bruno nodded. He didn't want to get into a discussion about religion. 'Anderson, thanks for the story... Thank you. I don't get much—' He lifted his leg and farted, '... friendly conversation from people.'

'I'm glad you enjoyed it.' Anderson cupped his nose with one hand and reached out for the can with the other. Bruno drank the remainder and passed it to him. 'Okay now, Bruno. Good luck with your sales.'

Bruno rose to his feet and picked up his selling-board. 'There won't be any.'

In the darkness of the trail he could hear people talking behind their garden walls, could smell their food cooking. He was hungry. Music from Main Street echoed as he approached the church to look at the bushes. He rubbed their gluey, lemon-scented leaves and was sure he'd read about them before. 'Vallena...Vrellixnila... Fraxinella!' In hot and dry conditions it could ignite in a flash. Big Mac's miracle had been nothing more than coincidence. The preacher had probably dropped a cigarette or had caused a spark, somehow. He looked closer at the stone around the base of the bushes and laughed. 'Flint.'

At the cross, he drew a hand over his body: 'In the name of the Father, and of the Son and of the Holy Spirit. A-fucking-men.' He snatched the chicken carcass from its foot and was about to set off for his shelter, when he froze, clutching the chicken to his chest. On the hill a crowd had amassed with their arms raised, ready to charge. He was about to toss the chicken away and make a run for it, but peered ahead for an extra second. There was something odd about their silence, their stillness. He focused both eyes on them and the tenseness of his body evaporated. It wasn't people at all. It was the cacti lit by the stars and the moon.

It was nature's way of beckoning to him. Tomorrow he'd go. The great river was calling out. He didn't have to prove anything to anyone. The chicken carcass bounced off his leg as he walked to the shelter. He looked up at the stars, picked out the constellations Crux, Centaurus and Carina, and took the flint from his pocket.

3

Bruno pulled the bed sheet over his head against the daylight strobing into his shelter. He tried to get back to sleep, but his mind had latched onto a knot tightening in his abdomen. Each twitch of his gut sent a jolt to his brain, cranking him fully awake.

'Oh, please no,' he said, rising to his elbows. He strained to see past the flapping tarpaulin. Blackened feathers and jagged, pink flesh lay amongst the half-charred fuel. The night before came back to him. He'd eaten the chicken near raw.

From his belly came the gargling noise of a clogged sink draining, along with the sensation of the entire contents of his gut screaming for an exit. He clenched his buttocks, rolled onto his knees and inched to his feet. Cold and weak, he set off in a hobbled run for the toilets, hopped two-footed up the steps and through the doorway. He found the first cubicle locked, the second locked, the third locked.

'Hurry the fuck up!' he shouted. 'Let me in!' There was no time. He ran back out onto the sand. In the warm haze of morning, people idled about the camp, oblivious to his emergency.

'Why can't you all fuck off?' he muttered. The hill was too far away. He ran for a neighbouring garden, but there was a man at the window. The back wall of the church offered the only refuge. He dropped his shorts to his knees and squatted, his backside pressed against the cool stone.

A puree of rancid bolognese exploded against the wall and squirted to the sand as a feeling of utter relief washed over him. He looked around for witnesses but there was no one there. Each convulsion of his gut was less severe than the last, and he began to relax. He searched for something to clean himself with and remembered the bushes. Reaching around the corner he picked at the small leaves. A door creaked, keys jingled, a lock clunked. He glanced towards the front of the church and questioned if what he saw was real or a drunken hallucination. It was turning to face him.

'God,' he said.

'Not quite,' said the moving statue of shining obsidian.

The giant stalked towards him, and despite the urge to run, Bruno couldn't move. He turned his eyes down, listened to its feet padding over the sand, and stared at them as they appeared in front of him.

'Vagabundo.' Mac paused. 'What's that awful stink?'

Bruno felt like crying. 'I'm sorry. The toilets were full. I… I'm ill.'

'Look at me, Vagabundo.'

Bruno looked from the feet to the red *abadas* with the circle of keys clipped to them, to the abdomen and chest. Ridged, heavy muscles, taut flawless skin. It was as if he had been cut full-size from ore instead of grown from a child. There was a hard beauty to his face that matched that of his body. An unlined forehead leading to a smooth, bald head. A narrow, rectangular nose and well-defined lips set in a square jaw. He wore a low-slung necklace of translucent beads and, gripped in his gigantic hand, the *berimbau* was like a toy. Despite the fear and embarrassment, Bruno felt awe.

'This is what you think of my church?' Mac took a measured look in both directions, then he crouched and wrapped his free hand around Bruno's throat. There was a reptilian coolness to his touch, a rank smell and a slickness to his skin. It was as if he'd been bathing amongst roots and fetid soil. 'This is a personal insult, you understand? But you've put the livelihoods of my people at risk and I can't accept that.' His voice was sonorous. He spoke with perfect enunciation.

Bruno didn't know what to say. Despite the pain in his thighs, he held eye contact and tried not to squirm. Struggling would only make it worse. He looked into Mac's unusual eyes. Hard black diamonds set in pure white candle wax.

'What if a tourist had seen you? Do you think tourists would come to a town' – There was anger in his voice now – 'where bearded, ragged, tattooed vagrants spray their stinking shit wherever they please?' He looked to either side again.

'I'm sorry,' Bruno started to say, but Mac's grip cut off his speech.

'My intention was not for this campsite to become a parasitic settlement. It was meant for tourists, not tramps. If your filth is here when I come back, you're gone. The lot of you are gone!'

With every word Mac spoke the pressure mounted in Bruno's head, until he felt his eyes about to pop out of their sockets. All feeling left him.

He woke. Shit was stuck to his hip, back and arm. He sprang to his feet, and with handfuls of sand and leaves tried to clean himself. He pulled his shorts up, scrubbed the spattered wall and dug a hole to tip the mess into.

Down the trail, behind Anderson's bar, he scaled the rocks and ran into the sea. The waves broke over his head as he trod water to stay afloat. *Swim out*, his inner voice said. *Keep going until your arms and legs give in. There's no shame in it. Drowning's the best way to go. At least you'll succeed in something for once in your life.*

*

The sun had dropped below the horizon by the time he got back to the campsite. A small red tent stood on the opposite side of his fire pit, blocking his view of the hill. He ignored it and to keep himself busy despite his tiredness, set about cleaning. He'd leave the site in good condition for whoever it belonged to.

After picking out the gnawed bones and feathers, he rebuilt the fire and began raking the sand with a long-spined cactus limb. He'd hacked the spines off either end to form handles. On his knees, shuffling in circles, he raked the sand into overlapping spiral troughs. A girl walked past him in the dusk. She sat cross-legged in front of the red tent and watched him.

Eventually she spoke. 'Hello,' she said in English. 'I'm Beatriz.'

He took a seat in front of his own tent and threw the rake aside. If she was shocked by his appearance, she hid it well. *Can't see me properly in the dull light*, he thought. 'Bruno,' he said, getting up again. He lit the fire and lingered over it, so she could see the full horror show.

Teenager, he guessed as he looked her over. *A bit young for this life*. He didn't bother putting his top on. Like the rest of him, his torso was covered in tattoos. There were anchors, boats, compasses and birds. *Fortune Favours the Bold* was inked in a scrawl across his abdomen.

'Been here long?' she asked. There was hesitation in her voice. *Is this man dangerous?* she'd be thinking. *Have I made a mistake setting my tent here?* He could tell by her accent that Spanish was her native tongue.

Faded jeans, which once would have been as black as her hair, clung to her slender legs. Sequins on her loose top sparkled in the firelight. She reached into her tent and drew out a tortoise-shell hairbrush.

'*Dos noches*,' he said, snapping dried mangrove roots and tossing them into the fire.

She sandwiched her hair between the brush and her palm

and made smooth downward strokes. He became conscious of his own hair, matted strands of uneven lengths and thicknesses. It had been years since he'd brushed it. Hers was so cultivated in comparison that he could barely hold back a smile when the brush snagged on a knot.

'I'm still not sure how long I'll stay,' she said, switching to Spanish. 'I met some people in the city. They had a spare seat in a pickup truck. I bought this tent and came along.' Her skin was unblemished, white porcelain, but her eyes were dark and puffed with fatigue, or grief. He wasn't sure which.

'Why aren't you on Main Street? That's where they'll be. You're missing all the action.'

She tossed the brush to the sand and worked at the knot with her fingers. 'It's been a long day. Maybe I'll see them tomorrow. How about you?'

'Don't like crowds.'

He followed her eyes as she surveyed the site. Only a few travellers were around. The majority would be in town making sales.

He fished a bottle of water from his tent and drank. Her fingers stopped working the knot. Her eyes were on the bottle. He offered it to her, and she gulped at it, straight from his mouth to hers, before he could even pass her a cup.

'Have you eaten today?' he asked.

She passed the bottle back. 'I have oatmeal if you want to use the rest for porridge.' She wiped her lips.

'I can do better than water for you.' He balanced a pot over the fire, opened a pair of coconuts and mashed their insides into a slurry. 'Get the oatmeal.'

She withdrew a crumpled box of porridge oats and emptied it into the pot.

'Here,' he said. 'Drink the rest of the water. There's plenty in town. You don't have to go thirsty.'

She drained the bottle and handed it back. He cut two vertical strips from its side, each encompassing one of the feet at the bottle's base. He folded them lengthways for strength and held them over the fire to round the edges in the heat.

'A spoon,' she said, her eyebrows lifting.

He cupped the porridge into one of the bowls he'd made and passed it over to her.

Her cupid's-bow lips drew back in a smile, unsheathing diamond-shaped canines at either side.

Look at those teeth, he thought. *Perfect for tearing fibre from branches, meat from bones*. He watched her as she stirred the porridge in her bowl. Her face had perfect symmetry. He could tell she would never have been in a bad photo in her life. *But those teeth*, he thought. *What a gift*. Her eyes rose and met his. Her mouth snapped shut.

'This is how you survive?' she asked after a few spoonfuls. 'You live off the land, make what you need from junk?'

Porridge stuck to his beard. 'It's not difficult,' he said, his mouth full. 'In the wild I can forage, trap and fish. In cities I can find anything I need in the bins. You know the supermarkets throw food out long before it goes off.'

'I tried to find a job today,' she said. 'Went from door to door, shops, restaurants, bars. I've got experience, you know? *I'm a hard worker*, I told them. *I'll do anything*.' She was an animated talker, eyes fixed on his, eyebrows moving, head bobbing. 'I almost begged. You know what they did?' Her jaw clenched. 'Soon as they realised I wasn't a tourist, they laughed at me. They said,' she spoke into the bowl, '*local jobs for locals only*.'

She was a runaway. He'd seen enough of them in the city dosshouses to recognise one. Meek little creatures, usually, sitting in the corner, afraid, noses twitching as the city's finest hobbled in wearing their rags, accompanied by the sour stench of filth and ill-health. But this girl was different. The clothes, her fine, arched eyebrows, slender nose and tapering jaw; there was a confidence in how she spoke, a quality in her mannerisms. Everything about her spoke of privilege.

'How old are you?' he asked.

She lowered the bowl to one side, drew circles in the sand with her finger and didn't answer.

'Shouldn't you be in school?'

'I'm twenty,' she said. 'I left school already. I wanted to explore the continent for a while before going back and finishing university.' There was a touch of defiance in her voice. She knew he'd read her but didn't want to give anything up. He pulled on his beard.

'Same here,' he said. 'Me too. I'm studying anthropology.' He looked hard at her when he spoke. 'But why not go back now? Get your family to pay the trip home. I'm sure they miss you.'

'What makes you think I *have* a family?' She stared at him. He was enjoying this. He was so used to being talked down to and abused by others. Now he could give a bit back to one of them. 'You'll never get a job here. They don't like outsiders.' She swept her hand over the circles she'd drawn. 'If we get up early enough,' he continued, 'we can have a good look in the bins. It'll still be cool then. Won't stink as much. See what goodies we can find. I got a nice baguette the other day. It only stank a little bit. Tasted great.' He rubbed his hands together and smiled at her.

'I don't want to look through bins,' she said, shaking her head.

Was there a quiver in her voice? He pressed on. 'It's not *that* bad. Who cares if the food's not served on a silver platter in some fancy restaurant?'

'It'll be covered in flies! Full of germs!'

'You can't beg here. They'll throw you straight out. Then what'll you do?'

'Beg?' She stared at him in disgust. He could see the tears were just about ready. He almost had her. 'What are you talking about, *beg?*'

'Pride will only hold you back. Beatriz, isn't it? Let go of it now.'

46

She lowered her eyes. Her shoulders rose and fell with burdened breaths. He leaned in to hear her whimpers, watched for her hand to reach up and rub the tears from her red lids, but neither happened. Instead, she cocked her head to one side, fed her fingers into her hair and tore the knot out with such force it made him wince. She threw the clump of hair in the fire. The smell of it singeing curled his lip.

He reached into his shelter, picked a piece of jewellery from his selling-board and threw it over to her.

'What's this?' she asked, holding it up in the firelight.

'A welcome present.'

'To poverty?' She smoothed her hair back and held his gaze until he looked away. The hard exterior he'd been trying to maintain softened. She inspected the bracelet again. 'It looks strange,' she said. 'Almost like it's been grown instead of made.'

'You don't like it? Give it here.' He held his hand out.

She closed her fist around it. 'I like it fine. It's beautiful.' She tied it around her ankle. 'I've never seen one like it. Where'd you get it?'

'I made it. Made lots of 'em.' He brought the board out to show her. 'I wanted to sell to the tourists, but they weren't interested.'

'So you're hiding here because of that?'

He flushed. 'Hold on,' he said, trying not to get flustered. 'You're the one hiding. I'm just passing through here.'

'If you say so.' Her smile had his jaw clenching. 'Where are you going?'

'The rainforest. If it's not been cut down by the time I get there.'

'Why?'

He exhaled. 'To do something about... To take something... Oh, I don't know. Just to go there, see what we can learn.'

'We?'

He held his arms out. 'Civilisation.' He spoke through his teeth, drawing out every syllable.

'I bet I can sell them.'

'The jewellery? You're welcome to it.' He tossed the board towards her.

'But you have to teach me how to make them.'

'No, no, no. I'm done. Take them. They're yours.'

'Just the basics. Surely you can do that?'

'Look, people are ignorant and I don't fit in here. I don't belong. I wouldn't buy anything from someone with a face like this, either. Nobody wants anything to do with me, and I'm fine with that now. I'm on a different path.'

'Why go to the trouble of making them, then? People are people. What if they just sense how you feel about yourself and mirror it? We all have problems, you know? Maybe they're just as self-conscious about something you can't see?'

'Jesus, I didn't ask for a psychiatric consultation. I know it's not *all* their fault. I'm just better off alone.'

'So you're just going to leave, without even trying?'

'I tried! Can't you fucking see? I've tried everywhere. There's nothing for me.'

'Everyone has issues. I saw how you looked at my vampire teeth. How'd you think that made me feel?'

'I was admiring them!'

'Bullshit. In school I got teased so much I never opened my mouth.'

'I'm serious. They're perfect.'

'Don't lie. I wanted to be taller, too.'

'You're not that small.'

'Want to know what I did?'

'Not really,' he lied. 'But if it makes you feel better.'

'I joined basketball training… swimming… skipped two thousand times every day. I ate calcium pills every night, took medicines from the Far East, went to the orthopaedics for a grow-tall-injection—'

'A what injection?'

'One where they check the bone condition and inject you with hormones to make it grow better.'

'Surely you didn't go through with it?'

'No. Unfortunately my bone condition was fine.'

'Yes, how unfortunate.'

'I used a machine that pulled my neck and legs in opposite directions.'

'A rack? You're crazy.'

'I hung by my feet from a bar across my door frame. I persuaded my doctor to give me X-rays to check for scoliosis.'

'And what's that?'

'It's a spine condition. If your spine is bent enough, they can give you surgery to correct it. But again,' she sighed, 'mine was normal. I even drank a glass of long bean juice every day from the age of twelve until I don't know how old, and I fucking hate long bean juice.'

He shook his head. 'It contains some kind of mineral that increases bone density?'

'I don't know. They must call them long beans for a reason, though.'

'You were teased really badly, weren't you?'

'What? No. I mean, I was teased about my teeth but not my height. Of course, I knew if I'd fixed them, they'd have teased me about my height instead. And everyone in the magazines and on TV is tall, slim and beautiful, so…'

'They're poisonous! Made of plastic and full of drugs. I threw my TV out the window years ago… Here.' He got to his feet. 'Stand up.'

They stood facing each other.

'See,' she said. 'You're massive.'

'I'm one eighty-eight. That's tall even for a man. But you're not that much shorter. What are you? One seventy?'

'One fifty-five.'

'Well don't worry about height. It's not important.' He sat back down, looked at his feet and spoke with sincerity: 'You're perfect.'

'I don't have any boobs either.'

'Well I'm sure it suits your body type. There's more to a woman than boobs.'

'But you see what I'm saying? We all have problems. It's not you against the world. We're in it together. And I *did* try everything. I'm sure I tried a lot more than you have.'

'Thanks, Beatriz. I really appreciate it. But I can't stay.'

Her shoulders fell and her eyes closed. 'Please.' Her voice grew small. 'Just one week. Give me a week and I'll sell them. I know I can. If you go, I…' Her lips stopped moving and on her eyelash a single tear fluttered red in the firelight. It ran down her cheek.

Bruno gazed at the hill, at the beckoning limbs of the cacti and the slit of the new moon smiling out at him. He was so close to the forest that he could almost smell it. She had come from nowhere. She was nothing to him. Why should he care? Who had been there to help when he needed it?

*

They started the next day. Bruno walked her through the town and took her to the top of the dune. She was another person entirely. Her hair was tied back, and she'd drawn thick lines over her eyelids, that gave her an Asian appearance. Much of the jewellery from the board was gone, wrapped around her wrists and ankles. Necklaces draped over her low-cut vest, sea glass anklets sparkled below her harem trousers. She was like an ancient traveller on the Silk Road. Although small, she wasn't skinny. There was a perfection to her, nothing excessive or lacking. As she walked, her muscular shoulders and strong legs moved with a grace and efficiency that reminded him of the *capoeiristas* performing in the *roda*.

'Okay,' said Beatriz. 'Give me your pitch.'

'What's that?'

'You know… Sell to me. Pretend I'm a stranger. Go.'

The board almost fell from his hands as he raised it for her to see. 'Hi,' he said. 'These are natural pieces of—'

'Nah.'

'I made them myself.'

'Can't you see I'm busy? I don't *want* any.'

'They're the cheapest you'll find in Las Bri—'

'Yuck.'

He dropped the board and held his palms up. 'What do you want from me?'

'Do you have any sales experience at all?'

'Of course I have.'

'No need to get defensive.'

'I've sold street papers in the cities. And photographs.'

'What's a street paper?'

'A paper homeless people can buy at one price and sell at another.'

'A *higher* price, I hope. Well, that's a start I suppose. I volunteered in a shopping mall for six months. Charity work. We had to get people to sign up for a regular donation or donate whatever they had in their pocket.'

'Doesn't sound like selling.'

'They put me through a day course in sales. I was probably the only one there who listened to the instructor *and* bought the books on the reading list *and* actually read them. Okay. Let's give it a try. I'll take the lead. You stay behind me and a little to the side so it's not weird-looking. Don't say anything unless I ask you a question.'

The music from the day-bars became louder between the gusts of wind as they rounded the bay and turned up Main Street. She carried the board with ease and exuded confidence, her head high, padding over the sand like a model on the catwalk.

A young man in board-shorts, carrying a towel, walked in their direction, his head down against the wind.

'Hey there,' she shouted. He stopped and took her in. 'How's it going?'

'Good, good,' he said, standing to face her. He glanced at Bruno, who inched further to the side, hoping he was in the right position. The man lifted his sunglasses.

Beatriz raised the board to show him. 'You wanna—'

'Oh no, no, no.' He pulled his sunglasses down and waved a hand. 'Not interested,' he said, walking off. 'I'm in a hurry.'

With a shrug of her shoulders and a smile at Bruno, Beatriz continued up the street. She approached a group of four girls who'd just descended the steps at the Dolphin cafe, which was packed. Three wore straw hats, sunglasses and beach kaftans. One was in linen trousers and a bikini top.

She could blend right in with them, Bruno thought. *But you can't find her kind of beauty in a make-up bag, and presence like that can't be taught. She's just like Flora.* He winced at the thought.

'Hi girls, I'm Beatriz, this is Bruno. Where you from?'

'Italia,' said the one in linen trousers.

She focused on her and switched to Italian: 'Last summer I waited a whole hour on Rialto Bridge to get a spot by the railings. I was so close. Little by little, I edged through the crowd, and I was just about to get a space, my hand almost touched the railing, when a busload of cap-wearing Chinese, like an army of wind-up toys, muscled in and forced me to the back!'

They all laughed. Bruno, who hadn't understood a word, watched her with a bemused smile.

'You won't get these on Rialto Bridge, though. The necklaces are fifteen *contos*, but we can offer a group discount.'

They looked from the jewellery on the board to the pieces she wore.

'*Non è il mio stile,*' said the leader, shaking her head.

'It wasn't my style either, but they look pretty good once they're on, don't you think? Anyway, what's respected today is ridiculed tomorrow. Best to get out in front. Interesting trousers, by the way. I used to have a pair like that.'

One of the girls stifled a laugh. The leader's neck stiffened. 'When do you leave?'

'Tomorrow morning,' another answered.

The leader whispered to the girl next to her, and they walked away. The other two stayed.

'I'll tell you what,' Beatriz said, lowering her voice. 'I'll give you any of the bracelets for three *contos*.'

They stepped in closer.

'They're selling pretty quick,' she added. 'Bruno, how long will it take to stock up again?' Not giving him time to answer, she shook her head. 'Not by tonight, anyway.'

'*Bene*,' said one of the girls. She plucked off two bracelets beaded with cowrie shells. 'Six?' she asked, dropping them into her bag and taking out her purse. Beatriz nodded. The second girl swivelled a bracelet on its hook to inspect it.

'Ah, the blue gemstone,' said Beatriz. 'I was going to keep that one.' The girl's hand snatched it up.

'Sea glass,' Bruno muttered.

'A nice choice,' she said, ignoring him.

She took the money and they moved off in opposite directions. '*Addio*,' she called after them. 'Say sorry to Giuseppe! It would never have worked between us!'

'We will,' the one with the gemstone called back. She smiled. '*Addio*.'

'See that,' said Beatriz, holding up nine soiled *conto* bills. 'Start with something expensive and concede to something a bit cheaper.'

'But the necklaces aren't fifteen *contos*.'

'They're worth whatever the customer pays. This is business. How will we work it? Fifty-fifty?'

'Sounds fair.' He'd have accepted any split she'd offered.

She handed him four and put five in her pocket. 'I'll give you the fifty *centavos* later.'

They spent the rest of the day selling. More people turned

53

them away than bought from them, but in the end they'd made enough to pay for a few days' food.

As he walked, Bruno kept an eye out for Mac, ready to run down the nearest side street if he spotted him, but it was Beatriz who ended up hiding. They'd been trying to sell outside Anderson's bar, when she dropped the board and ran for the trail. Bruno turned to see three young gringos reading a menu at one of the kiosks. A slim guy in a fitted singlet had his arm around a dark-haired girl; the other guy, with spiked hair and a bad complexion, held a ukulele. Bruno gathered the jewellery, picked up the board and chased after her.

'What's going on?' he asked, catching up to her halfway up the trail.

'Those were the guys I came with,' she said, looking past him to see if they were coming.

'If you're embarrassed of me I'll go back to the site. It's not a problem.'

'What? Don't be silly. I just don't want to be seen doing this. They think I'm a tourist.'

'It's not because of me?'

'Of course not. Bruno, don't be so insecure! Look, they're only here for a few days. You got a good look at them?'

He nodded.

'If you see them again, let me know and we can avoid them. Can you do that, please? It's only for a few days.'

He nodded. 'I'll keep a lookout. Tell me, doesn't all this rejection get you down?'

They began walking towards the campsite. 'The last time was for charity, so there was no need for embarrassment, but anyway, these people don't know us. Why take it personally? The stuff you've made is great. It really is. If they don't want it it's their loss. But it's different with those three. I didn't do anything to stop them from thinking I was just a normal tourist. I knew they had their doubts, though. I can't deal with the look they'll give me if they see what I'm really doing here.'

'That look of pity, masked by a nervous, reassuring smile that says everything's okay?'

'Something like that.'

'I deal with that look every day, except there's no pity because I did this to myself.'

'Well you're better for it, then. Who wants to be pitied?'

They headed over the hill and walked along the coconut palm beach.

'You ever tried it before?' she asked, looking out at the kite surfers.

He shook his head.

'I'd love to. I've only done normal windsurfing, though.'

'You'd probably get blown away.'

'You'll pull me back though, won't you?'

'Of course.' He smiled at her.

They walked around the bay and cut between the dune and the corral. All twelve donkeys were there. The owner, who Bruno had seen outside the tourist centre, was dragging a brush down one's flank. They crowded around him like children. Beatriz shouted and waved at the man. He walked over, the donkeys following in a huddle. One rubbed its neck on the barbed wire fence. A pair poked their heads through and tore at the scrub-grass. Bruno stayed behind and looked over Beatriz's shoulder.

Up close, the man's hair was spun like candyfloss. His eyes had the same docile look as those of the donkeys. He smiled a big, gap-toothed smile.

'How's it going?' she said. 'I'm Beatriz.'

'Nice to meet you!' He extended a meaty hand on the end of a ham-hock forearm. 'I'm Tonino and these are Oshum, Eshu, Ochumaré, Yemanjá, Oshala, Omulu, Nana...' He pointed each one out. 'Ossaim, Zhango, Oshosi, Ogum, Iansa.' He nodded benignly at Bruno.

'Strange names,' she said.

'Blame the big man, not me.'

'God?'

'Mac,' said Bruno.

'There you go.' Tonino wagged a finger at him. 'He knows.'

'Bruno, come pet them,' said Beatriz. 'Look at the pattern on that one. It's like a van Gogh painting.'

'That's Iansa,' said Tonino. He cupped his mouth and whispered, 'My favourite.'

'Nice area you have for them,' said Bruno.

'I'd like it to be bigger and greener but they're hungry animals. They'd strip a football pitch faster than Pele.'

'Not as fast as El Diego, though.' Bruno put on an exaggerated smile.

'Ah ha! If you say so. I've not seen jewellery like that before,' he said to Beatriz. 'Looks good.'

'Take a bracelet.'

'Well,' he said, 'I can't. If it's not for sale in the shops, I shouldn't be seen with it.'

'It's a present, take one.'

Tonino smiled and looked over at the streets. 'You want to feed them?'

'Can I?' said Beatriz.

He took a handful of feed from a bucket and crumbled it into her hand. 'Just hold your palm out flat and keep your fingers together.'

She giggled as Iansa munched in her palm. Tonino offered a handful to Bruno.

'Nah,' he said. 'Thanks.'

'Oh, come on,' Beatriz said. 'It's fun.'

He edged beside her and took a handful of crumbled pellets from the bucket. The donkeys pushed and bumped heads, vying for space. He could smell their hair and breath, the fermented straw of their waste. Moist, stubbly lips tickled his palm and hot breath blew between the gaps in his fingers. He felt a warmth well up inside, smiled at Beatriz, and petted the donkey with his other hand.

Tourists arrived at the opposite end of the corral. 'You've got more guests,' said Beatriz.

Tonino looked over at them. 'Suppose I better get ready for the next tour, then. See you guys later.'

They walked around the corral and passed through the copse of *caju* trees. Bruno picked up the empty bottle that lay where he'd left it and put it in the bin by the supermarket.

Tourists loitered outside. Each just like the other; gaudy, plastic sunglasses, branded board-shorts, thong-style sandals on their feet. Most had floppy, dark hair, some had dyed it blonde. The girls were all dressed the same as those they'd made their first sale to.

'They're like clones,' Bruno whispered.

'Social proof,' said Beatriz. 'We're programmed to follow the herd. Safety in numbers.'

'Maybe that's why the world's in such a bad state.'

Before Bruno could stop her, she walked into the supermarket. He looked at Luis, who stared straight ahead but kept his good eye on her via a series of mirrors mounted to the walls and racks. Luis was smiling when he served her, head turned just enough so his good eye could take her all in. He even packed the bag.

So much has changed, Bruno thought. Where had she come from, this beautiful, confident, smart girl who was turning everything around for him?

They walked past the temple to the upside-down tree. Bruno showed her how to strip fibres from the inside of the trunk. As he stripped the bark, Beatriz looked out from the hollow, scanning the streets for potential customers.

'Bruno,' she whispered. 'Come here. You have to see this guy.'

Bruno stayed where he was. 'What does he look like?'

'Dark as night and just as big.'

'Mac,' he said. 'Come here. Don't look. Has he seen you?'

She stayed put. 'No, he's headed for the temple. There's another guy.'

Bruno peered out over Beatriz's head. She held onto his elbow and watched. 'That's Ivo,' he said, 'and Faka and… I don't know that last one.'

After a short while they emerged from the temple. Mac, Faka and Ivo carried *berimbaus*. The other man lugged a conga drum over his shoulder and carried a tambourine in his hand.

'You see Mac, there?' Bruno said. 'He choked me unconscious yesterday.'

The whites of Beatriz's eyes flashed in the shade. 'What did you… I mean, why'd he do that?'

Bruno hesitated, reliving the warm, joyous feeling of his bowels emptying. 'I was outside the church. He said I was trespassing.'

'That's assault. You need to talk to the police.'

The men disappeared behind the buildings of Beekeeper Close.

'It doesn't work like that out in these towns, Beatriz. The police are in the city, and you know how far away that is. They'll not bother about anything that happens out here, especially with a tramp like me as the victim.'

'I wonder what he's hiding in there.'

'Where?'

'The church.'

'It's nothing to do with that. He just hates everyone in the campsite. He admitted it to me.'

She grabbed his arms. 'Let's follow them!'

'We've had enough for one day, no?' He took the grocery bag from her and stuffed the fibres inside. 'Let's go eat.'

*

After a dinner of vegetable broth and bread, to accommodate Beatriz, who was a vegetarian, Bruno took her to meet Anderson. A woman of at least sixty, with a shock of peroxide blonde hair, wearing denim shorts cut far too high and a bikini top covering sagging, sun-withered breasts, hopped off the stool at Anderson's bar. She peeled a drunk young tourist from the counter, cradled him in her arms and shuffled past them towards the *carrinhos*. '*Boa noite, queridos*,' she said to them. She had several small, neat tattoos on her body. A honey bee, a smoking cigar, a diamond, a one hundred US dollar bill.

'Who was that?' Bruno asked, as Anderson led them to the back door. The sultry night air held the floral, musky scent of the woman's perfume.

'Present company first please, Bruno.' Anderson brought his hat to his chest and eyed Beatriz. 'I'm Anderson. It's a pleasure to meet you.'

'It's my pleasure,' she said. 'My name is Beatriz.'

He took her hand in his and raised it to his lips. 'Welcome to Brisas.'

Bruno noticed the look Anderson gave him. *Wondering what she's doing with me, eh?*

'Could we trouble you for a couple of beers?' she asked.

'You most certainly could.' Anderson stepped inside and returned with three cans from the fridge. He waved away her attempt to pay him.

'Look,' he said. 'I'm more than happy to have you here, but my boss—'

'I told her,' said Bruno. 'We'll only have one can.'

Anderson nodded. 'That woman, Bruno *and* Beatriz, is Honey. She came here a few years before I arrived, and she's the only traveller who's ever managed to cross over and become a local.'

'How'd she manage that?' asked Bruno.

'She provides a service that no local is willing to do.'

'Which is?'

'She's a prostitute.'

Beatriz's eyebrows jumped almost to her hairline. She glanced at Bruno.

'Bit old for a prostitute, is she not?' asked Bruno.

'The name gives off a different connotation, don't it? But you'd be surprised how much business she gets.'

Beatriz opened her can and took a sip.

'She's accepted completely?' Bruno opening his. 'She fits in?'

'Yep. She's got a basic house at the top of the town and she holds her head high. I'm sure the elders and the Jingubans might have a grumble about it now and again but Mac's crowd aren't prejudiced people.'

'Unless you live in the campsite,' Bruno added.

'Yes but that's a financial thing. No offence, but them in the campsite, they take what they can but give nothing back.'

'Why are they so unprejudiced?' asked Beatriz.

'People say it's their religion. It's not based on sin and salvation. It's about balance and order.'

'Maybe I could do something like that,' Bruno said. 'Provide a service no local can.'

'I don't think there's a market for a male prostitute here, Bruno.' Anderson laughed at his joke. 'Aren't you on your way to the forest, anyway?'

'He wants to be one of you,' said Beatriz, a playful smile on her face.

'No I don't. I never told you anything like that, Beatriz. I'm on my own path.'

'He does,' she said, ignoring him. 'Don't listen.'

'And what brings *you* here?' Anderson asked her.

'She's a runaway,' said Bruno.

'Bruno.' Beatriz's smile disappeared. 'I'm taking some time out.'

Anderson pointed his can at the selling-board between them. 'Business is looking better. I saw you guys working the crowds today. You're quite the saleswoman.'

'She's teaching me to sell. I'm teaching her to make.'

'Perfect team,' Beatriz said, but her smile hadn't returned.

4

Over the next couple of weeks, they combed the beach for materials and made jewellery in the campsite. At nights, they stood between Ivo's and the *carrinhos* with their selling-boards on display. The tourists came to them. They never had to chase. Bruno suggested Beatriz shorten her name to Bea, knowing a single syllable name would be easier for the tourists to remember.

He'd stand behind her and slightly to the side, as she conversed with people. Too self-conscious to interrupt or add to the conversation, Bruno would let his mind drift. Sometimes he thought of the rainforest, imagining its sounds, animals and plant life. Other times, he tried to come up with great ideas to integrate with the locals and fit in as a contributing member of society. He fantasised about people smiling at him and calling him over for a chat. Almost unconsciously, he analysed the difference in the tourists' mannerisms towards Bea and himself. He constantly worried he might be holding her back. Every other night he told her he could return to the campsite if she wanted space – after all, unlike him, she was a complete, fully functioning person, and he didn't want to be a burden on anyone; but each time he suggested it she told him to be quiet.

Surrounded by so many people, he'd catch a look, a phrase or an action that reminded him of Flora. Despite feeling stronger with Bea at his side, if he allowed thoughts of her to stay in his head for more than an instant, the same old panic took hold, so intensely that he wanted to run and never stop. He'd whisper some excuse to Bea and rush into the darkness to calm down.

'I'm sure my hands are getting bigger,' Bea said one day at camp. She had fibres from the upside-down tree looped around her big toe and was braiding them into Celtic knots.

'You look good,' said Bruno, whittling a piece of driftwood into a lizard. 'You seem calmer... more relaxed.'

She nodded. 'I feel good.'

'"And what is it to work with love?"' He looked up at the sky. ' "It is to weave the cloth with threads drawn from your heart... even as if your beloved were to wear that cloth... It is to build a house with affection... even as if your beloved were to dwell in that house... It is to sow seeds with tenderness and reap the harvest with joy... even as if your beloved were to eat the fruit... It is to charge all things you fashion with a breath of your own spirit... and to know that all the blessed dead are standing about you and watching."'[2]

'I don't know how you remember all these quotes you come out with.'

'If you read something enough times, it sticks.'

'You're different with me,' she said. 'You'd never speak like that in front of other people.'

'I'm not good in crowds, you know that.'

'But you don't need to stand behind me all the time.'

'I don't want to get in your way. You've got a presence with people. I don't want to ruin it.'

'You could have that too, though. Just work on it. Test yourself. With practise you'll get it.'

He shook his head. 'Never. I'd need to live most of my life again before I could even try.' He was about to start

2 The Prophet – Kahlil Gibran

whittling again but hesitated. He looked at her and put his things aside. 'Bea, you're so confident and natural. You should have everything going for you. Why did you do it? Why did you run away?'

The look of comfort drained from her face. The braiding hung limp.

'I'm sorry,' he said, shocked to see the change in her. 'I shouldn't have asked.'

'No. Sometimes the more you try to ignore something, the more you need to confront it. It might help to tell... I'll try.' She drew her hair back and rubbed at her eyes. She watched him briefly then gazed at the sand. Her shoulders dropped as she exhaled. 'I should have been starting my last year of university a month ago... No.' Her fists opened and closed and she bit her upper lip. 'We'll start from the very beginning.'

Bruno crossed his legs and waited for her.

'My parents own a hotel, or they *owned* a hotel. I don't know any more. They worked their asses off to get it. My dad started out as a barman, learned everything he could about the trade... Makes the best cocktails even now.' She smiled. 'If you got him here, he'd have the most popular cart in no time. At nights he went to school and then on to college to learn about finance and business management. He got promoted to bar manager at a young age, then restaurant manager, and eventually general manager. My mother worked as a receptionist in the same hotel. Like him, she was ambitious, did night school, improved her Spanish, her English, and even though she was just a receptionist, she had a great mind for business. Her opinion has always been one you can trust. She has this intuition like nobody I've ever met. So one day a bouquet of twenty-two roses arrived for her with an anonymous note.' Bea stroked her hair and looked at Bruno. 'She's Russian. Never give a Russian girl an even number of flowers. That's for funerals. She knew straight away who they were from. She knew his handwriting from the customer logbook. Obviously, she forgave him, or I wouldn't be here.'

'So, you're half Russian! You speak it?'

'*Konechno*. That means of course. It was very important to them that I was brought up speaking both languages and English. After they got married, they decided to try for their own hotel. It was a huge risk but they worked well together and like I said, they're both ambitious.' Her hands moved as she spoke, her eyebrows arched. Even without make-up her eyes could take on an Asian quality. 'They bought an old hotel just outside the centre and completely turned it around. It became one of the best in the city. I arrived as soon as they were settled. I'm an only child, by the way. I wanted for nothing.

'A couple of years ago the floods came.' Her voice thinned. 'The regime ordered all the hotels to take in those who'd lost their homes, on a temporary basis, but the people never left. The help promised from the regime never came. The hotel lost all its paying guests. It started to get run-down. The blackouts and hyper-inflation didn't help any. My father had to let go of staff to pay the bills, and he was taking more and more responsibility on himself. He and Mother began arguing.' Her voice trembled. 'One afternoon I heard noises from a storeroom. I opened the door and found my dad crying. He was on a stool, slipping a noose over his head.' She stopped talking and turned away. Her back shook as she cried.

Bruno wanted to say something, to go over and hold her, to kiss her, but he couldn't. The words weren't there, nor the courage. He sat still and waited. 'I'm sorry,' he mumbled, but wasn't sure if it was loud enough for her to hear.

'I ran in and stopped him,' she said, wiping the tears from her eyes and turning to face him again. 'I got him down from the stool and wouldn't let go. I could see it in his eyes; he'd had some kind of a breakdown. Everything had got on top of him. He told me that by killing himself the insurance money would free Mother from the hotel debt and leave enough for me to finish university. I left them almost everything I had and snuck out that same night. I caught the first bus heading south.'

'Bea, I shouldn't have asked. I'm really sorry.'

'No,' she said, her eyes puffed and bloodshot. 'It's good to get it out. I needed it. I needed to cry. I feel so guilty, Bruno.' She looked up at him. 'About leaving them, I mean. But what could I do? I panicked. I tell myself it was the right thing to do.' She nodded. 'As crazy as it might sound to you, they'll worry more about me than their own problems, and it'll keep them going, it'll keep them together. As long as I continue sending my letters, they'll know I'm fine and they'll keep going.'

'You'll see them again, Beatriz. I'm sure you will.'

*

The tourists took to Bea as if she were one of their own, and without the selling-board she was often mistaken for one. She was a confident speaker, and could put people at ease like Bruno never could. His mind always raced forward when he spoke, as if it were a game of strategy. Even before a word had been spoken, he'd consider what and what not to say, imagine every direction the conversation could take. The fear of offending someone or making a fool of himself was paralysing. In the end he stayed quiet. He knew if it wasn't for Bea he'd be well along the river by now, but he was glad he'd stayed. He'd gained so much from her.

Bea used her femininity to sell; playful eyes, pouting smile. She wore low cut shirts and T-shirts, showing the skin of her flat chest, once porcelain, now a shade of gold. She never wore a bra, and the snagging of her nipples on the fabric of her tops had Bruno struggling to look anywhere else for weeks. She was as comfortable speaking to a crowd as she was to an individual and could charm both men and women with a nature that Bruno had only ever seen in

Flora. She never forgot a name and had a great knowledge and understanding of things. He knew she had what it took to survive anywhere.

'I always get what I want,' she told him after some cut-price cocktails from Kart de la Revolución. Her smile would come alive after a few drinks. She'd lose all self-consciousness about her teeth and would part her lips in a smile so penetrating that everyone around couldn't help but return it. Despite the manipulation and exploitation techniques she'd learned for her charity work, and used on the tourists, she had an integrity about her that all could see. They wanted what she was, not what she was selling.

Because of her, his jewellery almost sold itself. He saw either a necklace or bracelet on at least one in three people, although Bea said it was more like one in two. The money they made allowed them to eat twice a day, with food and charcoal bought from the supermarket, and to drink more than enough at the *carrinhos* every night. He soon realised he was becoming dependent upon her. It frightened him. If she were to leave, he'd be back to square one again. He made plenty of sales on his own, but was sure it was only because of his association with her, and the way she pushed him. He'd never have managed by himself.

He knew there could be no romance between them. There was the age difference, the respect he had for her, and the reality that she was everything he was not and never could be. She deserved much better than he could ever offer. He tried to fill the gap left by her family and friends, but didn't want to get too close. The last time he'd given himself completely it had almost killed him. If he did it again and it went wrong, he'd never recover.

One night, he found a canvas and some paints and brushes in the skip. Although the paints were nearly empty and the canvas a little worn, he took it all back to the campsite. He'd never been a painter, but he'd spent enough time watching

Flora to know the basics, and Bea encouraged him to give it a try. He spent hours in front of the canvas, waiting for an idea. Finally, after much indecision, he chose a church scene, but with brushes so old and frayed it was impossible to do anything fast. Day after day, under the hot sun, he worked at it. He painted the church with its driftwood cross; the bell with its coarse cord hanging to the ground, holding his breath and using a single brush-hair to get the fraying of the cord right; Mac and Ivo holding their *berimbaus*, Tonino with a donkey, Honey, and Faka the butcher with his knife. For a moment, he thought about putting himself in there, squatting against the wall, but in the end decided it was in bad taste. Bea tried to sneak a look at it every day, but he pushed her away and covered it up until it was finished and dry. When he finally showed it to her, he held his breath and inspected her face for the slightest betrayal of her true opinion. She didn't laugh. She said it was good in a strange kind of way, the way the colours blended and blurred, the small details when she looked at it closely; the way he'd captured each person seemed to show their character instead of their appearance. 'It'll definitely sell,' she told him.

At night, on his own, he carried it to Main Street to find a buyer. Without Bea to hide behind he was completely exposed, but it was time to push himself, to take a long overdue step forward.

By a lit-up *caju* tree in front of a live music bar, he watched a group of tourists at the closest table. A female guitarist by the back wall strummed songs about the south. The tourists sang along with her.

The longer he waited the less likely he'd be to do anything. He wiped the sweat from his brow with the desert scarf, put it back in his pocket. Three difficult steps forward and he was at the edge of the table, with only the railing separating him from the tourists. Eight faces turned to look at him. Condensation pooled around their beer bottles and dripped through the table slats. Candles in jars wrapped in brown paper flickered. The noise of the guitar and the singing went quiet in his ears. Everything closed in on him, leaving only the tourists' staring faces. He raised his eyes to meet theirs, cleared his throat and went to speak, but the man at the far end of the table, with dreadlocks and a bent nose, spoke first.

'Come on then, make your pitch,' he said in a native English accent. 'We're trying to listen to the music.'

Muffled laughter. The periphery entered Bruno's senses again. The music in his ears, the hushed voices of the sellers behind him. Laughter. Were they all listening in and laughing at him? He held his breath against the anger rising inside him.

'What I have here,' he said, clearing his throat again, 'is an original Brisas painting.'

'Wow,' said the girl next to the man. She made an exaggerated turn in her chair and faced the musician.

'Here,' he pointed, 'the beautiful church with its drystone walls and the flaming, yellow-flowered bushes, Mac the town ambassador, or the leader of the *capoeiristas*, as you might know him, Ivo the club owner, Tonino and his donkey, and Honey, the—'

'Who's the painter?' asked a male voice in hesitant Spanish.

Bruno pointed to his signature at the bottom. 'I'm the painter. It's literally just dried.'

'Is it a finger painting?' Dreadlocks asked.

Bruno stared at him as the laughter stabbed at his ears. 'No. I did it with very old brushes. I even bought an export stamp from the fucking tourist centre.' He looked down the street. 'It cost me ten *contos*.'

'It looks like shit, mate. I don't want it.' Dreadlocks turned to watch the guitarist.

Bruno's grip on the canvas tightened. A bead of sweat ran down his back. He went to rip the painting up, but paused. Setting it on fire with one of the candles on their table would have a bigger impact. The others stared at him as he tried to make a decision. In the instant that passed he realised how stupid he must look, standing there idle. He was unable to make even the smallest choice. With their eyes still on him, he remembered Bea's words and tried to calm down. 'Don't take it personally,' he whispered and hurried off down the street.

He tried many other tourists that night but there was no interest. At the *carrinhos*, he found Bea, seated himself on the sand next to her, and drank one cocktail after another. The man from the first group, the one who'd asked who the painter was, lingered nearby for a while then came up to him.

'I'm sorry about earlier,' he said.

'You can speak in English,' Bruno replied. 'It's fine.'

The man crouched beside them. 'We were all strangers at that table. Most of us, anyway. We're staying in the same guesthouse. That guy, Craig, the one with the dreads and the broken nose, he's an asshole. Been putting people down all night to impress the girls. Can I see it again?'

Bruno dusted the sand off the painting and handed it over. The man held it to the string lights above the street.

'I'd like to buy it,' he said.

'You really want it?' Bruno asked.

'I do. It's different. It's something real. Not some junk made-in-China thing.' He took a bundle of notes from his pocket and counted out fifty *contos*. Bea nudged Bruno in the ribs.

'Fifty's too much,' Bruno said. 'I can't take that.'

'He'll take it,' said Bea.

'It's priceless. I'll sell it on for twice that much in a few years.' The man pushed the notes into Bruno's hand. 'Fifty's a bargain. This is my last night anyway, and you can't use *contos* where I'm going.' He walked up the street. Before he'd gone more than a few paces, Bruno stood and called after him. 'Are you one hundred per cent sure?' he shouted.

The man turned and walked backwards. 'It's going straight on my living room wall. Of course I'm sure! All the best.'

Bruno returned the man's wave, pocketed the notes and sat back down next to Bea. He put his arm around her and skulled another drink. 'Bea,' he said, 'some defeats are more triumphant than victories.'[3]

*

After seeing Honey that first time at Anderson's they began to notice her all over town. She had a set route she'd follow every night, passing all the popular bars and weaving amongst the tourists on Main Street and at the *carrinhos*. After a few conversations they became good friends.

'Bea, dear,' she said in her hoarse voice, one evening. 'I like the style you've got here. You got a pretty face and a cute body, but a little bit of make-up and some lashes wouldn't hurt. You could be beautiful.' Honey, all rouge and hairspray, with caked foundation cracking like a clay desert, drew on her slim cigarette and continued: 'A push-up bra, some padding at the backside, a little heel on those sandals. You'd give me some real competition around here.'

Honey loved to look at their jewellery, and one night a piece on Bruno's board caught her eye. 'Oh, I adore it,' she said. She glanced at Bea. 'Cover your ears, sweetie.'

'Bruno,' she whispered, her mouth so close to his ear he felt the tip of her tongue touch his skin, felt the heat of her breath and smelled the tobacco on it. 'I'll suck your cock for that necklace.'

He'd been feeling sluggish all evening but that comment rang in his ears like an alarm bell. Even with Bea right next to him it was difficult to turn the offer down. He hadn't felt a woman's touch in years, and he'd all but forced the idea of sex from his mind. With this offer, images flooded

3   Michel de Montaigne

his head. He knew by the way she fluttered her sea-blue painted eyelids, that if he handed over the necklace, in a few minutes he'd be led to a secluded corner, and that mouth, so wrinkled from smoking that, when she puckered it, it looked like a lip-sticked anus, but a mouth none the less, would be wrapped around his penis, bringing him to a shuddering climax. The thought alone was enough to give him an erection. He pulled the selling-board over to hide it.

He had never been with a prostitute before and couldn't bring himself to do it. If intimacy was ever going to happen it had to be through mutual desire. Not some business transaction. With a slight pang of regret, he slipped the necklace from the board and gave it to her for free. He excused himself, hurried straight past Anderson's and scuttled up the trail. In the privacy of his shelter, he masturbated with such fury that the sweat stung his eyes and the ache in his groin had him doubled over. Bruno lay awake for hours afterwards; when Bea hadn't returned after a longer time than he thought normal, he went looking for her.

In these early hours, the tourists were drunk and voracious. All around the streets, amorous couples clung to each other as they left bars. He passed a pair in the doorway of a shop, grinding together. The girl's skirt was hiked up around her. She dug her fingers into the man's heavily tanned back and breathed into his neck. The waist of the man's jeans gripped his milk-white buttocks. A group of men staggered by singing a football anthem. Teenage girls lingered on bar stools waiting for the barmen to end their shift. It was a celebration of sexuality and self-indulgence, with a complete disregard for anyone not taking part. This is what the town thrived on. It was a sanctuary where anything could be done without concern or consequence.

Bea was standing in the same spot as he'd left her. She was surrounded by tourists, laughing along with them and enjoying herself. Her selling-board was near empty.

'What's up?' Bruno asked when he got through the crowd to stand beside her.

'Not much,' she said. 'Just been having a good time. Thought I'd stay out a bit.' Her eyes were glazed. The tourists had been buying her drinks. He noticed hostile glances from some of the males around. *Who is this tattooed intruder? Does she need my help?* All of them were ready to protect and defend her.

Over the weeks, many men and even some women had tried to seduce Bea, but she'd blocked their advances with such compassion that there was never any embarrassment or hurt feelings. Bruno knew, of course, that eventually someone would come along that she liked.

He noticed a pair of men about Bea's age over by Cart Smile. One was muscular, with a shaved head and dark stubble on his chin. The other was tall with wavy blond hair, light blue eyes and an aquiline nose. Bea watched him between the group of tourists, all coy-eyes and pouting lips.

'Go and talk to him,' said Bruno.

'Excuse me?'

'Go talk to that blond guy who's staring at you.'

'Who? I haven't noticed anyone.'

'How long have you been looking at each other? I'm going to get a drink.' He slipped away from her.

'Wait!' she called. 'What're you doing?'

Bruno bought a cocktail, walked over to the pair and handed it to the man. 'That's from the girl over there. You better go and thank her.' He glanced back and saw the anger in her eyes. Maybe he'd taken it too far. 'Her name's Bea.'

'You've got no right to interfere, Bruno!' she said when he returned to her, and was about to add more but had to stop when the pair came through the crowd and introduced themselves. After a quick chat, the friend left, saying he had to get up early for kiting lessons. Bea, who could speak proficient English, was only just able to cope with the blond man's accent. His name was Sean. He was an Irishman.

'Are you going to be okay?' Bruno asked. The crowd was thinning, and his eyes were heavy.

'Yes,' she said, looking straight ahead.

'I'll leave you to it then.' He looked at Sean. 'Be nice,' he said as he walked past him. He felt good about himself, despite the jealousy gnawing at him. He was being selfless. He was being a good friend.

Bea returned in the daylight as the campsite was waking. Bruno was cooking coconut porridge and brewing their morning coffee. In trees in the nearby gardens, silver-beaks sang. The soft purr of dune buggies could be heard from town. Despite the tiredness in her eyes, she was happier than he'd ever seen her.

'Want some porridge?' he asked. 'Some coffee?'

'Nah,' she said, taking a seat at her tent. She reached inside it and took out her toothbrush. She scrubbed her teeth and spat the suds to the coals.

'How'd it go, then?' he asked, the smell of peppermint hitting his nostrils.

'Good.'

'Happy I pushed you together?'

'You had no right,' she started, but her stern expression evaporated into a smile. 'We talked all night,' she said, rubbing her eyes. 'He's one of the most interesting and intelligent people I've ever met. Honestly, you'd really like him.'

'How long is he here for?'

'He's been everywhere, Bruno. An engineer. Works for the fourth-biggest oil company in the world. Grew up in a town with only two shops, can you believe it?'

'You realise you're talking in English now?'

She laughed. 'No, I didn't!'

'Bea, don't get too attached. It's good to have fun, but remember, he's a tourist. He's not staying here.'

'I know,' she said, reaching back into her tent, 'but don't

worry. We're both adults. We know how it works.' She took out her notepad, *La Reina* – the name of her parents' hotel – embossed on its cover, and unclipped the fountain pen with a floating snowflake in the tip of its lid.

'Sure you don't want any?' he asked again, helping himself to porridge and coffee.

'No thanks,' she said, pen cap in her mouth. 'I'm already awake enough. I need to sleep, not wake up more. I'm meeting him on the beach soon.'

'Keep your distance, Bea. Trust me. Build a wall or you'll get hurt.'

'I'll be fine,' she said. The nib of her pen began to scratch across an unlined page.

Bruno was forced to work the tourists alone for the next week. With the techniques Bea had taught him, he scraped out a living. He saw Bea with Sean at the *carrinhos* on some nights, and at camp he'd talk to her for brief moments when she showed up to change her clothes.

Being with Sean afforded her entry into the restaurants and bars. The grudging staff hid their disapproval well. Tourists provided their livelihood; they had to be looked after no matter what kind of person they chose to associate with. Sean took her on all the tours available from the tourist centre, trips to distant beaches, a walk over the sand at Jinguba, a visit to the farming allotments, where she learned how Brisas grew enough fruit and vegetables, and farmed enough livestock to supply almost all of its needs. She even got a ride along the coconut palm beach on the back of her beloved donkey, Iansa.

During their short encounters, she told Bruno all about it. Apart from the hostility of the locals towards the travellers, it was exactly the type of town Bruno hoped it would be. A self-sufficient community protecting its environment and conserving all its resources. A town built on respect rather than exploitation. A town he'd be happy to call home.

One afternoon, approaching the day-bars from the trail, Bruno saw Anderson waving him over from the back door of the kiosk bar.

'Enjoying the book?' Anderson asked. He'd swapped the old book for him at *A Gata Preta*.

Bruno took the new book from his pocket and gave it to Anderson. 'Rough sea,' he said, watching the waves crash on the outer sand bars. Only a few kiters were out.

Anderson looked at the sea then back through the kiosk, towards the crowded tables and loungers. No customers were waiting. 'Forecast says it'll be like this for a few days. Full moon tides. You finished it already?' Anderson drew his thumb over the pages. 'How was it?'

'Passed a few hours. Nice story but I'm not sure if it was original. I read something very similar in *Arabian Nights* years ago. Can you get me some non-fiction?'

'I'll see what I can do. Anything in particular?'

'Something on the rainforest.'

'Thought you wanted to stay?'

'You know Bea's with a tourist guy just now? She's pretty good at the jewellery, too.'

'I've seen her taking advantage of the extra privileges. Much else happening in the site? Chatter? Drug dealing?' He gazed through the bar again.

'Nothing I've noticed.' Bruno watched a kite-surfer jump, land and then fall over. 'I want to be prepared for all scenarios, you know? All these years my one thought has been the rainforest, and now I'm so close I can almost see the tops of the trees. I can just about hear the river. But now I find this town and all these thoughts and ideas jump out from the back of my stupid head. I suppose I don't truly know what I want.'

'So you *are* thinking of staying? You know that most of the travellers leave for the low season. It's coming fast. There won't be much money to be made selling jewellery then.'

Bruno rested the selling-board at his knees. 'I've spent so much time alone... It's just... Sometimes I feel like I turned my back and hid myself away from society instead of making a real effort. I want to be a part of something. Something bigger than just me. Look at you, you manage a bar. How many people have you served drinks to over the years? I bet you've made an impact on hundreds, if not thousands, of lives. You can make someone having a bad day feel better. I want a piece of that.'

'Bruno, I'm just a barman. I sell beer, you sell jewellery, there's no difference. This is an end-of-the-road tourist town, son. There's nothing to achieve here. People come to escape, not to be a part of something. Do what makes *you* happy. That's what I say.'

Bruno looked out again at the heavy waves and noticed vultures high above them, gliding on the wind. Long, black wings with feathers stretching out like fingers, they scanned below for their next meal. That's what his life was, constant movement, one meal at a time, alone with his books, ignoring the real issues. 'I don't want to be selfish any more,' he said.

'You think too much. Brisas will still be here if you decide to come back from the forest. Why not take some others from the campsite? Start a commune.'

Bruno left Anderson leaning on the door frame and climbed down the rocks to the sand. Maybe he was right, maybe all this thinking was useless. Making a decision and sticking to it would be much better for him. On the deserted coconut palm beach, he looked for materials amongst the flotsam. A solitary black towel with *GUINNESS* written on it lay on the sand. Stones on each corner held it down against the wind.

The waves rolled into the centre of the beach, and a rip tide ran back out to sea past a formation of rocks. There were no surfers out here. A strong smell of kelp clung to the air. Wandering amongst the cockle and whelk shells, the driftwood and pebbles, he bent to pick up a cowrie shell, when a guttural cry for help sounded out. He looked towards the horizon and saw someone clinging to the rocks. The swell fell around the man, exposing his full pink body before swallowing him up again.

Bruno stripped to his boxers, grabbed the towel and ran into the sea. The rip tide pulled him out to the rocks. The man held on in desperation. His whole body was trembling from the effort. His hair was matted to his skull, snot and tears mixed with the saltwater dripping from his nose and mouth; blood seeped from a graze on the side of his head.

'Help me!' he screamed in English. 'Help me! I'm drowning!'

'You have to let go,' Bruno shouted back. 'You can't fight the current.'

'I can't swim!'

He got alongside him, passed the towel around the man's waist, and tried to pull him off.

'Stop, I can't fucking swim. Are you crazy?'

It was Sean. Bruno was almost paralysed by panic. If he messed this up Bea would never forgive him. 'Sean!' he shouted. 'The rocks are sharp, you have to let go. Hold the towel. I'll pull you in.'

'No!' he screamed. 'I'll climb, I'll get on top.'

'Impossible! You have to be brave.'

Sean wouldn't let go. His fingertips and toes were digging into the barnacle-covered rock crevices. Every wave slammed him against the rocks, opening fresh wounds.

Bruno timed the swell and, as the water receded, he hauled Sean on top of him. Sean spluttered and shouted in panic as his head dipped under the surface. He threw his arms out at Bruno, making a grab for him. Bruno kicked as hard as he could to keep them both afloat. He wrapped the towel behind Sean's neck, pulled it under each armpit and got him onto his back.

'I'll die,' Sean shouted, coughing and retching from the seawater he was swallowing.

'Stay on your back or you'll drown us both,' Bruno roared. 'Point your toes out and kick!'

He pulled the ends of the towel in one hand, stretched out and swam with his free arm. He dragged Sean amongst the waves to the centre of the bay. Wave after wave broke upon them, each nearly tearing them apart, but Bruno gripped the towel with every fibre of his being, and between the waves, he swam as hard as he could towards the beach. After fifteen minutes, with almost nothing left, he raised Sean to his feet amongst the seaweed and froth in the shallows. They waded in then collapsed on the dry sand.

Sean's skin had been shredded by the barnacles.

'We need bandages, antiseptic,' Bruno said, not lifting his cheek from the sand. His voice was a whisper.

'Bea,' was Sean's barely audible reply.

'I don't know where she is. We need to get you fixed.'

'Campsite,' he said.

Bruno pulled his shorts back on, wrapped Sean's arm around his neck and helped him over the hill to the campsite. Bea was hanging her clothes on the line between the tents.

'Sean!' she yelled. She ran over to grab him. Blood dripped from yellow-edged cuts all over his body. 'What happened?'

'He saved my life. I almost drowned.'

'Bruno.' She switched to Spanish. 'We have to get him to a clinic.'

'There is no clinic.' He coughed into his fist. 'The supermarket might have bandages.'

'The barber's,' she said. 'There's a red cross on the sign… It's going to be fine, Sean. Don't worry. There's nothing serious. They're not deep.' She ran back to her tent and got a bottle of water. 'Drink.'

He drank and passed the bottle to Bruno, who finished it and tossed it aside.

They passed the church with Sean between them, an arm around both of their necks. Despite his tiredness, Bruno noticed some kind of entrails glistening in a turtle shell bowl at the base of the cross. At the top of Main Street, tourists and locals stared at them as they staggered towards the barber's.

Faka charged from his doorway and knocked Bruno to the ground. 'What the fuck have you done?'

Bruno rose to his elbows. 'I'm helping him, you fucking idiot!'

Bea put her hand on Faka's forearm but he shrugged it off. 'He saved his life,' she said.

'Tell me what happen,' Faka said to Sean in English. 'Hermes!' he called toward the barber's.

'I can't swim,' Sean answered. 'He saved me.'

Bruno got to his feet. 'He was caught in the rip, clinging to the rocks. That's why he's cut.'

A crowd was forming. Hermes appeared with a plastic chair and helped Sean sit.

'Did you push him?' Faka eyed Bruno. 'Tell me!' He turned to the crowd. 'Can't trust them! None of them! Parasites! Trying to ruin us.'

Bruno took a step forward. *One kick to the balls*, he thought. *I'll take any kind of a beating for one good kick to the bastard's balls.*

Faka's top lip contorted into a smile. 'Oh, you think so, do you?' He beckoned Bruno on.

'Faka,' the barber said. 'I need to help this boy. There's a crowd. Go back to work.'

'Know your place, faggot,' said Faka. He stalked back to his shop.

Bea leaned over Sean, wrapped her arms around his neck and pressed her cheek into his.

'You know I can't swim,' he said to her. 'I was jumping in the shallows, slipped and got pulled out.'

'It's okay. You're okay now.' She covered his cheek and neck in small kisses. There were tears in her eyes.

Hermes went to his salon and returned with a bundle of cotton wool, a bottle of iodine and rolls of bandages. 'Sean, isn't it?' He spoke in a mothering voice. His bald head was shaved to the scalp. His tweezed eyebrows and curled lashes complemented the gentle features of his face. 'My name is Hermes.' He lifted Sean's left foot. 'This is going to sting but we've got to get the sand out, leave no chance for infection.' Iodine spilled over his manicured nails as he tipped the bottle into a cotton wool swab. Sean gripped the edges of the chair and jerked as the brown liquid touched the sole of his foot. Bea held him tighter. 'Hush,' she whispered, her lips against his ear.

Mac arrived. Bruno noticed the way the locals and tourists looked at him; not with fear, like he did, but with admiration. Even Sean turned with moist eyes and smiled a hello.

'Hermes,' Mac said, fixing him with his black pearl eyes. 'What's going on?' He spoke in English.

'Sean here got pulled out by the rip tide. This man saved his life.' All eyes turned to Bruno, who looked down at his feet.

'Vagabundo,' said Mac. '*Bom trabalho*. Good work!'

'Thank you,' Bruno replied in English.

'Okay, people!' Mac addressed the crowd. 'There's nothing you can do here. I'm sure Sean appreciates your support but please return to your holidays,' he switched to an even-toned Portuguese, 'or your jobs.' The locals scattered. 'Hermes,' he continued, as the tourists ambled away. 'What's your opinion?'

'City,' Hermes said. 'They can treat him better there, make sure the infection doesn't set in. Keep him away from Yemanjá.'

Fresh tears came to Bea's eyes. Sean nuzzled his chin into the crook of her arm.

'Yemanjá?' Bruno whispered to himself.

'Sean,' said Mac, loud enough for the straggling tourists to hear. 'We're sending you to the city where you'll get the best treatment available. There's nothing to worry about, it's just that this environment is not good for foreigners' skin to heal. No expense will be spared. I'll arrange the transport now. Which guesthouse are you in?'

'Sunshine Reggae House,' he said.

'Travelling alone?'

'No.'

'Who else?'

'Steven Browne. Room nine.' Sean looked up at Bea as Mac left for the guesthouse. She cried into his neck. He closed his eyes and winced at each dab of iodine. Bruno helped Hermes clean the wounds and tape the bandages.

Minutes later a 4×4 made a circle at the top of the street and came alongside them. The driver hopped out, leaving the engine running. 'We have to go now,' he said to Hermes. 'The tide's on its way up.'

'They're taking you now,' Bea said to Sean. 'Will you come back?'

'Of course,' he said in a thin voice.

They all helped him into the 4×4. Bruno put a hand on Bea's shoulder as Hermes turned the salon sign to *CLOSED* and came back to the side of the vehicle.

'Amigo not in guesthouse,' said the driver to Sean. 'He bring bag *amanhã*.' He went to close the door but Sean stopped him. Bea tore away from Bruno and ran to Sean's beckoning arms. Sean put a bandaged hand around the back of her head and pulled her close. He kissed her. 'I'll come back,' he said, his forehead against hers. 'I can't say when but I'll come back, I promise.'

They stayed with their foreheads touching until Hermes eased Bea away and closed the door. Bruno held her by the shoulders as Hermes and the driver jumped inside. Sean raised his bandaged hand to the window, speckles of blood already seeping through.

'Come back to me,' she whispered in Spanish, watching him through the glass. 'Please come back to me.' As the 4×4 started off, Bruno put both arms around her and pulled her in, feeling the trembling of her body as she cried. They watched the 4×4 head down the street. When it passed out of view, Bea turned and cried into Bruno's chest. He stroked her hair.

*

She didn't leave her tent for the rest of the day, and didn't stop crying. Bruno pottered around the site, making more noise than he needed to, so she would know he was there for her. He set the fire, raked the sand and organised things he'd salvaged from nocturnal visits to the skips. He'd have to add another compartment to his shelter to keep everything organised.

'I'm here when you need to talk,' he said. He wanted to share the pain with her somehow, to take the edge off it. 'It's not good to keep everything inside. You need to be with people. You know that.'

'Thanks,' she replied. 'Just give me time. Give me space.'

He crept off to the beach to find his selling-board, but it was gone, taken by the sea or this Yemanjá Hermes had mentioned.

At the supermarket he bought two baguettes from Luis, who dabbed at his bad eye with a handkerchief.

'The humidity makes it weep,' he said.

Bruno was going to ask how it happened. He could feel a kinship with him. One ruined face to another. He wondered if Luis could see anything out of it, why he didn't wear a patch, but then he knew the answer already; better to be out in the open with these things, or you only draw more attention to yourself.

'They're going stale,' Luis said. 'I'll give you one for free.'

'You're a gentleman, Luis.'

'How's Bea? I heard about her tourist friend.'

'It'll take her a while.'

'You did well to save the guy. You must be a good swimmer.'

'Almost lost him in the breakers a few times.'

'You got him in though. Impressed a lot of people.'

'It could've gone either way, really. Got lucky. Anyway, thanks for the bread, Luis. I better get back. I'll tell Bea you're asking for her.'

Bruno filled two water bottles at the nearest faucet. He unzipped Bea's tent enough to push one through, along with a baguette. 'You have to eat,' he said, zipping it up again.

'I can't, Bruno. I feel sick.'

'Come out and get some air.' He wanted to take her in his arms like some hero in a story, tell her everything was going to be alright. The travellers at the other tents were loud and cheerful. As wrong as he knew it was, he wanted to shout at them to keep quiet, to embrace her sadness. He tried to eat his own bread but lost his appetite and tossed it, half finished, into the coals.

'Bruno,' she whispered.

'What, Bea? Tell me.'

'Take the bread away. I can't stand the smell of it.'

Agave plants covered the southern side of the hill. With the beam of his headlamp lighting up the dark, Bruno hacked off leaf after leaf until his sacks were full. He brought them over to the campsite and worked into the early hours, softening the fibres and weaving and splicing them into cordage.

At the skips, he found short wooden stakes that he brought back to camp. He bound them together for strength, and drove them into the sand at either side of the fire.

When Bea emerged late the next morning, the hammocks

were complete. Bruno lay in one, Honey in the other. Flames tickled a blackened pot of soup. Bea's face was swollen and red, but she didn't lower her eyes. She bore her sorrow with the strength and stubbornness that Bruno had seen in her on that first night. She pursed her lips and raised her eyebrows to say *good morning*.

'Bruno told me all about it, dear,' Honey said. She rose to sit on the edge of the hammock.

Bea nodded and pulled her hair up into an untidy bun.

'First love?'

She nodded again.

'First one is always the hardest.'

'It'll take time, Bea,' said Bruno. 'Just put one foot in front of the other, keep up a routine; concentrate on your work. The minutes will pass, then the hours, then the days. The pain will fade away and eventually it'll be gone.'

'Yes, Bea.' Honey always pronounced her name with an 'ah' sound at the end. 'Bruno's right. Every day as it comes.'

Bruno ladled the coconut and seaweed soup into three bowls. He handed one to Honey and put another down beside Bea. 'You need more water?' he asked.

'I still have some,' she said. 'Thanks.'

'This is delicious, Bruno.' Honey scooped another mouthful with the transparent plastic spoon. 'Be-ah, even if you don't feel like eating, you need your energy. You could do worse than have a few mouthfuls of this.'

Bea looked up at her; a quickness to her voice: 'I just don't feel like eating, okay?'

'Bea,' Honey said, her eyes softening. 'I know it's hard to take, and it only happened yesterday, but let me say this. I don't know where I heard it, but anyway... To love someone is to want them to live. So even though you're in pain, don't stay in pain too long. Know that John—'

'Sean,' Bruno corrected her.

'—wants you to be happy, as I'm sure you want him to be happy too.'

Bea took a breath and her shoulders fell. She reached into her tent for the water bottle. 'More than anything, I regret not telling him I love him. It's been on the tip of my tongue but I couldn't find the right time, and I felt so silly, you know? After only just meeting him.'

'But he said he'd be back, didn't he,' said Bruno. 'He was devastated in that 4×4.'

'Yes but he would have been leaving today anyway. He'll be on the plane now. On his way home. His life is there, and mine is...' She looked around the campsite. Kids ran around, Golias strummed his guitar, some drunkard facing their direction was taking a piss outside his tent. She closed her eyes.

'Life is full of tragedies and triumphs, Bea. I know it doesn't feel like it now but you're going to be okay. Know that you're going to get through this.'

'Be-ah,' Honey said, mopping the soup from her chin. 'Like I told you before, you're far from ugly. Make yourself up just a little bit more and there'll be as many men lining up for you as there are for me.'

Bruno watched Honey's face for a playful smile, but realised she was completely serious.

'Thanks, Honey,' Bea said.

Honey leaned towards her and hushed her voice. 'And let me tell you something else,' she glanced at Bruno, 'woman to woman. Make 'em slip on an eel-skin, bend over doggy, and they all feel exactly the same.'

Bea looked at Bruno, whose spoon hovered between his lips, then lowered her eyes. 'I didn't actually sleep with him.' She began drawing zigzags in the sand.

'Ah, a virgin.' Honey leaned back in her hammock and glanced at Bruno.

Bea shrugged. 'I've been waiting for the right person. I wish I just did it, now. I might even have done it tonight.'

'You'll fall in love again,' said Bruno. 'Everything will be fine.'

'But I don't want to fall in love again. I only want him. Have you ever even *been* in love, Bruno? Do you know how hard this is?'

He dropped his empty bowl to the sand and tried to let his anger dissipate. 'You think I—' He took a breath and steadied his voice. 'Of course I have.' He pictured Flora. *Let it out*, he told himself, but the void was already pulling at him. 'She was everything to me... A teacher, a lover, a parent...' His voice wavered, his breathing grew shallow. He turned away.

'Are you okay?' Honey asked.

He couldn't speak about her. Not Flora. Not yet. He turned to face them. He'd tell them about his second and final relationship. 'I'm sorry,' he said. 'I'll start again.'

He cleared his throat. 'I wasn't obsessively in love, but she was in my head, that's for sure. Her name was Sara, and I liked her from the day I started the job. I worked in a machine shop and she was the office girl; the boss's niece. I always wanted to talk to her but never had the courage. Even though I was dying to, and knew that she wanted to, we'd never say more than a passing hello. I'd practise conversations in my mind, but whenever I came face to face with her I couldn't find my voice.' He sighed. He'd never told anyone this story before. 'But one night at a guy's retirement party, I was at the table beside her. I got so drunk, ignored everyone else and talked non-stop. I've no idea what I said, probably bored her to death about all the problems in the world, but she sat, listened and smiled. Anyway, after that we began meeting at lunchtimes, and soon we were getting together after work. It went on for a few months. It was the closest I'd been to happy since... Well, for a long time.'

'Bruno,' said Honey, easing a slim cigarette from her silver case. She lit it up. 'This is boring. Get to the fucking!'

He held his palms up. 'Bear with me. I'm getting there.' He cleared his throat and looked up. 'It was early spring. An endless blue sky and sunshine. The jacarandas were in bloom, all purple. The flowers were everywhere. Even the air felt different. Winter was over. I can't say I wasn't sad and afraid.'

'Why were you sad and afraid?' said Bea, but Bruno cut her off.

'I was also filled with wonder. I was stepping out from under a cloak that I really hadn't wanted to shed. I wanted…'

Honey faked a snore and the cigarette popped out of her mouth.

'I *wanted* this feeling of spring, this sense of new beginnings, but not with… Anyway, forget it. I'm not going that way. It was all going good. Sara was fun. I liked to talk, but she was more into action. She wasn't a bit shy. Whenever, wherever, however. Obviously, it didn't last or I probably wouldn't be here, but she knew what she was doing, let's put it that way.

'The guys at work used to brag about what they'd done with her long before I got near. But I never paid any attention to that. You know how people lie to impress each other. So…' He looked towards the hill, remembering. 'One day, I noticed one of the delivery trucks parked out back for way longer than usual. She was in charge of filling out the paperwork and receiving the materials. I knew the driver. He was so fat he had to tuck his stomach in under the steering wheel. It took him forever to turn the truck around out there. He was old and had a chronic cough. I was worried he'd had a heart attack or something, so I went looking for him.

'I heard it as soon as I reached the storage area, a strange, wet, slapping noise. I thought it was an injured seagull squawking. I looked between the boxes and pallets in the racks. I'll never forget her nodding head sticking out from between the shelves, or the panic in her eyes when she saw me. It took me a second to realise what was going on. I didn't see the driver behind her for all the boxes. She was bent over the shelf, with two dirty fingers of each of his hands prising her mouth open. When she saw me, her squealing became grunts and she tried to pull away. He must have had her arms pinned somehow. I wanted to beat them, even picked up a metal rod from the rack, but as I walked towards them, I realised how little it all actually meant to me. It was as quick as that. It just didn't seem worth it. Nothing seemed worth anything any more. I went back to my machine. She ran over and tried to speak, but I had nothing to say. I quit the job soon after. That was probably when everything changed. I guess it was inevitable. If it hadn't been her, something else would have triggered it, but there was no going back after that. Fucking rotten whore.'

'Hey!' said Honey.

'I'm sorry. I—'

'She wasn't getting paid, was she?'

'No, I don't think so.'

'So she was a slut, not a whore. There's a big difference.'

A flicker of a smile appeared on Bea's face. 'How about you, Honey? You ever been in love?'

'Love,' Honey said, looking down at her cigarette case. She nodded. 'A lifetime ago. His name was Pavel. He was a sailor. Big and strong, not like this skinny wreck.' She pointed at Bruno.

'All core strength,' said Bruno, flexing a bicep.

'I'd see him a couple of nights then he'd disappear for months at a time. I'd sit at the end of the pier for hours looking out, wondering where in the world he was, when he'd be back, and what toy he'd be bringing me.'

'What kind of toys are we talking here?' Bruno asked. 'How old were you?'

She peered up and moved her fingers as she counted. 'Fourteen. I was fourteen when we first met. He approached me and my mother on the Malecón. I was more interested in keeping my kite flying, but he handed me some candy and they shared a cigarette.

'The next night we met at a hotel and he gave me

a Russian doll. I remember taking it apart as he and my mother talked on the bed. Inside each doll was a smaller and smaller version until there was a whole set.'

'A *matryoshka*,' said Bea. 'I've got one of those.'

'After they finished speaking, he came down onto the floor and played with me. I was getting a bit old for toys, but what can I say? I was a young, simple girl. The next time he came, my mother left us alone. That time he brought me a toy train he called Tiny Ding-Dong.'

'He was more of a father figure, then?' asked Bea.

'Oh no.' She shook her head. 'He was young at heart. He loved playing with toys more than I did. One of the rules was that I had to bring all the toys with me each time we met. We first had oral sex just before I was fifteen. I didn't have a clue what was going on. It seemed wrong, but man did he know how to use his—' Her tongue flapped around in her mouth like a beached fish. 'And once that explosion had me bucking like a feral horse, when I realised it wasn't going to kill me, I didn't care if it was wrong. We had full sex soon after. I was terrified but he kept me calm. *"It's only little Príncipe Alberto,"* he said, *"coming to play with you."* His Spanish was terrible!' She laughed then looked at Bea with a serious face. 'Of course, Bea, there's pain. I don't want to put you off, but that pain!' She raised a fist. '*Puta que pariu!* It doesn't last, though, I can say that much. These holes are God's greatest gift to women. You'll know that as soon as you start using them. You'll forget John in no time.'

5

Bea took Bruno's advice and concentrated on work. She struggled to sleep and took to walking the streets at any hour. She was by far the best seller in Brisas, the envy of all the other travellers. They'd approach her in camp and linger by her in the street, trying to learn her secret, but to no avail. She managed to keep them, and everyone else, at a distance. She'd built up a wall so thick that even Bruno struggled to pass through.

He saw the change the day he asked Honey to help out. He'd hoped it was a temporary thing and watched her closely over the following days, but there was no return to her former self. Her smile could still charm anyone, but the warmth behind her eyes was gone. When Honey left that day, Bea let her dark hair fall around her like a widow's veil. She had withdrawn so deep inside herself that Bruno was beginning to worry she might never recover. He knew what she was going through. He'd gone through the same thing with Flora.

He was amazed at how fast she'd learned all the weaves and knots for the jewellery. It hadn't taken her long to reach his level. She didn't need him any more. She'd lost her family and friends, and now Sean. It was a gap too big for him to fill. The fear of losing her tormented his sleep. She was his first true companion and his only real link to society.

Even though she went out and sold on her own, and

made many more sales than he did, Bea always gave Bruno a decent share. He didn't want to accept it at first, but it angered her so much that he had no choice. He now had more money than he could spend, and started burying it under his shelter in the tin alongside his camera.

Bruno knew she wanted more time to herself, so he gave her space; but he made sure she always knew where to find him. He made all the food, washed the dishes, and kept the area tidy, feeling both privileged and pleased that he was doing all he could for her. He'd have washed her clothes if she let him.

In his hammock, while reading the books Anderson swapped for him, he'd glance over at her and try to hide his sympathy; she was so sad lying there and there was nothing he could do. He'd close his eyes, fix his mind, and try to project all his positive energy towards her. *Please, Bea,* he thought. *Listen. Take this energy, take my strength. Let me get you through. You're too great a person to be down like this.* She'd given him so much that he would gladly have taken all the sorrow from her to pile it up on top of his, if it would only make her happy.

'Before sleep and after waking are the worst times,' she said one night, after hours of silence. 'He's gone. That's all I can think about. I dream of him all the time.'

'It happens,' said Bruno. 'You want sleep to give you a rest from it all, but the dreams don't let you. I know.'

'One morning I heard him say, "Kiss me." I hesitated. I was like: "What, here? In front of everyone?" And then I went to kiss him, but just as our lips touched, I woke up. It's torture.

'In another dream he wanted to come back. I was on one bed in the hotel room and he and Steven were on the other. I pleaded with him to come, and I knew he wanted to, but Steven stopped him! He told him not to be foolish, that he should forget me and get on with his own life.

'Just last night I dreamt I was under him and he was

kissing me so hard, but then I wake in this fucking tent. Bruno, even my soul hurts! What can I do?'

'Time,' was all he could say. 'Give it time.'

Respite came only for short moments, either while petting Iansa, haggling with a tourist, or listening to one of Bruno's stories. But the dragging minutes, and hours, and days, slow as they were, kept passing by.

She was writing so many letters that she had to buy another notepad from the supermarket. While preparing meals or cleaning, despite the pervading melancholy, Bruno couldn't help smiling as he watched her write. Her sleek hand led the pen across the page, leaving a wake of ornate, Atlantic-blue script. She wrote with the same care and skill as she put into her jewellery. He wondered how many of the letters were for her parents and friends, and how many were destined for Sean.

'Eight pages,' she said one morning, dropping her pen and closing the notepad. 'Eight pages straight from here—' she touched her chest, 'and he'll never read them because I didn't get his fucking address.'

Bruno built the second compartment and filled it with everything he'd collected from the skips. Over the weeks, he'd collected tubing, valves and angle-iron, but it was only when he stacked it all together in the shelter next to some empty beer kegs, that an idea came to him. He would build a microbrewery.

With his pinion drill and some tools Anderson lent him, he set about making a frame, modifying the kegs, and fitting the pipes and valves. It took him longer by letting Bea help, but he was glad of the company, and knew she needed the distraction.

As he worked, his instructions were addressed to Bea, although he was really talking to himself. 'Okay, Bea, what we're going to do here is a three-tier gravity-fed system. The hot liquor tank goes up here like this; we need a good base to put a fire under it, isolator valve here, mash tun... next tier down... round and round and round the cooling loop; you listening, Bea? Gravity fed to the kettle, like so.'

'How'd you learn all this, Bruno?'

'Books. Home-brew was one of my few luxuries when I was stuck in that apartment. Anything you want to learn is already written in a book. Where were we? Okay. Sealed fermenter at the bottom, wait two weeks, crack open, drink, repeat.' He thought hard for a moment, scratched at his beard and smiled at her.

'What is it?' she asked. 'Why you looking at me like that?'

'This is how we get in, Bea. This is what we can do that the locals can't. I know brewing inside out. We can save this town a fortune!'

'Come on, Bruno, *we?* Even if it does work, I never said I wanted in. I never said that.'

Bruno wasn't listening. His mind raced with visions of microbreweries popping up in every bar on Main Street.

Bea was crying hard in her tent the next morning. She'd been out on one of her twilight walks, selling to the drunks on their way back from the bars. It had been a profitable night, Bruno saw. The selling-board was lying outside her tent, only a few pieces left on it. He noticed an uneasiness about her when she finally came out for breakfast. At the slightest noise, her eyes darted towards the other camps, and across to town.

'Are you okay?' he asked.

'Fine,' she said, not looking at him. He didn't press her. Something had happened, he was sure, but she'd tell him in time.

He got her to help pull the keg brewery out of the shelter, and they brought it over to the fire. 'Okay, Bea. We need to fill the hot liquor tank. I want to test this thing for leaks. Then we're going to place an order, with young Omelette

Eye over at the supermarket, for malt, hops and yeast. He might actually—'

'You shouldn't call him that. He can't help what happened to him.'

'I'm not a pretty picture myself, you know.'

'But his was an industrial accident or something. Accidents happen all the time.'

'Mine was an accident too. Society did it to me. I'm fragile, you know I am.' He smiled at her.

'Sometimes I believe you're fragile. Sometimes I think you're just full of shit, playing games with everyone.'

'I use humour to deal with things. That's all.'

'Humour helps you avoid them, Bruno. Look at Honey. She's a real victim of society. What she has to do with those horrible, disgusting men. I feel so sorry for her.'

'Honey knows what she's doing.'

'They're watching us, by the way.'

'Who?'

'Those guys.' She nodded over his shoulder at Abilio's circle of tents. 'Three of them.'

'Thought you'd be on first name terms by now, the way they follow you around trying to learn all your selling techniques.'

'I haven't paid any attention.'

Water spilled over the sides of the cooking pots as they carried them back and forth from the nearest faucet. When the tank was full, Bruno opened the valve and let the water flow through the whole system then locked it in. He ran a dry cloth over the pipework and held it to the sun to look for moisture.

Abilio and Golias, along with Fortunato, who belonged to the group of tents next to Abilio's, huddled together by Bruno's shelter and watched. They spoke amongst themselves.

'It's for making moonshine,' said Golias.

'No it ain't,' said Fortunato. He was dark skinned, with

a shaved head, and had a curled upper lip that gave him the perpetual look of someone exposed to a bad smell.

'What is it, then?' asked Golias.

'It's a meth lab.' Abilio dragged his forearm under his nose. 'Sooty's gonna get us all thrown out for this.'

Bruno tensed at the word *sooty*. 'It's not a fucking meth lab,' he shouted over at them. He emptied the water from the lower kettle. Bea took a seat by her tent and started brushing her hair.

'What's it do, then?' asked Abilio, clawing at his ribs.

'Golias was closest,' said Bruno, refilling the hot liquor tank. 'It's a keg brewery. For beer.'

'How does it work?' asked Golias. Bruno noticed Abilio's eyes scanning the loaded shelter. He reached over and closed the flap.

'Don't touch it,' he said to Fortunato, whipping the cloth at his hand.

'No need to whip me, Sooty!'

Sooty, again. He took a breath and let it pass. 'Want to know how it works or not?'

'Go on then,' said Abilio.

He pushed his hair back and explained the brewing process in great detail, taking his time, watching as their eyes glazed over and they shifted their weight from one foot to the other.

'And how much beer can it make?' Golias stifled a yawn.

'About fifteen gallons.'

Golias raised his eyebrows and nodded.

'How much is fifteen gallons then, Gol?' Fortunato punched Golias's shoulder. 'Not a clue, have you, mate?'

'Tell us in cans,' Abilio said.

Bruno counted it out in his head. 'Round about seventy litres.'

'That's a lot of beer,' said Fortunato.

'A lot of beer,' Golias repeated.

'How about we buy some off you?' Abilio asked.

'It takes two weeks to brew. I still have to get the ingredients.'

'Plenty of time to be done for Christmas, then.'

'How much would you want?'

'We'll take it all.'

'Yeah,' said Fortunato. 'That'll do for everyone.'

'Bea,' said Bruno. 'What do you think?'

'Up to you,' she said, dragging the brush down her hair. 'Fifty per cent up front, isn't it?'

Bruno nodded. 'I'll give you guys sixty, and we'll keep ten.'

'How much?' Golias rubbed his thumb and finger together.

'Since it's for Christmas, let's say one hundred and fifty *contos*. Give me seventy-five *contos* now and I'll go order the ingredients.'

'Seventy-five is impossible!' said Abilio. 'We can scrape thirty together.'

'Seventy-five,' said Bea.

'*Puta que pariu!*' Abilio faced her. 'Forty.'

'Sixty-five,' she said, unblinking. 'Final offer.'

Abilio took a breath and gave a nod. He marched back to his camp, the others following after him.

*

That night, Bruno and Bea walked around town. They weaved amongst the tourists and watched the travellers hawk their wares under the string-lights of the *caju* trees. The travellers had never so much as glanced at him in the past, but now they were waving and smiling at him as if he were a friend.

'So popular tonight,' said Bea in a cheery voice, but Bruno could tell by the way she looked around that something was still bothering her.

'Beer brings people together,' he joked. 'It's pathetic

when you think about it, though. Always looking for what they can take, never what they can give.'

Bea held her selling-board by rope handles she'd had Bruno fit to it that afternoon. Bruno carried the new one he'd made a couple of days after Sean was taken away. He'd splattered it with the leftover paint from his art project, rounded the edges and polished the hanging nails to a sparkle. They made sales on the move. As Bea's board emptied, Bruno topped it up with jewellery from his own. She called out to smiling tourists, and with minimal words and compliments, had them tearing the jewellery off and pulling the *contos* from their pockets.

At Cafe La Mouche, Bea signalled through the heat waves of a grill to a cook who was so short his chin almost grazed the coals. He waved a blue and white handkerchief at her, removed his hat and wiped the sweat from his bald head. He jerked a thumb at the footpath alongside the restaurant and mouthed a question: 'Two?'

Bea nodded.

'New friend?' asked Bruno as they waited down the path for him.

'I couldn't help but meet people when Sean was here... Hey, Papa Rouge,' she said as he came round the corner. 'How's tricks?'

His stiff neck, hunched shoulders, and chin pressing into his chest gave him the cartoonish appearance of someone who'd been dropped head first from a high-rise building. There was a sunburned sheen to his face. He wore a thin moustache.

'Looking forward to the low season, Sugar Dumpling. I can't wait to shave this bloody moustache off!' He spoke through gritted teeth. 'Wish I was back in Jinguba, sitting on my porch, listening to the football on the radio... before the sand came, of course.'

'You can listen to the radio here.'

'Nonsense! All I do here is stand at the grill. A rumour's

97

going round that Big Mac's ordered chains.' He ran gravel through his voice. 'Chains, brothers and sisters. Chains to keep the cooks at the grills. Chains to keep the balance.' He coughed into a hand and wiped it on his trouser leg.

'Mac gets chains, we get a chain cutter, Papa. Don't worry.'

'Anyway.' He traced a finger over the moustache. '*Huit contos s'il vous plait, mon petit.*' He produced a pair of halloumi, courgette and red pepper skewers from behind his back.

'*Merci, monsieur!*' said Bea.

'Thank you,' said Bruno, taking the one he was offered.

'My pleasure,' said Papa Rouge. 'You two have a good night.' He shuffled away.

'Nice guy,' said Bruno.

'One of the best.' She pulled a slice of greasy red pepper from the skewer. 'Mac makes him grow that moustache. Can you believe it? They made a compromise. He keeps it for the high season and can shave it off for the low.' She laughed. 'But he says the high season keeps getting longer.' She watched Papa Rouge shuffle around the corner. 'Have you noticed any difference between the Jingubans and the locals?'

Bruno tore off a chunk of courgette. 'I see the farmers walking to the allotments some early mornings, coming back at night. They hold themselves with pride. They have integrity and are always friendly.'

'Friendly. Exactly! Tonino, Luis, Papa Rouge…Who else?' She picked at a piece of halloumi that had stuck in her teeth. 'Anderson's friendly but he's not Jinguban. Not local either, though. You don't think there's something strange about the locals?'

'I don't think so. They just have a sense of ownership or responsibility towards the place. They don't want it to fail.'

'Oh come on, Bruno. You pass that church every day. How many crosses have sacrificial offering bowls under them? What's in it today? Wings? Intestines? Fish heads?'

'So they have a quirky version of Christianity.'

'Quirky isn't how I would put it. What about the high walls at their temple and all that drumming and music that comes from there?'

'Drumming comes from there?'

'After the capoeira they hold some kind of ceremony in there. How haven't you noticed?'

'Never been interested.'

'And Mac's always at that church. I'm telling you, he's hiding something in there, not to mention the temple.'

'They've got no one to hide from.'

'Bruno, I know there's something odd going on here, and so do you.'

'So what? Maybe that's why I like the place. The locals look after each other. What is it Papa Rouge just said? Balance. Anderson mentioned that too. It must be their mindset. Balance instead of the instability I've seen everywhere else. Whatever Mac's doing, he should keep doing it. They're all happy here, have you noticed that? The Jingubans, the locals, the tourists, even the travellers. This place works, Bea, it really does.'

She popped the last chunk of halloumi between her lips. 'You're just odd, too,' she said. 'That's why he didn't throw you out for what you did against his church.'

Bruno took a sharp breath and turned away. 'Anderson told you about that?'

'Come on,' she said. She took the stripped skewer from his hand. 'It's nothing to be embarrassed about. Let's go.'

Halfway down Main Street a crowd had gathered. Bruno wrapped his arms around Bea's thighs and hoisted her up to look.

'Tell me what you see,' he said, straining under her.

'It's an artist.' She moved her head to get a better view. 'Asian screens, drawings. Oh wait, is that Honey? It's a tattoo artist. He's tattooing Honey!'

'What's she getting done?'

'I can't see. She's facing the other way. I think it's something on her boob. Let me down.'

He followed her to the front. Honey sat in a leather and chrome chair. As the tattooist reached over to a box of tissues on a bench, Honey spun the chair around to face the crowd. The left cup of her bikini top was pulled down just above the nipple, exposing the wrinkled, white skin of her breast. The cigarette hanging from her lips glowed red with each breath.

'Hey Bruno,' she called. 'What d'ya think?'

'Looks good, Honey.'

She spat the cigarette to the sand and knocked back the dregs in her glass. The tattooist wiped down a pair of cherries he'd inked on her and held up a dusty mirror for her to see. He was barefoot, wearing black jeans as tight as leggings, and a white vest. Though the lights of Main Street flashed off the tattooist's black-rimmed glasses, Bruno noticed the man's eyes, magnified by the lenses to bug-like proportions, lingering on him.

'*Perfeito*,' Honey said. '*Obrigada.*'

'And about payment,' the tattooist whispered.

'You know the score, Nik. Tomorrow at five? Bring your own tissues.' She got to her feet, threw her handbag over her shoulder and scanned the young men in the crowd. 'Okay, boys,' she said. 'Which one of you wants to pop Honey's cherry?' She pushed through the crowd and made her way down the street in a piston-hipped strut.

The crowd thinned after she left, but a continuous throng of tourists filed by to look at the designs pinned to the screens.

Bea picked up an album from the tattooist's bench and leafed through it. 'What should I get, then?'

'I don't know,' Bruno said, uncomfortable under the tattooist's gaze. 'How about we go to the *carrinhos?*'

'Maybe a butterfly, like this, on my ankle or shoulder?'

'Don't do it, Bea. He has good lines but what if he messes it up? Can we keep moving, please?'

She took his arm and put the album back on the bench. 'Okay,' she said, 'let's go.'

'Hi… Hey… Wait!' The tattooist chased after them. 'What's your name?' He removed a latex glove to shake Bruno's hand. 'I'm Niki.'

'Bruno.'

'I can fix it, Bruno,' he said.

'Excuse me?' said Bea.

Niki hovered a finger in front of Bruno's face. Like a surgeon planning an operation, he traced over the cheek bones, jaw and eye sockets. Bruno stared straight ahead. *This isn't happening*, he thought. *This is me now. I don't want any changes.*

'A few lines,' Niki said. 'Some skin tones, following the contours of your facial structure, skull, muscles. I'll bring your face back to life, my friend.'

'Got no money for that,' said Bruno, edging away.

'All I'll charge is food and beer.'

Bruno couldn't look at him. He was supposed to be on his way to the Amazon, what the fuck was he doing here? 'I can't,' he whispered.

'Pardon?' asked Niki.

'I can't!' He tore his arm away from Bea and walked off.

*

'Have you thought about it?' asked Bea, over porridge the next morning.

Bruno hadn't slept well. He dreamt he was in a city dosshouse when a mob of office workers poured in through the door. They chased the occupants into corners, bludgeoning them to death with axes and hammers. He made it to the roof and was forced to the edge. He had to make a decision. Suicide or murder. He woke before he could choose.

'I haven't been able to stop fucking thinking about it. How can I trust anyone? Half the night I thought I should do it. It can't be any worse, can it? The other half I thought no. I don't want to end up looking like a made-up drag queen, you know?'

Bea topped up his coffee. 'I watched a TV show once. One of those rich *gringo* reality TV ones. Trophy wives of such and such a county, or something. These two women were on a sofa, chatting. One was telling the other that she'd just been diagnosed with cancer. There was something strange about it. She might as well have been telling her the time. It took me a while to figure out what was wrong. They'd both had Botox and it had frozen their faces so much that they couldn't show emotion. They were blank, like wax dummies. When Niki said he could bring your face back to life, it made me think of that. Not that you resemble them at all.'

'I've been dealing with this for years now, Bea.' He held his cup in both hands and sipped. 'Do you know how bad it feels to be judged every day for a mistake you made years ago? You could walk past a rapist and give him more respect than me, because you can't tell, right? But all I did was get a fucking stupid tattoo.'

'I'm just using the Botox as an example, Bruno. I told you before; most of your problems are because of how you treat yourself. Other people see that in you and treat you the same. You know about the fight or flight response? We've evolved to see angry or uncomfortable expressions before happy ones. It's a survival mechanism. I think a little confidence is all you need, and maybe the tattoo will help get you it.'

He shook his head.

'If you're worried about his competence, get him to

change some of the others first. Then he can earn your trust. But do this for how it'll make you feel, not for how you think it'll make you look.'

He stared down at the faded, bluish anchors and swallows, the chicken-scratch Latin script across his belly, the freakish Sailor Jerry imitations on his legs. *That might work*, he thought. *Start slow, work up.*

He invited Niki for dinner the next night. The three of them sat down to a meal of roast vegetable stew and fresh rye bread straight from the Jinguban baker. Bea had found him one sleepless dawn, when the smell of pastry reached her nose and led her to the window of his house, where he was selling in secret. Still waiting for the ingredients for his own beer, Bruno bought a crate from Luis.

They listened to Niki talk about his life, about his two daughters, Mariana and Amelia, about his wife Rita, and his tattoo parlour being watched over by his apprentice. His hands shook so much at first that he had trouble raising the bread to his mouth. With stew dripping from his chin, he spoke about the performers he'd seen in Brisas over the years, contortionists, sword swallowers, magicians; and a missionary who'd been thrown out by Mac after setting up a barrel organ on Main Street and playing 'Old Hundredth' over and over for hours. After four beers, the shaking of his hands began to ease. He talked of how chronic back pain had almost forced him to quit tattooing, but a diet of four Ultracet pills a couple of hours before work every day had allowed him to continue.

'You probably shouldn't drink alcohol with those pills,' Bruno said.

Niki waved him off, took the pills from a black leather pouch attached to his belt, and washed them down with his seventh beer. His hands were now as steady as a watchmaker's. 'What'll happen? Heart attack? Kidney failure? Spontaneous combustion?' He struck the sand with the heel of his foot and laughed. 'I'd rather crash and burn than fade away, my friend.'

After eating, with Niki unable to assist because of his bad back, Bruno and Bea helped Hermes lift a chair from his salon to the corner of Main Street, passing the capoeira procession on the way.

Bruno tried to hide behind the chair as Mac approached from the front, but Mac's eyes were only on Hermes. 'Not happy with your house, Hermes?' Mac said.

'He'd rather have a tent,' Faka called over his shoulder.

Niki set up the screens again, pinned his designs to them and ran the cables to the connection of the lights on the nearest tree.

The warm leather of the chair stuck to the backs of Bruno's legs. He closed his eyes and caught the familiar scent of disinfectant. The dry safety razor burned as it stripped the hair from the first tattoo he'd ever got. He looked at it one more time. Once a skeleton with long, bony fingers poking out through a crescent-moon-shaped tear in the skin, it now looked more like a spindly-legged prawn. There came a sudden feeling of sadness. In a way he was painting over his past, burying his memories. It took a dose of calming breaths to stop him from jumping out of the chair.

Bea spoke to him as Niki rolled a cigarette. 'Everybody and everything changes, Bruno, from each cell in our bodies to the most distant star in the universe. Every moment is a chance to take the next step. We can't allow ourselves be held back by the past.'

With a cigarette dangling from the corner of his mouth and a can of beer within arm's reach, Niki snapped on the latex gloves and began.

Night after night, they carried the chair from the salon to the same spot on Main Street, passing the capoeira procession each time. It was the quietest part of the day, and Bruno sat meditatively on the chair, watching as his old tattoos were

104

covered over with dragons, koi carp, passages from books and films, or conversations that he recited from memory. The work was a truer reflection of himself, but what Bea had said got him thinking. Who would he be in a few years? Where would he be? He wished he could just wash all the ink off and be free of it.

Despite the quiet hour, there were still enough tourists to form a crowd. Bea took advantage of the situation. She sat in front of the audience with both selling-boards on the sand, and made all the daily sales targets she'd set for herself right there.

Niki charged eighty *contos* an hour to the tourists and was working long hours and making good money, but he suffered. Every night at dinner he spoke of the pain in his back and about how much he missed his family. He was already sick of the place. 'Sand everywhere!' he said. 'Why don't they ever lay asphalt? I'm leaving, my friends, I've had enough. Tonight will be my last!' But as the empty beer cans were tossed aside, so too was the passion of his complaints. He needed the alcohol to steady his hands and numb his mind. Tired of his constant moaning, Bruno and Bea pushed can after can to him, some laced with *cachaça*, and watched for the trembling to stop.

As well as tattoos, Niki did piercings. He pierced everything from ears to septa to nostrils, nipples, lips and tongues. One girl, who couldn't have been out of her teens, got a studded hoop through the frenulum above her front teeth. 'You know why she got that?' Niki asked Bruno. He drew his lip up and nodded like a feeding rabbit. 'That stud will be tickling some lucky bastard's pee-hole before the end of the night!'

Hermes was a constant visitor to the booth. Each night he stuck the same sign on the screens: *Sponsored by Hermes's Salon*, and stayed around helping tourists choose tattoo designs and piercings. He even gained Bea a few sales by taking her jewellery around the tourists, to show how much it suited them. Since the day he treated Sean, he'd ignored the locals' collective face of hostility and had taken Bea in.

Through the day, scabbing and itchy, Bruno made piercings for Niki to sell. The tattoos were flawless. Food and beer just wasn't enough to pay the debt he owed.

Despite the quality of Niki's work, Bruno still felt uneasy. With each cover-up, the stability of mind he'd enjoyed since meeting Bea weakened. As much as he tried to ignore the issue during the day, at night on his frond matting, his subconscious wouldn't leave him be. He hadn't slept so badly since the city years before. In every dream he was running from some great terror. He knew exactly what he was being told. A decision had to be made.

Bea nagged at him every other day. 'Have you made your mind up yet?'

'I'm still thinking,' he'd reply.

'He's leaving soon,' she'd say. 'You have to make your mind up!'

He couldn't. At one moment he was sure he'd do it. An instant later he'd changed his mind.

One day, an arc of lightning fixed in his eyes and he couldn't leave the campsite. As the arc dissipated, it was replaced with a headache so bad he had to lie in the shelter with the sheet pulled over his face. It was the first migraine he'd had since Flora's disappearance. In the days that followed, he spent more time in the campsite. There were too many people in town, too much noise. He needed silence, isolation. His appetite disappeared. Only at Bea's insistence did he take any food, and never more than a few mouthfuls. He drank nothing but coffee.

'Stop skipping breakfast, Bruno!' she shouted at him one morning. 'You need nourishment!'

'Fuck nourishment!' he shouted back. He threw his cup against the pot and headed for the coconut palms, ignoring her calls for him to come back.

*

At the start of December, Lagarto, Mac's head of construction and maintenance, supervised his workers in preparing the town for the holiday celebrations. In dune buggies fitted with ladders, they hung streamers between the buildings and changed the white bulbs on the street and tree lights for blue, green and red. Tinsel draped from the trusses of bars and restaurants and climbed like ivy up the wooden posts. Painted plywood effigies of strange saints sprung up around town. A tarpaulin banner with the words *Festa De Yemanjá* was fitted from poles at the entrance to Main Street.

After the decorations went up, the atmosphere around town became subdued. The tourists seemed to suppress the more hedonistic part of themselves. With such decoration around, the deep-seated faith, embedded in them since early childhood had come to the surface.

Bruno hated Christmas. Christmas at the orphanage was parade and hardship. The peso-eyed priests with plastic smiles for Samaritans making donations. The extra ceremonial duties. The hymns. The prayer.

He watched the tourists, locals and travellers interacting, saw how aligned they all seemed to be. They knew their standing and were happy with it. Each one did his small part for the bigger whole. The more Bruno thought about it, the more he realised he had no place in this life, this ecosystem. He'd never known what he wanted to be. Flora had always told him he could do anything, but after she left, all he ever did was float from one thing to the next, hoping that all the decisions would be made for him. He had no real ambition. What he had was an instinct to learn and pass that learning on to a family. A family with Flora. Why couldn't he just accept his lot now and be satisfied? Why didn't he know where he wanted to be, what he wanted to do? It was encouraging to see these people so content, but at the same time it was distressing, because all he'd wanted was peace, and he'd never been able to find it.

As he lay in his hammock one morning, reading an

English book, *In the Heart of the Amazon Forest*, Bea came running over, clutching a small bag. It was brewer's yeast.

She held it out to him. 'Your ingredients are here.'

He hurried to the shop with her and they hauled everything back to the campsite. They inched the brewery into position, and Bruno lit the fire. With Bea helping him as best she could, he set about filling the hot liquor tank, adding the barley and stoking the fire. His vest was off and sweat stung the raw flesh of his scabbing tattoos.

Abilio appeared. 'How's it going, mate?'

'Not now, Abilio,' Bruno said without turning to look at him. 'I'm working.'

Bea smiled.

The water went in clear, and after brewing for a couple of hours, ran through the system and turned the cooling loop golden on its way to the kegs. Niki approached as they were dragging the last keg into the cool storage compartment where the fermentation would take place.

*

'Right, then!' Niki wiped down Bruno's final cover up and applied some cream. It was a Haida design of an orca covering up a bottle of River Queen Scotch Whisky that Bruno had got after losing a drinking competition with a squid fisherman in a harbour bar. 'I know I've been saying it a lot, but now I'm serious. I'm ready to go. It's been a pleasure working on you, Bruno, but I want to surprise my girls for Christmas. If you'd like to finish what we started, it'll have to be tomorrow.'

Bruno's mouth went so dry he couldn't speak, and when he raised his hand to shake Niki's, it was limp.

'Let me know over supper if you want to go through with it.'

Bruno nodded and walked straight past Bea and the crowd of faces. He walked, though instinct was telling him to run. There was no point in running. There was nowhere to run to. He passed the *carrinhos*, removed his sandals and hiked up the dune. He lay down and looked up at the stars. Tears came to his eyes. He thought about going to Anderson for advice, but that would put him near alcohol, and he knew if he started drinking he wouldn't stop, not with this hanging over him. He wondered what advice Luis could give him. He'd never asked him *his* story, or Honey, or even Papa Rouge, but none of them would know what to tell him. The one person he needed to ask was the one who'd caused all his problems in the first place, and she was long gone. This was a decision he had to make alone. Adrenaline coursed through him. He needed to think, to put every idea, every fear, every hope through his brain, then he would sleep and the answer should be there when he woke. That was all there was to it. Why the fuss?

He remained still and waited for sleep as the stars tracked across the sky, but it didn't come. It was hot, unnaturally hot. His heart beat against his ribs so hard it felt almost painful. His eyes were open and alert. He massaged his temples, his beard, and focused on the discomfort of the scabbing tattoos, trying to stop his thoughts from blurring. His body was tense, sweat seeped through his skin and ran down his sides. He stood up, stretched, and went through his breathing routine, trying to push all thoughts away. He wanted to think one thing through at a time but had no control. It was as if the voices of a hundred different people were crowding inside his head.

'Think!' he said, wiping the sweat from his face. 'Make a fucking decision.' He beat the sand with his hand, grabbed a fistful and rubbed it between his palms. He felt like scouring his face with it till the tattoo came away, taking all the skin with it.

In the silence, a couple appeared on the edge of the dune. They lay down together in the darkness. He heard the smacking of their lips as they kissed, the rustle of their clothes under each other's hands. He didn't want to be near them or anyone else, so he descended to the beach and walked to the coconut palms.

He lay under the tallest tree and hoped a coconut would fall on his head. The voice of the police sergeant from years ago came to him. *'You can tell a lot about the way a person lived by examining how they died.'* This would be the most fitting death for him. A comedy death for a joke of a man.

'Here lies Bruno Expósito, who—' He stopped himself. There would be no memorial for him, no eulogy. How could there be? He hadn't made the slightest impact.

'Why didn't you throw me in the fucking river instead of abandoning me to the priests?' he shouted.

Why was it all such a big deal? The decision was there. It had already been made. Why couldn't he just follow through with it instead of torturing himself?

The heat was incredible. He'd never felt anything like it. He writhed against insects buzzing and crawling all over him. Sweat saturated his clothes. On the edge of sleep, half-dreams and thoughts of the past roused him again. He'd blocked everything out for too long. Now it was blocking his way when it should have been long forgotten. The stars were like eyes, twinkling with laughter. He could hear it all around him and from the tops of the trees came the noise of the fronds rubbing together. They were forming a voice and hissing a name at him. 'Stop,' he yelled. 'Leave me alone.' He held his ears but the name was already echoing in his head, dragging him back to the past. Santi.

The dank concrete stairwell stank of urine. Rubbish piled up on the landings next to rotten doors. Graffiti covered the cement walls. He adjusted his footing to avoid dog shit. There was a dollop on each step. The owner must've dragged the animal up as it shat. He heard it barking inside the apartment, pushed the unlocked door open, and saw it standing in a cage in front of him. A Dogo Argentino made vicious through mistreatment. Cigarette butts lay blackened in the base of its cage. Its skin was covered in welts where they'd been stubbed out on it. The sour smell made a physical impact as he stepped inside. It was the smell of self-neglect and squalor, mixed with the aroma of burning heroin. He embraced it all and smiled. This was it. This was *bottom*. He tried to shake the freshness of the cold from his jacket and spat the saliva welling in his mouth to the floor.

A man in boxer shorts and an open robe came through from an adjacent room, scratching at his balls. He flicked a glowing cigarette at the dog. 'Shut the fuck up!' He noticed Bruno. 'Who the fuck are you?'

'Ventura Expósito sent me.'

The man's eyes flashed. Yellow-tipped fingers scratched at his patchy beard. 'You're the guy,' he said, a smile filling his hollow cheeks. His voice was nasal and pathetic. He turned and looked through a doorway at two comatose men on a spring-bare sofa. '*Boludos, ese es el tio!*'

Their eyelids rose. One man attempted to speak. His drooping mouth moved and a soft, idiotic whine sounded out before his eyes closed again and his head fell forward.

Bruno laughed. 'Junkie fuck.' The man beside him didn't seem to hear. He led him to a filthy kitchen.

'I'm Santi,' he said, ushering him to sit at the table. He slid over a box of designs and opened the window. Cold air flooded in. A siren wailed nearby.

Bruno grabbed a handful of the designs and flicked through them as Santi prepared his equipment. He felt an instant hatred towards him, but it made no difference. He hated everyone, from the rich to the homeless, from infants to the elderly.

'Look,' said Bruno, taking the design from his jacket pocket. 'Fuck this bullshit. This is what I want.' He unfolded the paper and handed it over.

The tattooist wiped his nose. 'Right you are, son. Right you fucking are.' He scratched his chin, picked something off and rolled it between his fingers. He smeared it on the underside of the table. 'Ventura sent you. He knows what I can do. My best work's straight from needle to skin. None of this stencil bullshit. That's how I work. You don't want it, fine, fuck off.'

Bruno nodded.

His ears rang with the buzz of the tattoo gun. The ink smelled like bubbling tar. He could almost taste it. Eyes shut, he welcomed the searing pain. It cut like a rusted blade, like a shard of glass.

'It's done,' Santi said an hour later. He sat back, crossed his legs and flicked snot from his nose with two knuckles. There was fear in his eyes.

No more indifference, thought Bruno. *No more bravado.* Just as he'd hoped. They'd all see him now. He went to the bathroom and looked in the filth-spattered mirror. The air shot from his lungs as if he'd been hit in the chest with a hammer. This wasn't it. This wasn't what he wanted. He fell to his knees and held his mouth to stop from screaming. 'No!' he cried. 'You fucking idiot.' He shattered the mirror with his fist and rushed at the tattooist, grabbing him by the hair and hauling him to the sink. 'You fucked it up!' he shouted, and turned on the tap. He gripped the back of Santi's head, as Santi swung at him, and smashed his face down on the clutter of pots and plates, cutlery, and knives. Blood mixed in the scummy water, bubbling with Santi's screams. The men, roused from their torpor, tried to pull Bruno away. They punched and kicked at him but he was too big, too strong. One of them got a belt around his neck and pulled him to the ground.

The tattooist dropped to the floor, gurgling and convulsing, his face a sodden red mess of gaping cuts. His eyes were intact. Bruno sprang for him again, but the belt cut off his breath. As the man with the belt fought to hold him, the other ran out of the room.

'Kill him!' Santi shouted through his fingers. 'Kill the fucker!'

112

When the man came back, Bruno felt a sting on his leg. His eyes went heavy. He was losing control of his body. He reached back for the belt, pulled it towards his neck and got a finger in the man's eye. The belt loosened enough for him to slip it over his head. He took the belt up and whipped the buckle off the other man's face.

Amid the shouting and barking, he limped to the stairwell, and passed staring faces at every door, as he hauled himself down and out. He woke in an alley a few blocks away, numb with cold, under a winter-blue sky. In his apartment, he saw again what he'd done and locked himself away until starvation drove him out.

Under the coconut palms, trembling and sweating, he saw Flora. She stroked his face, and he breathed her scent of lychee, sweet almond and patchouli. He reached amongst the coarse coils of her black hair tickling his face and chest, and smiled as her finger made circles around one of his nipples and ran down towards his navel. In her rescuing, velvet voice she sang to him then whispered in his ear. He woke.

It was dawn. The lemon hues of the sun were just visible over the interior. He sat up and leaned against the tree trunk, tears in his eyes. He didn't know if she was alive or dead. Everything since her had been a mistake. If his life amounted to anything, it was having her. That was his peak, his real life's quest, not this pilgrimage to the Amazon. He'd burn the fucking Amazon to the ground if it would bring her back to him. She was everything, and everything should have stopped with her. He looked at the dark sea and grew calm. He knew what had to be done. He would watch the sunrise then follow it through.

6

Flora was in her late twenties when he first met her. She'd visit the orphanage almost every week, donating clothes, food and books. He was well over fourteen at the time. The first thing he noticed about her was her perfume. It was the smell of the world outside the gates. A world he barely knew a thing about. He'd watch for her arrival, the woman with the black curls that fell to her waist, and a stiff, slow gait that made the other boys laugh.

She used to smile at him as he sat by the door, reading. He'd smile back and after a few weeks she asked his name. She began to ask him questions about the books he was reading. One day, after many months, she pulled a book from within her dress and slid it on top of his. 'In the fire, Bruno,' she whispered, 'after you're done with it.'

He looked at the title: *Manifiesto del Partido Comunista*.

It was the first of many books she brought for him, books completely different from the ones he'd read until then. He read them in quiet corners, outhouses, storerooms, and in the toilet. Book by book, she gave him an education the priests would never have allowed. He savoured every word before tearing the books up and throwing them in the dormitory fire.

He'd never been able to accept religion as it was fed to him. He listened to the preaching, could recite the Bible and the Catechism, and never missed Mass or refused the Eucharist, but it was all empty ceremony to him.

These books were what he needed, his secret companions. They gave him purpose. Through them, he learned about the world beyond the gates, and prepared for life as an individual instead of an indoctrinated member of the church. Flora was his teacher, strengthening and maturing him. He developed a secret self that his brothers and the priests would never know of or understand. As time passed, he realised that the books had made him a free man amongst slaves; slaves to a set of boundaries their religion imposed on them, while he was free to explore any path his mind took him without fear or guilt.

After his fifteenth birthday, Flora was permitted to take him out of the orphanage on day trips, and on these trips his lessons continued, in museums, parks and markets. He was overwhelmed by the city, the buildings, the noise of the traffic, the colours and the people. Out here, he realised how different she was to everyone around her. Her mass of helical coils attracted everyone's attention. They stared at her mechanical gait and watched her actions with intrigue. Everything about her stood her out from the crowd, from the starched, colourful blouses and pleated skirts to her gaudy necklaces, bracelets, rings and earrings. She was unique, and he felt proud to be with her.

Her brown eyes were so intense that he avoided looking into them, fearing she could read his thoughts. She seemed to sense what he was going to do before he thought of it. Instead of looking in her eyes, he found himself looking at her bushy eyebrows, which met in a cross above the bridge of her nose.

She often took her camera with her, slung around her neck in a waxed leather case. In her slow, deliberate manner, she stopped to take photographs of street life. She photographed people without permission, and sometimes they'd take offence. Bruno knew her better. She didn't mean any harm. It was just that her interest in the world around her overcame her inhibitions.

'Never live in fear, Bruno,' she told him. 'What you do doesn't have to make sense to anyone. The most important thing is to be true to yourself.'

She talked to him in a direct manner about everything: herself, architecture, nature, style, colours and forms. Her confidence was something Bruno tried to emulate, but never could. It was out of his reach. It was an external reflection of her inner self. She knew exactly who she was and what she wanted.

He had always viewed her through child's eyes. In a quiet cafe, months after their first day out, that changed. She ordered a coffee with milk and another with tequila. Bruno had a covering of soft stubble on his chin, and was tall. He easily passed for a young man instead of a boy. When the waiter brought the cups, he placed them on the centre of the table, unsure who wanted the stronger of the two. As she lifted her arm and pulled her cup over, Bruno became aware of an odour under her perfume. It was the smell of her body. He grew hot, pulled his chair further towards the table and stole glances at her. She lit a cigarette, leaned back to expel the smoke and reached a hand behind her head. A moss of hair covered her armpit. Bruno adjusted himself under the table and took a mouthful of coffee. She spoke incessantly, but he wasn't listening to her any more. He was watching the movement of her face and hands as she talked, watching her lips press into the rim of the cup as she drank, seeing the smear of lipstick they left behind. He stared at the bare, tanned skin of her arms and slender neck. She reached for the ashtray, and he saw the soft motion of her breast through the armhole of her blouse.

'You're tense today, Bruno,' she said, gripping the back of his hand. 'Is everything alright?'

He nodded, tried to act indifferent, but when she knocked back the rest of her coffee and stood up to leave, he panicked. 'Already? We just got here. Can't we sit a while longer? Please? I haven't even finished.'

'I want to walk, Bruno. The sun's out, the birds are screaming at us. Can't you hear them?' She took his hand. '*It's spring, they say, Bruno, Flora, come out and feel the sun on your faces, smell the wind.*'

She tried to lead him away, but he gripped the table and pleaded with his eyes. She let go of his hand and rubbed her thumb and fingers together. His palms were sweating. With a softening of her eyes, she smiled, sat down and watched him. *One glance*, he thought, *and she knows it all.*

*

The next time they met, she took him to her home. Her courtyard garden was filled with animals: birds, dogs, monkeys in a cage. There were tropical plants, fruit and nut trees. A strangler fig climbed the wall of her quarters, and almond trees lined that of her husband's. Bruno hated the husband without ever having seen him, without knowing a thing about him. He didn't even want to know his name.

'I'll never bring you here when he's in town,' she said.

Past the squawking parrots and screeching monkeys, she led him through a door and down a narrow, blue corridor. At the end of the corridor was a large room where a dozen canvas-mounted easels stood, most hidden beneath paint-spattered sheets. She closed the door behind him, in front of one of the dogs that had followed. Next to an unmade bed in the corner of the room was an easel and a straight-backed chair. On the canvas was an unfinished self-portrait.

'You look like an Indian princess in it,' he said.

'Sit down on the bed and take a closer look.'

She sat next to him and described the painting. He watched her left hand hovering over the canvas, bringing his attention to every detail. Her right hand slid upon his knee.

He pulled the quilt over his waist and cleared his throat.

'It's okay,' she whispered, her lips brushing his cheek. She threw the blanket off him. Her breath was a hot vapour of coconut and lime. She turned his mouth to hers and kissed him. Her tongue was soft, her mouth sweet like honey dew. She lowered him on the bed, gathered her skirt up and climbed on top. Her dark eyes peered at him from under the fur of her eyebrows. He could almost see his reflection in them. Her knees gripped his hips as she pulled off her blouse and let it drop to the floor. He'd never seen a woman's body and turned away. She followed his eyes and noticed the camera on the chair.

'Take my picture.' She picked the camera up and handed it to him. She draped her hair on either side of her neck and arranged the coils to cover her nipples, dark as the Eucharist wine.

He lifted the viewfinder with trembling fingers and held it to his eye. She adjusted the focusing knob and set the shutter for him. He lined the camera up to capture her still, seductive face.

'Smile,' he said, and just as he clicked the button, she burst out laughing.

'Put the camera away, Bruno.'

He gathered its tether and placed it back on the chair.

She rose up on her knees, reached under her skirt and unbuttoned his trousers. She pulled them down, along with his underwear. Sweat ran down the sides of his face. He gasped as she sat back down on him, feeling the warmth of her soft, moist flesh, the prickle of her pubic hair. Blood surged through his body. His breathing grew shallow.

'Relax, Bruno,' she said, taking his hands and raising them to her breasts. He felt their softness, the nipples pressing into his palms, and reached his fingertips for the damp moss of her armpits. She rose again, tilted her pelvis forward, caught him, and eased herself down.

'You're a bit big,' she said, wincing.

He stared into her eyes as she took him fully inside and

rolled her pelvis. Every exhale was a visceral moan straight from her throat. She took one of his hands from her breast and bit into his thumb. Her skin grew hot and clammy. He turned his hand, cupped her jaw and let her kiss and bite at the heel of his palm. She rocked faster. His other hand moved from her breast to grip the hair at her scalp. He pressed his thumb into her forehead. He wanted her to feel what he was feeling, tried to project the love from his soul to hers. She bit harder and ran her tongue over his skin. Her moans came louder as her breath quickened. Her back arched. Her face tilted up to the ceiling. He closed his eyes and tried to hold back as all his energy began to flow into her. She moved faster still, her rhythm becoming jerky and violent. He was gasping, unable to stop the sounds escaping his throat. He forced himself into her and felt her tighten on him.

'*Despacio!*' she cried. '*Suave. Suave.*'

But he gripped the skirt at her knees and pushed deeper, feeling as if every cell in his body was flowing to the point where their bodies joined. As her pelvis twitched and shuddered, he let himself go and all the energy, all the electric charge that had built up, released into her. Euphoria erupted from him. His body convulsed then went limp. His mind emptied. She folded over, sweat from her hair and forehead smearing his face. She kissed him.

He stroked her hair as her lips pecked at his face and neck. Blood seeped from a mark on his hand where she'd bitten him. He sucked at it and smiled at her. There was no going back from this now. He was hers completely. This was the love he'd read about in all the novels she'd given him. This was what she'd been preparing him for, not an individual life beyond the gates but a life with her. She smoothed his hair back from his forehead and kissed his eyes, his nose, his mouth, and nuzzled into his neck.

'You're beautiful,' she said to him. 'So beautiful.'

His eyelids grew heavy, and he let them close. As she

separated from him, he turned into her pillow, breathed in her scent and smiled.

*

Life changed. He was no longer alone. His was to be a shared life with someone who loved and wanted him. By the time he'd walk out of the orphanage on his eighteenth birthday, she would have divorced her husband and would be his to marry.

He withdrew further from his brothers, struggled to concentrate on his studies, and couldn't even read the books she gave him. There was no space or time. There was only her, and he waited for her visits with the longing of a man, not a boy.

She continued to take him to cafes but now there were bars as well, where she'd let him drink whatever he wanted. She taught him what should be drunk with certain foods, and which drink was most suited to a particular time of day. Society's view, not hers. 'Always know what they expect of you, Bruno. Then you'll have no fear in doing the opposite.'

He felt as if he'd doubled in age overnight, and noticed a change in how she treated him. He wasn't a kid any more. He was an equal.

She told him about the mentors she'd had during her life, and how they helped mould her into who she'd become. 'But you'll find more mentors on bookshelves than anywhere else,' she said. 'Pick up the right book at the right time, and you'll have all the learning you'll ever need.'

She knew everyone from the lumpenproletariat to the haute bourgeoisie, from politicians and businessmen to underground freedom fighters and homeless drunks, from university lecturers to young students, from other artists, writers and poets to ballet dancers, stage performers and film stars. Although she never took him to any, she talked constantly about parties. Hundreds of names passed her lips, linked to affairs and scandals, achievements and failures. 'Of course you should never take an interest in gossip, Bruno. There are more important things to talk about.'

She spoke about society, about inequality, injustice and corruption, about perpetual war. 'Nobody talks about themselves, though,' she said, and made a nasal voice: '*If I want something I get it... no matter what.*' She flicked the ash from her cigarette. 'Bruno, how can society improve with this kind of selfishness, with so much greed in our nature?'

Every word she uttered was etched on his brain, just like the books she'd had him read. He was the perfect student, and his love for her had him searching her every word for meaning. But it was when she talked of art that his love was most awakened. He felt a joy nearing euphoria when she talked of nature, colours and forms. She was an artist before anything else, and through words alone she could turn the most commonplace, everyday thing into an object of wonder.

The sun rose fast behind the trees. He rocked back and forth in the blistering heat, sweating, shivering and retching. He could still feel the insects crawling all over him, but couldn't see any of them, and no amount of scratching would get them off. The shadows of the trees pointed like arrows toward the sea.

As the weeks passed, stuck in the orphanage, Bruno's restlessness grew. Although the ceremony of it all hadn't been completely without benefit, having taught him to focus his thoughts, take pleasure in the present, and find peace through the repetition of everyday tasks, it was ceremony built on a belief system he could never accept. His learning needed to continue beyond the gates, and his desire to be with Flora every day had turned into a need. He was already more of a man than anyone in there. Unlike the other boys and the priests, he'd known a woman, and he knew romantic love. He had to get out.

They made love every time she took him out, whether it was in the toilets of cafes and bars, down alleyways behind the dumpsters, in the bushes of the parks or back in her home. Each time, he pressed his thumb into the centre of her forehead, and channelled the love from his mind to hers. *I love you*, he projected to her, *I love you, I need you.* Afterwards they relaxed, still coupled, and if they were in her bed, she'd sing to him as he fell asleep, and she'd sing to him as he woke.

She never mentioned her husband, and as much as Bruno wanted her to raise the subject and tell him she'd ended it, he could never bring it up himself. He wanted her to think of him, alone. Talk of the husband would jeopardise that.

She'd sit naked in her room, painting her portraits, slowly mixing the colours and touching the brush to the canvas. He loved to watch her work. Each stroke made with care and precision. An idea, a thought, made visible. These weren't paintings to Bruno, they were manifestos. He belonged here; he knew that with absolute certainty. *She* was home. She was part of him. He watched her body as she painted, wishing he could lay against her and be absorbed into her flesh, to blend as one unique being. That way they'd never have to live or die alone.

Six months before his eighteenth birthday, her visits became erratic. The first time she didn't appear, he almost went hysterical. He waited and waited, wondering what had stopped her. Something awful had happened, he knew it. When she didn't come the next day, he was sure she'd been in an accident, but still he composed himself enough to wait. 'Tomorrow,' he told himself. 'Tomorrow she'll be here. The long arm of the clock ticked. Each hour the bells rang with increasing torment. That evening, he couldn't calm down. Ready to jump over the wall and run to her house, he talked to one of the priests.

'A note arrived this morning,' said the priest. 'She's ill. Nothing serious.'

'Nothing serious! And you didn't think to tell me? All this time?'

After that, she could miss two to three weeks, then would turn up as if nothing had happened. 'Pain,' was all she ever said. 'Pain from the accident years ago. I couldn't leave my bed.'

He nodded and told her he was happy that she felt better, but inside he wondered how she could stay in bed when there were no servants, and she had no family. Who would help her eat and wash? It had to be the husband, but he couldn't bring himself to even think it.

She took him to the house less and less, sometimes blaming the untidiness of the place, other times saying she was working so hard on the paintings that she needed space from them.

A nervous energy crept into their meetings. He noticed hesitation in all her actions, and at his touch, she tensed almost imperceptibly, but enough for him to notice. He felt an urgent need to be out of the orphanage, and began counting the weeks to his birthday. There were nine weeks to go.

When she took him to her home for the final time, the monkey and parrot cages were empty. He opened his mouth to ask why, but stopped. He didn't want to know the answer. In the room, most of her paintings and easels were gone. Only three remained. He felt something pop inside him and stumbled to the chair to catch his breath. He made love to her with an urgent desperation that day. Again, he wanted to absorb her or be absorbed by her; to blend his energy and thought with hers and create a single, shared soul. He gripped her head, ground his pelvis into hers and stared into her dark eyes, searching for her inside them. All he could see was emptiness. He pushed his thumb into her forehead with such force that it left a white print. He dug his fingers into her head so hard she clenched her jaw in pain. *Don't leave me*, he almost screamed at her, *please, please don't leave me*.

Of the three paintings left in the room, all were covered

in colourful sheets, including the most recent one that stood next to the bed, the one he'd watched her build from nothing. He'd seen every brush stroke and translated it into a story. Their story. This would be her masterpiece. She sat naked on the edge of the bed.

'You finished,' he said, pulling his trousers up. 'Are you happy with it?'

Her hair bobbed as she nodded.

'Can I see it?' He sat up beside her and was startled to see a tear run from her eye.

The sheet slid off and fell to the floor. He held his breath. 'You should have just stabbed me in the heart,' he whispered.

'I'm sorry,' she said, crying fully now. 'I'm so sorry.'

On the self-portrait, in the centre of the forehead, where he placed his thumb every time they made love, was a miniature portrait of another man.

'Your husband?' His voice trembled. He hated himself for having to ask it, and resented the tears filling his eyes. Rage exploded within him. He grabbed the canvas in one hand and raised a fist.

She jumped from the bed and reached out for it, but he pushed her away. 'Don't do it!' she screamed. 'Don't ruin it.'

He let it drop and uncovered the other paintings. She'd done the same thing to them, too.

'I'm not going to recover from this,' he said. His brain was shutting down, he stammered, vomited. He could barely see her. 'I'm not going to survive.'

She cried into her hands.

'This whole time!' he shouted. 'I thought it was me, but the whole time it's been him! You never loved me.'

'I did!' she screamed. 'I swear I did.'

'*Pain*. Always that same excuse. *Pain!* There was no pain. You were fucking him.'

'There was pain! I couldn't get out of bed. I swear!'

'You think I don't know how pain feels? Look at me. Is this not pain?'

124

She wouldn't look.

'Beautiful, you said, so beautiful. You want beauty?' He made for the window, punched through it and held a shard of glass to his face.

'Stop it!' she shouted, and ran for him. She grabbed his arm. 'You're bleeding!'

'Don't fucking touch me!' He dropped the shard and pushed her to the floor. His hand left a bloody print on her chest. He threw the door open and walked out.

'Bruno!' she called after him. 'Bruno! I'm sorry!'

*

The orphanage offered no shelter from his thoughts. Every minute of his day was taken up by thinking of what she'd done and the anger and hurt she'd caused him. He suffered in his sleep as much as he did awake, haunted by her in nightmares from which he'd wake with a start, only to suffer more. He realised how little he had in life. He had nothing and no one. These other boys were not really brothers. Some shared hatreds for the priests and the church, though others were followers and servants of it. Most hated themselves for their own reasons, others because of the priests, but he turned his hatred outward. He was the victim in it all.

He tried hard to hate her, but only succeeded for a short time, and as the days passed his anger abated, doubts formed and he started to question everything he had first believed. He convinced himself that the husband had put her up to it. Why would she have cried so much if she didn't love him? And in her final painting she was wearing some kind of white dress. It had to be a bridal dress.

It must have been the husband! he thought. He must have heard about their affair, found out she wanted a divorce, but wouldn't let her leave him. He forced her to add his portrait to hers. It was the only explanation. As soon as Bruno had this theory mapped out, he began to doubt himself again. There was no way to be sure of anything on his own. He had to wait. It wouldn't make any sense to act out when there was still a possibility that she'd walk through the gates.

His energy would change from one day to the next: from weak and powerless, when he was so depressed he had to burn himself with the acid of *caju* shells to stop from thinking, to becoming so impassioned by anger that he punched the courtyard wall until the skin came away, and kicked the *caju* tree trunks until his shins blistered and bled. The priests forced him to kneel on the concrete at the altar and pray for forgiveness. Instead of praying, he played out dramas in his head, dreamt up scenarios of what would happen when he saw her again, what he'd say, how she'd reply, and how he'd respond to it.

Just before his eighteenth birthday, or what he thought was his birthday – on the handwritten note he'd been left there with as a baby, torn from a packet of Jockey Club cigarettes, the first number of his date of birth could have been either a seven or a one – a letter arrived from her. He tore the seam of the envelope and closed his eyes, catching a trace of her perfume.

Dear Bruno,

I'm sorry for everything. I never meant to hurt you, please believe me. I do love you, I always did, but I thought I wasn't in love with my husband any more. I've realised that I am.

You'll always have a special place in my heart. You have such a beautiful soul. I know you're going to be a great man someday. Never give up on that.

I have to tell you I'm leaving. We're going overseas. A curator has commissioned an exhibition of our work. You know that art is my breath, Bruno. It makes me who I am. Keep reading, keep learning, and you'll find your path. You're young, Bruno. Don't wait for me. I'll never return here. Go and live your life. I want you to be happy. You deserve it.

All my love,
for you,
Flora.

126

He read it twice then looked it over word by word to make sure he hadn't missed or misunderstood anything. '*We're* going,' he said aloud. '*We… Our…* What about me?'

He cupped the letter to his nose and mouth, breathed in as much of her scent as he could and, glancing at her jagged, black handwriting one last time, tore the letter up and threw it in the fire. As soon as the flames took hold, he was burning his hands trying to save it.

'*All my love, for you,*' she'd written. '*I thought I wasn't in love with my husband. I've realised that I am.*' She didn't write plainly: *I am in love with my husband.* How could she love her husband when she'd written: '*all my love, for you*'?

Could the husband have put her up to this as well? Was he forcing her abroad to keep them apart? It was impossible to tell. He had to catch her. He needed to see her face and hear her voice. Only then would he know for sure.

He begged the priests to let him leave. He only needed a few hours to find her. He was dismissed with an ignorant callousness. These priests hadn't experienced what he was going through and had no empathy. They talked to him as if he were a boy, but he was fully grown now and stood taller and broader than any of them.

'It's better for you if you let me go,' he said. 'Please understand that. I don't want any harm or trouble.'

They had God on their side. There was nothing to fear in an orphan boy, an *Expósito*. But everything Bruno lived for was being taken, and with no time left to spare, he had no choice. He beat one of the priests until he got hold of his keys, and when the rest fought to get them back, he attacked them with his fists and elbows and knees until, amid pleading and crying, the other boys hauled him off.

He took the documents he needed in place of a birth certificate, tore the last pages from the registry of graduated boys, opened the gate and ran for over an hour in the winter cold until he reached her house.

He climbed the padlocked gate of her property. The

silence and emptiness were more numbing than the cold. No dogs barking, no monkeys. In the dull moonlight he found the door to her quarters, knocked and shouted, then kicked it in.

'Flora,' he said, shuffling down the unlit corridor. He opened her door and switched the light on. She wasn't there.

The bed in the corner was stripped to the mattress. Empty paint pots lay discarded on the floor. Frayed brushes stewed in jars of turpentine on the windowsill. The pane he'd punched through had been replaced. Gone was the scent of her perfume, starched blouses, and the coconut oil she used on her hair. Only the smell of emptiness and decay remained. The room seemed as if it had died. Plaster crumbled from the walls. Cobwebs clung to every corner. Black mould speckled the curtains like soulless imitations of her paint-spattered sheets.

Under the bed he noticed a tin bread bin. Inside, upon a pile of photographs, was her camera: the Rolleiflex TLR Tele. He flicked through the photos: photos of parks, trees and animals, photos of beautiful people in fancy bars and theatre halls, photos of street scenes and homeless sleepers. Hot tears welled in his eyes when he found the one he was looking for. Topless, with a hand on her head, Flora played with the black coils that draped her breasts. She was staring out at him with lips curving into the smile that had become laughter an instant later. With the photo in his hands, he curled up on the mattress and shouted out to her: 'Did you leave this for me? Tell me! You left this for me?'

He dreamt he was chasing after her, looking all over town, not knowing where she was. He'd catch glimpses of her, but just before he could get a better look she'd disappear into the crowd. At one point he was sure it was her. She stood with her back to him, not twenty metres away.

'Flora!' he shouted. 'Flora! Flora!' She didn't turn around, either not hearing or not listening. The despair he felt in his dream was so intense it woke him up. She was gone.

He'd have preferred it if she'd killed him, had driven a knife into his heart as they climaxed together, and let him bleed out with nothing but love for her. Instead, she'd disappeared with everything he understood and needed. She'd left him as a crumbling shell of dust and rot.

*

The light amongst the palms was golden-yellow. He wiped away the tears and twisted the sweat from his hair. He stared into the full sphere of the sun, insentient creator of all life on earth that would one day become its destroyer. In the uncommon heat, he struggled to focus. All sense of time had left him. He didn't know if he was still in the past or living in the present.

Maybe Flora was waiting for him. If not, he'd be the one waiting for her. There was nothing for him here but one disappointment after another. He was completely and utterly alone. He rose to his feet and held a tree trunk until his legs steadied. He stripped his clothes off as he crossed the beach, feeling the heat of the sun scorching his bare skin. He stepped into the cool, calm water, picked up a handful of sand and rubbed it between his palms. He washed his face and wet his hair. The taste of salt and smell of kelp made him smile. He turned to see the sun one more time then ran through the shallows and dived in.

He'd swim until his legs and arms gave out, until his lungs heaved, then he'd sink under the water and disappear. There was nothing tragic in this. He'd done everything he had to. ' "The obstacle is too solid to move?" ' he shouted, spitting water as he swam. ' "Failure does not lie with you! You must depart as gracious in death as one who does achieve his purpose, and at peace with those who stood in your way!" ' [4]

'Flora!' he called. 'I'm coming!' Some trick of consciousness had him hearing her reply. Maybe she *was*

4 Meditations – Marcus Aurelius

waiting for him. *You're going to fall asleep,* he thought, *and she'll sing to you as you wake.*

He knew what death would be like. It wasn't the suffocating black tar of his sleep paralysis. That was no more than the trickery of fear. In real death dimethyltryptamine would flood from his pineal gland to his brain, giving him psychedelic euphoria and removing any fear or suffering. He'd feel like a star exploding, a transfer of energy from one source to another. There was nothing to be scared of. *Bruno!* There it was again, her calling his name. It jarred his thinking. He didn't want to hear it. This was *his* moment. There shouldn't be any intrusion. He was growing cold now, his head was beginning to ache. That strange, searing heat he'd felt all night disappeared. *Bruno!* He heard it again. He threw his head back and trod water. He scanned the beach, and there she was. 'You're supposed to be there, not here!' he shouted. Her mass of black hair bobbed as she ran through the waves breaking in the shallows.

'Bruno!' she screamed, her voice hysterical. 'Don't do it!' She was in up to her waist and swimming. 'Come back. Please come back!'

He rubbed the blur from his eyes, unsure what was going on, and swam towards her. 'Flora,' he said, as he wrapped his arms around her. She gripped him so hard it hurt and cried into his shoulder. He got an arm free and swept the hair from her face. It wasn't Flora at all. It was Bea.

I feel a bit sorry for them.
Maybe we overdid it?

7

The wind had died down, as it did most nights, leaving the streets stagnating in the heat. He sat in the chair and looked at the sand around its base, strewn with hair from all who'd been tattooed over the weeks. He thought about what Bea had said after getting him out of the water, while leading him to his shelter to sweat out the fever. She'd taken a handful of sand and rolled and flicked at it until only one grain remained. 'This is all you get, Bruno!' She'd been hoarse from exertion and was coughing up seawater. 'Look around you! This is all you get out of infinity. Don't you dare cut it short.'

He was ashamed but happy, because he knew she really cared about him. He made a silent promise that if she ever needed him, now or fifty years on, he'd knock down mountains to be there for her.

'Okay, Hermes,' said Niki. 'Take the beard off.'

Hermes ran his clippers through the entangled mass. Knotted clumps dropped to the sand. With a shaving brush, he worked a bar of soap into a lather.

'No,' said Niki, laying the cigarette he'd just rolled onto the bench with the others. 'Shave it dry. It'll help with the pain.'

After shaving him, Hermes stood back and smiled. Bruno worked over his burning jaw. Bea turned from the crowd to look at him. 'Bruno,' she said. 'You've got the jaw of a Spartan.'

Niki positioned the screens so the onlookers couldn't see. They circled around and tried to peer through the gaps.

With his purple pen and beer-steadied hands, he drew the lines that would give Bruno his new look. The lines curved out above his eyebrows, down his nose and circled his nostrils. They followed the contours under his eyes, around his cheekbones and down to the edges of his lips. The hollow under his bottom lip was filled with a convex cross.

Bruno closed his eyes and kept still as the tickle of the pen left wet trails. Niki ordered him to smile and frown, and made adjustments until he was happy that each line did what it needed to. As Niki worked, Bruno ran over all the things Bea had said to him as he drifted in and out of consciousness in the shelter. *You'll never be happy if you rely on someone else... Face your past and walk forward instead of running away... It's better to choose one road and follow it than to be paralysed by indecision and have nowhere to go.*

All this time he'd been trying to hide from his past. Doing so had ruined his present. Now it was time to start again. No regret. No guilt. No fear.

Bruno wished she'd listen to her own advice, too. Not to hold herself back, but to walk forward, figure everything out and go home, but he kept quiet. In time she'd realise. She was smarter than him and much stronger.

'Okay, Bruno.' Niki raised the tattoo gun and rolled his neck. He smiled. 'You don't have to grip the seat so tight, we won't be going that fast.'

The needle cut trails of fire on his skin. Bruno tried to send his mind far away, but the pain and the noise kept him right where he was. There was no escaping it, so he focused on it, let it be the punishment for all the mistakes he'd made in life. He was being reborn, and birth was never a pleasurable experience. Everything from this point forward would be different.

After four hours, with only short breaks for Niki to grab a beer or light up a cigarette, the tattoo gun whirred to a stop and Niki stretched out his back.

'Bruno, my friend. It's been a pleasure working on you. I appreciate the opportunity.' He placed the mirror on Bruno's thigh.

Bruno held his breath and closed his eyes until the mirror was in position. Though his face was burning, the rest of his body was cold with fear. He inhaled, opened his eyes and exhaled evenly. He peered at himself in the mirror and was overwhelmed by a sense of relief. He smiled then frowned, turned to the side and raised an eyebrow. He touched his jaw where the beard had been and worked it around, watching all the lines moving with the muscles of his face. His expressions were distinct. There was no mistaking them.

'Niki,' he said, springing from the chair and wrapping his arms around him. 'It couldn't be any better. See how it moves? Bea, come and look at me!'

Bea slipped between the screens and gave a nervous laugh. 'Unbelievable,' she said. 'It's perfect!'

'Thank you so much, Niki. I can't take it in.'

Hermes popped his head between the screens and smiled. 'Bruno, let me cut your hair.'

Bruno felt lighter and stronger all of a sudden. He handed the mirror back to Niki and looked around. The street lights seemed brighter, the noise of the people in the street was joyous, the music from the nearest bar almost had him tapping his feet.

'I'll need a chainsaw to get through this,' Hermes said, sitting him down again. He began hacking away until Bruno's hair reached only to his nose. He got Bea to hold the hair up on top of Bruno's head as he clipped the sides short, shaped the sideburns and trimmed around his ears. He washed it as best he could with the bar of soap and water from a bottle, then brushed the wavy hair straight back from Bruno's forehead and took a step back to look. 'You'll have to wash it properly; then come to the salon so I can get it right.'

Niki held the mirror for Bruno to see.

'I look like a gangster.'

'You look great,' said Bea.

'It's my best work.' Niki sat on the bench and crossed his legs. 'I wasn't sure how it would turn out but I think we got it right.'

'It's Maori style, is it not?' Bea asked.

'It's a mix of cultures. Maori, Tufi, the Chins, the Kayabi, the Kayapo. I've done my research. You're far from alone, Bruno.'

As Bruno helped move the screens and fold them up, the hushed voices of all the tourists who'd been waiting to see him merged and amplified. People of all different nationalities and languages were smiling at him. 'Bravo,' said one girl. Another smiled. Everyone there was smiling. A man asked for a photo with him.

'Thanks,' Bruno said to them. 'Thank you, all.' He posed for pictures with whoever held up a camera.

A 4×4 arrived for Niki, and they loaded it with all his things, along with Hermes's chair. They carried the chair into the salon then surrounded the passenger door of the cab, where Niki sat with the window rolled down.

'Not coming out to give us a hug, Nik?' asked Hermes.

'You know how it is,' said Niki. 'I couldn't slip away during the night this time. Have a good Christmas, New Year and all that bullshit. I mean it. Bruno, it's been good.'

'Thanks again, Niki.'

'Goodbye,' said Bea.

Niki patted the roof. The driver set the motor in gear and drove off down the crowded street.

*

A few nights before Christmas, Honey approached Bruno and Bea at the *carrinhos*. She looked around and beckoned them away from the tourists they were talking to.

'I was in the campsite toilets with a client the other night,' she started.

'But you have a house,' said Bruno.

She raised her palms. 'We all have our kinks, Bruno. Anyway, I heard some guys come in. They were talking about you two.'

'What did they say?' asked Bea.

'They were talking about beer. Said they'd take it without paying.'

'Fucking bastards.' Bruno shook his head.

'Look,' said Honey, taking a cigarette from her case. 'I'm not one for interfering in other people's affairs. I'd appreciate if you guys keep me out of it.'

'Of course,' said Bruno.

'Thanks for telling us,' Bea said. 'Want a drink?'

'No thanks, darling. I'm meeting a client for a massage.' She lit the cigarette.

'You do massage? Can you teach me?'

'Nothing to it, sweetie. Just rub them up and down a bit and when the time's right—' She pulled the cigarette out of her mouth along with her teeth. She chomped her gums together. 'Never had a complaint yet.'

They returned to the crowd and Bea bought a couple of *caipiroskas* at Kart de la Revolución. 'What are you going to do?' she asked, handing one to Bruno.

'Well, it doesn't surprise me,' he said, catching the straw between his teeth. 'We still have a few days before bottling. I'll come up with something.'

He woke that night after only a few hours' sleep, and without waiting for the day, grabbed his machete, rope and canvas bags. He made his way to the coconut palms. Under the half-moon, he climbed the trees and cut down the ripest coconuts. After four trips, emptying the bags in his storage compartment, he knew he had enough for the job.

He worked as quietly as he could, lit the fire, and with sweat dripping from his brow, halved the coconuts and scooped their innards into the pot. The oil rose from the slurry and turned brown as he stirred. He strained it through a muslin cloth into another pot, repeating the process until all the coconuts had been used. He re-boiled the oil and strained it again and again until all the impurities were gone. He was left with a few litres of highly concentrated coconut oil. In the dim light of morning, he left it to cool in his shelter and threw the coconut shells in the skip.

Later that day, with cans of spray paint Bea got from Luis, they painted over the clear plastic bottles.

'Remind me why we're doing this,' she said.

'It stops the sunlight damaging the beer.'

'Let it be ruined, they're going to take it anyway.'

'We need to give it a name,' he said. 'What d'you think?'

She shrugged.

'Let's call it Burro Beer,' he said, 'after your beloved donkeys.'

'Burro means butter in Italian, you know?'

'Even better. It'll appeal more to all the Italian tourists. Here.' He passed her a dry bottle. 'You're the calligraphist. I'll keep painting them black, you add *Burro Beer* in white.'

'Bruno, there's no point. They're going to steal it.'

'"And if you grudge the crushing of the grapes, your grudge distils a poison in the wine."'[5]

'Osho?' she asked.

'Gibran.'

'Hold on.' She lowered the bottle and glared at him. 'Are you crazy? You can't poison them.'

He leaned towards her and lowered his voice. 'Not

5 The Prophet – Kahlil Gibran

poison, but I've got enough pure coconut oil to make them shit pond water for a month.'

Her lips curled into a smile and she shook her head. 'We're painting the bottles so they can't see it. Bruno, what if they taste it?'

'We won't add it to the first few bottles. Once they drink them they won't notice any difference.'

'You *are* crazy.' She looked over at the closest group of tents. 'Maybe we should mix in some laxatives just to be sure.'

'Can't hurt,' he said. 'Have a chat with Luis. See how many packs he has.'

On Christmas Eve, in Bruno's shelter, they filled the bottles up.

'Leave a gap of three fingers,' he said, 'and I'll add the oil.'

'How many pills per bottle?' she asked, reading the back of one of the boxes of laxatives.

'Four, maybe?'

'Says here, one to three a day. Let's go with two and see how many we have left over.'

They left ten bottles untarnished, prepared all the others and stacked them upside down in crates Bruno made from palm fronds.

'This way the oil will mix with the beer when they turn them around.'

They carried the loaded crates out of the shelter and called over to Abilio. He brought Golias along. Both were shirtless and had a stale odour about them. In all the time Bruno had been there, he hadn't seen either of them enter the toilets with a towel.

Bruno kept one bottle for himself, handed them a bottle each and passed another to Bea. 'It's all ready to go,' he said. 'Enough to drown in. I hope you boys like it.'

He held up his bottle to them. 'Merry Christmas.'

All three uncapped their bottles and swigged. Bruno nodded at the flavour and saw Bea smiling.

'Not bad,' said Abilio, wiping his mouth.

'Fucking good.' Golias tipped the bottle back again.

'Drink up, lads. It's worth every *centavo*. Speaking of which, we agreed on one hundred and fifty *contos*, did we not? You paid sixty-five already. So,'. He held out his palm. 'I'll take the rest now.'

'Well… Erm…' Golias's mouth closed under Abilio's glare.

'Help us over with it first,' Abilio said. 'Adelina's got the money.'

With Golias carrying two crates, Bruno with one on his shoulder, and Bea reluctantly sharing with Abilio, they got all the crates over.

Adelina was breastfeeding the infant. Golias dropped his crates, sat in his deckchair and picked up his guitar. Fortunato appeared with his brother, who had the same sneering nose and lip.

'Bruno.' Abilio cocked his head and looked him clean in the eye. 'We don't have the money, mate. We'll pay you as soon as we can.'

'I'll take it all back then.' Bruno stepped towards the nearest crate. 'Bea, come help.'

Abilio nodded to Golias, who rose from his chair and shouldered Bruno to the ground. 'He said we'll pay when we get the money.'

'No you fucking won't,' said Bruno, dusting the sand off his clothes. 'It'll be low season after New Year. All the tourists will be gone. You won't be able to make any fucking money! I'll give you the beer when you pay. Not before.' He made for the crate again.

'Bruno!' Bea shouted. 'It's not worth fighting over.'

'Listen to her,' said Abilio. All of them were smiling, even Adelina, whose nipple had escaped the infant's mouth. The infant's lips fished for it.

Bruno started towards Abilio but Golias blocked his path. He pushed with all his strength but only managed to wobble the folds of fat on Golias's greasy torso. Golias brought one hand up and pushed Bruno to the ground again.

'Come on then, fat fuck,' Bruno said, rising to his feet. 'Let's go!'

'Enough!' Bea shouted. 'Forget about it.'

'Take it easy, Sooty,' said Golias. 'You'll be hurting.'

'Hurting? You hear him, Bea?' He talked to them all. 'Give me that crate or you'll all be fucking hurting!'

Golias raised his fists, as the others began to laugh.

'Give him a fucking crate,' said Abilio. 'He's a fool. Just give it to him.' He looked at Bruno. 'Take your lovely crate and fuck off.'

'Consider yourself lucky,' Fortunato said.

'Haul your skinny ass away,' said Adelina, as the infant reattached itself again to her breast.

Bruno picked the crate up and walked with Bea at his side.

'What are you playing at?' she whispered. 'You could've been killed.'

'It had to seem realistic.' He winked at her. 'Now they'll think we're drinking exactly the same beer as they are.'

That night, they brought a couple of bottles to the last day-bar for Anderson. He was sitting on the back step, panama hat perched on his freshly clipped head, stubby cigar bit between his teeth. He was reading a paperback.

'Ah,' he said, taking the hat and cigar in his hand. He rose to greet Bea with a kiss on each cheek. 'Merry Christmas, Squirrel.'

'It's not even midnight,' said Bruno.

'She might be gone by then, and I'd have missed my chance.' He reached out to shake Bruno's hand.

Bruno noticed how her face lit up when Anderson called her Squirrel. He hadn't heard him call her that before. He wished he could come up with a pet name to make her look at him in the same way she beamed at anyone who directed endearments towards her. He still kept those softer touches locked up inside, leaving no chance for them to slip out.

'We thought we'd bring the beer to you for a change,' Bruno said. 'Got some glasses?'

They took a seat by the step as Anderson went inside.

'It's not poisoned, is it?' Anderson asked and laughed at his joke. He held the glasses for Bruno to fill.

'Not these bottles anyway,' said Bea, raising an eyebrow at Bruno. 'Cheers!'

'*Za zdorov'ye!*' said Bruno.

Anderson touched the beer to his lips, ran his tongue over them then finished the glass. 'Bruno,' he said, 'this is good. This is very good.'

'All brewed at the campsite using other people's junk; sterilised junk, don't worry.'

'You made a lot?'

'One hundred and fifty *contos* worth,' said Bea. 'We gave most to the travellers.'

'Gave away?'

'They were supposed to pay for it. We're still waiting.'

'Can't be trusted,' Anderson said. 'I told you already, son. They only take. I don't know why Mac doesn't just throw the lot of them out. You know, a few weeks ago, some drunk tourist almost lost an eye. Hermes had to stitch him up. The guy said Honey had attacked him, but he was so drunk he couldn't remember anything about her. He couldn't even remember where it happened. But he said she was young and pretty. Sound like Honey to you?' He looked at Bea.

'Oh come on,' said Bruno, noticing Bea's face whiten. 'If Mac threw *them* out, *we'd* be thrown out too. Where would we go?'

'You'll be fine, Tarzan. I mean the others. They're bad people. I know some of those tourists should get what's coming to them, but most are just here for a good time.

Not like those gypsy sellers. You sure there's no drug dealing going on up there?'

'People are people,' said Bea. 'The tourists love walking past the sellers every night. Where would it stop? If you got rid of them you'd end up without the street performers. They use the campsite as well.'

'Anyway,' said Bruno. 'Take a look at them. They're not happy people. The best way is not to let them get you down. Just get on with things. Here.' He handed Anderson two books. 'Can you swap these for me?'

'I've never met anyone who can read so fast,' Bea said.

'Do you think he's actually reading them, or just wants to look smart?' Anderson asked her.

'Every word,' said Bruno.

'Are you a reader, Bea?'

She shook her head. 'I'm more of a visual person, you know? Film, theatre, talking, socialising.'

'More into the present.' Anderson nodded. 'That's what I'd say you are.' He held up his paperback. 'I read these just to escape, to walk in someone else's shoes for a while. Not like this guy.' He dragged on his cigar and rolled the smoke around in his mouth.

'There are thousands of years of experience in books,' Bruno said. 'Only two things are more valuable as far as I can tell: air and water. By the way, I've been thinking about what you said Honey does. The real Honey, not this drunken illusion the guy dreamt up. I'd bet the guy imagined the whole thing. You said Honey provides a service none of the locals can. Maybe this beer could be a hit with the tourists. I could sell to the *carrinhos*. None of the locals can make beer.'

'Forgotten the coconut scenario already?'

'So I shouldn't try it?'

'It's a risk is all I'm saying, and low season will hit soon. Maybe it's time to get moving again?'

'I think you should do whatever you want,' said Bea. 'You've spent a long time on the road already. So what if it takes you a little longer to get to the forest? And who cares if they throw you out of town? Ha! You were leaving anyway. Don't put yourself in a place where you spend the rest of your life regretting what you didn't do.'

'Easy there, Squirrel.' Bea's face relaxed into a smile again. 'I'm not saying you shouldn't, Bruno. I'm not that good at thinking on the spot. Tell you what, I'll change these books, have a think, and give you my opinion later. Now, pour me another beer.'

'What will you do tomorrow?' asked Bea.

'Business as usual. Christmas is for the tourists, New Year's for the locals. Anything much happening in the campsite? Any chatter?'

'No chatter at all,' Bruno said. 'Same boring people, usual boring things. We're not invited to their party. Will everything close here at New Year?'

'Restaurants close at six on New Year's Eve.' Anderson tapped the ash from his cigar. 'Only the *carrinhos* will be open at night.'

'Why's that?' asked Bea.

'You don't know about the ceremony? Every year, on the 31st of December, they perform the *Festa De Yemanjá*. This year is extra special because of the black moon. The whole town will be there. Starts at 11p.m. at the church.'

'I told you there was something weird going on here,' said Bea, as they walked under the clear night to the campsite. 'I bet it's…' Her eyes flashed open and her tongue stuck out. 'Voodoo!' She collapsed to the ground, convulsed then went still. She spoke with gravel in her voice: 'I bet they take poor travellers from the campsite…' Her hand rose and she pretended to stab herself, '…drive a ceremonial dagger into their chests and cut out the beating heart.' She threw the invisible dagger away, tore her ribcage open and reached inside. She offered the invisible, throbbing heart to Bruno.

'Come on, joker,' he said.

'And Big Mac takes the beating heart in his mouth and bites down on it, and the blood runs down his chin, and the victim sees him chewing on his heart, and Mac says,' she deepened her voice, ' "Where's the fries?" and the traveller spasms out dead!'

He pulled her to her feet. 'You're a good actor,' he said. 'I was going to run to Hermes for a second there.'

'Shhh,' she said, serious all of a sudden. 'Listen.' Carol singing came from one of the houses. 'It's 'Silent Night'.'

'Nothing weird about that,' said Bruno. 'A good old-fashioned Christmas carol. Would it bother you if their religion really was a bit weird?'

'If they're sacrificing people? Yes, I'm pretty sure I'd get out of here as fast as I could.'

'But what if there's no danger in it? What if it's just different?'

'It's creepy enough seeing the stuff at the cross every day, Bruno. I'm certain it's different but I'd definitely like to find out what's actually going on.'

'Bea,' he said. 'Why didn't you tell me what happened that night?'

'What night are you talking about?'

'That morning your board was lying empty. You haven't been out on any of your middle-of-the-night walks since. The guy thought you were Honey?'

'I really don't know what you're talking about.'

He stopped walking. 'Bea, we've been through enough to be honest with each other.'

'Look, I just didn't want you to worry, okay?'

'What happened?'

'The street was empty and a drunk came from nowhere.' Her voice grew hollow. 'He put his arm around me and gripped me so tight I could barely move. You should've heard what he was saying. Yellow teeth. Stinking breath. Spitting all over me as he spoke. He told me all the things he was going to do to me. I was so scared. I had no choice. I swung the board and caught him with the corner. If I didn't, I've no idea what would have happened.'

Bruno ran his hands through his hair and closed his eyes. 'You should have told me, Bea. I'm here with you. I'm here for you. Never forget that.'

*

All through the night, Bruno's sleep was broken by the noise of the travellers' party. At one point their tuneless singing got so loud that he considered running out smashing the guitar over Golias's head. He visualised throwing each of them, one by one, into the bonfire they'd made. The only thing that stopped him confronting them was the knowledge that the coconut oil and laxatives would already be inside them, silently making magic. He got up to make breakfast. Bea was already out of her tent, running the tortoise-shell brush down her shroud of hair. She nodded over at the toilets.

'I feel a bit sorry for them. Maybe we overdid it?'

Bruno stretched his arms high over his head and smiled. People were squatting all over the site: beside their tents, at the toilets, up on the hill by the cacti. The sound of their groans was sweeter than any song he'd heard on Main Street.

'Not a cloud in the sky,' he said. 'Merry Christmas, Bea. You're the best present I ever had.'

Abilio hobbled over.

'And a Merry Christmas to you, Abilio, my man!' Bruno reached out to offer a hug.

'You fucking bastard,' Abilio said, swatting Bruno's hands away. 'You poisoned us!'

'Poisoned! You hear that, Bea? Must've been the food.' He looked down at his belly and gave it a rub. 'I'm fine. Bea, how about you?'

'I'm okay.' She had a look of such unquestionable innocence that it took even Bruno by surprise. 'The children are sick,' she said. 'It *had* to be the food. No decent parent would give their children alcohol. You *are* a decent parent, aren't you, Abilio?'

Abilio's lips unsheathed his stumpy yellow teeth. 'This is bullshit! You're fucking liars—' His face contorted and he doubled over, groaning. 'Won't be the end of this,' he said, scrambling away.

'Get well soon!' Bea shouted.

'They'll know not to steal again,' said Bruno. 'I hope all this excitement hasn't ruined your appetite?'

'I've got some letters to finish first.'

'Take your time. Don't mind me. Just help yourself when it's ready.'

They didn't leave the campsite all day. Bea had decided to cook lunch and made a green vegetable risotto with flaked parmesan and garlic bread that she baked in foil amongst the coals.

She'd invited Honey over, and the three of them sat on the sand by the fire with the food set out on a frond mat. Bruno dug his camera out, set the timer, and snapped a photo of them together.

He'd been keeping an eye on Golias, Fortunato and his brother, but could see by the way they moped around that any fight in them had gone.

'So,' said Honey. 'Almost the new year. What do you want out of it?'

Bea had been quiet since morning. Her mind had been relieved of her troubles when cooking, but now, with nothing to keep her busy, Bruno could see the hurt.

Here I am, he thought, *finally happy. Here with a real friend, but she's so sad she can barely hold it together.* He wanted to tell her to go home, but every time he tried, she silenced him with the same force she'd hauled the knot out of her hair with on that first night. She had a quick temper that rarely surfaced, but when it did she could be as intimidating as anyone he'd ever met. He looked at those eyes that seemed both Western and Asian at the same time, and at her compact body, all padded muscle that most people would never have noticed, and wondered how far back her Russian ancestry went. He saw something primal and nomadic in her; he was sure that if she traced her lineage far enough she'd find herself to be a descendant of the Mongol Empire.

'I don't think either of us know, Honey. Maybe I'll have a *carrinho* of my own. Maybe I'll get kicked out of town and be on my way again. How about you?'

'*Contos*,' she said. '*Contos, contos* and more *contos*. In another couple of years I'll retire, live in a small apartment, eat nice food like this every day.'

'You won't miss your young men?'

'I'll enjoy them for free! It's not the same when business is involved. It's all about them. I'll make it about me after I retire.'

'Will you stay here?' Bea asked.

'Why would she leave?'

'Why would I stay?'

'You're accepted here,' Bruno said. 'You're a local.'

'Bruno, I'm tolerated, just like the farmers and the fishermen; less than them, actually. Anyway, I'm a city girl. This is a tourist town. There's nothing here but money. Once I reach my goal – and I'm nearly there – I'll go live in a nice coastal city, take a small apartment with a sea view over a cafe, and I'll sit watching the boats steam by.' She coughed and cleared her throat. 'I need a cigarette.' She reached into her pocket. 'I thought you were a city-boy, too, Bruno. Can you see yourself spending the rest of your life in a place like this?'

'Cities are all the same,' he said. 'Exploitation. Decay. Greed. The rich and corrupt driving fancy cars past emaciated children cupping stagnant water from potholes. And even the poor don't want to help each other! All for themselves!'

'Here we go,' said Bea. 'Saving the planet. Won't even stop for breath.'

'Bea, I just don't want any part in it. This is the first place I've seen hope. Everyone gets a share, no? I don't see anybody at the side of Main Street starving to death, do you?'

'Where there's power there's corruption, Bruno.' Honey tapped the ash from her cigarette. 'Greed is the nature of the beast. Someone's always getting a bad deal somewhere, and even the unhappiest of people can smile... Bea, you made a great meal; I brought the dessert.' She opened her bag, tossed packets of shortbread amongst the plates and scattered a handful of teabags, sachets of sugar and thimbles of milk onto the mat.

'I haven't seen these in ages,' said Bea, picking up a shortbread finger in tartan wrapping. 'Thanks, Honey.'

'All the luxuries of home,' said Bruno. He got up to clean the pot and boil the water.

'They steal them from the big city hotel suppliers and use them in the guesthouses,' Honey said.

*

In the late afternoon on the 31st of December, Bruno took a walk around the streets. The locals rushed to finish their duties, performing their tasks with minimal courtesy towards the tourists. The waiters removed plates from tables as soon as the tourists put their cutlery down. The shopkeepers lowered shutters on people's heels. All they wanted was to close up and get ready for whatever celebration they had planned.

He went to meet Bea on the dune to watch the final sunset of the year, passing the cart-boys dragging their *carrinhos* on the way. He smiled as the staff in the closing bars and restaurants heckled them for having to work as usual.

He sat still and silent next to Bea and considered all that had happened in the past year. Despite the thoughts and noise pulling at him, he felt relaxed and he lay back and smiled.

After sunset, they had a few drinks at Kart de la

Revolución before returning to the campsite. While Bea rested in her tent, Bruno lay in his hammock, watching Mac and Lagarto work at the church. They hung a light above the door and staked unlit pairs of torches from the doorway to create a path that curved out towards Main Street. Bruno let his eyes close and fell asleep.

When he woke, the torches were aflame and the light above the church door glowed red. A few cool-box-men lingered. They were dressed completely in white. Bruno watched people arriving, and as the crowd grew, went to wake Bea.

They walked past the gathering of travellers looking on from beside the campsite toilets and joined the crowd around the church. At the front, locals had packed themselves in, leaving only the torch-lit path free. All were barefoot and wore white clothes. Girls had white flowers in their hair. Men and women wore necklaces of blue, pearl and transparent beads. Behind them stood the tourists and some locals dressed in simple clothing. 'Jingubans,' Bea said.

From elevated ground by a neighbouring house, they watched more white-clad locals arrive and push into the crowded area. People who'd been sitting got to their feet. Children who'd been playing in the sand were lifted into their mothers' arms.

A pair of women walked up the path to the church. Conga drums slung under their arms, they wore white *abadas* and matching crocheted bras. They set the conga drums down on either side of the door and faced the crowd. Strings of beads hung from their necks and blue paint smeared their eyes. Bruno recognised them as the twins from the bookshop.

Cool-box-men edged through the growing crowd of tourists selling beer and fizzy drinks. Excited locals laughed and joked amongst themselves while everyone else stood in near silence, nervously sipping drinks and watching the doors of the church.

'Look,' said Bea. 'There's Anderson.' She waved to him.

Anderson lifted his hat, and Bruno gave him a wave over the mass of bodies.

'What's the time?' Bruno asked, but before Bea could answer, the twins struck up a polyrhythmic drumbeat that had the adults hushing their children, and everyone turning to watch. Conversation faded to only a few voices that fell off one by one until the only sound was the beating of the drums. Everyone, apart from the drummers, was still.

Mac strode barefoot between the flames, followed by Faka, Ivo and Lagarto. The locals cheered as he held his circle of keys aloft and spoke. They joined him in murmuring voices.

'Oh Yemanjá, Goddess of the Sea. Mother, have mercy on us all. Blessed are the blessings that come of thy kingdom. May hearts and souls open to receive the blessings of Yemanjá. Dear Mother, take all impurity, all negativity, every broken thing and all the bad magic of our collective aura to the depths of the sacred sea. Mother who protects. Mother of *Os Orishas*. Mother who cares for all her children. Yemanjá, your light guides our way. Your waters wash over our heads. Pour over us your protection. Instil in our hearts the respect for *Os Orishas*, oneness with the force of nature, the balance of all things. Do this for us, our dear mother. Our saving grace. Yemanjá.'

Whistles and cheers erupted from the crowd. The drumbeat grew faster. Mac unlocked the church door and pushed it open. Faka, Ivo and Lagarto passed under the red light, following Mac into the darkness.

The locals began to sing and sway, some with eyes closed, some gazing, trance-like. The warble of their singing mixed hypnotically with the rhythm of the drums. A commotion amongst the tourists caught Bruno's attention. A young girl had fainted. She was carried out of the crowd towards the campsite to recover.

The men reappeared under the red light, Mac and Faka first, side by side, passing through the door with some kind of wooden frame between them. Cheers rose again as the statue appeared from the shadows. On the frame, between the four men, stood a garish, dark-skinned version of Our Lady. Golden hair flowed from the wood-carved head. Clusters of pearls adorned the crown and spilled from the hands. The blue and white dress was lined with gold, and out of the bottom, instead of legs, spread tentacles like those of an octopus.

They carried it along the path, Mac and Faka picking up the first pair of torches, Ivo and Lagarto the second. The twins followed after them, drums slung under their arms, keeping the heartbeat of the congregation pulsing. The crowd's singing resounded with fervour as they pushed in behind. Young men fought for the remaining torches as they followed the statue to Main Street. Bruno and Bea stayed behind the locals, near the tourists. Children ran alongside the statue, jostling each other for space to get a better look, reaching out to touch it. The singing echoed in the street as they made for the bay.

The crowd of tourists at the *carrinhos* separated to let the procession through, and even the cart boys followed as it passed. The tide was almost fully out. The boats had been dragged to either side to make room. The cool-box-men ran ahead and took up position by two large trunks. They handed out small candles on folded palm leaves to all who wanted them. The twins stood their conga drums by the trunks, lit wicks and walked through the crowd, lighting the candles.

Bruno pointed Anderson out to Bea. He was walking towards the water with his hat pressed to his chest, a lit candle in his free hand. Bea ran to the nearest trunk and took a candle for herself and one for Bruno. She passed one of the twins on the way back to have them lit. They edged to the shallows with the rest of the crowd. The lights of a freighter moved east in the distance.

The singing hushed to silence. The only noise came from

the slushing of the tide and the rustling of clothes. Mac and the men hoisted the frame onto their shoulders and waded out into the calm, dark sea. Bruno looked around at the locals, tourists and even some travellers, all mixed together, poised at the water's edge, with their trousers rolled up and their skirts hiked. The flickering candles in their hands bathed their faces in soft, ephemeral light.

All at once the church bell rang out, hollow and clanking. The men in the sea lowered the statue beneath the surface. Like the tourists, Bruno and Bea followed the lead of those dressed in white. Shoulder to shoulder, they placed their candles on the surface of the water and let the tide drag them out. Girls tore the flowers from their hair and threw them to the sea. Some locals corked champagne and poured in a share before passing the bottle around. Others lingered with their candles, whispering into them before setting them off. A drunk tourist was about to pour some beer in, but thinking better of it, he drank it and tossed the empty bottle in instead.

Hundreds of glowing candles drifted out towards the men like a bloom of bioluminescent plankton, each carrying a wish or a message of thanks to Yemanjá from her followers. Even those faithful to other religions or no religion at all set their candles off with positive intentions. To Bruno, these candles carried a message of happiness, hope and unity.

As the glow from the tiny, flickering flames illuminated the men's bodies, straining from the weight of the statue and the pull of the water, they hoisted it back to the surface and made for shore. Applause from all present met them as they set foot on dry land. The most enthusiastic applause came from the locals, but even Bruno found himself clapping. The drums started up again and the procession headed to the temple, where everyone dressed in white entered behind Yemanjá, and everyone else was politely turned away.

'It was quite beautiful in the end, wasn't it?' said Bruno, as he and Bea made their way back to the campsite.

'The candles, the silence...' she said. Her eyes glowed in a way that Bruno hadn't seen since Sean. 'It was enchanting. Bruno...' Her face grew solemn. 'I'm glad you're here with me. It's been such a big year. I'd never have got through it without you.' She reached up and kissed him on the cheek.

Emotion filled his eyes and a tear escaped. He couldn't say anything, knowing he'd cry if he did. 'You're my family, Bea,' he managed to say before his voice broke. 'Family.'

He watched her crouch into her tent, took a moment to breathe in the night and looked up at the stars. He rubbed the coarse stubble on his chin and tried to force out the despair drifting in amongst his happiness. *Someday I'm going to have to let her go,* he thought. *Someday I'll turn from her and never, ever see her again.* He took a sharp breath and stepped into his shelter.

Faka held the knife above his head

8

During the first week of January the Christmas decorations were removed and the street lighting was changed back to its usual white and yellow. Almost overnight, the number of tourists halved. Lagarto and his team embarked on a programme of maintenance. Week after week, they worked on the restaurants, bars and guesthouses. They painted signs, sanded and varnished wooden railings, replaced broken planks on the patios and repaired tables and chairs.

On his nocturnal visits to the skips, Bruno was faced with so many materials to choose from that deciding what to take and what to leave gave him headaches. The storage compartment of his shelter was stacked from ground to ceiling with plastic, metal and wood. Bea teased him about it every time she looked inside.

'You never know when it'll come in useful,' he always told her, but she didn't seem to understand.

As he collected more books from Anderson, Bruno asked again about his idea to sell the beer to the *carrinhos*.

'Okay, Bruno, I've had a think, and if you wanted to sell direct to the tourists I'd say a straight out no. But because you're going to the *carrinhos*, the town still gets its share, so I can't see a problem. As long as nobody gets ill, that is... Obviously, if anything happens or you get caught, I never knew a thing about this.'

'Of course not.'

'And Bea told me about what you did to those guys up

in the campsite.' He whistled through his teeth. 'Good job, son. Good job.'

Bruno had started on his next brew before talking to Anderson. His intention was to hand out bottles to all who'd been nice to him and Bea. Anderson, Tonino, Luis, Honey, Papa Rouge, Valter from the Kart de la Revolución, everyone would get their share, excluding Hermes, who was too close to Mac's inner circle. He wanted to keep up the momentum he'd first felt when the tattoo was done, and then at the candle ceremony, and to contribute to the community in any way he could.

He took more of an interest in the locals and their ways. While pitching the jewellery to the tourists, he and Bea would wander off their usual route to observe how all the locals went about their lives. Bea had a more inquisitive eye than he did, and even spoke to some locals as they tended their gardens or passed by in the street, although most of those she met were Jingubans.

With fewer tourists to cater for, the pace of the town slowed. The strain that had built up during the high season dissipated. People took on a more relaxed air, and their faces, relieved of stress, were aglow with renewed vitality. They spoke to each other more, lingered in the streets and enjoyed the quiet days and nights. Papa Rouge stood over his grill with a clenched-teeth grin on his clean-shaven face. On his nights off, he sat at a table by the corner of the restaurant playing dominoes with his fishermen friends.

Young locals hung around at the *carrinhos* talking to tourist girls during their time off. They held impromptu capoeira sessions on Main Street.

Along with the tourists, much of the campsite dwellers had left, and with fewer sellers to compete with, it was as easy as ever for Bruno and Bea to make a living.

'It's nicer with the campsite almost empty,' said Bea. 'More homely.'

'Homely,' Bruno said. 'You feel like home to me. This

154

here, our meals, raking the sand, making the jewellery, cleaning up, this is home.' To him it seemed that the whole town was bathing in the afterglow of those twinkling candles.

Amongst the tourists one evening, just before sunset, they watched a full capoeira session. Local children dragged their heels in the sand to mark out a large circle.

'It's called a *roda*,' Bruno told Bea, remembering a conversation he'd once had with an old *capoeirista* in a city dosshouse. '*Feel them all round you when you step into the roda*,' the man had said. '*Who?*' Bruno asked. '*Os Orishas.*'

The shirtless locals, in their *abada* trousers, eased through the crowd and took a seat behind the children at the *roda's* edge. Most were young adults, few over thirty.

Mac, Faka, Ivo and Lagarto arrived with their instruments. They stood at the opposite edge of the *roda*, and after Lagarto passed a triangle and a tambourine to the nearest kids, they began to play. Mac's voice bellowed, and all the *capoeiristas* repeated after him:
'They say the *capoeirista*,
'Is that dirty guy,
'But they don't know.
'They say the *capoeirista*,
'Is just another bum,
'But they don't know.
'The *capoeirista* has no race.
'The *capoeirista* has no colour.
'Capoeira is in one's blood.
'Capoeira is simply love.'

They stopped singing and changed to another rhythm. A young man who worked in one of the Main Street restaurants, and a girl of a similar age, entered the *roda*, bowed to Mac, and started their acrobatic dance in time with the music. Slow at first, they performed gentle handstands, the backward stepping movement and front and side kicks, then as the music grew faster they became more aggressive.

Sweat sprayed as they spun and kicked, jumped and swept, ducked and dived. It was a violent ballet played out with grace, timing and precision. The music worked them up until they were lashing out at one another, muscles straining, chests heaving. Then the pace of both the performers and the music slowed. Out of breath, the pair bowed and stepped back into the crowd. Another couple were called in.

After the majority had taken part, and just as the sun touched the horizon, a tourist shouted in English for Mac to go in.

'Me?' Mac widened his eyes in mock fear. 'The man asked me to perform,' he told the local children in Portuguese. 'What do you think?'

Amid their excitement, he handed his *berimbau* to Faka, and the instruments were passed down the line. He slung his beads around the neck of a pretty blonde tourist and called two youths into the *roda*.

He attacked the pair from all angles with spinning aerial kicks and assaults, using all available space. He let them come at him with attacks of their own, and with an unnatural speed and agility, avoided their strikes by millimetres and countered at will. It was the display of a master in prime physical condition performing at such a level of expertise that his movement seemed perfectly choreographed, while that of his foes was clumsy and superfluous. He left the pair on their knees, sweat dripping from their bowed heads, and called in another pair, then another. He brought the display to an end when the sun had almost set and called all the *capoeiristas* into the *roda*. They bowed as the sun disappeared below the horizon.

As they formed a procession and headed up Main Street, Bea turned to Bruno. 'Let's go see what they get up to in there.'

Before he could reply, she was off and walking. They crossed the beach and passed between the dune and the corral. Iansa separated from the herd and trotted over to the fence. With her fingers, Bea made circles in the fur of Iansa's neck and talked to her like a doting parent to a toddler.

They carried on up Beekeeper Close and watched from a distance as Mac let the locals in, turning the tourists away. When all the tourists had wandered off, they crept to the side wall of the temple and climbed the closest tree. A rusted corrugated roof, dusted with sand, blocked their view.

'Let's just go back to the campsite,' said Bruno.

'No. There has to be a place we can watch from.'

Bruno followed her around the building. 'Look.' She pointed at the top, back corner. 'The bricks are gone.' They climbed the tree by the corner and stretched out on its branches. Past a roof post, they could see right into the building.

Ivo and Lagarto weaved amongst the people, lighting beeswax candles on multi-branched candelabra. In the corner to the right of the door, a chalk-white statue of Yemanjá rose to the roof. Its tentacles curled out from underneath and climbed up the wall, each one looking as alive and conscious as a Gorgon's hair. Cut into the body, without any order, were wooden drawers labelled in brass. Strings of flowers and colourful beads hung from every point they could be attached to, and scattered the ground beneath. Amongst them, pots of incense sent spirals of smoke up towards the roof.

'Have you seen a graveyard here?' Bruno asked in a whisper. He'd noticed a heat-tempered mortician's table propped up against the wall beside the statue.

'No,' she said. 'The tour guide took us to one near Jinguba, though.'

'See the heat marks on that metal table? They must cremate people on it. Those drawers in the statue probably hold the ashes.'

People sat around on plastic chairs while others swept the floor or tended to the potted plants lining the wall. 'Look at the pots,' Bruno said. 'Mint, basil, the bushy ones are patchouli and rosemary, dwarf sandalwood trees, lavender shrubs, orange blossom, asafoetida, ginger.'

In the centre of the space a cylindrical patio about the size of the *roda* rose the width of a brick from the floor. Nine chickens, tied together by their feet, were lying next to a metal post in the patio's centre. There were nine conch shells set around the edge of the patio, and three large, hollow turtle shells laid out in a triangle around the centre post.

In the corner across from Yemanjá was a hut, and outside the hut Mac and Faka lit coals in two half-barrel grills.

'It's beautiful,' Bea said, 'apart from the chickens.'

The whites of the walls were barely visible behind drapes of blue, green, red and yellow, strings of fist-sized cowrie shells and dried starfish.

A chair adorned with tropical flowers and green leaves stood against the back wall. Mac donned a white trilby hat and took position in front of it as the twins, swathed in black robes, with red paint smeared over their eyes, stepped behind their conga drums. Lagarto, whose deep tan and wrinkles gave his face the look of a prune, extinguished his wick and positioned himself at the bongos. He rubbed his palms together above the drum skins. The percussionists began to play a slow beat that reverberated off the walls. The congregation gathered around the patio, formed three circles and joined hands. Others sat on the chairs by the walls and watched. The three circles spun clockwise around the patio in time with the rhythm of the drums.

Mac quietened the musicians with an outstretched hand and spoke in his unwavering, confident manner: 'The high season has provided and now the low season has arrived. This is balance, brothers and sisters. With unity and respect we shall continue to flourish. The low time is as important as the high. The town continues to be maintained as we rest and refresh. Respect the deceased, respect our families and respect our friends. And as ever, brothers and sisters, we praise and appease *Os Orishas*.'

All present spoke in unison as they spun in their circles:
'*Estamos agradecidos Yemanjá,*
'*Ogum, Oshosi, Oshala, Nana,*
'*Estamos agradecidos Ochumaré,*
'*Zhango, Eshu, Iansa,*
'*Ossaim, Oshum, Omulu,*
'*Os Orishas estamos agradecidos.*'

The spinning stopped and they knelt down at the patio. The drumbeat grew louder and gained momentum. Faka hopped onto the patio and pulled a knife from the cord of his *abadas*. Nine of the people who'd been sitting took a place on the patio at the conch shells. Faka held the knife above his head and grabbed the first chicken.

'Enough,' whispered Bea. 'See you at the campsite.'

Bruno watched her climb down and disappear into the shadows.

In the centre of the patio, Faka was approached by the first of the nine helpers who lowered to her knees and held the conch shell aloft. One by one, unaffected by the frantic flapping of their wings, Faka slit the chickens' throats and drained their blood into the shells. All the while, the unceasing beat of the drums slowed and accelerated, quietened and grew loud. It was the writhing of a snake, the stampede of a herd, the thrashing of wings. Bruno watched the swaying mass of people, unconscious of his grip tightening on the branch.

Mac stepped onto the patio as Faka dismembered the birds. He received the dripping entrails in his hands and separated them into the turtle shells. These, along with the conches, were taken into the hut.

'Adriano, Cloé,' Mac shouted.

A young couple got to their feet and joined him and Faka. It was the same pair who first entered the *roda* during the capoeira session. Four women, holding two conch shells each, exited the hut and gathered around them. Of those, Bruno noticed a waitress and a shop attendant. They

159

undressed Adriano and Cloé, and with the drums beating a loud staccato, poured the bloody concoction over their heads and smeared it into their skin. It matted their hair and ran in rivulets down their backs. The four women worked the mixture into their flesh then bowed at their feet. Again, Mac led the crowd in prayer:

'Estamos agradecidos Yemanjá,
'Ogum, Oshosi, Oshala, Nana,
'Estamos agradecidos Ochumaré,
'Zhango, Eshu, Iansa,
'Ossaim, Oshum, Omulu,
'Os Orishas estamos agradecidos.'

The women scooped water from the turtle shells and washed the youths, who then turned and bowed to the statue of Yemanjá before following the women to the hut.

With their hands still joined, the crowd rose up and began to circle again. Their movements were languid and loose: swaying shoulders, hips and arms, rolling heads. The intoxicating rhythm of the drums shifted and the circles broke up. People danced with a new energy and aggression. Some had their palms raised to stir the air around them, others had their fingers intertwined and moved as if they wielded a weapon, some lurched and twitched, crouching low and springing up again. Louder and louder came the pounding of the drums. Bruno looked at the twins straining with exertion, their hands a blur upon the bleached drum skins of the congas. Sweat sprayed from the tips of Lagarto's hair as he whipped his head from side to side.

Bruno's whole body began to stiffen, his jaw clenched and the nails of his fingers turned white as he gripped the branch. He almost screamed when someone dropped to the floor and began to convulse. The others danced on as if nothing had happened. It was Hermes. He was having a seizure.

'Help him,' Bruno whispered. 'Fucking help him.' Two

men rushed from a small crowd of onlookers by the hut and carried him inside. They were smiling.

The drumbeat slowed, and the dancing calmed. After a few minutes, Hermes reappeared from the hut. Bruno's concern for him was replaced with a feeling that some ridiculous joke was being played. With a blonde wig on his head, Hermes wore a purple, sequin-covered dress and danced around making extravagant gestures of femininity at everyone.

'Nana, Goddess of the Rain,' said Mac. 'It's an honour. May we prepare a meal for you? Will you accept?'

Hermes replied in a high-pitched voice: 'I will.'

The dancing stopped and the plastic tables were grouped together and draped in cloth. Pots of black beans, mashed potato and vegetables were taken from the hut. Bottles of champagne, wine and beer were presented. The smell of grilled chicken drifted up to Bruno. He'd had enough. He slid down from the tree and made his way back to the campsite.

*

The following morning at breakfast, Bruno told Bea about what he'd seen.

'How can a whole community believe in something like that?' she asked.

'It's what they've been brought up with. It's no different than how other religions get you.'

'It's ridiculous. You're saying they have twelve gods and the gods communicate with them through possession?'

'Young and weak minds are easy to manipulate. You think the boys from my orphanage would ever question the existence of God? Why do so many junkies and alcoholics turn to religion? They're vulnerable, that's why. They need something to hold on to, something with ready-made answers so they don't have to think for themselves. The church sucks them in.'

'They don't go around slitting hens' throats in Catholic churches.'

'In some places they still do. Clergymen do whatever it takes to get followers so they can keep that tithe money coming in. Educated Christians and Muslims don't want blood on their hands any more than you or I, but in isolated towns like this people don't get the kind of education that makes them question things. It's all they know.'

'You think it's safe for us here?'

'We've been fine so far. There's a big difference between chickens and humans, Bea.'

'They breathe and bleed just like us. They feel fear. Anyone who can kill a defenceless animal can kill a human.'

He went into his shelter, sifted through his bag and found his whistle. 'If you ever feel threatened,' he said, throwing it over to her. 'Blow as hard as you can on this and I'll come running.'

She slipped the cord over her head. 'If you hear it you better be fast. I'm going to see Tonino and the donkeys. Why don't you come down more often? It's peaceful around them. They're amazing animals, and Tonino's always asking about you.'

'I'll come down when I've got the beer ready.' He gathered up the pots and bowls and headed to the faucet to wash them.

Every night after that, Bruno climbed the tree at the back corner of the temple to watch the ceremony. Nothing much changed from one night to the next. The drums would drive someone to the point where they either fell in a convulsing heap, or lost control of their limbs and had to be secured by helpers. They'd be taken to the hut and would reappear dressed as one of their gods or goddesses.

Over the following weeks, he saw Faka fall twice. First, he became *Oshosi*, the hunter who wore green and danced like he was shooting a bow and arrow. On the second occasion, he appeared as *Ogum*, God of Metal and War, who wore armour and marched around with a shield and spear.

A young barmaid from one of the day-bars was possessed by *Iansa*, Goddess of the Tempest, who wore a yellow dress and danced like the billowing sail of a yacht.

A god or goddess could possess a person regardless of their gender. Men became *Yemanjá*, *Iansa* and *Nana*, while women became the axe-wielding *Zhango*, or the white robed *Oshala*.

There were animal sacrifices during every ceremony: mostly chickens, but on occasion sheep and goats.

On the surface it all seemed so ridiculous, just as Bea had said. He'd need months of observation to know what it was all about, to see if there was any real structure to it. 'It's too easy for the modern world to brush off these cultures, though,' he said to Bea. 'There's always something to learn, something important we can take from them.' He decided he'd keep watching until he figured it out.

After breakfast, Bruno got Bea to help him bottle the beer. They took a couple of bottles to Tonino, who was at the corral surrounded by the donkeys, feeding them chopped carrots from a pail.

'Ship those carrots in by the tonne?' Bruno asked.

'Ah, good morning.' Tonino waved them in, and they jumped over the fence. 'I took over my mother's allotment when she left. The guys up there help me with it. Can't give these gluttons too much though, don't want to spoil them.'

'They're way past spoiling,' said Bea, touching her head to Iansa's and rubbing her ears.

'Here,' said Bruno. 'A present for you.'

Tonino took one of the bottles in his big hand. 'Bea told me you were making another batch. Let's see if it's as good as she says it is.' He put the bucket down and went to unscrew the cap when a tourist couple arrived at the gate.

'Only two for the tour this morning.' He looked up the

quiet streets and hushed his voice. 'You guys want to come along?'

'We'd love to,' Bea said.

'I'm a bit busy,' said Bruno, speaking over her.

'Bruno.' Bea gave him one of her looks. 'The beer is safe in the tent. You don't need to sell any jewellery today. You're coming and that's all there is to it.'

The tourists, called Jason and Lauren, were a couple in their late twenties from California. Tonino got them all saddled up and led the way on his donkey in a slow, heavy walk around the foot of the dune.

Only a handful of surfers were out. A pair of dune buggies was parked between twisted, windswept trees whose exposed roots gripped the sand like strained fingers.

They followed the curve of the coast and entered the mangrove forest. Its green canopy cast them in shade and cooled them from the sun. They threaded their way through the trees and puddles. The donkeys' hooves squelched in the silt and mud. Under the leaves, red-necked tanagers called out in warbling birdsong. Honeybees hovered around flowers and shrubs.

'Hey Tonino,' Jason shouted. 'Why's that street back in town called Beekeeper Close?'

'Not hear of honey we make?' Tonino answered in English. 'Mangroves full of bees. We keep the honey in well. Mac dig it himself. The path to well is where all bee houses stay. It take nine months to fill the well, then jar, and sell. You not taste better than Brisas honey.'

'Do they have it in the shops?' asked Lauren.

Tonino smiled. 'Too late. Go down path, see beekeepers at work. Maybe they give you taste.'

'How do you know where you're going?' asked Bruno, in English for the benefit of the tourists. 'There's no clear path.'

'Same thing every day, Bruno,' Tonino replied in Portuguese. 'And the water always flows to the sea, so I never have a problem finding my way.'

Curlews and crabs scuttled out from under the donkeys' feet as they traversed deeper into the forest. Water trickled around the tree roots, forming small streams that sparkled when the sun broke through the leaves.

It was peaceful here, putting one foot in front of the other, away from all the people, noises and smells in town, surrounded by nature. After an hour's trekking, Bruno heard a rushing sound above the rustling leaves. The mud grew firmer. Stones stuck out from the ground, round and dry.

Tonino talked non-stop about the birds and the crabs, the trees and the shrubs. Despite his broken English, his voice seemed as natural to the forest as the birdsong. 'Five minute more,' he said, 'and we find first surprise of tour.'

The trail curved up into the trees. Hoof prints from previous tours were visible. The rushing noise grew louder as they climbed. The mangrove trees thinned, making way for fan-leaved cecropias which grew in abundance. They ducked under the leafy branches, found the bank of a deep, slow-moving stream and followed it to its end under the full glare of the sun. They were at the top of a waterfall.

Tonino helped them tie off the donkeys and led them to the edge of the falls. Bea held onto Bruno as she looked over at the water crashing on the surface of a pool far below.

'How far do you think?' she asked.

'About ten metres,' Bruno said.

'What's that in feet, Bruno?' asked Jason.

'Thirty-three, or so.'

Up here, with the heat of the open sun on their heads, they could see all the way over the mangroves to the sea and back towards the green hills of the interior. The dune dwarfed the town in the distance.

'Is it deep enough to jump into?' Jason asked Tonino. Away from the turbulence of the falls the water was so transparent the bottom was visible. Fish nipped at algae on submerged rocks.

'I don't know,' Tonino said. 'Let me try.' He stepped out of his espadrilles, took his shirt off and rolled it around them. He placed the bundle in the saddle bag draped over Zhango, padded over the stones to the edge and crouched low. He swung his heavy arms and threw himself off, landing with a splash that sent a wave rebounding off the boulders that surrounded the pond. The wave ran down the outlet stream, catching the overhanging branches and rustling their leaves. Birds took flight from their branches.

Jason let out a whistle.

'Yeah, Tonino!' Lauren yelled. They rushed to their donkeys and stripped to their swimsuits. 'Come on, guys!' said Lauren. 'Let's get on it!'

Bruno watched Bea at Iansa's side, petting her. He could tell she was scared.

Lauren sailed over the edge, followed by Jason. Their splashes had the newly re-perched birds flapping skyward again.

Bruno removed his vest and shorts, and put them in the saddle bag. 'You next, Bea,' he said, standing in his underwear.

'I think I'll lead the donkeys down and meet you there.'

'That's worse than jumping. The trail's slippery.'

'Come on, guys!' Lauren called from below.

'You can do this.'

'I can't. I won't.'

'You want to. I can see it in your face.'

She avoided his eye, pushed her hair back and let out a breath.

'Just come to the edge for another look.'

They walked up to the edge. Bea gripped Bruno's wrist as she lowered herself into a squat and peered over. The others shouted up, beckoning them down.

'Shit,' she said. 'They saw me. I have to do it now or they'll think I'm a coward.'

'Calm down.' He touched her shoulder. 'You want to do this.'

'I *don't* want to do this, Bruno. I'll go down the way I came up.' She headed back to the donkeys.

'Let's go, guys,' Tonino shouted up.

'Just a second,' Bruno replied. 'Bea, you'll regret not doing it. Just try. I'm right here beside you.'

'Okay,' she said. 'Just... Okay...' She undressed to a beige bikini.

Bruno tried not to look at her figure as she moved over the rocks, the lithe muscles, the sleek curves, the glow of her skin. She hesitated at the edge. Bruno went to stand beside her.

'Did any of you touch the bottom?' she called.

'Nowhere near it,' Lauren shouted back. 'You'll be fine.'

Jason slipped under the water for a while then resurfaced. 'It's at least twice my height,' he said.

'We'll count for you,' said Tonino. 'Three!'

She shook her arms loose and forced the air from her lungs.

'Two!'

She bounced on her knees.

'One!'

She threw her torso forward but her legs remained planted. She stepped back and swore.

'Bruno,' she said. 'You go first, please. I'll watch how you do it then I'll jump.'

'No, no, no. You first... Come on, guys, one more count... Three!'

She stepped forward, frowning at him, then focused her eyes on the landing point.

'Two!'

She balled her fists. Her toes curled around the edge of the rock. Bruno stepped in close.

'One!'

She leaned forward, sprang on her knees, went onto

her tiptoes. As her heels lowered towards the rock again instead of taking to the air, Bruno nudged a hand into her lower back a little harder than he'd intended and sent her flying.

Her scream had the birds squawking into the sky. Her arms sprawled and she plunged into the water.

'You bastard, Bruno!' she shouted as she resurfaced. Hair stuck flat to her face. 'How could you?'

But the others swam around her, congratulating her on the jump.

'The water's great, isn't it?' said Lauren

'I suppose.' Bea dipped her head and smoothed the hair back from her face.

Bruno took a little run, hopped over the stones, and dived out with his arms spread wide. He hit the water, making the smallest of splashes. As soon as his face rose above the surface Bea splashed him, then jumped with both hands on his head, forcing him under again and again.

After swimming around, they relaxed on the large boulders at the side of the pool and dried off in the sun. Tonino went to fetch the donkeys.

Bea spoke to Jason and Lauren, who'd spent a couple of nights in the city before journeying on to Brisas.

'It was a bit rough,' Jason said. Lauren nodded in agreement.

'Compared to what we're used to,' she added. 'The whole place was so run-down. Potholed roads, restaurant and bar signs not working, barred windows, trash everywhere, the street lights barely lit a thing. We didn't like to go out at night. It seemed too dangerous.'

'So what did you do?' asked Bea.

'Well,' said Jason. 'During the day we went to the beach but didn't swim 'cause the water was too dirty.'

'And at night,' continued Lauren. She looked at Jason and shrugged. 'We just hung out at the hostel.'

'You should have come straight here from the airport,'

Bruno said. 'Every city this side of the equator's the same. Decayed, corrupted, polluted.'

'No they're not, Bruno.'

'Bea, nobody cares about anything any—'

'There must've been something good about it?' Bea asked. They looked at each other.

'Well,' said Jason. 'It's made us appreciate this place a lot more. Nobody's even heard of Brisas back home. We only found out about it a few months ago.'

'And the people in the hostel were interesting. A real backpacker crowd. People from all over the world.'

'And they had good food there,' added Jason.

'We all ate together.' Lauren spoke more to Jason than to Bruno and Bea. 'The vegan from Canada, the Swedish couple, that French guy who everyone hated because he only ever spoke to the girls. He was such a sleaze.'

'There was a model maker, an Australian girl who slept with a different guy every night.'

'That's right, the model maker!' said Lauren. 'He made these amazing models out of wire.'

'What was it we saw him making, Laur? A frog. I swear if you put some green skin on that thing it would've hopped away.'

'It was so good,' said Lauren.

'So good,' agreed Jason.

'He was hot, too.'

'Oh, come on! With that moustache? He looked like an evil version of Friedrich fucking Nietzsche!'

'The doctor was hotter,' said Lauren. 'He was from Chicago. He said that one time he de-gloved the hand of a cadaver and slapped a nurse in the face with it.'

'Disgusting!' said Bea. Jason nodded.

'Special treat today!' shouted Tonino as he climbed onto the boulders beside them. 'From our man Bruno here, the Brisas brewer.' He handed out enamel cups, and served Bruno's beer.

'Wow, you made this?' Jason swilled the beer around in his cup and swigged. 'Tastes awesome.'

'Indian Pale Ale,' said Bruno. 'Only my second batch.'

'So this is what you do here?' Lauren looked into her cup.

'We make and sell jewellery,' said Bruno. 'But we're thinking about doing this, too. It's still a secret, though.'

'Expanding our empire,' said Bea. 'First the jewellery, now the beer. Soon we'll be employing Tonino.'

'As long as you don't interfere as much as Mac,' Tonino said. He switched to English. 'Bruno, this too good. I open second bottle.'

'You should definitely sell this stuff,' said Lauren. She picked up the bottle Tonino left on the rock and read. 'Burro Beer... Catchy.'

They sat in the sun, drinking, and made light conversation. Bruno finished his cupful and lay back with his hands under his head. He smiled to himself, happy at how easy it all was.

Jason got his camera out. He and Lauren wandered around the waterfall shooting photos of each other.

'So, Tonino,' said Bruno. He was eager to learn more about the local customs. 'Mac interferes in the business a lot?'

'Mac's just Mac. He works us as hard as he can during the high season. It can be tough but we get a rest in the low season, short as it is. He's not all that bad.'

'And you never go to the temple?'

Tonino refilled their cups. 'No, that's just a Brisas thing. I'm from Jinguba. We have the Son, the Father and the Holy Spirit. Those three are enough for me.'

Bea kept silent as Bruno pushed on. 'They didn't force you to join when you came here?'

He shook his head and drank straight from the bottle. 'I was too old to change by then. It'd be like telling someone to ignore everything they've learned growing up and believe in something completely different. Impossible.'

'So they've never forced anything on anyone?'

'Mac's a fair man. I'm sure he'd love everyone to take part... Many of us do enjoy that Festa De Yemanjá thing, but most of us Jingubans and the elders could never truly accept his religion. He knows that, and he's... What's the word?'

'Tolerant?' asked Bea.

'*Exactamente.* He's tolerant about it. The only disappointment anyone has is that he took the church. The elders asked if they could build a new one, but he said no.' He looked for Lauren and Jason and lowered his voice. 'We practise in private, all the same. You don't need any church or icons. All you need is in here.' He touched his heart.

'Exactly,' said Bea.

'But you mentioned that your parents left,' said Bruno.

'Mother and Father couldn't accept it. There were a few like that. They were devout.' He laughed. 'They tried to get me to come away with them, but I was too much in love by then.'

'You didn't tell me you have a girlfriend.' Bea pouted her lips in disappointment.

'The donkeys,' he said, patting her shoulder. 'I couldn't leave them. They're like my children.' He looked at his watch. 'Okay, guys!' he shouted to Jason and Lauren. 'Let's look at final surprise of tour.'

They waded through the stream behind him. Here, the mangroves grew thick along the banks, their roots reaching into the clear, knee-high water. He stopped, crouched low. They crowded around him. Jason raised the camera to his eye. Tonino cupped his hands under the water and lifted out a small, orange creature.

Bea and Lauren sighed in admiration. Jason's camera clicked in rapid succession. The creature had a long nose and a curled tail.

'*Um cavalo-marinho,*' Tonino said. 'A seahorse.'

'Have you ever seen one, Bruno?' asked Bea.

'Only in books,' he said, wishing he'd brought his camera along, too.

'Can I hold it?' Lauren asked.

Tonino eased it into her hand. It flopped onto its side and lay helpless, with its transparent dorsal fin fluttering. 'So cute,' she said. Bea patted its head with her finger and cooed at it. Jason took a few shots of Lauren smiling with it in her hands.

'Maybe we should put it back now,' said Bea. 'We don't want to hurt it.'

Tonino returned it to the water, teasing its tail around a root and holding it until it righted itself against the current. A few steps forward they saw a blue one, then a yellow one, then a green one. For a hundred metres the stream was full of them, tiny dots of brilliant colour like a Seurat painting. After seeing all different sizes and colours, and hearing a hundred clicks of Jason's camera, they mounted the donkeys and started for town.

*

The town lights came on as Bruno and Bea walked to the *carrinhos* with a bagful of Burro Beer. The capoeira procession had passed, and the handful of tourists there stood by Cart Smile and Cart Passion.

Bea had already told him how to play it, and Bruno insisted that she wasn't to get involved in case it ended in him getting kicked out of town.

He approached Valter, who was resting on his elbows at the counter of Kart de la Revolución.

'Quiet start,' said Bruno.

'Can't win. It's either nothing at all or a hundred at once.'

Earlier that week Anderson had told Bruno about a league involving tourist girls that the young townsmen ran every high season.

'I thought you *liked* a hundred at once.' Bruno tilted his head and eyed him.

'What do you mean?'

'How many'd you get this season?'

Valter stood back and smiled. 'Who told you about that?'

'I've got my sources.'

Valter hushed his voice and leaned in. 'You know who won? Davide, the waiter at Cafe La Mouche. Averaged more than one a night. Bastard got two at the same time again this year.'

'That slim guy who never stops smiling? He looks so innocent.'

'It's those green eyes. Lucky bastard. Anyway, the innocent-looking ones are the craziest. Some of those tourists will do *anything*.'

Nobody needed to tell Bruno how crazy the tourists could get. If it wasn't for the town cleaners, the streets would be littered with condoms and panties, cups, cans and cigarette butts. They pissed, fucked and vomited all over the place without caring who cleaned it all up.

Anderson told him that Hermes dealt with a lot more than cuts and bruises. Without Mac's knowledge, he smuggled in condoms with his salon supplies and dispensed them amongst the young locals for free. Bruno gained more confidence knowing secrets could be kept from Mac. Maybe selling this beer actually had a chance.

It was like Flora had said, society could only improve at the speed of individual change. He smiled. There was no hurt when he thought of her. He looked at Bea. She was handing a bracelet to a tourist. Another sale. Easy.

'Two cans of cat piss and two empty cups please, Valt.'

He picked up one of the cans as Valter slid them across the counter and read the label. 'Look at the ingredients,' he said. 'Full of additives… beta-glucanase, propylene glycol alginate, silicone!'

'I never read the ingredients,' said Valter. 'Just find the can with the highest percentage.'

'You know these companies don't care about your health. All they care about is getting our money.' He rubbed his thumb and finger together.

'*Contos*.' Valter nodded.

'I bet the barley and hops they use in this stuff are full of pesticides. Do you know that thousands of sugarcane workers die from chronic kidney disease every year because of the chemicals they work with? It'll be the same with barley and hops, we just don't hear about it yet. Even tap water isn't pure. They add fluoride to it, calcifying the pineal gland, blocking our creativity, controlling us!'

Valter's chin rested on his hands. Bruno followed his gaze to see what he was looking at. Nothing. Oblivion.

'Our food isn't safe either,' Bruno continued, unabated. It was nice not having Bea there to cut him short. 'You eat beef lasagne, don't you? Know what's in it? Well?'

Valter shook the mist from his eyes. 'Excuse me, what? Beef? Cows?'

'Not cow! Horse! That's what you get! All these bastards are out to rob us of our money and our health, while they're flying in private jets over our heads. Now, if I was to make a beer, Valter, I'd have four ingredients.' He held up four fingers and counted them off. 'Malted barley. Hops. Water. Yeast. Everything organic, nothing genetically modified or damaging, no pesticides, and all in the right quantities. The best taste, quality and price, straight to the consumer.' He glanced over at Bea, who stared at him and tapped her wrist.

'Back soon,' he said, picking up the other can and cups.

'What took you so long?' Bea asked. 'You were just supposed to get the cans and come right back.'

'I got carried away. You know it as much as I do that the planet's fucked.'

'Fuck the planet, Bruno! We've been through this; you're not going to save the world on your own. Jesus! Look, you're going to die someday. That's for certain. Enjoy your life. You're trying to do something for yourself here, don't ruin your chances by getting it mixed up with what you can't control.'

He passed her a can with a plastic cup pinched under the ring-pull.

'Start small,' she continued. 'Do what you can and that's enough. Everything else will figure itself out.' She laid her selling-board flat on the sand, stood the cup between the jewellery and half-filled it.

'I saw you sell a bracelet.'

'I sold three already *and* a necklace.' Her eyes narrowed with pride. She took a swig from the can then emptied the rest onto the sand. She shook out all the dregs then refilled it halfway with Burro Beer.

Bruno poured half of his can into a cup and took the other can from Bea.

More tourists were arriving, the girls all made up with red lips and coloured eyes, the men tanned, with oiled hair, necklaces hanging over their shirts, wrists looped with leather and chrome. Many had fibrous pieces of jewellery made by Bruno or Bea. Bea waved, smiled and chatted with them as they passed.

It was a humid night. Bruno wiped the sweat from his forehead and approached Valter again. The music from Ivo's was loud over the mingling voices of the tourists.

A trio of girls plucked their drinks from the counter and stepped aside. Bruno nodded to them and smiled.

'Valter,' he said. 'Taste these. They're different.'

Valter took a can in each hand and gave him a look.

'Don't worry, we drank from the cups.'

'If I knew which was Bea's I wouldn't care,' he said, wiping the rims with a dishcloth. 'It's only you I don't want to share spit with.'

Bruno overheard the three girls talking in Italian. He'd picked up some words over the months.

'I did,' insisted the petite one who had short, asymmetrical hair.

'No,' said another. 'No. I don't believe it.'

Bruno watched them from the corner of his eye.

'Si!' She shrugged, smiling.

'No you didn't,' said the tallest girl. She turned to the other. 'How long was she with Stefano, and she never—'

'It was... fantastic.' She tucked her hair behind her ear and lit a cigarette.

The tall one closed her eyes and waved for her to pass one over. 'You let a *barbone* with a moustache like a... What's that moustache like?' She touched the third girl on the arm.

'A black octopus,' the third girl said, holding the back of her hand to her nose and wriggling her fingers.

'You let him do that to you? You're crazy.'

'He was charming. I never met a man like him.'

'No. No. Tell her, Marta.'

'Yes,' said Valter, tapping Bruno's elbow. 'This second one is off.' He poured it onto the sand and crushed the cup. 'I'll get you another.'

'Wait!' Bruno pulled the bulky two litre bottle from his back pocket. 'The good one is Burro Beer. Made right here in Brisas. All ingredients obtained through local resources. By Brisas, for Brisas.'

'Okay... Tastes good.'

'I have six bottles here. Twenty-four *contos* a bottle and they're yours. That's two *contos* a cup. You sell for four or even five and we both make a living.'

Valter tore a sheet of paper from the roll hanging from the cart roof, removed his glasses and polished the lenses. 'Bruno, if Ivo found out, I'd get my ass kicked.'

'Don't tell him. Hide the bottles under the counter. You'll be serving it by the cup anyway. Give a bottle to each cart. Spread the risk.'

'You know we're all on a salary here, right? We make the same money as the waiters and waitresses and the baristas at the day-bars. If we start earning on the side, they'll soon find out.'

'But surely they make a lot more tips than you do.'

'It all goes into a pot and gets shared with everyone on the same pay grade.'

'Put the beer money in the tip jar too, then.'

'I should really run it by Ivo. But you know how it is. They won't deal with travellers.'

'Okay then,' said Bruno. He turned away. 'I was just trying to do something good, to give back to the town, but if you say you can't do it, then...'

'I'm sorry, Bruno.'

Bruno turned to face him again. 'Look, Valter. I'll tell you what. I'll give you these bottles for free. Give it away to the tourists if you won't sell it. See if they take to it. If they actually like it, *then* you can talk to Ivo. If not, he'll never know a thing about it.'

Valter looked around blindly, took a breath and put his glasses back on. 'What time is it?' he said then checked his watch. 'Ivo won't be here for a while. Pass it over. I'll give it to anyone who orders a beer.'

As Bruno handed him the bottle, Bea appeared at his side with the bag containing the rest of them. She placed it at the side of the cart.

'Look, if Ivo does come and asks questions, or if anyone gets sick, I'm going to have to say you forced me to do this.'

'Of course,' said Bruno. 'Only, make sure that Bea isn't mentioned. She has nothing to do with this. It's completely my responsibility. Okay?'

Bruno, I'd like you to meet Carlos

Through his regular visits to the temple, Bruno pieced together more of the religion and got a better picture of how the town operated. Each practitioner had three gods or goddesses assigned to him. Collectively, these gods and goddesses were called *Os Orishas*. All the faces he saw there worked directly with the tourists or in Lagarto's small maintenance team. None of the fishermen or allotment farmers, who were either older or of Jinguban descent, ever showed up.

Labour in the town was organised so that everyone involved in the religion could visit the temple at least every second day while allowing the restaurants, bars and guesthouses to operate as normal.

The ceremonies always started with Mac addressing the congregation from his floral throne. '*Brothers and sisters,*' he'd say, his hands clasped together. '*Keep the balance, respect the deceased. This town is built for the people of Os Orishas. We are both the guardians and the guarantors. We must strive to ensure sustainable growth, protection and benefit for both our time and the future.*' Bruno noticed some paranoia in the way he spoke of the travellers. He believed they were a genuine threat to their way of life but had to be tolerated because of the rapport they had with the tourists, and because any course of action that could be taken had to be done within the natural confines of balance inherent in the religion.

After his nightly speech, they all joined in the prayer to *Os Orishas*:

> *'Estamos agradecidos Yemanjá,*
> *'Ogum, Oshosi, Oshala, Nana,*
> *'Estamos agradecidos Ochumaré,*
> *'Zhango, Eshu, Iansa,*
> *'Ossaim, Oshum, Omulu,*
> *'Os Orishas estamos agradecidos.'*

Night after night, the drums thudded and hammered with a violence and rhythm that clouded Bruno's head. The beat seemed to seize control from his heart and course the blood through his body at its will. Sometimes, he got so tense that he thought he was going to faint. Before that ever happened someone in the temple would fall into a trance, the rhythm would change, and he could relax again. The person would be led into the hut and returned as an *Orisha* embodied. It was frightening to see such a sudden change in people. He could never tell if they were acting or truly were possessed, and wondered if there was some kind of mass hypnotism or hysteria at work. They fell so hard at times that he couldn't understand how they recovered so quickly without broken bones or a concussion. *Os Orishas* each had their favourite foods. *Oshosi* liked game meat, for *Oshum* it was creamy fish stew, *Ogum* liked brown beans with prawns. The smell of the meat and the sight of such an abundance of food drove him away each night. He'd turned vegetarian for Bea, but when the aroma from the grills reached him, his mouth would well up and his stomach would become almost painful with hunger.

He had watched so many ceremonies that Bea encouraged him to take a look inside the church. She was sure Mac was hiding something in there. In the middle of the night, as Bea kept a lookout, Bruno climbed up to the circular window.

His unlit headlamp strapped on, using Bea's shoulder for support, he got a foot onto the round, rusting door knob and pushed himself up to grab the top edge of the door lintel. He reached with his other hand, gripped a stone and gained a toehold on the door lintel and slowly pulled himself up. With the fingertips of both hands secure on the windowsill and the toes of both feet on the lintel, he went to turn on his headlamp.

'What do you see?' Bea asked.

'My torch isn't even on yet!' With his chin tucked into his chest to aim the unlit headlamp down through the church, he let go of the sill with one hand and twisted it on.

The beam shot through the darkness of the church, reflecting off the dust particles inside. He scanned the room from wall to wall.

'It's amazing,' he said, 'all twelve of them are here.'

'*Os Orishas?*' Bea asked.

'Yes. The floor's covered with some kind of bush grass and... Hold on... There's a big vat in the middle... It's full of liquid... Roots and leaves.' The sight of it reminded him of some experience he'd had not so long ago, but he couldn't place it. A smell, maybe. He hugged the wall and drew the beam of light up the length of the vat. The roots were tangled inside the opaque liquid and overhung the vat's concrete edges. He followed a thick root along the side. Smooth and bulbous, it turned inward, the smaller roots twisting around it. He traced its curve to the top of the vat, and paused on what looked like a huge and highly detailed *Orisha*. Its closed eyes, nose, and mouth were just above the liquid's surface. 'Fuck!' He ducked his head under the sill, grabbed at the headlamp to turn it off, but his other hand slid, his foot came away and he fell. He threw an arm out and caught hold of the bell cord as he thumped to the ground. The bell clanged out, all hollow brass echoing in the night.

'Quick!' he gasped, getting to his feet and hobbling away from the church. 'It's Mac!'

'Your light!' she rushed after him. 'Turn it off!'

All the fires in the campsite were long extinguished

and there was no moon to provide any light. They heard travellers, roused from their sleep by the noise, talking to each other. Tents were being unzipped.

The church door clattered against its stop and Mac appeared in the soft light. They halted in the darkness.

'Who's there?' Mac shouted. Laughter came from Main Street, and he marched off in that direction.

'I'm going to have a fucking heart attack,' Bruno said, doubled over, hands on his knees.

'You fell so hard. Are you hurt?'

'I don't know.' He grabbed at his legs. 'I think I'm okay. Wait, my hip's sore. My head's throbbing, Bea. Fuck! He sleeps in that fucking place!' They crept towards their camp.

'He's coming back,' she said, holding a hand out to stop Bruno from moving.

Mac appeared in front of the church again and faced the campsite. 'Who rang that bell?'

Townsfolk began to appear from the streets. Mac's attention turned to them as they formed a congregation outside the church, their faces illuminated by lights shining from the adjacent house windows. Most were elders. Fishermen and allotment farmers. More appeared: dayshift workers from the shops and cafes, Tonino, Silvia. Anderson arrived, silver stubble on his chin.

Two members of the group had buckets. One had a cloth tied over his nose and mouth. He pulled it down to his neck. They huddled together, mumbling and looking from Mac to the rooftops.

'Did he see you?' whispered Bea.

'My beam was right on his face. I don't know. I don't think his eyes opened.'

Mac turned from the townsfolk to the campsite and back to the townsfolk.

'Where's the fire?' one asked.

'Where's the fire?' Mac repeated, gravel in his voice. 'How will you fight it? You have no bucket.'

'It's never happened before,' said another, his glasses aglow in the light from the houses.

'There's no sign of flames,' Tonino said. 'No smoke.'

'What took you all so long? The town could've burned to ashes already!'

Travellers gathered by the campsite toilets and watched.

'Two buckets!' Mac continued. 'Only two of you useless old fools took buckets. Next time you'll be here before that bell stops ringing. Each with at least one bucket!' He turned and marched up to the travellers. 'And if I find out that any of you parasites rang the bell, you'll all be thrown out. Every one of you. It's the low season. There's nothing for you here. Go back to your city slums! Go!'

'Nothing to do with us, Mac,' Adelina said.

'I saw them,' said Fortunato. 'Pair of tourists, it was. Ran off down Main Street. They were laughing.'

'Yeah,' said others in the group, latching onto his lie. They began talking over each other.

'It was tourists, Mac.'

'You won't catch us doing nothing like that.'

'We're just here to make a living, too.'

'Enough!' Mac roared. They fell silent. He went back to the townsfolk. 'All of you go home. Ten per cent of your salary will be deducted this month. Next time you'll arrive sooner.'

'What did you see?' Bea asked, watching the townsfolk shuffle off.

'My heart's still not slowing down,' Bruno replied. 'That's what I smelled on him before. He must sleep in there. It's some kind of herbal bath. Every night, he's been right there. Not a hundred metres from us!'

'I told you he was hiding something. What else is there?'

'Twelve statues.' He massaged his hip. 'The *Yemanjá* one's at the back. All of them in the same style. *Oshala* with his staff and the bird, *Ogum*, swinging his sword, *Oshum* in her yellow robes. They're quite nice, actually.' He pushed his

182

hair back. 'Palm leaf parcels were set out in front of them all. Rice, coins, melting candles... There was a big turtle shell with cowries in it.'

'Probably like tea leaves, you know? Shake them around and see what they say. A divination tool.'

'Bea, imagine if he saw me!'

'He didn't. If he did he'd have come straight over.'

'Straight over and fucking killed me! Maybe he's holding out?'

'Calm down.' She placed her hands on his chest. 'He didn't see you.'

'I'm not going near that church again.'

'You were like Tarzan swinging on the rope.'

'The fire alarm,' he said. 'I rang the fucking fire alarm.'

*

The next morning, as Bea went around town making her sales, Bruno stayed in the campsite. Later, taking two bottles of beer along with him, he met her at Anderson's.

'Perfect arrangement,' Anderson said. 'You bring the beer, I bring the glasses.' He reached in through the door and passed Bruno a flyer. 'Seen this?'

Bea snatched it and read aloud in Portuguese:

'*The church bell shall only be rung in the event of fire or another emergency.*

Anyone can and must ring the bell if required.

However, misuse will result in immediate expulsion from the town.'

The note was typed in Portuguese, Spanish, Italian, French and English.

'You guys see anything?' Anderson asked. 'It's costing me ten per cent of my pay!'

'No,' Bruno said, unable to look him in the eye. 'It woke us up.'

'Fortunato said he saw tourists running away from it.' Bea handed the note to Bruno.

'Mac won't stand for any of that.' Anderson whistled through his teeth. He got up and went inside for glasses. 'If he catches them, they'll be on the first 4×4 out of here… *If* they're lucky! I don't think any tourist would've done it.'

'So you're saying it had to be a traveller?' Bea tucked her hair behind her ear. 'Who's to say it wasn't a local?'

'Anyway,' Anderson passed Bruno the glasses and seated himself down again. He leaned against the door frame. 'How'd it go at the *carrinhos*?'

'Well, they took it.' Bruno tried not to smile too hard. 'And the first six bottles sold out within a few of hours.'

'Within one hour,' said Bea.

'I had to get more from the campsite. I'm already making another batch.'

'How much are they selling for?'

'Five *contos* a cup. I sell to them for two.'

'Not bad.'

'What'll happen if Mac finds out?' Bea asked.

'*When* Mac finds out,' Anderson said. 'I'm not sure. Mac's a businessman. I guess we'll find out as soon as *he* does.'

'I'll run away before letting him choke me again. Seriously, I'll just carry on to the forest. At least I've given this place a go. It's been a good time here, really. It's changed my life. A few months ago I—' He turned to Bea. 'Before meeting you, I never had the courage to try something like this. I mean, I was leaving that night we met. I'd be long gone if it wasn't for you.'

'What if he likes the idea and asks you to stay?' Anderson asked.

'Then I'll stay… at least for a while. Try to settle down, maybe. Fit in. And who knows, a wife? Kids?' He looked from Anderson to Bea. 'Whatever happens, I've proved I can take chances. I'm not locked inside myself any more.'

'If you had the choice right now,' Anderson said, 'what would you do?'

'I've had this whole regret hanging over me because I

never pushed myself as hard as I should have. But now that I've actually put myself out there, I know I can do anything. Nothing's holding me back any more. Who knows what I can learn up there? Here could be good, but imagine I got in with the indigenous tribes up there. I can find out what they know, how they do things, and come back to show everyone the changes we can make to improve our way of living.'

'Sounds like you still want to go to the forest.'

'I want everything. I'm not getting younger. I put women out of my head long ago, but now that I've taken a chance on one thing why can't I take a chance on another? I could just as easily forget the forest and live here if I got completely accepted for who I am. But I just have to wait and see if I have a choice to make or not.'

'Don't worry about age or time, Bruno,' said Bea. 'Do what you enjoy now and the future will take care of itself. You can always choose a different path. You don't owe anyone anything, not even yourself.'

'Spoken by a woman much wiser than her years.' Anderson held his glass up to her. 'You're a flower amongst nettles, Beatriz.'

Bea beamed. 'A flower amongst nettles,' she repeated.

Bruno heard a touch of hypocrisy in her words, though. She wasn't allowing herself complete freedom. Every time she saw a 4×4 arrive, her eyes would linger on the tourists jumping from its open doors, always hoping Sean would be amongst them. If she'd only realise there were a million Seans out there, maybe she'd go home to her family and friends. As well as the idea of Sean coming back, another thing was keeping her in Brisas: Iansa.

The next week, Bruno walked with Bea to the corral. She'd been going there every day after breakfast since the tour and had decided to make furnishings for the donkeys. Bruno helped her weave twelve sets of fly masks, collars, tail guards and ankle wraps, all made from agave fibres and decorated with coloured sea glass and whittled wooden trinkets. He had told her about the appearances of *Os Orishas*, and they'd made the garments to suit.

Iansa had separated from the others and was walking towards Bruno and Bea as they rounded the corner of Main Street.

'I'm sure that donkey has a sixth sense when it comes to you,' Bruno said.

'I'm her big sister,' said Bea, climbing the fence and tickling Iansa's ears. 'Look how cute you are in your new clothes,' she cooed. 'Isn't she adorable?'

Tonino led Oshala over. They began fitting him with his white accessories when the noise of a *berimbau* had Bruno gritting his teeth. Mac, in his red *abadas*, strode barefoot towards them.

'Here he comes,' Bruno said. 'I'm fucked.'

'Take it easy, Bruno.' Bea placed a hand on his arm. 'Just wait and see what he says.'

Bruno moved to put Oshala between himself and Mac. As Mac's shadow enveloped them, Bruno felt as if he were being thrown into an open grave. Oshala jerked when Mac stroked his mane. Tonino held the reins firm and hushed him.

This was the closest Bruno had been to Mac since being choked. The pungent, earthy smell revived the pain he'd felt in his throat, along with a tinge of the embarrassment, but most of all it intensified the image of Mac lying asleep in the vat.

'Tonino,' Mac said. 'How's business?'

Tonino spoke at the ground. 'Two tours a day. Rest two donkeys each tour. That's eighteen tourists a day, but you know it's never as busy during the low season.'

'Must we rest them? Don't they get enough rest as it is? We're almost down to a quarter occupancy.'

'If they don't have constant rest they'll get injured or sick. They work hard enough.'

'Must we rest them in pairs, then?'

'They've never been alone in their lives. Business is good enough.'

Mac looked at Bruno and Bea. Bruno couldn't tell if the knowing look in his eyes was real or a reflection of his own paranoia.

'Good enough is not how we do things here, Tonino. You know that. We provide the best.' Mac eyed the donkeys, and his voice softened. 'They're like mini horses of *Os Orishas*. Did these tramps charge you for this equine haberdashery?'

'No they didn't.'

'Just because we stay in the campsite doesn't mean we're tramps,' said Bea.

'How should I call you then? Leeches? Parasites?'

'Epiphytes,' Bruno said, lowering his gaze as Mac fixed his eyes on him.

'Vagabundo, I have to admit your face is less horrific-looking nowadays. You almost look civilised.' He turned to Tonino. 'Be careful of the company you keep, Tonino. These types take but give nothing back. I want you to think about how we can get more productivity out of these beasts.' He turned and brought the *berimbau* up to play, but stopped. 'What's the lifespan of a donkey, Tonino?'

'They could reach fifty if we keep treating them right.'

'And if we don't?'

'Much, much less.'

His *berimbau* pinged into a warbling melody and the circle of keys at his hip jingled as he walked off towards Beekeeper Close.

'He's always pushing!' Tonino said. 'It's never enough.'

'He's just trying to keep the town moving forward,' said Bruno. 'He's ambitious.'

Bea stared at him. 'He loves himself, Bruno. Can't you see that? I've known guys like him before. They have some success, think they can do no wrong, then bang! The world falls out from under their feet… Tramps! Did you hear him? *Mamaguevo!'*

*

Bruno woke the next morning to find Bea in tears. She was leaning over her off-yellow notepad writing a letter. He kept quiet and set about making the porridge and brewing the coffee. He hadn't seen her crying for weeks, and thought she was getting better. Seeing her like this again gnawed at him. As the porridge bubbled, he kept an eye on her. She was in such a state that she could barely hold her pen. He had to say something.

He filled two coconut shell mugs with coffee and sat at her side. She took the mug he offered with trembling hands.

'Bea, you know how much I care for you. It'll break my heart when you go, but this is too much. You have to go home.'

'I can't,' she said, blowing on the coffee and taking a sip. She exhaled, staring at the flames licking the pot. 'What if it's got worse? What if something's happened to them? Maybe there is no home to go back to.'

'That's even more reason to go. At least you'll know what's happening.'

'What about Sean? What if he comes back?'

Bruno rested his palm between her shoulder blades and, after a moment of hesitation, massaged the back of her neck. 'Let him go, Bea.' He wiped a tear from her cheek with his forefinger. 'Don't be like me. Don't bury it all inside, waiting, hoping, fantasising. You want to end up covered in tattoos and so messed up you can't talk to people? You're much too smart for that nonsense.'

She put her coffee down and wiped her eyes.

'You will get over him. Months have passed already. There's no such thing as a special one. We just fool ourselves into believing there is. It's love's illusion, but time shows us the truth. Your job now is to do whatever it takes to forget him. It's the love of your parents you need to think about. Get yourself home and be with them.'

'And what will you do?'

'They're still selling my beer, aren't they? And I haven't been thrown out yet. Maybe they'll let me stay. Imagine it, me with my own cart. There's lots I could make, not just beer. Maybe some wine, different spirits. There's so much I could do here, Bea. But if I get thrown out, I'll go to the forest. It's no exile.'

'But there's Iansa too. She depends on me now. I can adapt. I already did. You could teach me the brewing. I'll work the cart with you. When I'm ready I'll let my parents know where I am.'

'Iansa's a donkey.' He held his palms up when her eyes shot a look at him. 'I know you love her, and she loves you, but Tonino will take good care of her. And if Sean does come back, I'll be right here to tell him where to find you.' He sipped his coffee. 'Start your studies again, Bea. Release the pause button. Your future's at home.'

'And what a bright future it is. Father trying to kill himself. Drunken trash living off our money, trying to get into my bedroom at nights. I didn't tell you that bit, did I? Sometimes I think that's why he really tried to do it, because he couldn't stand up to them. There is no future in a place like that. We need a revolution. Every day I ask the tourists, every day I look at the same, shitty, week-old papers in the shop. Nothing's changed. The government's stealing the people's money to solve the problems they create. My father's life's work is in that bastard of a president's pocket. It was he who tied the noose around my dad's neck. It was attempted murder, not fucking suicide.'

Bruno kept quiet and let her calm down on her own. Tears fell from her eyes in silence. They drank their coffee without talking, then she lowered her cup and picked up her pen. He couldn't help himself reading what she wrote. His throat tightened and his eyes filled at the sight of it. She suffered so much to put these narratives together. Her heart was breaking because of that family bond. A bond he'd never known. He realised how much he wanted to experience it. He wanted children, a wife, a family.

'I better stir the porridge,' he said, coughing to hide his tears. 'You know, in another time I'm sure you'd have been a calligrapher for the most important emperor in Asia.'

She smiled at him. 'I'd have been the emperor.'

Bea headed off with her selling-board as Bruno carried the pot, filled with utensils, to wash. He cleaned the ash from the fire and rebuilt it with fresh charcoal. On his knees, gripping the spineless ends of his cactus limb rake, he smoothed out the sand between the tents.

He often joked with Bea that his campsite chores made him more like a wife and she his husband, but he actually felt more like a guardian who would always be there to look after her. He felt a responsibility towards her, like he'd never experienced before. Too long had he lived for no one but himself. Now, by turning vegetarian, by being there for her, he'd introduced obligations like all men his age should have. As well as providing a service for others, this sense of responsibility was playing a necessary part in his own growth as a person.

Since finding success with Burro Beer, although Bruno still enjoyed making the jewellery, he had less patience for selling it. He gave Bea whatever he made so that she could sell, and he could concentrate on supplying the demand for the beer. He dug a second fire pit to brew without interfering with their meal times.

He'd been having trouble sleeping since giving the first bottles to Valter. His dreams were filled with visions of townsfolk storming the campsite and throwing everyone out, all because of him; of Bea's disappointed eyes staring; of Anderson telling everyone there that they were never friends and he was nothing to him. It had gone on for weeks and was wearing him down. He decided not to hide the brewery any longer. Instead of moving it back into the shelter after each brew, he left it in the open for all to see. There'd be no more hiding anything.

Ivo, if not Mac himself, was bound to know about it by now anyway. Whenever he saw either of them, he waited for a finger to be pressed into his face, a barrage of words, maybe a punch or a kick, but they never took any notice of him. If they looked at him at all, it was with the usual expression of contempt they reserved for all the travellers. He only hoped that when the confrontation actually did occur, the cart-boys wouldn't get in trouble and Bea wouldn't be affected.

With the sun overhead and the fires burning under the kegs, it was too hot to concentrate. He gathered cuttings of tarpaulin he'd taken from the skips and stitched them together to form a solar shade. He elevated and stretched it out from Bea's tent to his own. As the brewery bubbled and hissed he lay in his hammock and read the latest book Anderson had brought him: *The Number Three: Its Occult Significance in Human Life*.

He prepared a soup of carrot, onion and coriander for lunch, and waited for Bea. When she didn't appear, as was often the case, he ate alone, washed the dishes again and prepared the fire for supper. He'd got used to this routine way of life. His chores brought him comfort, as they had in the orphanage. But those he performed here were far more important than those of his childhood, because these were benefiting someone other than himself. They gave him purpose.

He decided to take a walk through the town. A 4×4 was parked outside the church. Four people were visible in the passenger seats; only the driver was missing. He hurried by, but heard the church door shut. Mac's voice called out, 'Vagabundo!'

He's going to bundle me in the trunk, he thought. *Beat me and leave me for dead at the roadside.*

'Vagabundo, that camping area of yours is an eyesore. It's even worse now that the rest of the bottom-feeders have left. Why are you here? It's the low season. Leave!'

'There're still tourists here. Still a living to be made.'

'Not sick of taking *our* money, hassling *our* tourists?'

Bruno noticed the chicken wings and beaks in the turtle shell at the bottom of the cross.

'Breakfast of *Os Orishas*. Not yours.'

'I had my porridge oats already, with coconut milk and cinnamon all bought from the shop. All the money Bea and I make goes straight back into the town.'

'Nonsense. You're all the same. Mosquitos. If you had your way you'd drain all our blood and move on to the next place without a care.'

'Mac, I only have good intentions for this place, and I'm making a contribution, however humble.'

'You're a consequence of our success, not a contributor to it. And another thing, the colours of those donkey costumes were quite accurate for someone who doesn't know a thing about our religion.' Mac glanced up at the window above the church door.

Bruno hesitated. 'Tonino,' he said. 'He talked to one of your guys… We talked to the cart-boys and got the colours.'

'Stay away from this church, Vagabundo, understood?'

Bruno nodded and walked on. The 4×4's engine started. Its wing mirror clipped his elbow as it sped past and turned onto Main Street. He watched it weave through the tourists on its way towards the dune.

Bruno ambled through the sparse groups of tourists towards Anderson's kiosk and slipped the book from his side pocket. Anderson nodded to him as he handed a pair of pink cocktails to a brunette in a beach kaftan. Behind the bar, Bruno stood at the edge of the rocks, looking down. The back door of the kiosk opened and Anderson leaned against the door frame.

'Learn anything?' Anderson asked.

'I'd like to know where they get all these books from.' Bruno passed it to him. 'So many old books, all different subjects.'

'Like I told you when you first appeared. Mac's mother had trunks full of them. The same trunks they use at the *Festa De Yemanjá.*'

'But in English?'

'You think anyone spoke English before Mac came? His mother taught him with those books. The others are either left by tourists or bought wholesale in the city. Mac's a big reader too, you know? Or so I hear. That's one thing you two have in common.'

'The *only* thing,' Bruno said. 'It's only a matter of time before I'm thrown out.'

'Why'd you think that?'

'I bumped into him just now. He wants everyone in that campsite out. He's waiting for the right time to do it. I hope this beer isn't a big enough excuse for it. He drove away with four other guys in a 4×4.'

'Faka's the big man for a few days. Look, it's politics. Mac took a stance, you know that. He needs to hold a firm line with most of them in the campsite or they'll run all over the place. Did you see the rubbish they left? Who cleaned it? The town. Mac knows there's value in having the travellers around. As long as they don't get too carried away with anything, everyone will be safe.'

'He's not acting, Anderson. There's real animosity there. I can see it in him. Faka's in charge, you say? I don't know what's worse, being found out by him or Mac.'

'How's things in the campsite now, anyway? Much quieter?'

'Just me and Bea, Abilio and Fortunato's groups.'

'If anything does happen up there, you'll let me know, won't you? You sure those guys ain't doing drugs?'

'Why are you always asking about drugs?'

193

'That Abilio's got the junkie pallor to his skin, don't you think?'

'He's probably just malnourished. I've never seen any drugs, but they wouldn't have that shit out in the open, would they? I smell *maconha* now and again, but that's not really a drug, is it? It's a medicinal herb. I keep myself to myself, Anderson, you know that.' Bruno felt a sudden coolness in the air. His ears nearly popped. He looked up at the wisps of cloud in the sky towards the interior. There was a flutter in the wind.

'What's up?'

'It's going to rain.'

'Rain?' Anderson looked up at the blue sky. 'How the hell can you tell it's going to rain?'

'I know it.' He pointed. 'See the clouds inland?'

'Don't get too excited. The mountains block all but the biggest storms. But when it does rain here…' He cocked his head. 'You'll want to be in a house, Bruno, not a tent.'

'You'll get me another book? Maybe two?'

'I gave you two. Where's the other?'

'Still reading it.'

'Okay, I'll see what I can do, but don't forget to return that one. I don't want them to think I've lost it. What flavour this time?'

'Maybe something about Confucius. I haven't read much of him.' He looked up at the sky again. 'It's coming fast. Look at those clouds. See you later.' He hurried up the trail.

He had just stepped into the clearing of the campsite when the first crack of lightning split the sky above the mountains. He rushed to fill as many plastic bottles as he could, watching the unnatural dark approaching.

In his hammock, he watched with delight from under his watertight solar shade as Abilio, Golias and Adelina stood motionless looking up at the sky. Arcs of lightning drove from heaven to earth all around. The air became damp and

194

cold, and he could feel the static from the lightning cling to the hairs of his arms.

The rain fell lightly at first, but in an instant was crashing down, saturating the sand. Bruno sprang from the hammock and dug a channel that curved alongside Bea's tent and his own. He built up the sand on the tent side of the channel to stop any water flowing into the tents or seating area. He sat down again and waited for Bea.

For hours, he paced back and forth within the confines of the shade, wondering if she was okay, scanning the trail and the opening by the church for her. He didn't allow himself to go into town and look, deciding to test himself in resisting the need to check on her. He had just sat down when she rounded the corner by the church, walking along as if it were a beautiful, sunny day. She wasn't alone.

A man strode next to her. Bruno gauged him to be about the same height as himself, but that was the only similar attribute. The man had the arms and shoulders of a powerlifter. Like Bea, he moved with an effortless grace, but where her gait was light and sleek, his was one of harnessed power. A backpack slung over one of his shoulders, he carried a black holdall in the other hand. A flash of lightning lit a coil of wire around the man's neck. Sparks seemed to fly from his beard. Bruno rose from his hammock and stood staring at them.

Bea led the man under the tarpaulin. 'God, it's good to get out of the rain,' she said. 'We're so lucky you put this shade together.'

The man laid his bags down and pulled the coil of wire over his head. It clanged onto the holdall.

'Bruno, I'd like you to meet Carlos.'

'A pleasure,' said Bruno as casually as he could, but there was something about this man he was unsure of. He seemed familiar, although he knew he hadn't met him before. Bruno reached out, and his hand was enveloped in Carlos's. Big and powerful, it was the hand of an artist, a labourer and a prize fighter all in one. His beard glittered with coils of silver and gold. Coloured amulets and trinkets were tied into its knotted strands.

Bea pulled her towel from the line running between the tents and began to dry her hair.

Bruno released his grip but held Carlos's gaze. His eyes were so dark they seemed to be sucking the remaining light from the day.

He sat back down in his hammock as Carlos took a seat in the one across from him. The fabric strained and the wooden posts creaked under Carlos's weight. There was a brutish look about him, a confidence in his hard, staring face. His ears were tucked tight to the skull under swathes of black hair held up in a samurai knot. He had a strong forehead and nose and a bullish jaw beneath the beard. His moustache fanned out over his lip like the tail of a Siamese fighting fish.

Carlos tugged off his drenched vest and slapped it onto the line. Its spray caught Bruno's face. The vein in Bruno's temple began to twitch. Carlos undid the samurai knot, and his black hair fell with the flap of a vulture's wings. Bea's towelling paused. Her eyes were on Carlos. Bruno's jaw clenched. The last time he'd seen that gaze was on the night she met Sean.

Carlos had an Olympian physique. The skin of his chest and torso was unblemished, flesh-coloured armour, but there were marks on his arms that held Bruno's attention. On each forearm, from a large circle below the bicep, an arrow extended towards the fist. Long healed and hairless, the pink gristle markings rose like mounds of sausage meat. He'd been branded. Bruno eyed them, trying to understand why a man so inherently masculine felt the need for overt symbols of manliness. He noticed Carlos's eyes on him, and through their near impenetrable hardness saw a flicker of weakness. Carlos hadn't chosen to make these marks himself, he realised. Someone had forced them on him.

Carlos's eyes remained fixed on Bruno. He brought his hand up above his forehead and chopped it down to his chin. His indifferent expression had changed to one of extreme grief. His hand waved up past his face again, and he was smiling like a maniac. He chopped it down again and was wild with anger. Each time he unveiled his face, he'd be looking at Bruno with a different expression.

Bruno hadn't felt such rage since Faka laughed at him. He wasn't about to be made a fool of in his own camp. He got to his feet, reached for the pot, and was about to crack Carlos over the head with it, when Bea began to laugh. She sidled up to Carlos, who stopped making the faces, sat down at his side and gave him a playful shove.

'Carlos is a big joker, Bruno. Don't pay any attention to him.'

Her words and smile calmed him but her unconscious action said more. For months he'd been her true friend and she'd been his, but by sitting next to Carlos, she'd shown what she truly thought. One day was all it had taken. Carlos had superseded him. He was sure he saw the curl of a smile on Carlos's lips. He'd understood her as well as Bruno had. For the first time since he'd met her, Bruno looked at Bea not with adoration but with bitterness. He struggled to form even a half-smile as her eyes lingered on him.

Bea helped herself to beer from Bruno's storage compartment, poured it into three coconut shell cups, and passed them around. 'Seriously, Bruno, there's too much junk piled up in there,' she said over the noise of the rain. 'One day it's all going to tip over and fall through the wall. You'll be crushed in your sleep.'

'Doesn't matter,' he said, rising to light the fire.

'Carlos is a model maker,' she said, gesturing towards the holdall. 'Carlos, may I?'

He gave a nod.

She unzipped the bag and set out four models on the sand. Bruno looked at them in the dim light: a butterfly, an anchor, a horse and a cross. He realised why he seemed familiar, now. This was the man the Americans had talked about on the donkey tour. Bruno looked at Carlos's moustache and remembered the three Italian girls he'd heard speaking at the *carrinhos*. It had to be him they were talking about.

'They look good,' Bruno said, looking at the models again. He tried not to sound enthusiastic. 'Pass one over.'

'Good?' Carlos spoke in a voice that had Bruno questioning his ears. It was the voice of a man twice his age, who'd breathed cigar smoke instead of air his whole life. 'Bruno, my boy, these are the finest wire models you'll ever see. Beatriz, pass him the horse.' His Spanish was without accent and there was a strange, eroded quality to his voice, like the static of an old record playing on a gramophone. 'See that horse? That's an ideal horse. That horse is the essence of horse-ness.'

Bruno spun it around, admiring the curves, the angles, the notches in its little hooves. It even had horse shoes. As much as he didn't want to admit it, it was as perfect as a wire model could be. 'What kind of tools do you use?'

'These hands.' Carlos spread his thick fingers. Rain dripped through the seams of the shade and hissed in the fire.

'No tools at all to get that hoof detail?'

Carlos parted his moustache to the sides of his mouth and raised his top lip. There were gaps between every tooth.

Bruno nodded. 'A natural wire bender you have there.' He handed the model back to Bea, who packed all four into the bag. She picked up her beer and sat down again next to Carlos.

'How long did it take you take to make them?'

'Depends on the piece. Little ones like these I can do in a few hours. Bigger ones take many hours.'

'Once he starts,' Bea said, 'he doesn't stop until it's done.'

'I see.' Bruno looked out at the pouring rain. 'But why did you come now? It's the low season.'

'I hadn't heard of the place before, but a lot of people in the city talked about it. It's *all* they talked about. When something calls, I listen. I had to come.' He looked at Bea. 'And I'm glad I did.'

Bruno took a breath as Bea beamed at Carlos in a way she'd never looked at him. He opened his mouth to ask about Sean, just to see her reaction. Had she really forgotten him just like that? But as she waited for him to speak, he decided against it. It was pure jealousy. She was his friend only, and he should be there for her no matter what. He looked at Carlos again. Despite the look of youth and vitality, and the absence of any grey in his ink-black hair, he guessed that he was over forty.

'He made a good decision to come now,' Bea said. 'There's no one selling wire models, and with fewer tourists you can make a better connection. That helps when you're selling something you make in front of them. You're selling an experience, a memory.' She uncapped the bottle and topped up the beers.

'You could do well here,' Bruno conceded.

'And he speaks all the tourist languages,' said Bea. 'Even Russian.'

'*Moy Russkiy ne ochen horoshiy* (my Russian isn't very good).'

'*Niet, odin mesyats so mnoy I vy budesh govorit ochen horosho* (no, one month together and you'll speak very well).'

'How'd you learn?' Bruno asked, not having a clue what they'd said.

'*Ya brodil…* Ah.' He laughed. '*Izvinite…*' He switched back to Spanish. 'I drifted around for many years and picked up the languages. I was as a labourer, going where the work

199

led me. My fellow workers taught me their languages. All the bad words first, aye? Then the not so bad ones. Parrot listen, parrot repeat.'

'Yes, of course.' Bruno stood. 'I'll prepare supper.'

'I'll set up my tent.'

10

Bruno chopped the vegetables and ground the tomatoes, watching Carlos rearrange the camp. With Bea commanded to stay put under the tarpaulin, Carlos was out in the driving rain feeding his tent-tubes through the sleeves. He erected his tent next to hers.

When Carlos crouched into his tent with his bags, Bruno crept over to Bea.

'Why did you bring him here?' he whispered.

'He was alone,' she said. 'He seems nice, don't you think? I thought you'd be glad of the extra company.'

'Bea, you don't even know the guy. Are you attracted to him or something?'

'Of course not! I'm just being friendly. Nothing more.'

'You sat down next to him instead of me.'

'Don't be ridiculous. That's where I always sit.'

'I think he's dangerous, Bea. This is—'

'Nonsense, Bruno. He could help us if the locals ever get violent.'

'Bea, this is the guy that—'

Carlos's tent flapped open and he reappeared in a pair of black shorts, with a towel wrapped round his head like a turban. Bruno went back to his cooking.

Bea helped Bruno serve the vegetable stew. She tore fist-sized pieces from the fresh rye bread she'd bought the day before and passed them around. They sat down to eat by the glowing coals of the fire.

'What're those?' Bruno jabbed his bread at the amulets tied around Carlos's neck.

'These?' Carlos rubbed the wooden one between his fingers. 'This one's *Pinus Sibirica*. A present from a peasant.'

'Siberian pine,' said Bruno.

'Five hundred years old. I helped chop it down. This one here...'

'Chop it down!' Bea stopped chewing. 'That's horrible!'

'An act of necessity, Beatriz. These trees spend their whole lives collecting energy from the celestial bodies. If you don't cut it down, the energy is wasted. The tree wouldn't have served its purpose. Cutting it down was an act of kindness, yes?'

Bea glanced sideways at Bruno, who couldn't tell if Carlos spoke the truth or had made the whole thing up.

Carlos held up a stone that glowed purple and black in the firelight. 'Amethyst from Borneo. And this last one is jade.' He held it up and smiled. 'I won it from a ching-chong Chinaman.'

Bea giggled. 'A ching-chong Chinaman.'

'How'd you win it?' Bruno asked.

'Lifting.' Carlos fished through the stew with his fingers and stuffed their dribbling contents into his mouth.

'Use your spoon.' Bea waved hers at him. 'We'll have our work cut out with this one, Bruno, won't we?'

'Lifting what?' Bruno asked.

'A snooker table.' Carlos peered into the bowl and fished again with his fingers. 'Why,' he swallowed, 'why is there no meat in this?'

'We're vegetarians,' said Bea.

'We don't believe animals should suffer for our taste buds,' Bruno added.

'*Putain!*' Carlos spat onto the sand. He looked at Bruno,

his dark eyes unblinking. 'So you're telling me, a man whom I hear has lived off the land like a beast, who has walked the length of a continent, would rather starve to death than kill a lamb and partake of its nourishment?'

'Yes,' Bruno lied, holding Carlos's stare. All was silent but for the rain around them, and the constant drip and hiss from the shade to the fire.

Carlos's laugh resonated across the campsite. He raised his nose and sniffed the air in an arc, then winked at Bruno. 'Aye,' he said.

'Actually,' said Bea. 'Bruno only turned vegetarian to accommodate me.'

Bruno's grip tightened on his spoon and he glared at her in spite of himself.

Carlos clapped his hands together and smiled. 'Yes-yes-yes,' he said. He flicked his moustache.

'One has to be adaptable to ever changing conditions, don't you agree?' Bruno tried to sound smart, but it was something straight out of a Jack London novel. Carlos would see straight through it.

'No.' Carlos shook his head. 'I don't agree. Not in this instance anyway. A man must remain a man.'

Bruno had no reply. He stole the rest of the rye bread from the mat and dipped it in his stew.

'Do you have any family, Carlos?' Bea asked.

'Six brothers. I'm the youngest.'

'Seven boys! So much work for your parents.'

'Normal where I'm from. My father was a seventh son too.'

'And where are you from?' Bruno asked, trying to push his aversion aside. He knew he might have to spend a long time with this man. 'You look southern.'

'Really?' Bea inspected Carlos's face. 'I thought he looked northern.'

Carlos's teeth gleamed in the firelight. 'People always say I look like their people. I have a familiar face.' He looked at

Bruno and swept his hand from forehead to chin, but his expression remained unchanged. 'Not to be full of oneself,' he said, 'but I've been told I love like an Italian, have the passion of a Spaniard, the taste of a Frenchman and the fight of a Scotchman. Feel these muscles, Beatriz!' He made a fist and curled his arm. She dropped her bowl and wrapped her hands around his bicep.

'Hard,' she said, nodding from him to Bruno.

'Hard! Beatriz, that's prime Aberdeen Angus beef! That's Ravenscraig steel!'

'So where are you from?' Bruno asked again. Carlos looked up and around as if he was trying to find his bearings. Bruno pointed. 'That's east.'

'Ah, yes-yes-yes. Okay. I'm from...' He looked around again, touching the four cardinal points with his finger. He licked his finger and felt for the wind. 'That way! Si-si-si. That direction right there.'

'West?' asked Bea.

He cried out in laughter again. 'Yes! The west. That's where I'm from.'

Bruno exhaled into his bowl. He'd never met anyone who'd generated this much of a dislike in him in such a short time.

'And *you* have family?' Carlos nodded at Bruno and raised his eyebrows. 'Big, big family, yes?'

Bruno looked at Bea, wondering if she'd mentioned his upbringing to him, but she didn't give anything away. 'No I don't,' he said, and told him about the orphanage and how the note he'd been left there with was so badly written that he couldn't even be sure of his birthday.

The confession was supposed to inspire sympathy, and Bruno regretted it as soon as he'd told him. But the whites of Carlos's eyes grew bigger and his teeth glinted like wet cobbles under a street lamp. Laughter like the growl of a bear roared out of him, as if he'd just been told the best joke he'd ever heard.

Bea laughed along with him, but seeing Bruno's stern expression, protested to Carlos that it wasn't funny.

'What type of jobs did you do?' Bruno asked, after Carlos had caught his breath. He spoke in an even voice, determined to master his anger and not let Carlos get the better of him.

'Many jobs,' said Carlos. 'Yes-yes-yes, many jobs.' He lifted the bowl to his lips and slurped.

Bruno waited for him to elaborate, but his only action was to throw the empty bowl in the fire.

'How did you get into model making?' Bruno scratched his beard.

Carlos wiped the stew from his moustache. 'I used to work in a spring-maker's factory. Not little springs you'd find in a watch, oh no-no-no… Well, those too, but no. Big ones!' He threw his arms out wide. 'From bar this thick.' He curled one of his hands around an imaginary telescope and peered through it. 'I worked on a lathe, you see?'

'I used lathes, too,' said Bruno.

'A converted capstan, so it was. I'd feed the wire onto a jig and turn it around and around and around, like this, see? Like Archimedes, aye? And a spring would pop out.'

'Sounds like hard work,' said Bea.

'Labour intensive,' Carlos agreed. 'But there were bigger springs too and these took more time but were less labour intensive. It was while making these that I started to fiddle with the tiny wire, just to keep my hands busy, but soon I found rhythm and skill. I enjoyed the craft, and I'd sell the many tiny creations I made to workmates for beer money. It became a source of entertainment. They'd come up with more varied designs, trying to find my limit, but I'd oblige them every time. I never said no, and I never stopped. When work took me away from that job and on to another, I left with a coil of wire around my neck and as much in my bag as would fit.'

'All paid for?' Bruno asked.

'Not paid for, Bruno, my boy. I took it. I took it because I could!'

Bruno gathered the pot, Bea's bowl and the spoons, and went as far from them as the solar shade would allow. He knelt with his arms outside its shelter and scrubbed everything clean in the rain. He closed his eyes as he worked and breathed in long, deep breaths, trying to breathe all the aggravation out of him.

He found his beer topped up when he returned. Carlos was packing the chalk-white bowl of a pipe.

'He smokes a pipe,' said Bea with childlike enthusiasm.

'I do indeed, Beatriz. It's a meerschaum calabash. I found the meerschaum floating off the coast of Constanta and had a craftsman produce a pipe for me.'

'What wood is the shank?' Bruno asked.

'Alder, and the bit is amber.' He packed the bowl in three pinches, each tighter than the last. He pushed down with his thumb, twisted the pipe around and turned it upside down to tap out the loose tobacco. He lit a wick in the fire, held it to the top of the bowl and puffed until the smoke billowed from the side of his mouth. Its rich smell permeated the wet night air. 'This beer, Bruno,' Carlos said, nodding down at his cup, 'is marvellous.'

'He makes it with that thing,' Bea said, pointing at the keg brewery.

'I sell it in town.'

'To the cocktail cart guys,' Bea added. 'You saw them setting up earlier.'

'Even in this rain?' Bruno asked.

Bea nodded.

'Mac must have a big influence, even when he's out of town.'

'Or Faka. He's running things while Mac's away. Nobody likes him.'

'How do you know?'

'People tell me. Told me he's beaten his wife for the last time; she's run off to the city with their daughter.'

Bruno and Carlos shook their heads.

'Man should be strung up,' said Bruno.

'That's not a man,' said Carlos.

'You should see the size of him. Calf muscles like plucked hens.'

'Bulging muscle is nothing,' Carlos said, pipe bit clicking between his teeth. 'Real strength comes from the core.'

'He's a scary guy,' Bea added.

'What does he do?' Carlos asked.

'A butcher,' Bruno and Bea answered together.

The tobacco embers flared as Carlos pulled, and Bruno noticed him glance at the marks on his arms. 'All that time hacking at meat. Killing. Kills something inside.'

'Hardens him,' Bruno said.

'No, not hardens. Weakens. The killing empties him and the emptiness fills with anger.'

Bruno sipped his beer and was silent.

'Is this rain ever going to stop?' Bea said.

'I wonder if that's why Mac's gone to the city to get her back,' said Bruno.

'Maybe,' said Bea. 'But anyway, even if the rain doesn't stop, we have enough provisions in your shelter to last a year.'

Bruno smiled at her. 'Three months maximum.' He'd stored two sackfuls of rice, a few crates of canned vegetables and a container of dried fruit left over from when he'd shown Bea how to dry it over a low heat to preserve it.

'Thought a man like you would never need to store anything,' Carlos said.

Bruno stood. He'd had enough. He slipped into his shelter and went to bed.

On his frond matting, with his headlamp on, Bruno skimmed through all his tattered philosophy books from start to finish. He switched off the headlamp and waited for sleep, but his eyes wouldn't stay shut. Thoughts of Bea and Carlos filled his head. He turned over and over, trying to latch onto another train of thought. Finally, he was able to still his mind long enough for sleep to come.

A giant spider clung to the upper corner of his shelter. Its black hair stuck needle-like from its rigid body. Its numerous, unpitying eyes were fixed on him. He tried to rouse himself and escape but found he couldn't move. Instead of jumping on him, the spider arched its legs and curled its bulb-shaped abdomen. With a slick noise like a high-pitched scream, it shot silk from its spinnerets that wrapped around him like a constrictor snake. Helpless against the spooling silk, he didn't struggle. He was transfixed by the ominous mirror-like eyes. His reflection stared back from them. Helpless. He became aware of more eyes on him. They were staring through every slit and hole in his shelter, eyes he'd seen all over town. Eyes belonging to townsfolk, tourists, travellers, to Bea.

'Help,' he tried to ask her. 'Do something!' But his mouth wouldn't open, and somehow he knew she wouldn't help him anyway. She was gone. Something had happened to her. Her sense of self-preservation had kicked in and she'd chosen the better option for survival: Carlos. A boundless sorrow bore down upon him at the sight of her indifferent gaze. This was the girl who had saved him from himself, convinced him that he wasn't alone, and here she was, leaving him at the first opportunity. It was enough to make him submit. Silk flew from the spider with the whirr of a dental drill. Its jaws worked back and forth in silence. Soon it would liquidise his organs and suck out his essence, leaving only a withering husk. His chest heaved; but the panic subsided, and he accepted the suffocating dark clouding in. If she didn't need him, he didn't want to be here.

He woke. His body stewed in sweat. The thump of his heart reached his throat. Outside, the rain still poured.

The next morning, as Bruno set the fire, he watched Carlos's tent opening. Carlos emerged, stood on his tiptoes and stretched his fingertips up into the solar shade. The rain still hadn't let off.

'Good morning,' Bruno said.

'*Bonjour*,' said Carlos. He unzipped his shorts and urinated.

Bruno tried to ignore it but he couldn't. He stopped stoking the fire. 'You have to piss on your doorstep?' He pointed at the wooden hut in the near distance being pelted by rain. 'The toilets are just over there.'

'I needed to.' Carlos kicked dry sand over the sodden patch. He let his shorts fall and stepped out of them. He stood naked, stretched his neck, triceps and hips. He closed one nostril with a finger and breathed in, then closed the other and breathed out. He performed squats, push-ups and sit-ups, stretched his back, sat on his heels and stretched his shoulders. He dug his toes into the sand, pushed his behind up, and walked his hands to his feet. He rolled his body upright, threw his arms around in an arc and joined his palms at his chest. '*Namaste*,' he said, smiling at Bruno, his moustache fluttering in the wind.

'Even a pig doesn't roll in its own piss.'

'And all the better for it,' said Carlos. 'He's my bacon.'

'Use the toilets next time or go up on the hill and piss against a cactus. Not where we sit. And put some clothes on.'

Carlos gave a subtle bow then crouched naked into his tent. He reappeared with a towel and a bar of soap. He threw the towel over the line, stepped out into the rain and scrubbed himself. Bea appeared just as the towel was secured around his waist. Her oblivious, smiling eyes were filled with sleep.

'*Bonjour, mon trésor,*' Carlos said.

'*Bonjour,*' she answered, curling her hair behind her ear.

Bruno set out three cups of coffee and three bowls of porridge, and they sat down to eat together. Afterwards, he lay in his hammock pretending to read, listening to Bea tell Carlos all about the town and the temple, about Big Mac, Honey and Anderson, about Tonino and the donkeys, Papa Rouge and his dominoes-playing friends, Luis with his 'sore' eye, and about many others she knew. She told him as much about her life in that short time as she'd told Bruno all the while they'd known each other.

Bruno listened as Carlos told her his own stories, his strange, crackling voice, deep and resonant, saying much but giving nothing away. He had a poetic use of language unlike anything Bruno had heard. He was a natural speaker and entertainer.

'Let's sit a while and sip some wine,' said Carlos after his fourth coffee. He pulled a plastic bottle from his tent and beckoned Bruno over. It was exactly like the bottles Bruno had collected for beer and water, but had blood-red wine sloshing inside it.

As Carlos poured it into the coffee cups, Bruno sat down beside them. Although he wanted to hate the wine, he'd never tasted better.

'Where'd you get this from?' asked Bea, looking into the opaque liquid. 'It's perfect.'

'The faucet,' said Carlos. His laugh made Bruno's teeth grind.

Bruno turned to Bea, wondering if she knew what Carlos was laughing at. She shrugged her shoulders, and at this Carlos laughed even harder.

'Ah.' Carlos cleared his throat. He swirled the wine in his cup. 'Music and wine... Music and wine... It makes me close my eyes and smile like a loony... Curl my fists... Tap my feet...' He tapped both feet and patted his free hand on the ground. 'I can't help drifting off, can you? Think. Listen. Think things through... I need to listen again and again and again...' Bruno slipped back into his hammock as Carlos rambled on in a somniferous tone. 'I keep missing the tune... It sends me into my own head... Listen... Deep... Deep into my thoughts...' The beat of his hands and feet on the ground slowed. 'Hear it? My consciousness sings its own song. What's yours?'

Bruno let his eyes close. He listened for his own song, and wasn't sure if it was the sound of his breathing, or the patter of the rain, or even the continuation of Carlos's voice, his beating hands and feet, his singing to Bea that made him weary. His bones grew so heavy he couldn't even turn his head. He couldn't help but listen to the rhythm of the music and the sound of the rain and, despite having just woken up, he drifted off once more.

He woke. The rain had stopped and the sun was shining. He had to splash water on his face to clear the sleep from his eyes. The water felt sticky, like wine. After showering, he went for a walk. It was late afternoon. Tourists were crowding in the street outside Ivo's. A pair of them broke away and passed him.

'What's going on there?' Bruno asked.

'A model maker,' one of them replied.

Carlos was sitting cross-legged in front of the crowd, hair tied up in a samurai knot, moustache quivering in the wind. He teased the wire from the coil around his neck and was twisting and bending it into the fourth wing of a giant dragonfly. Every detail was perfect, every vein connecting to the next, the natural curves and kinks. Bruno could almost see the pulsing of its blood.

Bea was working the crowd with her selling-board, and Bruno went up to her. 'He's really good,' Bruno said. 'How long's he been at it?'

'Beautiful, isn't it?' She took money from a male tourist

whose eyes lingered on her body. 'He's been here since the rain stopped. Been hours now.'

'Why doesn't he take a break?' A tourist dropped some coins into a battered bowler hat at Carlos's feet. Another placed a bottle of beer at his side.

'"God doesn't take a break," he told me.'

Bruno smirked, but Bea's eyes hardened on him. 'It's his passion, Bruno. Don't be petty. He believes he's celebrating God's Grand Design.'

'Doesn't seem like any God-loving man I've ever known, Bea. I think this is the guy the Americans mentioned on the trip to the mangroves. I heard some Italian girls talk about him too. There's something not right about him.'

'Is that how you judge people, Bruno? On what strangers say? Make up your own mind. Don't depend on others.'

'Bea, the guy's a fucking pig. He pissed—'

'Hey!' called a hoarse voice from behind them. Honey's aroma of musky perfume infused with cigarette smoke enveloped them as her arms fell around each of their shoulders. 'What's going on, *queridos?*'

'Carlos is making a dragonfly,' Bea said, glaring past her at Bruno.

Honey craned her neck to get a better look. 'I love dragonflies… Oh,' she said, 'look at him. Quite a man, isn't he? That hair! He's gorgeous.' She pushed through the crowd. Someone whistled as she knelt by the beer bottle. Her thong dug into the sagging, sun-dried skin above her denim shorts.

Bruno knew what she'd be whispering in Carlos's ear, and he watched as Carlos turned to her, his mouth forming an inaudible reply. Honey's face contorted from a confident smile to a look of pain, then horror, then rage. She snatched up the bottle. Bruno drove through the crowd to stop her. The bottle smashed off the side of Carlos's head, but Bruno got a grip on her arm before she could thrust the jagged neck

212

into his face. Those in the crowd gasped in shock, but Carlos didn't seem to register the attack. His fingers never ceased from their weaving of the wire.

Bruno prised the bottle neck away from Honey and dragged her, as she lashed out at him, onto the beach. He shouted at the tourists to stay back, and led her up the dune, watching over his shoulder for Bea. She didn't follow.

The first tourists were already arriving for the sunset. Bruno bought two cans of beer from a cool-box-man and sat Honey away from the crowd. He opened the beers and handed her one. Dark trails ran from her ink-webbed lashes. The tears blackened the back of her hand as she wiped her eyes.

Bruno could feel and taste the mugginess left by the rain. He ran the cold beer can across his brow and rubbed Honey's back, whispering for her to calm down. She tried to talk to him between sobs but couldn't form any words. 'Stay calm,' he told her. 'Have a drink.'

They sipped their beers in silence. Out on the horizon, a tanker headed east.

'Oil,' Honey said when it was almost out of view. 'Steaming to Europe or China.'

Bruno nodded.

'Gold... timber... stone. They take the old from this continent and make it into something new and useful on another. Maybe I'll swim out and hitch a ride. Maybe I'll become something new and useful.'

'I'll come with you,' he said

'You're still young.' Her eyes followed the tanker. 'Maybe you can find another way.'

'We all can, Honey.'

'You know... Every time I see these ships... Any ship... I think of him... of Pavel. He's probably long dead now, but I still feel the hurt after all these years. For a long time I used to think, *oh, I should've done this, I could've been different, what if I...* For so long I dreamed of our reunion.'

'Honey, I did the same; everyone who's lost someone does.'

'Maybe he'd have a divorce and rush to see me, or his wife would die and he'd need me to mother his children, or he'd love me so much he never wanted any other, but had no money to come, so he worked for years and years only to arrive on my doorstep and pick me up in those big arms.

'Our last goodbye was so inadequate, Bruno. Two little kisses on a crowded pier, a smile, and he was gone. I remember thinking, that doesn't do it, that's not enough. I needed to see him again at least for a real goodbye... But it was all a waste of energy. The longer he was gone, the more of me died. Of course, there were others, plenty of others, but it was him, Bruno. It was always him! Even now, once in a while, I hear his voice.'

'But isn't it nice to hear his voice now? It brings a smile to your face, doesn't it?'

'No, Bruno. It's torture. Look at me. I'm a good woman. I was loved once, really loved. Now they play games for me, you know that? The fucking animals. They stand in a circle while I wait, and the slowest one to finish his drink has to fuck me. I wish I were deaf sometimes... the things they say, the shit they have me do.' She rubbed her eyes and Bruno put his arm around her. 'And the others, the ones that aren't joking, it's not just sex they're paying for, it's the power; it's domination. Some of them would torture and kill me if they could get away with it. I see it in their eyes. Of course, there are also those who are as gentle as lambs, as shy as rabbits. Some want to *be* dominated. But those... the bad ones... It's scary sometimes, Bruno. They hate themselves, that's why. They force me to do these things, to degrade myself, so they can hate someone more than they hate themselves for a while. Maybe they think I despise myself, too. That's what I show them. I play their game, but I don't feel that way. I gave up my body,' she pinched her arm, 'this flesh, long ago. Yes, I'm still a good-looking woman, still a catch, but I'm separate from it. It's my mind I've preserved. It's like it hasn't aged a day, and that's why it hurts so much to think that Pavel could have had it all. With him I was whole. Now I'm broken.' She took a long drink of her beer. 'I'll retire soon, Bruno. I almost have enough hidden away. Maybe I'll go and find Pavel, or at least visit his town, but I can't just let him go. Your health can be improved through diet and exercise, your intelligence by reading books and listening to those wiser than you. You can challenge yourself to overcome all obstacles. But love? You can't say to the person who once loved you that you're going to work harder, you'll be less selfish, be a better companion, be a better lover... It's too late. They don't love you any more. They're gone.'

'But Honey, there are others. You can find someone else.'

'You're wrong, Bruno. I've met others. I spent my life with others, but none of them came close. You're the same as me, Bruno. I saw right through your mask. That's why you got the tattoo. You loved her so much you knew there could be no one else. Part of you died when that relationship ended, and the tattoo was the lid on the casket. Am I not right? How many years have passed? When you see or hear her does that crack in your heart not open so wide you think you'll fall into the it? Is that not the truth? We're not meant for love any more.'

'Honey,' he said. 'You're wrong. You've held on too tight. Let it go. I didn't get the tattoo to stop me from loving anyone else. I got it to destroy everything she'd built. She said I was beautiful, so I became ugly. It was her I killed with the tattoo, not me.'

'But she didn't go away.'

'No, but that was through my own stupidity. I've let go now. It's the only way to happiness. We *can* love again, I know that for certain, but maybe happiness that's earned is more important than love that's given, and it can't be as easily taken away.'

'Don't let Bea get close to that man, Bruno.' Honey got

to her feet. 'And if you *can* love again, why don't you love her?'

'Of course I love her. I'd die for her, but this isn't her place. She should be home. She'd never love me anyway.'

'You knocked down one wall only to build another, can't you see it? She needs you, Bruno. She needs you to keep her away from him.'

Bruno watched her descend from the dune, and sat there until it got dark. As Honey made her way over the beach, the tourists pointed at her. He could tell they were laughing. Just as with him, they viewed her as a novelty, a sideshow, a freak. He watched them in their groups, all the same as the next, same clothes, same haircuts, same accents and speech patterns. They were the real freaks, too afraid to show themselves, cowardly conformists laughing at anyone who had the bravery – as if it wasn't a thing of nature – to be themselves. What they *really* did when they pointed and laughed, was expose their own insecurity. Behind all those gestures was the knowledge that they'd never have the courage to differ from the accepted surface standard of their chosen culture or group. They were followers who needed people like Honey as much as a flock of sheep needs a herding dog, but instead of respecting and admiring real people, they worshipped celebrities and saints: creations that manipulated and controlled them. They were blind. They were ready-made meals, paint by numbers and follow the instructions. There was zero individuality in any of them.

Alcohol and drugs were the only way to escape from their crowd. 'Everyone suppresses something,' Bruno said in the darkness, knowing that some of those who had laughed and pointed at Honey actually desired her, maybe even had already paid for her. With nobody around, and with their self-imposed prison gates open under the influence, they'd stop their judging and laughing. They'd take out their *contos*, and with fear and excitement, track her down and pay to be part of her world for a while. It was the same with the tourists who kept their distance from him, who criticised him in their groups, then sought him out when they were drunk and asked to hear his stories, stories of life in the dosshouses, selling street papers, or foraging and surviving in the forests. Just like reading a novel, they'd escape their conformist lives for a moment's respite, only for their cowardice to return with the hangover.

And of those who paid Honey, many would keep it secret, maybe feeling ashamed in sobriety, only to delight in it once again when intoxicated. Maybe some, in a moment of boldness, in an attempt to impress, might tell their friends what they had done, how they'd visited an exotic place in a far-off land and paid a much older woman for sex. And their friends, as sheep-like and cowardly as the other, would listen in awe, and wonder what they could do in turn to push the boundaries of acceptable behaviour and climb the social ladder like they all wanted so much to do, but never daring to climb high enough to escape the confines of safety and become a truly unique individual, to become their real selves.

*

Taking a bag from his side pocket, Bruno went around the cocktail carts collecting empty Burro Beer bottles to reuse for the next brew.

'We're nearly out,' Valter said, smoothing his frizzy hair down as he scanned the storage compartment of his cart.

'Sim,' said Lucio, from the cart alongside. 'Mine's already done, Burro. Get your ass moving.'

'Bottling in two days, Luc,' said Bruno. 'Sell the mass market stuff till then.'

'The rat piss,' said Valter.

'That's right,' said Bruno.

Amongst the tourists between the carts, Bruno spotted

217

Carlos. He was smiling at those around him, sweeping his dark eyes over them like a predator. Bea was at his side, all her troubles at home and Sean forgotten, warming herself in the haze of Carlos's spotlight.

With his bag full of empties, Bruno made for the day-bars, stopping to see Anderson before heading up the trail.

'Didn't drown, then?' Anderson asked.

'Almost. If I didn't dig a run-off we'd have been swept away.'

'How'd the others fare?'

'I'd say they'll need a month to dry out.'

'Maybe they'll leave?'

'I doubt that, Anderson. The bank notes are pretty resilient. As long as they don't tear, I don't think you'll see the back of anyone soon.'

Anderson looked at the bulging bag. 'Ivo said anything yet?'

'When he walks down the left side of the street, I walk up the right and jump into the first footpath. You think he knows?'

Anderson nodded. 'He must. Surely he must. Maybe he's waiting for Mac to come back.'

'Am I done for?'

Anderson patted his lips with a finger. 'I can't say. But it's selling very well, isn't it? I think you might be onto something.'

Bruno smiled. The sound of the positive opinion made him happier than he thought it would. Maybe he *could* settle here. 'Met the new guy yet?'

'Carlos? Charming fellow.'

'Charming? The same guy? Black beard full of metal coils and beads?'

'That's the one. He's funny. Smart. Nice guy.'

'I thought the opposite.'

Anderson cocked his head. 'Maybe... If you don't mind

218

me saying…' He held his hands up. 'You know I'm always honest with you, but maybe there's a little jealousy involved here?'

'Jealousy? Come on, Anderson.' Bruno cleared his throat as the blood rushed to his face. 'I'm not jealous.'

Anderson smiled.

'I'm not!'

'Okay! I believe you. Calm down.'

'Maybe I… Bea has never been more than a friend, okay? And I wouldn't let that affect my opinion of him, anyway. I find him to be a bit disagreeable, that's all.'

Anderson laughed. 'Disagreeable! Bruno, you hold back too much. If you think someone's an asshole say they're an asshole.'

Bruno forced the air from his lungs. 'I guess I don't know him well enough yet. Maybe I should try a little harder, just to be sure. Maybe we got off to a bad start.'

'Always best to be sure. More books?'

He nodded and handed the other over.

'Romance? Love triangles?'

'Anything, Anderson; preferably something serious.'

Back at camp, he cleaned out all the used bottles and stacked them ready for daylight when the paintwork could be touched up. He'd need to collect more from the skip.

He cleaned and rebuilt the fire and cooked supper. As it bubbled and spat, he raked the sand between the three tents, and when Bea hadn't returned at their usual hour, he ate in silence, alone.

With no sign of Bea or Carlos, he tended the fire so their share of food wouldn't burn, running scenarios through his head of what a future in Brisas might be like. He saw his own *carrinho, O Alquimista* where he'd serve unusual drinks of his own design, drinks with basil and elderflower, lavender and thyme, made with spirits distilled from rice, berries and palm. He'd forage for everything in the forests, make all the distilling equipment from materials he'd find there, minimal metals and plastics, everything as natural as could be.

Maybe he'd join in at the capoeira-meets, learn to dance like the locals at the bars and clubs. He'd play dominoes with Papa Rouge and his friends, hang out at the bookshop, drinking coffee and helping tourists find books they'd enjoy. There'd be conversation, laughter, friendship and maybe, or even inevitably, love. He smiled at the thought of it. Out there, probably closer than he could imagine, breathing the same humid night air as he himself, was a woman he'd come to love with intensity, a woman who'd bear him children with names like Sasha and Joe, Mik or Leo. But if children weren't an option for whatever reason, they'd have a dog, a big, ugly, stinking mongrel that they'd both adore as much as they would have their children. Maybe they'd build a cabin just outside of town. They could walk around naked all day if they felt like it, just as he'd done at times in the forests. They'd learn about languages together, about the universe, they'd practise yoga and meditation, they'd study physics, literature, natural medicine, anything at all. It would be home.

'Maybe you boys have taken me far enough,' he said, looking down at his feet. 'You'd like a rest, wouldn't you?' He reached down and massaged his toes. 'But you're still strong,' he said, feeling both happy and embarrassed at his arrogance. He gritted his teeth with pride and stroked his feet, having no doubt they could take him to the very north-western tip of the continent if he wanted them to, and he wouldn't have to stop there either. He'd swim the Bering Strait, stop for a while on Diomede, then continue through the land of the great writers, with air so cold his nose hair would freeze each time he inhaled. He pictured a great trip down through Russia, across Arabia, and over to Africa, following the trail of Livingstone and Hemingway to the vast fertile plains, where the great migrations of beast and bird rumbled louder than any man-made machine.

'Sleeping on the job, aye?'

The voice tore the smile from Bruno's face. Carlos stepped from the night and stood by the fire. The red glow cast his deep-set eyes in shadow, like volcanic craters. Bea stood at his side. A docile and smiling pet. All she needed was a collar.

'The stew won't be burned yet.' Bruno withdrew to his hammock. 'Help yourselves.'

Bea slopped the food into a pair of bowls, took out a bottle of beer and three cups, and waved him over.

'One hundred and fifty *contos*, my boy,' Carlos said. '*Oui-oui-oui*, from an onion-breathed little Frenchman.'

'Come on... It was his girlfriend who really wanted it,' Bea said. 'If it wasn't for her, he'd never have taken the money out.' She passed Bruno a cup. 'He tried hard to get the price down, but Carlos wouldn't budge.'

'She *wanted* it, alright.' Carlos gave Bruno a wink. 'They all do. Someone else would have bought it if they hadn't... And the Coke hat paid well, too... A blessed day if ever there was one.'

A blessed day, thought Bruno. He was waiting for the right time to ask Carlos to apologise to Honey. 'It's a bowler hat,' he said.

'Edward Coke,' Carlos replied.

'Bowler.' Bruno made the shape of a bowl with his hands. 'From the English word for bowl.'

Carlos shook his head. 'Thomas and William Bowler... *Bowler*, commissioned by Edward Coke. You've been to London haven't you, Bruno?'

Bruno looked into his cup.

'Wonderful place, but cold.' Carlos crossed his arms, trembled and rubbed his triceps. 'A chill bastard of a winter.'

'It'd take at a week for us to make that kind of money,' Bea said to Bruno, who knocked back his beer and refilled the cup.

Carlos looked at Bea with an air of surprise, 'I thought you said *you* made all the sales.'

The look of cool confidence fell from her face. 'No, Carlos... I didn't say that... Bruno taught me how to make our jewellery... He still makes most of it... I owe everything to him.'

'I see... I see,' said Carlos.

'I want you to apologise to Honey,' Bruno said, topping up the beers as an excuse to avoid eye contact.

'No.'

Bea brought the cup to her mouth and sipped.

'No? Just no? I've never seen Honey so hurt. She couldn't stop crying. What did you say to her?'

Carlos shrugged. 'She smashed a bottle over my head. Would Newton apologise?'

'What's Newton got to do with any of it? Take responsibility!'

'Responsibility, you say? Ask Newton if an action should apologise to a reaction.'

Bruno's grip tightened on the cup. He drained it. 'If there hadn't been an action in the first place, there wouldn't have been a reaction!'

'But in another scenario, my apology would've been the reaction, you see? In this scenario the bottle smashing over my skull suffices... and anyway, the first action was her proposition, so I suppose it's back to me again.'

Bruno poured the last of the bottle into his cup. The bottle clattered off the pot and melted on the coals. His hands were shaking. 'You're impossible! Thank me for stopping her from stabbing you in the face, then.'

'I'll thank you when I'm ready.' Carlos flicked the moustache from his lip.

Bruno looked to Bea, who wouldn't meet his eyes. He turned again to Carlos, watched him drinking the stew from the bowl, the stock trickling down either side of his mouth, matting the hair of his beard. There was a smile on his face when he lowered the bowl, a subtle, arrogant, conceited smile. Bruno hated him. He hated him more than anyone he'd hated in his life, and could tell that Carlos knew it. But there was nothing he would do, and Carlos understood this as well. He wanted to poison him, to kill him slowly and watch him wither and die in agony, but would only carry it out in his imagination, never in real life.

'Ah, silence,' said Carlos. 'Silence is never empty, is it?' His eyes fixed on Bruno. 'Silence speaks the truth.'

'I think I'll go to sleep,' Bea said, leaving her half empty bowl, cup and spoon where they lay, left for Bruno, her servant, her slave, to clean up. 'Good night.' She crouched into her tent, pulling the zip down behind her.

'Good night,' Bruno repeated. He left the utensils in the sand, stood, and slipped into his shelter. In the darkness, the vision of Carlos sitting there remained with him: his wet moustache and gapped teeth aglow in the firelight, sipping the beer *he'd* made, eating the food *he'd* cooked, from the bowls *he'd* cleaned. He threw the bed sheet aside and brought his fist down on the matting.

*

Early in the morning, before the sun had burned off the salty haze that lingered over the sand, Bruno sat on the dune watching the town wake up. A 4×4 came over the plank bridges through the mangrove forest, sped along the beach and skirted the dune below him.

Half an hour later, as the dune buggies purred in the streets, and as Anderson ambled to his day-bar, hat in hand, Bruno spotted Mac and the others riding on horseback. He followed their slow approach. Mac at the front, leading three horses behind him, the others following, each with a horse in tow. Twelve pure white horses. Bruno walked to the back of the dune and looked at the corral.

Tonino, who'd been gathering buckets, stood still as Mac appeared. At Mac's command, he opened the gate.

The donkeys moved off to one corner as the horses were led inside. Mac waved the men away, and they hobbled bow-legged up the street. He stood with Tonino for a while then strode into town.

'We don't have enough feed for them all,' Tonino said, when Bruno approached him. He had a look of despair on his face; one big hand resting in his bird's-nest hair.

'You didn't know he was bringing them?'

'No! "Just make it work," he said. Can you believe it? Never enough for him. I told you. Always pushing. "Cut costs! Work harder! Do your part for the town! Balance!" You know what happens when you keep cutting costs and pushing harder? It breaks. Everything breaks. *Foda-se*.'

Tourists were gathering at the gate. Tonino looked at his watch. He smoothed his spiralling hair and pursed his lips. There were tears in his eyes. 'I'll have to deal with it later. What else can I do?'

Bruno walked with him to the tourists then passed between the buildings and across Main Street, where one of the restaurants was full and the rest were empty – Bea's social proof theory in action. Tourists strolled towards the day-bars with their towels. He spotted Ivo coming down the street, turned back and walked past the day-bars. Anderson was tending three dark-skinned beauties. He'd just made it to the trail when heavy footsteps thudded behind him. A hand gripped his arm.

'Vagabundo!' Ivo's tobacco-stained voice sounded in his ears. 'Been a naughty boy, haven't we?'

Bruno pulled his arm free, his heart rate quickening. He cleared his throat and played dumb. 'What are you talking about?'

Ivo gave a wheezing laugh. 'The beer, Vagabundo! Burro Beer!'

Bruno looked down at the black-mirror sunglasses shielding Ivo's eyes. He couldn't lie. He wasn't going to hide.

'It was all my own doing,' he said, trying to stand taller. 'Nobody else's... I forced them.'

Ivo waved him to silence. 'We could throw the lot of you out for this, every traveller in that little refugee camp of yours. You know we've been looking for an excuse.'

'No need for that. This was my mistake. I took a chance, that's all. I had good intentions. I'll leave. I'll go to the campsite now, pack my things up and leave.'

Ivo's nostrils flared as he laughed. He coughed. 'Pathetic, aren't you? You'd like that. All the same, your kind... Take the easy route... The path of least resistance. Come with nothing but filth and disease then run off with your pockets full of *contos*, leaving only your shit behind.'

'Everything I make goes into the town.'

'Good with your hands, aren't you, Vagabundo?'

'My hands?'

Ivo pointed a hairy, cigarette-stained finger. 'Those things hanging at your sides with four fingers and the short, fat digits.'

'Thumbs?'

'Yes, you idiot. Thumbs. You made that lean-to as easy as pulling on a shirt. You made a brewery from junk...'

Bruno scratched behind his ear.

'Tell me...' Ivo dragged his sunglasses to the tip of his nose. 'Could you do that on a bigger scale?'

'A *real* brewery?' Bruno cleared his throat and drew a hand through his hair. 'You're serious? I'd need equipment, people, a location. It's not a one-man job. I don't know if—'

'Think about it and we'll talk.'

'How big a scale? How much beer does the town go through a week?'

Ivo pushed his sunglasses back up and cracked his knuckles. His lips moved silently as he counted. 'Let's say... High season... About five thousand cans' worth.'

Bruno bit his bottom lip and breathed in. '*Mucho cerveza*,' he said.

225

'Vagabundo, just tell me what you need and we'll take it from there. Otherwise you can pack your bag and fuck off.' He walked away through the day-bars, leaving Bruno staring in disbelief. Had the door really just been opened for him?

Instead of going back to the campsite, Bruno climbed down the rocks behind Anderson's and walked to the coconut palm beach. He looked out at the kite-surfers and with the music from the day-bars just reaching his ears he raised his fists above his head. 'Yes!' he shouted and faced back towards the town. 'Home,' he said. 'Hi, where are you from?... Brisas, and you?... Me? I built a brewery. Rich? No-no-no... Well, rich is only a state of mind, isn't it? Not a number in a bank account. Can I tell you a secret?' He leaned in as if he really were talking to someone. 'I was a homeless wanderer who walked thousands of kilometres before I came here.'

He sat down and tried to concentrate. 'How can it be done?' he asked himself. 'Water... Power... Supply of barley and hops... Waste!' He picked up a stick and began sketching on the hard-packed sand. He made his way along the beach, leaving a scrawling trail of words, numbers and diagrams. He forgot lunch, walked back and forth and up and down, as the hot sun brought steam from the sand. When the tide had turned and started to wash away his etchings, he'd developed a plan. He knew he could do it.

He went straight back to the campsite to tell Bea, but found only a smoking fire and more dirty bowls. To help calm down, he scrubbed the burnt residue from the pot, washed the dishes and raked the campsite. He left everything spotless and went looking for Ivo to tell him how it could be done. It would take a while but he estimated that within a few months, his brewery might be able to supply all the beer Brisas could ever need.

Ivo was smoking at the door of his bar. Nearby, Carlos, surrounded by tourists, was making another model.

Bea sat cross-legged with her selling-board on display beside him.

'Ivo,' said Bruno. 'I know how to do it.'

Ivo crushed the cigarette out between his fingers, flicked it to the sand and took a look up the street. He nodded towards the door, and Bruno followed him inside.

A few hours later, Bruno was standing in the crowd watching the capoeira. Big Mac was in his rightful place ahead of Faka. Now that all was known, the stress bearing down on him had lifted. He watched the action in the *roda* with a fresh interest, absorbed himself in every step, every swing of the arms. He listened to the thumping drums and the twanging *berimbaus*. The staccato of their rhythm was like three-syllable words: *bro-ther-hood... fa-mi-ly.*

Before the capoeira had finished, Bruno went to tell Bea. He saw her at the side of Kart de la Revolución with Carlos and his latest model. A spider. He nodded to Valter, who was taping a finger he'd just cut, and went to stand on Bea's other side.

'Bea,' he said, unable contain the excitement in his voice. 'They've found me out. They want me to supply all the town's beer. They want me to build a brewery!'

'That's great,' she said in an even voice. 'No more forest?'

'The forest can wait. This is huge. I'll be a leader of men. I'll have influence. There's time for everything.'

'You saw the horses?'

'Yes.'

'Who does he think he is? How's Tonino going to look after all of them?'

'Well, I wanted to talk to you about that, maybe you could—'

'A bully, that's what he is. Carlos knew it as soon as he saw him, didn't you, Carlos?'

'Arrogance,' Carlos said. 'Control freak. Impenetrable.'

'But look at all the good he's done. Bea, didn't you tell

him? This was nothing but a few shacks and boats when Mac arrived. He took nothing and made it into something. These people have work, they have a future.'

'Good is subjective,' Carlos said. 'Many may think he's done bad.'

'What do you mean?'

'You don't think the bright lights and colourful facades are like a whore's make-up? The restaurants, the bars, they line the street like a whore's wide open legs, leading the way straight to the rotten core.'

'It's business. The tourists come here for fun and the town provides it. Rewards are granted for services rendered... Bea, those are your words... Are they not?'

'Bruno, I...' She went quiet.

'It's prostitution,' Carlos said.

'Everyone gets a share here. It's not like the cities. Bea, you know how the cities treat people.'

'And he said unto me, the waters which thou sawest, where the whore sitteth, are peoples, and multitudes, and nations, and tongues... Sound like anywhere you know?' Carlos flicked his moustache.

'You know what?' Bruno looked Carlos directly in the eye. 'I can't be arsed with you any more. Bea, I need to talk to you later.' He walked off to the campsite.

*

Bruno had barely got the fire started when he caught sight of Bea marching past the church towards him, Carlos trailing after her.

'He took Carlos's model!' she said, throwing her arms up. 'That fucking bastard!'

Bruno almost smiled at the sight of Carlos's empty hands, the sparse coil of wire around his neck, the solemn look of shame on his face. 'Who?' he asked.

Carlos put the wire inside his tent. He unravelled his top-knot and let his hair fall.

'Big fucking Mac,' she said. 'He called it tramp tax!'

'Why didn't you stop him?' Bruno asked Carlos, who shrugged and turned away. He knew then he'd been wrong about him. For all his size and impressiveness, his confidence and his talk, Carlos was a coward. He was like the facade of a once great house, architecturally sound and beautiful, with a big heavy door and seemingly unbreakable windows, but if you looked through those windows you'd see inside was hollow, empty and weak. Bruno looked again at the gristle on Carlos's arms then up into his soft eyes.

'What was he supposed to do?' Bea shouted. 'With all of them there? If he'd done anything he'd have got us *all* thrown out. Let's get the others on our side. Let's stand up to them.'

'Bea,' said Bruno, 'sit down. Calm yourself. Look, it's low season, there's hardly anyone left. Abilio and Fortunato? They're only out for themselves.'

Bea flung open her tent, threw her selling-board inside and took out her hair brush. She brushed her hair in long, aggressive sweeps, her top lip puffing out as it always did when she was angry.

'Why you getting so worked up?' Bruno turned to Carlos. 'You've got plenty more wire, haven't you?'

'It's the principle,' Carlos said, not looking at him.

'You just have to accept it, my boy.' He couldn't resist adding *my boy* at the end. 'Or move on to the next town...' He stopped himself, fearing that Bea might leave along with Carlos. He glanced over and caught the look she was giving him.

'I can't believe you're just accepting this,' she said. 'The guy choked you unconscious. Now he steals Carlos's model – that he spent the whole day working on, by the way! Maybe we should all leave.'

'I won't leave,' Carlos spat to the sand. '*Putain!* I'll stay.' He leaned into his tent and pulled forth a book so thick his fingers barely reached around it. It was coverless, with fraying strands of binding-string around its spine. The corners of its yellowed pages curled into one another.

The violet sky darkened from the east. With only a sliver of moon, there was no light to read. Carlos reached again into his tent and brought out a perished leather satchel from which he produced a nickel-plated candle lamp and his roll-up pipe bag.

He held his wick to the fire, unscrewed the glass bulb of his lamp and lit the candle. He pulled the pipe from its thongs, packed it tightly and puffed it aglow. From the satchel, he withdrew a jar of orange stones, similar in size and shape to dried fruits. With the tip of his boot, he separated a hot coal from the fire and placed three stones onto it. Along with the fine smoke that rose from them came the smell of frankincense.

There was an economy to Carlos's movements that reminded Bruno of the way he himself cleaned the campsite, built the fire and carried out his chores. He and Bea watched in silence. There was something hypnotic to it all. The thud of the book opening on Carlos's lap jolted their attention to his face. His lips moved around the pipe-bit as he read.

'What book is it?' Bruno asked.

'The *Book of Verses*.' Carlos's eyes didn't stray from the page.

'Never heard of it.' Bruno looked at Bea.

'There aren't many in existence. I received this copy a long time ago, aye.'

'It's like a Bible?' Bea asked.

'Like a Bible?' Carlos smiled. One eye watched her from under a raised eyebrow.

Bruno pulled a hand down his face. He was sure the other eye was still reading.

'Everything of worth in the Bible,' Carlos said, 'is in here, along with every important philosophical thought.' He looked at Bruno. 'This is the only book one ever needs to read. It has every useful teaching from the *Diamond Sutra*, knowledge from the *Book of the Dead*, facets of the *Epic of Gilgamesh*, wisdom from the *Kabbalah*, the *Book of Job*, the *Yi-jing* and even the strategies of *Sunzi Bingfa*. Everything you *have* read, Bruno… And, Bea… And everything you ever *will* read is already written in here.'

'So what wisdom does it offer you in this scenario, then?' Bruno got up and poured himself a cup of water from a bottle he'd left with mint and lemon soaking in it. Since drinking Carlos's wine, water had been leaving a winey aftertaste in his mouth.

Carlos drew his moustache around his lips, closed the book and shut his eyes. He let the book fall open again, hovered his thumb around and plunged it onto the page. He opened one eye, looked down and smiled.

' "Then whoever shall call His name shall be spared." '

Bruno smirked. Carlos looked at him. 'Why do you laugh, Bruno?'

'Acts,' Bruno said. 'Two twenty-one. God.'

'God? But who's talking about—'

'The big man in the heavens, you know? Wants everyone stoned to death, wants to slice open pregnant women with swords, brings hunger and famine, stops the rain falling, sends plagues…'

Carlos smiled. 'Bruno, my boy, God is omnipotent, omnipresent and omniscient. The sentient creator of everything around us.'

'And who created God?'

'God was always there.'

'And you, Bea.' Bruno turned to her. 'You believe that too?'

'I don't know.'

'Well I don't think you need God to be who you are, or that *Book of Verses* or whatever you call it. All everyone should do is enjoy their time and try to achieve what they want to achieve without hurting anyone else. That sums it all up. "Your daily life is your temple and your religion," [6] he said, quoting from one of his books. He stood up and was about to walk off when Carlos spoke.

'The heart has been taken from this town. It's naught but a thoroughfare.'

'The temple is the heart,' Bruno said.

'From what I've heard, it's a *hounfour*, not a temple. It's the bowels! The arse!'

'Maybe it *is* a *hounfour*,' said Bruno, deciding to go and watch the ceremony, 'but it brings them together. Theirs is a religion of balance, a celebration of life, not an oppressive religion of salvation like yours, full of suffering and guilt, worshipping a hateful God who treats the world like the director of a play.'

'You speak as if God's a cartoon character!'

'No,' Bruno shot back. 'Your books do that already.'

Carlos's laugh hissed in his ears, pulling at him like sentient strands of smoke from a hundred stones of frankincense.

Bruno hurried over to Beekeeper Close, checking in every direction to make sure he hadn't been seen. He climbed the tree at the back corner of the temple. As soon as he sat on his perch, he saw it was no ordinary ceremony. There were more people than he'd ever seen there before.

Mac stood in front of his floral chair watching the writhing crowd move around the patio, hands joined, arms swaying over their heads. The twins, bare-chested with white lines painted under their eyes, beat the congas with an urgent violence. Sweat poured down the sides of Lagarto's face and dripped from his chin as he nodded in time with the pounding of his hands on the drums.

There were no chickens, goats or any sheep tied to the pillar tonight, nor was there any sign of Faka. The circumference of the patio was lined with turtle shells instead of conches.

6   The Prophet – Kahlil Gibran

From outside the walls, Bruno heard shouting, scuffling and the braying of a donkey. He looked between the branches of the trees and saw Faka in the dim light, hauling a donkey by a rope around its neck. It dug its hooves into the sand and pulled against him. Tonino was there with three men clambering all over him, holding him back as he tried to get at Faka. 'Please,' he called. 'Please don't do this! Don't do it!'

The men tried to calm him. They gripped his arms. 'Quiet, Tonino. Quiet or we'll have to gag you. It's necessary. It must be, Ton… Faka, make it nice and quick… Keep the balance.'

'No!' Tonino pulled against them. 'You can't!' He got an arm free and swung for Faka, who caught the blow on his forearm. Two of the men got hold of the arm and twisted it up behind Tonino's back. He yelled out in pain. 'Get off!' he shouted, trying to swing with his other arm, but the third man was hanging from it. His voice grew louder and more hysterical as they neared the front of the temple.

'Gag him,' Faka ordered. One removed his T-shirt and twisted it up. With Tonino shouting and throwing his head from side to side, the man got it tied around his mouth.

The banging on the temple door jarred against the rhythm of the drums. Mac made his way around the swaying crowd and hauled the doors open.

Even from his distant perch, Bruno could see the whites of Tonino's eyes as the doors opened. His struggling became hysterical. Mac shouted to the women sitting by the hut. One rushed inside and came back with something cupped in her hands. Mac took whatever it was and held it over Tonino's mouth and nose. Tonino's movements grew slow, his cries hushed and slurred. He slumped in the men's arms, heaving for breath. They struggled to hold him up. Head lolling, he tried to lift it to look for the donkey, and continued his pleading.

Mac took the rope from Faka and dragged the donkey through the crowd, its hooves scraping and clattering on the concrete floor as it tried to break away. It had no chance against Mac's inhuman strength. He tied it to the pillar. As the donkey bucked, kicked and jerked in an attempt to free itself, Bruno noticed its swirling white and brown flanks in the candlelight. It was Iansa. He was helpless. He had to either stop it, or leave, get as far away from the place as possible, but Faka closed the door and the three men appeared at the side of the building. They dragged Tonino to the tree by the front corner and held him against it. Bruno knew that if he got caught, everyone would be thrown out of the campsite.

Faka stepped onto the patio, and Mac moved back to his chair. The polyrhythmic drumbeat quickened. The crowd linked hands again and circled around the patio. Incense smoke rose from the palm-leaf parcels by the statue of *Yemanjá*. A gust of wind sent the smoke spiralling, and caused the draped strings of cowrie shells to rattle against the wall.

Mac silenced the drummers, raised his hands and shouted to the congregation: 'Brothers and sisters! She is with us!'

They all cheered.

'Sit down now,' Mac called. 'Everybody sit down.'

Iansa's cries became louder in the silence. She threw her head back against the rope and stamped her trembling feet. Bruno felt sick. He heard Tonino groaning against the tree, begging for her life to be spared. He wanted to help him, but had no choice but stay where he was.

'We're here to honour *Iansa*,' Mac said. 'Goddess of the Tempest. Without her, the winds would not blow the kites nor billow our sails. The tourists would not come.

'Brothers and sisters, we are a family. Strive, brothers and sisters! Strive to stay united.' He looked at Faka and spoke to him alone. 'We must treat each other as we ourselves would be treated. Here is no place for selfishness. We are as one in this community.' He closed his eyes, nodded and rubbed his hands together.

'May the winds always blow us in the right direction. Our path has long been chosen. Let us be ever vigilant not to stray off course. *Iansa*, guide us as ever you have! *Estamos agradecidos Yemanjá...*'

The crowd joined in with passion and fervour, faces from all over town, waiters, cooks, shop attendants, Hermes, Silvia, Ivo.

'*Ogum, Oshosi, Oshala, Nana,*
'*Estamos agradecidos Ochumaré,*
'*Zhango, Eshu, Iansa,*
'*Ossaim, Oshum, Omulu,*
'*Os Orishas estamos agradecidos.*'

The drumming crashed in, echoing off the walls, and the crowd came alive. They moved around the patio again. White-dressed women took up their positions. In perfect symmetry, they lifted the turtle shells above their heads. Between the branches, Bruno looked again at Tonino. His struggling was without strength, and the men easily contained him.

Faka's eyes never strayed from Mac, and when Mac raised his hand and clenched his fist, Faka produced the filleting knife and held it aloft. A handle of wrapped twine, a thin, curving blade glinting in the candlelight.

Iansa kicked out as Faka approached her, the white-tipped swirls of her hair bristling as she skipped away in the arc permitted by the rope.

Her hoarse screams were all but human cries for help, for mercy. Bruno felt tears run down his face. He swallowed to stop from vomiting. He should have left regardless of being caught, but his eyes were fixed, he couldn't look away.

Faka timed her kicks, got alongside her and threw a strong arm around her neck. He gripped her to him and leaned in with all his weight.

Tonino went silent. Bruno saw one of the men step back in the darkness and light three cigarettes. He passed them to the others, who kept Tonino upright against the tree.

He looked back to the patio as Faka drove the knife into Iansa's neck and twisted the blade. Her lips drew back. Her eyes flashed open. Wet breath spurted from her nostrils. Faka called out to the nearest helper, got hold of the first turtle shell and laid it on the ground. He pulled the knife out, tossed it aside and raised the shell to catch the spewing blood. It filled in an instant. Blood overflowed and pooled around the pillar. The helper carried it off the patio as the second one got hers under the crimson deluge. With Faka's weight still on Iansa, the fourth shell filled and her footing became unstable. In an attempt to lower herself to her knees, she slipped in the blood and fell onto her side with Faka on top. Her breaths came in irregular, bloody spurts. Her eyes rolled back, white and empty. The rising and falling of her flank slowed and stopped. She was gone.

In the silence, Tonino wept. 'Is okay,' said one of the men. 'Is done now.' He took the T-shirt from Tonino's mouth, and they let him go. Tonino shuffled drunkenly down the street.

The drums had slowed and stopped in time with Iansa's breathing. They started again as Faka skinned her body.

The three men lingered by the tree, smoking, preventing Bruno from descending. It was too late anyway. He'd seen it all.

Steam rose from Iansa's glistening flesh as Faka butchered her, placing her organs and body parts into each of the remaining turtle shells. His work was swift, his hands and arms red to the elbows, his *abadas* soaked through. Blood smeared his chest and face.

Amongst the blood and tissue, the shards of bone, the trimmings of flesh and hair, Faka stood up straight and looked about him. There was defiance in his eyes. A sick air of power and arrogance emanated from him. Bruno vomited in his mouth and spat it to the ground. He rubbed the tears from his eyes and smoothed back his hair. The helper women returned from the hut with a single turtle shell. They surrounded Faka and removed his *abadas*. They cupped the bloody mixture in their hands and bathed him in it.

So this is his cleansing for beating his wife, thought Bruno. *They're so fucking stupid they see this as the solution?*

The three men slipped in through the temple door. Bruno slid down from the tree and sneaked back to the campsite, disgusted with both himself for watching, and the people for their involvement. He vomited again in the toilets before lying in his shelter, awake and alert, wondering how to tell Bea.

He couldn't tell her, there was no way he could. *Pack up and leave*, the voice in his head told him. *Leave before sunrise and never return.*

He is the most important man in Brisas

11

From inside his shelter, Bruno heard Bea's wails on her return to camp. He kept still, staring past the needles of daylight piercing through from the slits in the tarpaulin. He hadn't slept all night, wondering how he could approach her, but when she'd called on him earlier, he'd feigned illness. Now she would know about it all through Tonino.

'They've killed her!' she shouted. 'They're all dead!'

Bruno squeezed his eyes shut, held his face in his hands and listened.

'Pardon?' said Carlos.

'Iansa! They killed her in the temple last night. Tonino's gone. He's put the others to sleep so they won't suffer like she did. And you watched it!' she screamed. 'Didn't you, Bruno?'

'I...' Bruno didn't know how to answer. He stared at the latch of his entrance.

'Come out!' she said. 'Come out here and face me.'

He rose, unlatched the tarpaulin and stepped into the daylight. The sight of her face shocked him. Red and swollen, eyes wet and creased from crying, she scowled at him from Carlos's arms.

'Bea,' he said, reaching for her. 'I'm sorry. I'm so sorry.' She beat his hand away.

'Don't fucking touch me. Don't you dare fucking touch me. Read this.' She threw the note to the ground. 'He thinks

I hate him, Bruno! It's not him I hate! He did everything he could.'

Bruno picked up the note and read:

Dearest Bea,

I'm so sorry I didn't come to you. Iansa was sacrificed in the temple last night. I couldn't stop it. They drugged me. I know you hate me now. But I won't let the others go through the same suffering. I put Olhos de Boneca in their food and watched them sleep. No pain. I promise. I can't stay. I'm sorry.

Tonino.

'The whole town was there, Bea. I couldn't do anything. They held him against a tree. If I tried to stop it they'd have thrown us all out, then where would you go, where would—'

'Where would *I* go? Don't use me as an excuse. You didn't leave because of that fucking brewery. That's what you were protecting. You don't care about me. You don't care about the rest of us. You left your city and were running off to the rainforest because you're selfish, Bruno.'

'No, Bea.' He moved towards her. 'That's not true.' Carlos pushed him back and he fell to his knees.

'You pretend you're a nice guy,' she continued, 'but you're not.'

'Don't say that. You're family, Bea. I love you. I mean it.'

'I'm not family. I have no family. You should've stabbed me in the heart.'

'Bea, I'm sorry. I'm so fucking sorry!'

She went to speak again but no words came. She gripped Carlos's shirt and cried into his chest.

'Bruno,' Carlos said. 'Go.'

*

After spending the rest of the morning amongst the coconut palms, Bruno went to meet with Ivo, who introduced him to Lagarto.

'I thought there'd be an apprentice,' Lagarto said in a frog-like croak. He shook Bruno's hand, his palm and fingers

239

cool and calloused through years of labour and banging on the drums.

'She won't be coming any more,' Bruno said. He'd taken the project on with the condition that Bea would be involved, but knew better than to ask her after what had happened.

'You'll still be needing one, though?' Ivo asked.

Bruno nodded.

'Then you'll get my nephew, Tiago.'

Bruno nodded again. Part of him still wanted to run away. He held resentment towards the townsfolk that hadn't existed before, and was disappointed in himself. Was there really nothing he could have done? He was also angry at Bea for how she'd reacted. She couldn't really have meant all she'd said. Surely her anger and hurt would subside soon enough for them to talk about it.

After a brief conversation about the expectations, the dos and don'ts, Ivo left him with Lagarto, who took him to meet the workers. Up by the skips, four stern-faced men aged between twenty and forty stood in a half circle around him. There was Rudi, the youngest of the group, who Bruno recognised by his prowess during the capoeira sessions, Riccardo, who wore glasses, had a heavily receding hairline and a head much too big for his slender neck, Joao, the plumber who, the whole time they were talking, was biting a hangnail until he drew blood, and Selmo, a young monkey-faced man with dark hair that stuck straight up from his head.

Without enthusiasm, Bruno explained his plans. They'd build the brewery next to the upside-down tree, because of its closeness to the town's water supply and because it had plenty of open space around it. One or two wind turbines would be erected to generate enough power to heat the water and mill the barley. They'd have to visit the city scrap heap every week until they had enough piping, cables, valves and any other materials they'd need. Ivo had told him that

Mac didn't want to spend one *centavo* more than Bruno's salary, so he had to find what he could and make do. As he stood talking, he hoped a feeling of pride and excitement would grow inside him; here he was, a leader of men, it was impossible, but all he could think of was getting back to the campsite to see if Bea had calmed down enough to forgive him. Any achievement without her was empty. He'd do whatever it took to prove his loyalty to her. If she wanted him to leave, he'd do it. If she told him to burn the temple to the ground he wouldn't hesitate.

When he returned to the campsite later that day, she wasn't there. He cleaned the dishes and the pot she and Carlos had used, raked the area and waited for her. He tried to read the latest book Anderson had given him but couldn't concentrate on it. All he could think of was her, and how badly she'd taken the whole thing.

When it grew dark, he decided to go looking, and found her at the *carrinhos*. He watched without understanding, as she and Carlos danced in the middle of an excited crowd. Her eyes were closed and she had a big, drunken smile on her face. Carlos's hands were wrapped around her hips. He was turning her like a spinning top. It was as if nothing had happened. There was no sign of sadness about her. She looked as happy as he'd ever seen her.

Confused and angry, but reluctant to cause any more harm, Bruno decided not to confront her. Instead, he went to the supermarket. He passed a soiled banknote over to Luis. 'Whisky,' he said.

'Get it yourself.'

The next morning, he woke in the copse of *caju* trees down by the corral. His head throbbed worse with every beat of his heart. Sweaty dew matted the hairs of his legs. His saturated shorts clung to his thighs. He'd pissed himself. He stood, struggled to focus his eyes, and tramped back to the campsite. Bea was making breakfast. By his tent, Carlos stood on one foot, bent over at the hip. The other foot was up behind him like the tail of a scorpion. His hands were out at his sides flapping to keep balance. He expelled his lungs in six short bursts then breathed in.

'Bea.' Gunpowder ignited in Bruno's throat as he spoke. 'You're always right, but—'

'I'm over it,' she said. Her voice and eyes were so unmistakably indifferent that, even with his senses dulled by the hangover, he knew she meant it. He sat in front of his shelter and watched her. Carlos sucked in the air again after another set of exhalations.

'Sit down, Carlos,' said Bruno. 'You're making my head worse.'

'Yoga,' said Carlos, pressing a finger to his left nostril and breathing in through his right. Bea brought Carlos a bowl of porridge and a coffee. They sat down together and ate.

'Can I grab some coffee?' Bruno asked.

'It's in the pot.'

He struggled to his feet, ladled a cupful and sat back down.

'I had a dream last night.' Carlos shook his porridge-dripping fingers at him.

'Yes?' Bruno looked over his cup. The coffee burned the roof of his mouth.

'Yes, I did. Aye.'

Bruno blew on the coffee and listened.

'Of all occupations, I dreamt I was a labourer for a butcher. My job was to unload the meat from the van and take it to the cold store. From the cold store, I had to take it to the display cabinet in the front of the shop. You follow?'

Bruno squinted at him and glancing to Bea. His eyes burned in the sun.

'The meat came in those woven bags, aye?'

'Hessian sacks,' said Bruno.

'Yes... Hessian sacks, that's what they're called... And they were sealed with those twisted, long, metal strands with the loops at either end.'

'Wire ties,' said Bruno. 'Bea, can we talk?'

'That's the one,' Carlos continued. 'Wire ties... Yes-yes-yes. And after opening a number of these hessian sacks I realised that I could unwind the wire little by little.' He pinched his thumbs and fingers together and turned them as he spoke. 'Each link not knowing the one before it had come undone. I could unravel it from the lowest point and the sack would remain sealed until I got all the way to the last link, the very top of the wire tie... And you know what happened?'

Bruno shook his head.

'Without the top link having a clue what was coming...' Carlos closed his fists and threw them open. A wire tie landed on the sand in front of Bruno. 'Pop! All at once the sack would open. That which was so strong had been torn apart from the bottom to the top. What do you think that means?'

Bruno looked at Carlos then at Bea, as she heaped small spoonfuls of porridge into her mouth. At that moment he remembered the whistle he'd given her months ago; he looked for it around her neck, looked for the bulge of it under her shirt. It was gone. Its absence knotted his throat. He watched her in silence and felt tears forming in his eyes. He got up and hesitated. 'I... I...' He was trying to answer Carlos's question but had nothing to say. He slipped into his shelter.

'Entropy,' Carlos called after him. 'That's what it means, my boy. Entropy.'

Bruno could tell that Bea wasn't acting. Over the months, he'd learned every detail of her face, knew each of her mannerisms, and could read every movement of her body. He could tell what she wanted or thought without her having to speak. She'd been a friend to him like no other, and to see her so vacant and empty of feeling for him was worse than any physical pain he'd ever had to endure. Without her, he'd have left this place before making any real effort, and have walked on with no progress made as a person. Here he was, being accepted into the town, granted a major role to play, and he couldn't even thank her. He knew that to her his words would now be as vacant and empty as her eyes when she looked at him.

She was projecting all the hate and blame for what happened to Iansa onto him. Not once did he hear her criticise Mac or Faka, nor did she show any hostility towards them when he watched her on the street. He went to speak to Anderson about it but found no solace. Anderson spoke in clichés about the ways of women and told him the best thing to do would be to give her time and space. He tried to take the advice because there was nothing else he could do, but struggled to stop himself from attempting conversation with her. He made it obvious that he was there if she needed him. It had all been so sudden and unjust, but he had to be strong, to respect himself and carry on.

He was introduced to his new apprentice in Ivo's smoke-filled office. Tiago was tall and gangly, sparse stubble on his chin and piercings in both ears. Bruno was relieved to sense an easy nature about Tiago after the hostility he'd felt in the workers.

'Tiago,' said Ivo. 'Take him to the shop for *abadas*, a shirt and espadrilles, and get his pay from the office.' He looked at Bruno through a fog of cigarette smoke. 'Bruno, I want you to explain every single detail about the brewing process to Tiago, from cradle to grave, you got that?' He tipped ash from his cigarette into the overflowing ashtray.

'Got it,' Bruno answered, eyes nipping because of the smoke.

'And Tiago, I already told Bruno how things work here, the salary, the clothes, the conduct, but you remind him, okay? Don't let him forget.'

'Okay,' Tiago repeated.

'Off you go, then.'

Bruno followed Tiago through the bar and out into the fresh air. Tiago walked up to a dune buggy, climbed onto the frame and slid into the driver's seat. 'Jump in,' he said. 'We'll need the salary first.'

While Bruno waited in the buggy, Tiago entered the bookshop. Minutes later he was back in the driver's seat handing over a pay packet.

Bruno looked at the pay packet in his hand, a white envelope padded by the banknotes inside. 'I haven't held one of these in years,' he said, as Tiago turned the key in the ignition.

'Welcome to the team.' Tiago drummed his fingers on the gearstick. 'You'll get one every month.'

Handwritten in slanted font was his name. Not Vagabundo, nor tramp, nor parasite but his full, *real* name; or as close to real as any orphan found in the south without a surname could expect; all being given the same surname: *Bruno Expósito*.

Without looking inside, he stuffed the packet in his back pocket. He didn't want to open it in front of Tiago. It could only cause animosity between them if Tiago saw such a big difference in pay, even though he was only an apprentice. They drove to Beekeeper Close.

Hollow wooden chimes knocked together as Tiago opened the door of a clothes shop and led Bruno inside. *Abadas*, linen trousers, shirts and espadrilles stacked shelves from floor to ceiling. The smell of linen, dry wood and citrus fruits hung in the air.

'Fatima!' Tiago shouted at a tall, light-haired woman with her back to them. She knelt, pulled out a few pairs of *abadas* from a cardboard box and slotted them into a shelf compartment.

'She's more or less deaf,' Tiago said. Bruno rubbed the short beard on his chin as he watched the woman. Her hair danced in the light from the window as she moved between the shelves and the box. Khaki shorts hugged her rear. From ankle to thigh her tanned legs were covered in golden fuzz like the fur of a stinging nettle.

Tiago walked up and placed a hand on her shoulder. She turned and gasped at Bruno, then smiled and held up a hand in apology. Bruno hadn't taken offence. He smiled back at her.

Her big, slanted eyes were a little further apart than normal. Caramel pips crossed her cheeks and nose. Her pinkish-brown lips parted to show large white teeth with a gap in the middle.

'Sohay,' she said in speech marked by deafness.

'It's okay,' answered Bruno in a whisper. 'You should see how people used to look at me.'

Her eyes were on his lips as he spoke. Tiago touched her shoulder again.

'We need clothes for Bruno,' he shouted. 'Two pairs.'

'What sigh?' she asked.

'I don't know,' Bruno mouthed, coming up beside them. 'It's been so long since I bought any. Used to be eighty-seven.' He circled his hands around his waist.

'Not any moh.' She beckoned him closer.

His legs trembled as he moved towards her. She swept up a roll of tape from her desk and fed it around his waist. He caught the smell of vanilla in her hair. Sweat dampened his forehead. He wiped it off, smiled uneasily at Tiago and noticed a paperback by the till.

She held the tape up to him, but he looked straight past it into her eyes. 'See,' she said. 'Sebenty eight. You between sizeh.'

He smiled at her.

'What colah?'

'You choose.'

She reached out to a shelf and picked out a pair of navy *abadas*, and from another a sky-blue, short-sleeved shirt.

'I'd rather have the linens if that's okay?' He looked again at Tiago.

'Shouldn't be a problem,' said Tiago.

She handed him the clothes along with two pairs of espadrilles and pointed to a curtained changing area.

Behind the curtain he opened his pay packet for the first time. It was filled with limp, cloth-like fives, tens and twenties. Pride flushed through him. This was progress. This is what courage and taking chances did for you. It got you accepted instead of cast out. He tried to push the feeling of guilt and regret surrounding Bea aside to enjoy the moment, and laid his pay on the stool.

He stripped off his patchwork shorts and torn singlet and stepped out of his sandals, aware of how significant the act was. There was emotion as he slipped on the linens and buttoned up the shirt. He wasn't simply changing his wardrobe. He was wearing one future and leaving another crumpled in a heap at his feet. He drew back the curtain. Tiago and Fatima stood shoulder to shoulder.

Fatima smiled and nodded at him. Tiago looked at his watch.

'I look okay?' Bruno held his arms out.

'Great,' Fatima said.

'Fine,' said Tiago. 'Let's get going.'

At the desk, Fatima packed a pair of khaki linens and a black, short-sleeved shirt into the bag, along with a pair of black espadrilles.

'Foh the night,' she said and, looking at the old bundle of clothes in his arms, added: 'Bin?'

He was about to hand them over but couldn't let go as her fingers gripped them. 'I'll keep them for now,' he said. He glanced again at the book by the till: *Perfume* by Patrick

Suskind. He wanted to ask her about it, but in the act of handing over the money, fumbling with the change, and with fresh sweat almost dripping from his brow, he couldn't bring himself to say any more. He hurried after Tiago.

'Where to now then, boss?' Tiago opened the door. Bruno followed Fatima's eyes to the wobbling, wooden chime. She looked back at him.

'Bye,' he whispered.

*

That evening, Bruno invited Anderson and Honey out to Cafe La Mouche to celebrate his new position. They met at Anderson's bar then walked past the tourists at the *carrinhos* and up Main Street. In his pressed linen trousers and shirt, the locals either ignored him completely or watched him with indifference. He felt taller and looked around without concern, smoothing his hair back anytime anyone stared. He'd always felt half-formed and weak, afraid to voice his childish opinions lest he be ridiculed by the fully-formed adults around him. With this acceptance, he felt as if he were shedding a shabby overcoat he'd been wrapped in for too long. He realised that he had something to offer too. He was an equal, and tonight he walked with a confidence he'd only ever felt in the presence of Flora or Bea. They were gone now. Both of them. Maybe Bea would return, but if she didn't, he was no longer afraid to stand alone.

'Evening, Papa,' Anderson said, tipping his hat at Papa Rouge as they passed the grill and climbed the steps. The smell of cooking meat and burning coal mingled with the fragrances of patchouli and lavender smoking from jars of incense on the steps.

Papa swivelled his stiff neck and looked at Bruno. 'Dressed up for a change, I see. And so you should be,' he teased an invisible moustache at the edge of his lip, 'with such a… a… a Venus! Such a *déesse. Tu es en belle compagnie!* How's tricks, Honey?'

248

She flicked her slim cigarette into his grill. 'Like a fairy tale.'

Davide, the waiter, his green eyes set like emeralds in his tanned, handsome face, led them to a table at the back. As they sat, he handed out the menus. 'The fish of the day is the sea bream cooked with butter, banana and garlic. The soup is *soupe à l'oignon gratinée*.' He clasped his hands in front of his navy hip apron, stepped back and turned off between the tables.

Anderson called at his back for a bottle of house red.

Bruno rubbed the cotton tablecloth, eyed the red paper napkin and the shining Inox cutlery wrapped within. He picked up the bundle, weighed it in his hand and smiled at Anderson and Honey. 'Heavy,' he said, laying it down again.

The wooden chair creaked as he turned to take in the artwork on the false-brick walls. On one side was a series of round, white canvases painted with black spirals, swirls and dots. On the other were fish made from mangrove roots tied together with thin strips of bark.

At the other tables, tourists laughed and talked in foreign languages. Glasses clinked, wine glugged from bottles, cutlery tapped and scraped on ceramic plates. There were wine-stained smiles, white, sparkling eyes, and a hubbub of excited conversation. It was a place of beauty and positive energy, and he was right in the middle of it.

'Look at this man, Honey!' Anderson reached over and rubbed the fabric of Bruno's collar. 'All dressed up in the finest Brisas garments.'

Bruno smiled at him.

'Who'd have thought?' Anderson continued. 'A salary man! How's it feel?'

'Feels good,' he said. A girl was laughing at an adjacent table. She looked like Bea.

'Now don't let your troubles with Bea ruin your night, Bruno,' Honey said. 'She'll come around in the end.'

'A woman scorned,' said Anderson, easing his half-moon

reading glasses from his shirt pocket. 'How did you fall out again?'

'I told her what I thought about Carlos.' He didn't want either of them to know about his spying on the temple, and hoped Bea would keep it to herself as well.

Anderson looked at him and went to speak, but Honey spoke first.

'A horrible man. But don't you worry. She'll find out for herself. Some people can only learn that way… I can't get poor Tonino out of my mind. He was an angel. He treated those donkeys like children. Why would he do such a thing?'

'Bea found a note,' said Bruno. 'It told her they sacrificed Iansa in the temple. He had to do the humane thing and put the rest down.'

Anderson looked over the rims of his glasses. 'Some people just flip, Bruno. Maybe that's his alibi? Who can say he didn't leave on Iansa after killing the others? He was always a bit work-shy, I bet the arrival of twelve more to look after got too much for him.'

Bruno held his breath and lowered his eyes. There was something in the way Anderson spoke. He opened the menu and read the silver font embossed on its creamy pages. *He can't be lying*, he thought. *Why would he?*

Davide returned with the bottle of wine, uncorked it, and nodded to Anderson, who extended a palm towards Bruno. 'The specialist.'

Before Bruno could stop him, Davide was pouring it into his glass. 'I'm not an expert in wine, or anything else for that matter, Anderson.' Heat rose to his face.

'Oh come on,' said Honey, 'don't be a pussy. All you're doing is tasting for cork.'

'You know all about cork tasting, don't you, Honey?' Anderson's deadpan comment had Davide clearing his throat.

'The more you joke, the more you pay,' she said, not

lifting her eyes from the menu. 'Why is it that the corks over at your place are so small?'

'It's fine,' said Bruno, after touching the glass to his lips.

Davide filled the glasses then backed away again.

Anderson licked his thumb and turned a page. 'So, are we having starters or just mains?'

'This is all on me,' said Bruno. 'Have both, and a dessert.' He picked up his wine and looked into it as he spoke: 'You've both been great friends to me since I arrived. I want you to know it hasn't gone unappreciated.'

'You've been good to us, too, Bruno.' Honey's hand slid up his thigh. 'I know I'm having a dessert. That *petit gâteau*'s calling out to me as always.'

Davide approached the table again. 'Have you made your decision?'

'Seafood stew and a *petit gâteau* please, Davide.'

'Same for me,' said Anderson, 'but spring rolls to start, and no dessert.'

Davide nodded and eyed Bruno.

'Just a pizza Regina.'

The wine went to Bruno's head and he spoke with enthusiasm about his plans for the brewery. Until it was up and running he'd make more keg breweries to at least supply all the *carrinhos* and the cool-box-men. Next phase would be supplying the guesthouses, then the restaurants, bars and clubs, and finally the day-bars. The whole process would take at least six months, dependent on what materials they could find.

Honey and Anderson were good company. Bruno downed glass after glass and listened to them talk. It was nice to sit at a real table, in a nice restaurant and learn more about other people's lives, to walk in their shoes for a while.

After finishing their mains, Honey's dessert arrived. She laid aside the fork provided and dug two fingers in from the top of the cake. She ate the sponge then licked and sucked at the chocolate oozing past her knuckles, all the while staring with her 'work eyes' at a nearby table full of male tourists.

After dinner they moved to Reggie Sunshine's, where a band played afro-jazz and couples danced pelvis to pelvis between the tables. Hermes ran over and gave Bruno a drunken hug. Immaculately dressed, with a scent of floral perfume and amyl-nitrate about him, he tried to pull Bruno up to dance.

'Hermes,' Bruno shouted over the noise of the band and the people. 'I'm the absolute worst dancer you'll ever see, don't even try.'

'Reggie calls the steps out between each song,' Hermes said, pointing at a man in sunglasses and a yellow blazer on the side of the stage.

'I'm sorry, Hermes. I can't.'

At the refusal, Hermes mocked offence, brought up his hand and chopped his fingers like a scissors. 'Come for a haircut, then. Don't be a stranger.' He swivelled on his heels and strutted back to the side of a floppy-haired tourist with an accessory bag draped over his shoulder.

They grabbed a table after a group of tourists moved on. Bruno drank one whisky after another, smiling at Anderson, who reclined in his chair, hat tilted ready to fall off, red-tipped cigar lodged between his fingers. He was almost zen-like in his calmness. Bruno imagined himself that content one day. An old man who'd done it all, whom nothing fazed, happy just to sit back and let the hours pass. Honey sat with her legs crossed and drank lemon-stained water from a champagne flute. Each time a tourist looked over, her legs would open momentarily as she re-crossed them in the other direction.

So this is life, Bruno thought, looking from the hypnotic tip of Anderson's cigar to watch the guitarist's fingers patter up and down the fretboard of his Gibson SG. Sweat had his shirt clinging to his back. The smell of spilled beer and body odour lingered as locals and tourists crowded every bit of space. They danced, smiled and sweated under a haze of tobacco smoke and condensation.

Bruno closed his eyes and listened to the music carrying through the speakers. He felt the throb of its bass and percussion in his bones. Thoughts of Bea crept into his consciousness, their first meeting, that smile, her eyes, hair, her stubborn confidence. He both hated and loved her. He rolled the peaty whisky around his mouth and swallowed slowly. 'You *are* family, Bea. You'll never take that away.' He had always been loyal to her, always would be, but she wasn't there for him any more. 'She'll come back,' he said to himself. Someday she'd come to him with her smiling eyes and make an apology, maybe even as soon as tomorrow, but until she did he'd have to push her out. He knew how dwelling on the past and pitying himself ended. 'No more,' he said.

The drinks kept coming. He opened one eye at a time to find the glass and drain it. When the effort to open an eye got too much, he kept the glass in his hand. Now and again someone tipped it upright against his chest to stop the whisky spilling out. He heard his name being called and prised an eye open. He squinted at Anderson's big face in front of him. 'Time to go home, son.'

'I'm fine,' he muttered, closing his eye again.

'You've had enough.'

He rubbed his face and turned away.

'It's two o'clock.'

He opened both eyes and looked around. Honey was dancing amongst a group of men. Most were laughing at her.

'Let me sleep for a…' He couldn't be bothered finishing the sentence. He let his eyes shut.

'Your work, Bruno! You start early.'

'One more minute.'

'Bruno! You have to go.'

'Fuck me! Anderson.' He got to his feet. 'You a spy,

or what?' His hip knocked against the corner of the table as he tried to squeeze past Anderson's chair. 'Bastard!' He brought his fist down on the table. He limped for the exit, rubbing his hip as he passed the smiling, glaring faces. He found the door, stepped onto the sand and walked into the night.

A smell of fish lingered in the camp. By the burned-out fire, plates and cutlery were clinging with fish skin and flesh. Fish heads and tails were amongst the coals.

'Fish!' he shouted, kicking a bowl at Carlos's tent. 'Stinking fish! And you expect me to clean it up. Bastards!' He flung open his shelter, dropped to the frond mats and pulled his sheet up to his neck.

*

When he woke a few hours later, with just enough clarity of mind to think despite his hangover, he decided the best way to deal with things at camp from now on was to pretend they didn't bother him.

He dragged himself out of his shelter and was relieved to find Carlos's and Bea's tents still shut. He set about cleaning the place, then had to scrub his hands with a slurry of sand and ginger as well as his soap to get the smell of fish off. He prepared the porridge and coffee. The cooking and cleaning had always been a ritual for him but today he had to push through it, struggling to convince himself that it wasn't an act of servitude or submission, but one of selflessness, beneficial for himself as much as anyone.

'*Bonjour*,' Carlos said when he emerged from his tent.

'*Bonjour*,' Bruno replied with forced enthusiasm.

When Bea came out she took a look around, hesitated, then sat down, her top lip puffing out. There was a frond mat set out on the freshly raked sand with bowls, spoons and coffee cups ready for them.

'Shall I serve the breakfast?' Bruno asked.

'*Oui monsieur, si'l te plait*,' said Carlos.

'I'll get mine later.' Bea took her towel from the line and walked over to the toilets.

Bruno watched Carlos leafing through the pages of his great *Book of Verses*. 'What's it telling you today then?' he asked, between mouthfuls.

Carlos closed it and smiled at him. 'Shall we check?' He shut his eyes. 'Open it.'

Bruno reached across, pinched a few pages and turned them over.

Carlos let his thumb hover in circles above the book. He let it drop, opened one eye then the other, and read: ' "And He considers the house of the wicked bringing the wicked to ruin." '

Bruno smirked.

'Bruno,' Carlos had a profound look in his eyes. 'It's time for you to show me the temple.'

'Whatever you say, Carlos. I'll never watch it again, but if that's what you want…' He clapped his hands together and stood. 'But now, I have work to go to.'

That night, from behind the upside-down tree, he and Carlos watched the capoeira procession pour in through the temple doors. Once the tourists had left, they sneaked around the back to the sacred fir trees lining the wall.

'Same time every night,' Bruno whispered. 'Always after the capoeira.' He put his hand on the trunk of the tree. 'This one here gives the best viewpoint. See the missing bricks? Keep quiet no matter what you see, or you'll get the whole campsite thrown out.'

Carlos raised a hand. 'No one will get thrown out.'

When Bruno got back to the campsite, he cleaned the mess left from Carlos and Bea's lunch and cooked a vegetable broth. Bea sat in silence, writing her letters.

'You eat fish now?' he asked.

'I eat what I eat.'

He sat in his hammock and tried to read, listening to

Bea's pen scratch across the paper, hearing the put-put-put of the bubbling soup. He remembered how she was before Carlos's arrival, so fragile, so distraught. It was hard to think of her as the same person. Could she really keep this up? Was he mistaken and it was actually just an act? Surely she hadn't got over Sean so easily.

'Work was good,' he said. She didn't look up. 'The guys seem a bit reluctant but it's not as bad as I thought it might be. Rudi's one of the best *capoeiristas* here. You should see what he can do.'

She let out a slow breath.

He removed his headlamp, got up and ladled broth into a bowl. 'Plenty here if you want any.'

She crawled into her tent.

Carlos came back just as Bruno was finishing his second helping. 'It's an outrage,' he said. Bruno thought he noticed a smirk on his face. 'An absolute outrage!'

'What did you see?' Bea had emerged from her tent and was fixing two bowls of broth.

'Heathens! Pagans! Voodoo! I saw voodoo in there tonight. Bruno, you call *that* a religion?'

'It is what it is,' said Bruno, lying back and holding his book up to read.

'It's a fetishist cult. I saw possession. Sin. Black magic. I could feel the evil. Those drums. By God, there's something terrible in those rhythms. That Faka's at the root of it, not Mac. He's more beast than man.'

'Did they sacrifice anything tonight?' Bea asked, handing him a bowl.

'A few chickens. Snapped their necks and bled them into conch shells, wings flapping even in death. Poor souls.'

'They probably didn't need to sacrifice anything big after murdering Iansa.' Bruno winced behind his book.

'What did you say she looked like again?' Carlos asked. Bruno spied on them over the book spine.

'Beautiful, Carlos. Swirling brown and white hair on

her sides, as if the wind had left an imprint on her. Like a masterpiece by Vincent van Gogh.'

'Mac wears her.'

'Excuse me?'

'A coat. Mac wears her hide like a great, armless coat.'

Bea placed her bowl on the sand and vomited. Her dead eyes fell on Bruno. He threw his book aside, slid out of the hammock and headed for the hill.

'I wondered if you were going to ask me,' Anderson said. It was lunchtime. He and Bruno were on their way to *A Gata Preta*. 'What took you so long?'

'My head's been full, Anderson. It's a big change. This brewery's such a responsibility. Got to get the guys motivated, teach Tiago, meet the demand at the *carrinhos*. And there's more and more tourists arriving. What's going on? It's supposed to be low season.'

'She'll be wondering what's happened to me after this. The most well-read man in Brisas back to one crime thriller a month!'

'I hope Mac's not there.'

'Don't worry about Mac. You're a local now. He hardly leaves the back office anyway… Wait here. I'll go in first and let Rosy know. Don't want the same treatment you got last time.'

Anderson opened the door and stepped inside. The sound of the metallic chime muffled as he closed it behind him. Bruno caught a glimpse of the wild-haired Rosy behind the counter. Moments later, Anderson had the door ajar and was beckoning him in.

Rosy busied herself stamping books. The percolator at her elbow was full to the brim and the same scent of stale coffee and old books met Bruno's nose.

A pair of tourists reclined on the brown leather couch beneath the window, their feet resting on the edge of the coffee table, strewn with magazines etched with coffee rings.

They looked up from their reading, and Bruno gave them a pleasant nod.

'I believe you've met Bruno already, Rosy.' Anderson held his hat to his chest. 'He's the one building the brewery over there by the upside-down tree.'

'Hmm.' She brought the stamp down hard, closed the book and picked up another. 'Welcome,' she said.

'Thank you, Rosy.' Bruno stepped forward and extended his hand. She looked at it as if it were the paw of a leprous rat and inched a limp hand towards it. He gave it a gentle shake.

'Books are my passion,' he said. 'I'll be in here quite a lot.'

'Hmm,' she uttered, stamping the next book.

As Anderson asked for two coffees, Bruno scanned the shelves. Adventure, Thriller, Romance, Classics. His eyes fell on Austin, Bulgakov, Camus, Dostoyevsky, Fitzgerald, Hemingway. 'Pushkin!' he said aloud and pulled *Eugene Onegin* from the shelf. Anderson came over and handed him a mug. He held the book to Anderson's nose and dragged his thumb over the pages. 'Breathe that in, Anderson. That's richer than any cigar... I can't believe this place exists!' He turned to Rosy. 'Rosy, are you the person I need to thank for this collection?'

'No,' she said in monotone. 'That would be...'

'My mother.' Mac stepped out from behind a shelf. He stood before them, head nearly touching the roof.

Bruno backtracked towards the door, almost dropping his coffee. 'She... she must have been an amazing woman.'

'You know who this man is?' Mac said in English to the smiling tourists. 'This is Vagabundo, but maybe Vagaburro is more apt now. He is the most important man in Brisas. The creator of Burro Beer. He's building a brewery that'll supply you with the best beer we could possibly offer.'

They smiled. 'Hope it's going to be strong,' one said. The other was pulling a camera from his pocket.

'And what will it run on, Vagaburro?'

'Mostly wind,' said Bruno.

'Wind!' Mac clapped his hands together. The whites of his eyes flashed and a smile spread across his face. 'Just like your kites,' he said to the tourists. 'When will it be ready?'

'Six months to eight months.'

'Six months! You can do it quicker. I know you can. Our finest tradesmen are working on this, and you have our full support.' Mac held up a finger to the tourists. 'I promise you,' he said, 'this brewery will be up and running by the high season. Tell all your friends.' He turned back to Bruno. 'The high season's approaching, Vagaburro. It's coming faster than ever. Keep your head out of the books and put it in the beer. Our tourists are thirsty!'

He made to walk away, but the tourist with the camera shouted after him. 'Mac, can we get a photo with you?'

'It's my pleasure.'

The tourists walked around the table. 'You come in too, Vagaburro,' the tourist said, as he handed the camera to Anderson. Mac threw his big arms around them, and Bruno stood at the side. Anderson lowered himself to a knee and clicked the shutter.

*

Bruno pushed forward and absorbed himself in his work, but kept a close eye on Bea for any sign of change in her feelings towards him. Instead of using the supermarket, he ordered all the barley, hops and brewer's yeast directly from Ivo, who sent a 4×4 to the city for what was needed. Along with the ingredients, Ivo handed him a few books on brewing, as he'd requested

'And the ones on wind and solar power?' Bruno asked.

'There wasn't any. The guy said he'll call headquarters and see what they can do. Next week we'll see.'

Bruno was uncomfortable with his position of authority, but was desperate to succeed. He managed to get Riccardo and Rudi constructing a base for the big brewery while he and the others put more keg breweries together. After building one while the guys watched, he left Selmo and Joao to build another as he walked Tiago through the brewing process. Tiago asked questions non-stop, and spoke over Bruno's answers. Selmo and Joao cried constantly for help. With all the distraction, the malt got burned, and the brew was ruined. They had to start over.

By the end of the second week things were improving, and with three times his previous capacity, Bruno had a lot of beer fermenting in the tanks.

Lagarto gave the keys of his flatbed truck to Tiago on the Saturday night of the third week, and he, Bruno and Riccardo left for the city early the next morning, when the tide was at its lowest.

After driving for an hour over the sand, crossing the mangrove plank bridges, and winding along on the dirt track hacked out of the forest, they turned onto the main road.

'Tarmacadam,' Bruno said.

Riccardo pushed his glasses up from the tip of his nose and looked at Bruno. 'You know what?' He spoke with the know-it-all-swagger the other guys made fun of him for behind his back. He pointed south. 'This road goes all the way to the end of the world.'

'Really, now that's a long road.' Bruno wound down the window and watched the road roll by in the mirror. The scent of salt and seaweed had gone from the hot air, replaced by the smell of bitumen baking in the sun. The warm morning breeze wafted in through the window. Bruno put his hand out and let the wind run through his fingers.

'You're from the south, are you not, Bruno?' said Tiago.

'Way down there,' he said, looking in the mirror. 'Yes.'

'Do you miss anything about it?'

He thought of Flora. He couldn't think of the south without her. She *was* the south. He remembered walking with her in the parks, the air so cold they could see their breath. 'Winter,' he said. 'The jacaranda trees, the *tipas*, the cold, fresh air, *café torrado*, *alfajores*.' He laughed. 'You ever tasted *alfajores?*'

'No,' they both said.

'Get yourselves down there. They almost make up for all the other shit.' Bruno closed the window, rested his head against it and watched the landscape. In all the hours of driving, it barely changed: grass, trees, mountains.

'There,' Bruno said. He lifted his head from the pane. A dusty grey blotch appeared in the blue sky. Soon the tops of tower blocks and cranes appeared. Roads snaked in between the trees from the surrounding hills, and the traffic increased as they drew nearer. The roads came together in a Celtic weave of grey amongst the green landscape. The trees, bushes and grass receded, giving way to dust and decay. For the first time in almost a year, Bruno found himself in the urban sprawl of a large city.

'The old hag,' Riccardo said, head tilted back, peering down through his thick glasses.

They rattled through the outskirts, passing run-down buildings, tyre and auto parts shops, everything thrown up haphazardly amid the roads and pathways. Shreds of polythene clung from concrete posts, plastic containers and bottles lay by dry thorn bushes that grew amongst the industrial scree by the roadside. Concrete storm channels, filled with trash and oil, followed the road and tunnelled under to join an open sewer grid. Telephone wires and electric cables were slung low in all directions, disappearing between buildings, many of which were unfinished: vertical columns of concrete and rebar with gaping holes and stacks of red-brick. People were squatting in the buildings. Soot from their grills stained the walls, clothes hung from the gaps between the concrete columns. Beneath each glassless window was a spatter of shit and piss where the inhabitants had slopped out.

The closer they got to the centre, the taller and more modern the buildings became. Behind a tall iron gate with a security guard posted outside, an old colonial building stood in a lush green garden. A leftover from the old world. There were high-walled communities with electric fences to keep the poor out and the rich in.

Bruno remembered a crippled man he'd met in a dosshouse when he first set off. He'd been stealing wing-mirrors from cars in a wealthy neighbourhood when a guard, who'd been asleep on a flattened cardboard box with a Kalashnikov for a pillow, woke and emptied the magazine into his legs. "Poor shooting poor!" the man had said. "For what? For the rich."

Bruno lowered the window to take everything in, but the air was filled with so much dust it left grit in his mouth. He caught a whiff of sewage as they passed a canal, and rolled the window up again.

'Look, Tiago.' Riccardo pointed at the open gate of a deserted construction site. A stack of plywood lay behind the gate next to a pile of timber posts. 'That wood will do for something.' He pushed his glasses back up.

The streets were quiet even though it was the middle of the day. The occasional group of poor people walked by in the distance. Immaculately dressed in clean, pressed clothes, leather-bound books in their hands. They were on their way to church. The rich never walked anywhere. They drove.

'Looks like the construction site will be using that,' said Bruno.

Riccardo looked at him then raised an eyebrow at Tiago. 'Let's take a look anyway.'

Tiago pulled in by the kerb and reversed up to the gate. Bruno hopped out to let Riccardo pass. 'You two wait here. I'll check everything out.'

'I'm not sure I like this, Tiago.' Bruno stood on the pavement with his hands on the truck seat.

'It's okay,' Tiago said. 'It's normal.'

'It's theft.'

Tiago shook his head. 'Riccardo will make sure it's all done right.'

Riccardo marched out of the site rubbing his hands together. 'Right, boys,' he said, repositioning his glasses again. 'He said it's ours.'

'Who?' asked Bruno.

'The guy in there. The boss. C'mon, help me lift it.'

Bruno looked up and down the street, as Tiago jumped out and took a corner of the stack. 'Quick, Bruno, it's heavy.'

Bruno skipped over and bent to grab a corner. They loaded all the wood onto the truck, and Riccardo wound it tight with heavy-duty straps. They scoured site after site, taking all they could; cables, wood, piping. Bruno knew it was wrong. He wanted to speak up against it. They could make money from the sales of the keg beer and buy what they needed. It would take much longer but the job would get done. Every time they stopped the desire to speak intensified, but each time he couldn't bring himself to do it. They always spoke first, and wouldn't lift anything by themselves. He was going to spend a lot of time with these guys. They were depending on him. He couldn't let the project end before it even started.

'These are huge companies,' said Riccardo. 'They won't miss a thing.'

Bruno latched onto the words. How many people had the companies cheated in the first place? Let go of a hundred staff one month, report record profits the next. He had a lot more to lose than any company did.

They missed the tide on the way back and had to park up on a plank bridge and wait for a few hours. They finally arrived in Brisas at dawn. The street cleaners, in their green uniforms, were scattered about town, their filled black bags leaving trails in the sand as they pulled them along at their heels.

Tiago flashed his lights at a pair of tourists lying on top

of one another on the beach, tops hitched to their shoulders and shorts lowered to their ankles. The man lifted his face from the girl's naked breasts and squinted into the lights of the truck. He managed to raise his middle finger before the girl pulled his head back down again. As they drove up Main Street one of the cleaners was helping a drunken tourist from a doorway.

Tiago smiled at Bruno. 'The high season's coming quick this year.' They parked the truck at the top of the town, and Bruno walked back to his shelter.

12

Bruno decided not to go back to the city. He explained, made sketches and wrote lists of what was needed, and let the guys sort it out. He knew it wasn't honest, wasn't the right thing to do, but it was the only way the project could go ahead. He'd have to set his own views aside for the benefit of the town. He could use his influence once he'd established himself.

With the decking almost complete, the whole thing began to feel real. This was actually happening. At night, he'd bite his lip and stare at the roof of his shelter, thinking about it. He was finally part of something bigger than himself. Flora had her paintings. He'd have his brewery.

The more time Bruno spent with Tiago, the more he came to like him. Unlike the others, who sneaked off every chance they got to smoke and gossip over card games, Tiago showed a genuine interest. He read and reread the books on brewing, and involved himself in all aspects of the project. Because of his enthusiasm, Bruno tried even harder to explain everything properly, and give him the best education he was able to provide.

'Make every mistake only once, Tiago, and you'll be the best brew-master... In fact, the best anything in the world. Don't be afraid to make mistakes; just don't make the same one twice.'

*

As Bruno hauled the kegs around and manipulated beams for the construction of a frame that would become the skeleton of a full-sized, gravity fed brewery, he realised how unfit he was. Three sizes, the beautiful Fatima told him he'd dropped. He gripped a bicep, touched his hands together around his thigh, reached back and patted his bony shoulder blades. What had once been dense muscle was now atrophied and weak. He had to do something about it.

He began to pay more attention to the movements of the *capoeiristas* in the *roda*, and watched Carlos perform his morning yoga and breathing routine. During lunch breaks, when the men were at home or occupied in a game of cards, he would slip down behind the decking towards the mangroves, and copy both workouts.

One afternoon, with sweat dripping off him, he was trying the side-back step that all the *capoeiristas* began with. He was throwing his arms up and out, kicking his legs back and forth like a speed skater in reverse, when he thought he heard laughter. He stopped, looked about and waited. When nobody appeared, he started up again. Laughter, unmistakable laughter.

Tiago stepped out from the side of the temple. 'Nice moves.'

'You're spying on me? Come down here.' He drank water from his bottle and poured some over his head.

Tiago descended, red-faced and trying not to laugh again. 'You'll be ready to take on Mac in no time.'

'I can't believe you've caught me. I just want to get fit. I've wasted away.'

'Don't be embarrassed. Watch.' Tiago crouched into position. 'I'll show you how it's done.' He performed the move at a slow pace. 'It's called the *ginga*.'

Bruno drank again (the taste of Carlos's wine in water had disappeared since having the house red at the restaurant), re-capped the bottle and threw it aside. 'Now, don't laugh,' he said. In slow, unbalanced steps, he performed the manoeuvre.

'That's it.' Tiago joined him and counted out the steps. 'The arm comes up to block any strikes to the face, like this, and from this position you can choose your attack.' He threw a low, spinning kick and stood upright again.

'Could you maybe teach me some stuff?'

'Of course! But you should get *abadas*. The ass will tear right out of those linens. Hermes will be after you.'

Bruno nodded. 'Next pay day, I'll get some.'

'I'm sure Fatima will pick out a good *coh-lah* for you.'

Things were not improving between him and Bea. She seemed to be tunnelling deeper inside herself. He'd catch a look in her eyes before she turned away and see only empty hollows. She was gone. She never started a conversation and always replied with the minimum of words when he asked her anything.

The further she withdrew from Bruno, the closer she got to Carlos. She prepared all his food, washed his clothes, and even read the *Book of Verses* for him. One time, Bruno came back to the camp to find her dragging her turtle shell brush through his hair. She did it all with the kind of adoring, dependent nature of an infant for its mother. It was as if an unseen umbilical cord held them together.

At the *carrinhos*, surrounded by tourists, Bruno noticed how she watched Carlos. The look in her eyes couldn't have been more different from the way she looked at him. It was full of passion and care rather than indifference. Whenever Carlos wasn't paying her attention, she headed to the nearest man, put a hand on his shoulder and flirted with him, constantly looking at Carlos for any reaction. There was none. He didn't seem to be aware. Bruno watched it all from the shadow of the carts. It sickened him to see Bea throwing herself at Carlos, and it was worse still to see how her jealousy caused her to run to the closest person, with no thought for how it might affect them – she was still sought after by those around her. Carlos had done this. He'd made her this way, and Bruno hated him for it because he couldn't bring himself to hate Bea.

One afternoon, when Bruno returned to look for a pipe-fitting he thought might be in his storage compartment, he found Carlos and Bea sitting together at her tent. Carlos was dictating a letter to her.

In his shelter, trawling through the scrap, he caught only some words of Carlos's dictation, '*enterprise, old world values, apocalypse... This paper is my body, this ink is my blood.*' Empty handed, Bruno slipped out of the shelter and was about to make for the brewery, when Carlos called him over.

'Bruno,' he said, holding the letter up. 'Tell me, what colour is this writing?'

Bruno leaned in and looked at the beautiful script. She'd got hold of a calligraphic nib for her pen somewhere. 'It's red,' he said. 'Crimson, if you want me to be specific.'

'Exactly!' Carlos beat a hand on his thigh and handed the page back to Bea. 'Yes-yes-yes... Crimson. Deep blue crimson.' He shrieked with laughter.

With Carlos and Bea cooking their own food and eating meat with every meal, Bruno returned to the campsite each day to find the place in a mess. Pots, cutlery and utensils were covered in fat and gravy. The coals of the fire teemed with bones and fish scales. The sand was never raked, and was strewn with bloody polythene torn from meat packaging. It became too much effort for him to pretend nothing was wrong. He stopped cleaning and had every meal at a restaurant. Without seeming to notice, Bea began washing whatever she and Carlos needed before they used it, but the fire was never properly tended to, and the place was never raked again.

One hot day, Bruno was trying to read in his hammock, but there were so many flies buzzing around him that he couldn't get through a sentence without having to swat a fly away. He unseated the hammock netting and carried it in a bundle to the brewery. After that, he read between the frame posts on the decking, and if he wanted company, he'd visit Anderson at his day-bar. He only ever went back to the campsite to sleep.

Bruno longed for and dreaded the coming pay day because it meant seeing Fatima again. He'd thought about her every day since their meeting. He had looked out for her everywhere he went, but never once saw her in the bookshop where he took his coffee breaks, or the supermarket which he frequented more than was necessary in the hope of seeing her.

Much of the time, his thoughts of Fatima didn't occur independently. His head was still full of Bea and how she'd reacted. He knew it wasn't right, but every time he found himself dwelling on her, he forced himself to picture Fatima instead. He used her image to live out the deep-seated desires he'd buried since losing Flora.

At night, before sleep, he'd call back the sight of the golden down on Fatima's toned legs, and in the morning he'd wake, push all other thoughts aside and see her smiling, gap-toothed mouth and slanted, sleepy eyes.

Over the passing weeks, he learned all he could about her from Tiago and the other guys, asking them in indirect ways so as not to arouse any suspicion of his interest. Apart from Bea, she was the most beautiful girl he'd seen in town. He learned that she lived in a bedsit above the shop, with a terrace on the roof, where she supposedly lay naked and read books under the sun. Originally from Jinguba, she was home-schooled by her parents, who'd had her late in life, and died before she was out of her teens. Fearing that the other children would abuse her because of her disability, they'd installed the roof terrace to their Jinguban home to keep her isolated. She'd go up there to watch the normal children play, but was never allowed out amongst them. Her only friends were the characters in the stories she read.

Here in Brisas she was only ever seen walking from her shop to the supermarket and to the bookshop. She never went to the restaurants or bars or wandered on Main Street to see the travellers and tourists, as many of the farmers and fishermen did. She was content living her life in the twenty square metres of her building.

Bruno dreamt up all kinds of scenarios about how his next meeting with Fatima would go. It always started with him mentioning the book on her desk, and would lead to long, passionate conversations about favourite authors and books and characters, and then to taking her out to the restaurants for the first time, where, having never touched alcohol before, she'd drink wine and wince at its strength. They'd dance near the speakers in bars so she could move her body to the vibration. The locals would be so surprised at how well she danced, but Bruno would know better. On occasion, he'd take her to the *carrinhos*. Bea and Carlos would come up alongside and Bea would say, '*Who's this then?*'

'*Just a friend, Bea,*' he'd reply. '*Just a friend.*' And he'd leave the three of them standing together while he got drinks for himself and Fatima alone. '*Where's mine?*' Bea might ask, and Bruno would look at Carlos and say: '*Better get moving, my boy, your girl wants a drink.*' Tourists and locals alike would sense something special about them and want to feed off their energy, but they'd be oblivious to it, focusing only on each other. They'd become closer as he expanded her world from that twenty square metres and brought her out into the open, just like Flora had done by taking him out of the orphanage.

His imagination played like a film. They would become best friends then lovers. He'd take her virginity – gently, of course, very gently – and she'd find such an unrestrained pleasure in sex that neighbours would blush whenever their paths crossed; her deafness preventing her from hearing the volume of her enjoyment. Eventually, they'd move to a house just outside town, grow their own fruit, vegetables and herbs, or pick them straight from the tree. They'd have great philosophical debates and arguments over the dining table. She'd win most of the time but not all, and there'd be tearful apologies and blissful make-ups. Inevitably, he'd grow old. With her arms around him, he'd close his eyes for the final time, having found, in the end, absolute love and happiness.

In his imagination all this happened and more. It was fun to think about these things, but he knew how ridiculous he was being. He should be concentrating on designing the first wind turbine and processing more constructive ideas. He was also aware that every thought of Fatima carried with it an undercurrent relating to Bea.

When Tiago handed him his pay packet, Bruno marched off without telling him where he was going. Before he'd even got his hand on the door handle he was sweating. After a few calming breaths, he wiped his forehead dry and pushed the door open. His foot hovered mid-step. The game of strategy whirring in his head halted. In all the scenarios he'd visualised, not one of them had accounted for another customer being in the shop.

*

'Vagabundo,' said Faka. 'The Parasite Prince. Look how you walk around in those new clothes and neat hair. You look almost normal. Don't stand! Come in… Browse.'

Bruno mouthed 'Hello,' to Fatima. She smiled at him.

'As I was saying,' Faka said to Fatima, then turned to Bruno so she couldn't lip read, 'before this piece of shit interrupted us.' He turned back. 'I want everything black. Black *abadas*, black shirt, black T-shirt, black espadrilles. Everything. Black. D'ye hear that?'

'Yeh, I hear.' She stepped out from behind the desk and

began picking the items from the shelves. Bruno watched her as she moved, her tanned legs and caramel hair, the curve of her breast within the fabric of her shirt.

Faka spoke to her back. 'Maybe I'll bend you over that desk later. Bet you'd enjoy that, wouldn't you?'

On his way out, Faka nudged Bruno with his shoulder. A trace of body odour lingered in the shop. Fatima wedged the door open.

'He's not a good man,' she said. 'Bad eneh-gy.'

'And smell,' Bruno whispered. She shrieked with laughter. 'He's a bully,' Bruno added. 'Does he intimidate you?'

She shook her head. 'No. You?'

'A little bit.' He looked at the book. *Ask her about it.* 'I need *abadas*,' he said. 'My apprentice is teaching me some moves.'

'Why?'

'I want to get fit again.'

'Squat, push-up and yoga. All you need.'

'I... I'll do that too.' He wiped his forehead and cleared his throat. 'Maybe you can teach me the yoga part?'

She smiled but glanced at the floor.

He took a breath and changed the subject. 'What colour of *abadas*, do you think?'

'White,' she said.

'Two pairs, then.' He stared at the book. 'You like to read, don't you? I mean, you have the book on the table, so I'm just assuming you do. I like reading too. I read all the time.'

'Yeh. Love this book.' She touched her ear. 'I can't hear, so I read authors who describe smell and texture.' She tapped her nose. 'Suskin, Murakami.'

He smiled. 'That's great.'

'Because I can't relate to sound,' she said, tugging her earlobe.

'I get it,' he said. 'I like psychological books. Dostoyevsky is my favourite.'

'Oh, I love him too, and Pushkin, and Dickens, London, and Orwell.'

He beamed. 'I love them all! You read in English?'

'Only Portuguese.'

He cleared his throat again. 'Maybe I, I mean, if you want, I can take you to the bookshop sometime and recommend a book for you?' He held his breath and pleaded to her with his eyes.

She smiled but looked down again and went to get the *abadas*.

He didn't like to ask any more. He had imposed himself enough on her already. He left the shop, desperate to ask Bea for advice, but had to accept that it wasn't a possibility. He'd have to figure this out on his own, or speak to Honey.

That night, surrounded by kegs, he lay in his hammock under the electric lights that Riccardo and the guys had finally installed on the half-built frame. He tried to read through his philosophy books, but his mind kept wandering. He switched all the lights off, looked up at the constellations and pushed all thoughts of Fatima, troubles with Bea and pressures of work aside. He concentrated on the river, visualised his trek along its bank, heading upstream amongst the trees and bushes, amid nature, hacking with his machete, deafened by the birdsong and the scratching percussion of the cicadas, keeping an eye out for the snakes and tarantulas. The butterflies fluttered like falling purple petals of jacaranda trees. With heavy feet and a tired body, he arrived. He was in the heart of the rainforest. He breathed the fresh forest air, his eyes full of wonder, excitement and a sense of achievement. He slept.

Early the next day, watching to make sure no one was around, Bruno imitated Carlos's yoga and breathing routine. He washed under a hose at the keg brewery manifold and made for Horizon Cafe on Main Street.

Horizon was the first place to open each day in Brisas.

Since he'd stopped eating at the campsite, he'd been going there every morning for breakfast. He took his usual table by the railing, a few back from that of the town cleaners, and waited for Gina, the glum-faced waitress, to bring him his banana pancakes and black coffee. He watched her slow approach, hypnotised by her pendulous, funeral-march gait. The plate slammed on the table, making him jump. 'Thanks, Gina,' he said. 'Good morning.'

'If you say so.' She walked off.

Why are you so different in the temple? He wanted to ask her. She was one of the most enthusiastic dancers, was always cleaning the place and tending to the plants and herbs. How could someone be so much one thing at one time and something so different at another? *Balance, Vagabundo. Balance!* Mac's voice boomed in his head.

There were only two street cleaners at the table this morning. Their rakes, garbage pliers and bulky refuse bags were propped up against the patio on the sand below. Normally there were five of them, boisterous women, talking over each other in shrill voices about what they had seen and put up with that dawn: waking drunk tourists, filling bags with cigarette-ends and cups, raking spilled beer, the piss, the condoms, the vomit, the shit! But they were a team. They did their part for the town and kept each other going.

Today there was no talk. Bruno watched the pair, sitting silently side by side, sipping now and again from the mugs in front of them. Their food was barely touched. They were too quiet. Something had to have happened. He glanced in the direction of the campsite, fearing for Bea.

Halfway through his breakfast, he heard agitated voices out on the street. Mac, with his hard black eyes sloe-glazed with sleep, appeared alongside the cleaners' table with another of their number and Hermes, who was dressed in silk pyjamas and looked like Mac had reached in through his roof and plucked him straight from bed.

'Are they still down there?' Mac demanded. 'They're still asleep?'

'Still at the corral, Mac,' one of the cleaners said. 'Horses are all worked up.'

Mac slammed his hand on the railing and started moving again. He glanced at Bruno. 'Vaga— Bruno! Come.'

Bruno dropped his cutlery, took a swig of coffee and dropped a few *contos* on the table to cover his bill. He ran down the street after them.

Two male tourists were lying against the back fence of the corral. The gate was open and the horses cowered together, moving as a herd away from a horse with mud all over its legs. It had an oozing, bloody stump where its tail should have been. It threw its head and neighed, trotted on skittish legs and tried to merge with the herd. They kept their distance by kicking out whenever it got close. Two cleaners, standing over the tourists, backed away as Mac approached.

'Get the gate, Bruno,' Mac said.

Bruno closed the gate and looked at the unconscious men. One of them had a roll of duct tape in his hand, the other held a bundle of orange fishing twine.

'When did you find them?' Mac crouched to check each man's neck for a pulse. He held the back of his hand to their lips.

'Maybe two hours past,' one of the cleaners said, looking at the other.

'Two hours! Why didn't you inform me?'

'We thought them just drunks. Smell the drink on 'em. Didn't see no rush.'

'We didn't notice the horse was gone till it came back,' said the other.

Bruno counted the horses. 'There's another one missing,' he said.

Mac glanced at him then scanned the horses, working his fingers into the oily skin of his neck as he counted them out.

Hermes knelt by the men. 'Wake up, boys,' he said. 'Time to get up now.'

'Go wake Silvia,' Mac said to the cleaners. 'Tell her to see to these damn horses!' As they hurried off, Mac prodded one of the men with the sole of his foot, crouched again, and slapped the man's face. 'Wake! Wake up now!' He peeled back the man's eyelid.

'Drugs?' Hermes asked, unbuttoning the pouch of his shoulder bag. He produced a brown bottle, uncapped it and held it to the man's nose and mouth. His nose and eyes twitched, his head inched away, his hand, still clutching the duct tape, rose to his face and tried to swat the bottle. Bruno stared at the man's grip on the tape. He was holding it so tightly his fingernails were white.

Mac reached over and tried to pull one of the man's fingers loose. 'It's not normal,' he whispered to Hermes. He stood, looked towards Main Street then crouched again.

Hermes held the back of the man's head, keeping his nose to the bottle. Mac took the man's hand and whispered in a language Bruno had never heard before. It sounded ancient and tribal.

He listened to Mac's voice and smelled the roots and earth on him. His mind filled with visions of camp fires, in forest clearings enveloped in darkness. He saw the pounding of drums, and tribal women dancing. He saw sacrifice, could feel the heat of the fire, the reverberation of the drums. One by one, Mac peeled the man's fingers from the tape.

The man strained with more force to tear himself from the bottle, but Hermes held firm. His eyes began twitching as if a nerve were trapped. They shot open and he bent forward with such momentum that Bruno and Hermes jumped clear. The man's eyes were alert and staring. His first breath was so deep it was as if he'd been brought back from the dead rather than roused from sleep. He began to hyperventilate. Mac held him by the shoulders against the fence. 'Calm down,' he whispered. 'Calm down.' He looked at Hermes.

'I'll get a buggy,' said Bruno, staring at the man's eyes, unable to comprehend what he'd seen. Both the men reeked of alcohol, but Bruno had never seen a drunkard come round like that. Could it have been the concoction in Hermes's bottle? The strange words Mac whispered? Both? Maybe it was the result of some party-drug the guy had taken. He'd witnessed possession in the temple, but up close, this was different. It seemed real.

'What do you remember?' Mac asked. The man's eyes didn't even flicker. There was no sign that he could hear or see him.

'I'll go and get a buggy,' Bruno said again.

'Don't just say it!' said Mac. 'Get one!'

Bruno knocked on the door of Tiago's parents' house and shouted for him until his mother opened it. 'I work with Tiago,' he said between breaths.

'I know who you are. What do you want?'

'The keys of the buggy.'

Tiago opened an upstairs window and squinted down. He looked at his watch. 'What's up, Bruno?'

'Need the keys!'

'Mum, give him the keys. You need me now?'

'No. I'll see you at the brewery.'

Tiago's mother came back through the hall, dropped the keys into Bruno's hand then closed the door.

Both men were awake and talking when Bruno returned.

'I don't know what happened,' one of them said, in Italian. They looked around in confusion.

'Start with what you remember,' said Mac.

'We were at the cocktail carts,' said the other. 'Drinking, dancing.' He looked at his friend.

'Yes... Like everybody else. Having fun. That's what we're here for. That's it. I can't remember anything else.'

'Look at that horse,' Mac said. 'See the blood? Why did you do it? Why the tape? Why the twine?'

'I… We didn't do anything!'

'We didn't!'

Silva came running over. 'We think Honey's missing,' she said. 'She didn't appear at Andre's with the tithe this morning. She's never been late.'

Mac stared at the men. 'Tell us what you've done!'

'We haven't done anything!'

One tried to stand, but Mac's hand landed on his shoulder and almost forced him through the fence. 'Drink? Drugs? What did you take? Who were you with?'

Bruno looked at the mud on the horse's legs. 'The mangroves,' he said.

'Hermes,' Mac said. 'Take Bruno. Get twenty men. Go search the mangroves. Silvia, get Faka, then deal with the horses.' Hermes and Bruno began walking. 'The keys, Bruno!' Mac shouted. 'Give me the keys.'

Bruno tossed the keys to him and took another look at the men. 'If you've fucking hurt her!' he said, but didn't finish his sentence. He chased after Hermes.

They crossed over to Main Street, where shop workers were dragging out their postcard and sunglasses stands. Bruno looked towards the bay and fell behind Hermes. Carlos, with his great, broad back bared to the sun, was up to his knees in the water, helping a pair of fishermen push their boat out.

'Hermes,' said Bruno. 'I'll get Bea. You get the rest. Make sure you take Anderson. He'll want to help.' He ran to the campsite.

Bea was sitting by her tent, filling a page in red ink. 'Honey's missing,' he said. 'We think she's in the mangroves. Let's go.'

Her eyes softened for a moment. 'What happened?'

'Something fucking strange, Bea.' He ran his hands through his hair. 'We've found tourists with tape and rope outside the corral, a horse going crazy with a bloody stump for a tail, and there's another one missing. Honey didn't pay her tithe this morning.'

'It's this place,' she said. 'Carlos is right. There's a bad energy here.'

Bad energy. It was an echo of how Fatima described Faka. 'I'm sure we'll find her safe, Bea. Probably in bed with some young stud having the time of her life.' He smiled at her, but she didn't smile back.

'We better get looking. Come on.'

'I can't.'

'Bea, put our problems aside!'

'I'll only slow you down.'

'This is Honey. She's your friend.'

A tear fell onto her page. 'I can't, Bruno. I hope you find her.' She nodded, as if convincing herself there was nothing more she could do. Her pen began moving across the page again.

'Okay…' He looked around at the mess. 'Okay, well, at least ask around town. Maybe someone saw something.' He turned to walk away.

'I think I saw her at the *carrinhos* with two guys,' she said.

'You were there?'

'Two guys,' she repeated. 'Typical Italians. Sleazy, oiled hair, too much aftershave.'

Bruno drew a breath. 'We'll find her safe, Bea. Don't worry.'

In the mangroves, they split into pairs. Bruno and Tiago pulled their sodden, bare feet through the mud and trickling streams, sending crabs scuttling. Shouts of 'Honey!' echoed all around them. Bruno stopped by a tree with giant telescopium snails clustering on its roots. He removed his shirt and tied it around his head to stop the sweat dripping into his eyes. Tiago did the same. Tanagers and seedeaters watched motionless from their branches.

Bees circled around flowers and their bulb-like hives. Because of the wetness there were no tracks. Any footprint was sucked up in the mud or washed away in the streams or by the tide. With the pairs hacking branches and crossing paths time and again, it was impossible to find any signs of where she or the horse could have passed before them. The only trail to be found was the one Tonino had formed after years of trekking on his daily tours.

'Nobody knows this place better than Tonino,' said Tiago. 'It's a shame he deserted us. We could really use him now.'

Bruno bent to roll his trouser legs up again. 'It's a tragedy he's not here,' he agreed, and cupping his mouth, shouted out again: 'Honey!'

They searched into the early afternoon, coming into contact with the others numerous times, but nobody had seen a thing.

Bruno's water bottle was nearly empty. He filled it at a stream. As Tiago crouched to do the same, shouting came from the direction of the town. They rushed to higher ground. Down on the beach, the horse was limping along, its tail a bloody, black hole.

Two men emerged from the trees, got hold of it and started leading it back towards town. 'It's Joao and Azevedo,' said Tiago. He looked at his watch. 'Maybe we should go to the meeting point.'

They found the others already at the honey well, sitting on and around its heavy concrete covering. A beekeeper hopped on between them and poured the contents of his plastic jug in through a small metal standpipe protruding from the centre. The path winding back to town was lined with *dendê* palms, their orange fruits bunched around the leaf bases. Under the palms, beekeepers worked between the beehives. They wore no protective clothing, every movement slow and methodical to avoid aggravating the bees – *meliponines*. They had no sting but were ferocious biters.

'We've been everywhere,' said Riccardo, straddling one of the many rebar handles moulded into the concrete. He was the laziest of Bruno's workers, spending most of his days hiding behind the upside-down tree smoking roll-ups. 'If she was here we'd have found her by now.'

'It's a huge forest,' Bruno said. 'We haven't checked half of it. We should keep looking.'

A waiter from the Dolphin spat onto the mud. 'She's a hooker. Who cares?'

'She's a—' Bruno began, but Hermes shouted over him, 'She's a good person! A unique person, and this town's done well by her. What's a few more hours?'

The waiter began tapping his ring on a padlocked chain slung from a rebar handle to the well's base. The key of the padlock would no doubt be clipped to Mac's *abadas*.

'I'll keep looking till it's dark,' Anderson said, fanning himself with his hat.

'Me too,' said Bruno. 'All the brewery guys will.' He looked at Riccardo, Rudi and the others.

'We'll keep looking,' said Riccardo, eyeing Bruno, 'because it's best for the town.'

'Good,' said Hermes. 'Whoever wants to go back is free to do so. But you'll have Mac to report to. He arranged this, not me.' No one spoke. The only noise was the waiter's ring clicking on the chain. 'That settles it, then. We'll meet here again at six. That's not long, so let's get going. Search as far as you can. And remember, if you get lost, find a stream and follow it. If you face the same direction as it's flowing in, the town is on your right.'

Bruno and Tiago hurried away from the group, determined to get deeper into the forest. Espadrilles in their hands, they skipped over rocks and waded through streams. The forest was alive with noise: the squelching of their feet, the flow of water, the rustle of leaves, and the buzzing of the bees. Bruno couldn't believe how many hives there were. Here, the forest was filled with exotic flowers, colourful birds and trees of all shades of green.

'Look at this place,' he shouted back to Tiago, who was struggling to keep up. 'It's beautiful. God, I hope she's okay.'

'I've never been five steps in here before,' Tiago said, knocking the branches from his face. 'Don't think I've sweated as much in my life.'

'Keep drinking.'

They searched on, sodden with sweat and mud, and found themselves at one of the plank bridges. As Tiago looked around on top, Bruno searched underneath. She wasn't there.

'It's almost six,' said Tiago.

Bruno paid no attention.

Bruno continued into the forest with Tiago drifting farther behind. 'Maybe it's time to go,' Tiago called.

'Let's just search a little bit longer, there's still light.' They walked on, the darkness in the east reaching like a claw to the west.

'We should get back,' Tiago said. 'They're expecting us. We can't have them searching for us as well.'

Bruno ran his hand through his hair and shouted for her again. He crouched and rubbed his eyes. Tiago began walking towards the town.

'Fuck!' Bruno roared. The nearby birds flew from their branches. He got up and followed after him.

At the meeting point, they found Hermes sitting alone.

'Any sign?' asked Bruno.

Hermes shook his head. 'You're the last two. Nobody's seen a thing. Every guesthouse has been checked. She's vanished.'

'I'll keep looking,' Bruno said. 'I can't just give up on her. She could be lying somewhere. She could be in trouble.'

'Bruno, you've done your best. We all have. It's dark. Get some rest.' Hermes stood, put his arms around them and led them back to town.

The two horses were gone by the time they returned. Their frantic cries and attempts to reintegrate with the herd had been too disturbing and may have distressed the tourists. They'd been dragged off and disposed of.

*

Bruno went to let Bea know that they hadn't been able to find Honey, but as he walked past the campsite toilets he changed his mind. Bea and Carlos were at Abilio's area. Bea sat beating a tambourine against her palm, Abilio played a pair of bongos, and Golias strummed his guitar. Carlos, on his feet, held the infant in his arms and spun it around in circles. He spied Bruno and let the infant down. It waddled for Bea and tripped into her lap. Carlos's lips moved, and they all looked over at Bruno.

'Come here, Vagabundo!' Carlos shouted. 'Pick up an instrument.'

The scent of cedar wood caught Bruno's nose. He ignored Carlos's words and all their glares, and headed down the trail to the day-bars.

'Everyone deals with these situations differently,' Anderson said, taking a seat on the bar stool next to Bruno. 'Some people fall apart, some accept it and get on with things, others ignore it and preoccupy themselves.' His tongue darted out of his mouth, licked his upper lip and slipped back inside.

'You think those tourists killed her? You don't think she could be lying somewhere? She might need us. We should look more.'

'I don't know what to think.' Anderson lit a cigar. 'Wherever she is or whatever's happened, I know she wouldn't want us to make too much of a fuss. Maybe she finally swam out to one of those boats she was always talking about.'

'Oh, come on, Anderson. Those guys tied something to the horses. Bea said she saw her with them.'

'What can we do, Bruno?' He pulled on his cigar, inhaling the smoke. Bruno had never seen him inhale before. 'They've been in every room in town. She isn't here.'

'We should search some more.'

Anderson expelled his lungs toward the tube-light. Flies beat against it on their way to the blue zapper. He licked his lips again. 'Mac had Lagarto rig up a gate on the upside-down tree. He's locked them up in its trunk. If they've done anything, he'll get it out of them. You and I just need to hold tight and stay calm.'

'We need to search more.'

Anderson shook his head and slid off the bar stool. 'Fuck, Bruno. You think too much. Let it go. It's in God's hands. Here... Let's drink.' He walked into the kiosk, pulled a bottle of whisky from the top shelf and snapped two glasses together. 'A Scotsman left this a while ago. Told me it was from a small island. I forget the name, but he said it has a horseshoe-shaped waterfront where all the houses are painted different colours.'

Bruno picked up the bottle and read aloud: 'Ledaig.' He handed it back to Anderson, whose yellowed eyes were more bloodshot than usual.

'Anyway. He said that all the rich people owned these colourful houses by the water, and all the poor people lived in the houses up on the hill looking down on them. Said it was the only place he knew of where the poor looked down on the rich.'

Anderson poured three fingers of whisky into each glass. 'What's this got to do with Honey?'

'It's not about Honey! Honey's...' He waved his hand and shook his head. 'The poor look down on the rich here too.'

'And in Rio.'

Anderson ignored him. He peered into the darkness, towards the interior. 'From up on those hills, toiling in the allotments. You're the man with all the philosophy books, all the psychology. You should know how things are.'

Bruno realised that Anderson was drunk. He'd never seen him drunk before. There was no slurring of words, no lack of coordination in his limbs, just a subtle change in his demeanour, and this rambling, pointless speech. So this was how Anderson dealt with things. The same way as he himself had done most of the time. The bottle.

'You read all these books, Bruno, these giant books that you quote from, but you rely on them too much.' He patted his finger against his lips and dragged again on the cigar. 'On the one hand, you want to control what you can't control, and on the other, you don't have the confidence to say what you really mean. What *you* really think and mean, not your books. I'm a lot older than you, son. Don't be afraid to be yourself, but know that everyone else has to be themselves, too. Don't dwell on the inside, look out and take an interest. They have their own things going on. If people judge me, you know what I say?'

Bruno shook his head.

'Fuck 'em. I've done the best I could with what I was born with. I go to sleep satisfied every night.' He looked around. 'This is my lot. I've looked after myself. Don't be too afraid to live on instinct.' He skulled his drink and poured another. 'Stop standing under these giant books, Bruno. There's a whole world around you.'

Bruno sniffed at his whisky.

'Anyway,' Anderson continued. He raised his glass. 'To Honey, or you and me, or Carlos or Bea or whoever the fuck really gives a damn. I'm going to look after myself, that's all I know, okay? Everything else will work out on its own.' He drained the glass and lowered it.

Bruno emptied his glass and slammed it on the bar next to Anderson's.

'I don't know what you're trying to tell me.'

'Do what's right for you.'

'I think they've killed Honey.'

'And what made them kill her? What if they had no choice?'

'What are you saying, Anderson?'

'There's a bad energy, Bruno. Something's not right here any more.'

Bruno couldn't sit and do nothing. He grabbed his headlamp from the campsite and went searching again. He wandered through the coconut palms and then went down onto the beach and scoured the sand. He walked every street and went back to the mangroves, crossing the plank bridges and wading through the silt and the wash of the rising tide. Before dawn, he spoke to the street cleaners, who said they hadn't seen or heard anything.

After a strong coffee at the Horizon to lift the weight from his eyes, he followed the allotment farmers all the way out to the fruit trees at the foot of the hills. He was tired and anxious from the coffee on an empty stomach and a lack of sleep. They had no information. They told him to go home. Not knowing what to do with himself, he tried to help some of them pick oranges, but realised through their subtle glances and mumbling that he was making a nuisance of himself. They didn't want him there. He headed straight to the brewery, where the men waited for their orders.

A crowd of tourists gathered to protest the imprisonment of the two men in the cavernous trunk of the upside-down tree. Each day the crowd grew larger. The prisoners shouted at Bruno and his workers, as they went about their construction work, and as much as Bruno didn't want to feel any remorse for them, he couldn't help it. He'd see them looking out from between the bars of the makeshift prison and knew they had no space to lie down. There was barely enough space to sit. Their constant kicking at the trunk, shouting and crying, affected the workers so much that the job was progressing faster than before. The noise of hammers, drills, welding and grinding drowned out any sound made by the prisoners.

The men pleaded their innocence no matter how hard they were questioned. Mac tried everything to get answers. He and Hermes took turns questioning them, hoping a turn of phrase or a different angle would trip them up and lead to the truth. Their story never changed. They had no story. All the while, Mac was unable to rule out the chance that Honey had left of her own accord, just like Tonino.

There was much more pressure from the protesters than had been expected. These men were potential murderers. How could the other tourists stand so united with them? With the crowd over a hundred strong on the morning of the fourth day, Mac could no longer put relations between the town and the tourists at risk. There were already many more tourists here than normal for this season and more were coming. He had to make the best decision for the town, and that was to let the prisoners go. Under the concerned eyes of the protesters, he had Lagarto grind off the gate. The crowd gave the men a hero's welcome, and received a public apology from Mac. After a long talk with all who'd gathered by the tree, Mac justified his actions, regaining some favour with the crowd, and sent the men off to the city. He ensured that the protesters were treated with extra care for the remainder of their holidays, minimising any animosity they had towards the town, and limiting any damage their stories back home could cause.

Bruno found it impossible to focus. In a matter of days, everyone else seemed to be getting back to normal, but he couldn't let it go. His work suffered. Numerous brews were ruined because of him burning the malt, getting his ratios wrong, or mixing up the dates on the fermenting kegs. His instructions to the men were hesitant and confusing, and when they finished one job, he didn't have anything else ready for them to do. He stopped training, forgot to eat and when he tried to read, he'd be so preoccupied with what could have happened to her, that he had to reread complete sections multiple times.

He went to see Anderson again, and found him cleaning out the kiosk. All the bottles had been removed from the shelves and crowded the middle of the floor. Anderson was wiping down the counter as Bruno approached. A book lay open with Anderson's glasses resting on it.

'Still managing to read?' Bruno asked, catching Anderson by surprise.

Anderson snatched the book. His glasses fell off the counter. Bruno picked them up and handed them back. The book had been placed out of sight, but Bruno had seen enough copies to know what it was. The Bible.

'Think you'll find more answers in there than the bottom of the bottle?'

'Don't patronise me, son. Thought I'd wipe the dust off, that's all. I heard you're struggling.'

'I can't stop thinking about it. Something has to turn up. Anything. Even a fucking body would be better than this. I keep looking for clues: one of her cigarettes, a piece of clothing, the smell of her perfume. I can't concentrate on anything else.'

'You're going to have to, Bruno. You have a business to run.'

'This is bigger than any business. Honey's a friend. She needs us.'

Anderson sighed. 'Sit down, Bruno.' He came out and sat next to him. 'I haven't told anyone this before, but I'll tell you now in case it helps. My dad was a fisherman. He was a worker, a real good worker and was always in demand.

He'd be gone for days on end. I'd be lucky to see him once a week for a few hours. He'd come home, wash, eat, sleep, play with me for a while, take care of Mum then be off again. That was his life. I'd beg him to stay but he'd say "I'm doing this for you, son. I'm working hard for you." He'd make me touch his hands, big strong things, skin as tough as pig skin. "You'll have a clean hands job," he'd tell me. "A banker. That's what you'll be."'

Anderson pushed his cuticles back and spoke at his fingers. 'One day my dad didn't come home. A boat had gone down. The skipper radioed in as it was going under but didn't say who was aboard. The boat wasn't found, nor any bodies, no nets, nothing. We didn't even know if he was on it. He was a freelancer, he'd get picked up by whoever was going out that day. The men who came to tell me and Mum said he'd been seen hopping aboard, but we couldn't know for sure. Think about that. There was no trace of him. He didn't turn up that night or the next. We waited for him, and we waited for word from the search party. The search was called off after three days. We begged for them to continue but they just looked at us. I'll never forget their eyes. They knew he was gone, drowned, but they knew we'd always have hope, delusion or whatever you want to call it. Even now, I still wonder sometimes if he's alive.' He rubbed the bridge of his nose. 'So when this happened, I'll tell you straight, I didn't want any part of it. I can't open my mind to that again, Bruno. You asked me if I think those tourists killed her. I think they killed her alright, but there's not a damn thing we can do about it, and I'm not going to sit here and wait for any evidence or her body to show up. I'm going to get on with my life. I hope to God something turns up; I even hope I'm wrong. Who's to say she hasn't just left? It's not impossible. A couple of drunk tourists and mutilated horses don't mean shit. But I won't be torturing myself waiting. I've been through that already, and once is enough.'

'Anderson, I'm sorry.'

'A lot of eyes are on this project of yours, Bruno. Don't get yourself in a rut. You can't let what happens to other people affect you so much that you lose sight of yourself, okay, son? Don't wait. Waiting kills. Don't mess up those brews any more. Lead the men and get the job done. Look, I hate to turn you away like this, but I've got some things I need to do.' He walked around and into the kiosk.

Bruno stood and watched him.

'Goodnight, Bruno.' The shutter clattered down on the counter. Before it reached the bottom, Bruno noticed Anderson's hand grasp at the book.

Bruno tried hard to concentrate on his task. He pushed into training again, wrote job lists for himself and the men, and checked up on them every hour. He made some improvement after a few days but was unable to find the clarity of mind he'd first had.

The men had lost motivation. They'd sit around the table smoking and playing cards, while he either wandered about thinking of Honey, or rushed here and there, trying to complete an ever-increasing list of jobs on his own.

Ivo called Bruno to his office. He sat in the tobacco smoke haze, breathing through his nose, trying not to cough.

'Everything alright?' Ivo asked, pressing his cigarette out in the ashtray, causing a few butts to spill over.

'Fine,' he said. 'Progressing.'

'That's not what Lagarto told me. He said the men play cards all day while you run about like an idiot. Tiago makes more money from playing poker than his fucking salary!'

'I'm getting on top of it. Look.' He held up a notepad. 'I have a job book. It's going to be fine.'

'You're leading the job. The men need your instruction. Tell them to get off their arses and do something!'

'I'm getting the work done.'

'Tell *them* to get the work done! Efficiency. You know

what efficiency means?' Ivo didn't wait for an answer. 'Efficiency is when a job can be done quicker and better with more people. You were given the manpower to do this job. Use them.'

Bruno looked at the empty beer crates in the corner. 'I'm having a hard time because of Honey's disappearance.'

Ivo cracked his knuckles and exhaled. 'You were close?'

Bruno nodded.

'Nothing we can do,' he said. 'I know it's hard, but you have to get on top of this. This project can't stop for her. It can't stop for anyone. Who else was she friendly with? Forget it.' He wafted the smoke. 'Look, I need Tiago for a while. It's that time again.'

'What time?'

'The well's full. We need to jar it. The beekeepers need help.'

'But he's still got a lot to learn. I'm using him. He's busy.'

'It'll only be for a couple of weeks. Three at most. You'll get him back then.'

'But I had a list of things for him to get in the city this Sunday.'

'Sunday's fine. He'll be able to get the jars as well. Full tide's around...' he counted it out, 'eight. Make sure they leave early enough.'

On the Sunday morning, Bruno watched Tiago, Riccardo and Selmo leave for the city, then set about tidying the brewery decking and uncoiling the copper piping for Joao to plumb in the next day. He swept away all the rod ends and slag from around the old dairy tank that Selmo had been modifying, and collected the cuttings of electric wire that Riccardo had been doing his best to waste.

He dug a fire pit behind the decking, where he had a view over the mangroves and out to the horizon, and prepared an early lunch of coconut soup with a stock ground from dried vegetables. He was sick of eating at restaurants every day.

When he'd gone to camp for the pot, Bea and Carlos hadn't been there. The whole, filthy place had been near empty and was quiet.

After eating, he packed a canvas bag with small green wallets he'd weaved from palm fronds, and set off through the town. It was time to try and get himself back on track. He walked south along the beach, following the same path from which he'd first arrived, then headed inland and wandered through the forest. He clipped pods and seed heads from flowers and shrubs, collected fallen berries and nuts, took cuttings from the *moringa* and *erva de mate* trees and placed them in the pouches he'd made. He happened on a well-trodden path between the trees, and followed it further inland. The path was straight and clear enough of branches and fronds so that he could see far in the distance. An old man and woman were walking towards him. They stopped and must have been talking to each other before the man hurried back in the direction they'd come, only to about-turn and continue towards him again.

Bruno stood aside as they approached. 'Thought you'd forgotten something?' he asked the man.

'Yes,' said the man, tipping his hat. 'That was it.' The woman raised an old, rheumatic hand, and they passed by.

He walked on and entered a clearing in the trees. Within a lattice of gravel pathways, stones arranged in crosses were set into the lawn. Flowers of all colours stood in grave pots by the headstones. He walked around seeing the violet of lavender and the white of jasmine in every bunch. Sheltered by the surrounding trees, the scent of it all brought a smile to his face. It was the Jinguba Cemetery. He thought of Fatima. Somewhere here, in one of these graves, rested her parents. He looked around for the most visual, most fragrant collection of flowers, but they were all one like the other. Maybe if he waited here she'd come along and he'd have the chance to talk with her again.

In the corner of the graveyard there was a water trough

carved into a log. He sat on its edge and watched a plastic pail floating inside. He put his bag down and listened. Silence. He closed his eyes and enjoyed the calmness of it. He thought back to his childhood, remembered how, surrounded by other boys and men, he'd dreamt of disappearing, of being completely alone. Flora had taken that desire from him. She'd made him dependent. He'd looked to her for approval, for a near maternal love. She'd built a false hope inside him for something he could never have. He'd wanted to fit in at all levels of society and had gone so far as to visit the expensive boulevards to try and meet people like those he'd seen in her photographs, but they'd looked at him as the orphan, the nobody that he was, and he hated them for it. He'd set off not with the hope and joy of wandering, but with the anger and resentment of someone rejected, of an outcast. It had been a spiteful retreat instead of a courageous advancement.

He looked at the pail again. It was half full. It was as if someone had been in the middle of filling it but changed their mind. The whole place had the feeling of being abandoned. He listened again and felt the silence clawing at him. Not even the birds were singing.

He thought of Honey and raised his palms as if she were in front of him. 'I tried,' he said. 'I kept going as long as I could. Know that. I can't do any more for you.' He wanted forgiveness from her, approval to move on. 'Anderson said you wouldn't want any fuss, so I won't fuss any more, okay? I know you're not coming back, but I didn't abandon you. You're a friend and always will be. I did my best, but I need to move forward. I can't fall back again. I hope you understand.'

He slung his bag over his shoulder and made the long walk back to town. He spent the rest of the day behind the decking, planting the seeds, nuts and cuttings in halved plastic bottles, old cooking pots and other receptacles he'd salvaged from the skips.

In the evening, after a late dinner at the Dolphin, he was on his way back to the brewery when the truck, its horn sounding out again and again, braked so hard the back tyres nearly lifted off the ground. Tiago flung open the door and rushed towards him, eyes wide and a huge grin plastered on his face. 'Bruno!' he shouted, 'Bruno! We found her!'

A strange smell and taste filled his senses
as the ground flew up between him
and the wall of faces

13

Bruno put his hands on Tiago's shoulders to keep his balance. 'Tiago,' he said, 'tell me exactly what you're saying.'

'We found Honey, Bruno. She's fine. There's nothing wrong with her. We were driving past the *Alencar*. It was Selmo who spotted her, saw the peroxide blonde from a mile away.' He laughed. 'We followed her around the corner. She'd seen the van already and was about to make a run for it, but we caught up and shouted that it wasn't about the tithe. As soon as we mentioned your name, she calmed down.'

. Bruno felt sick. He closed his eyes. 'What happened?'

'She said she's sorry and hopes you'll forgive her. Said to tell you she's finally taking the boat.'

'So she's fine? You're telling me she's fine? Tiago, look me in the eye. Promise me. You're certain that it was Honey. She's safe and she's catching a boat to Russia?'

'Bruno.' Tiago placed his hands on Bruno's shoulders. 'I know who I saw. I promise she's fine, and I only said she's taking a boat. I didn't mention Russia. I don't know where she's going.'

Bruno pulled him into an embrace. 'I'm trusting you,' he said in Tiago's ear. 'I know you wouldn't lie to me.'

'You're hurting my neck,' Tiago said, pushing away. He

reached into his pocket and pulled out a silver cigarette case. 'She said to give this to you.'

Bruno took the case in both hands and turned it over. His fingers were trembling. It had starburst ridges shining from a golden button inset with faux sapphire. It had Russian Cyrillic engraving on its underside. There could be no doubt. It was Honey's. He popped the button and sniffed at the tobacco-sweetened inside. Loose tobacco collected in the corners. 'It's empty,' he said.

'She took the last one out and sparked it up as she handed it over.'

Bruno began to laugh. 'Typical Honey.' He laughed harder. 'Why did she not fucking say anything? She should have said something, left some sign, anything!'

'She said you'd understand. She just had to go.'

'When's her boat? Why isn't she flying? Give me the keys, I'll go and see if I can find her. Did she say where she's staying?'

'Bruno, calm down! Her boat leaves tonight. It's probably left already.' Tiago put on a gruff voice. 'Tell him to look at the horizon sometime after midnight. Maybe he'll see me sailing by.'

Bruno laughed again and snapped the case shut. Hot tears warmed his eyelids. He had to tell Anderson and Bea. She was safe! Of all the scenarios that could have played out, this was the last one he imagined. The thing with the tourists had been a coincidence, completely unconnected. He crouched down and rubbed the moisture from his eyes.

'Did she say where she's been staying? What she's been doing?' He stood up again.

'Bruno, she's fine. She's happy. That's what she said, and that we should all be happy. She was in a hurry to get ready.'

Bruno nodded. 'I see. Okay, let's get this truck unloaded. We can talk more about it later.'

'I've been driving for hours! Can't it wait?'

'Of course! Of course. Go get some rest. I won't be able to sleep now, anyway. Not after this. I need to work the adrenaline off.' His whole body was shaking. 'Go home. I'll have it done long before daylight.' Tiago started back for the cab. Bruno chased after him and hugged him again. 'Thank you,' he said. 'Thank you for finding her... Selmo!' He held his thumb up to the cab. 'Good eyes, brother. You did good!'

Tiago hopped inside. 'I'll leave the truck at the brewery.' He closed the door and drove off.

At the brewery, Bruno lowered the side panel of the truck and began unloading everything he could carry alone. He spent hours unstacking the jars and carrying them to the opening of the mangrove path, where he re-stacked them in empty barrows ready for wheeling to the well.

As he worked, the initial feeling of relief and excitement wore off. He began to feel angry and tired. She really should have said something. Here he was jeopardising his own life and ambitions, while she sat in a fucking hotel room. She let him believe she'd been killed, or was lost or lying somewhere, wounded and desperate, when all it would have taken was one word to let him know her thoughts, one minute of her time, even if it was just to say, 'fuck off!' He'd completely lost focus, and had forced Ivo to reprimand him for his incompetence. He was fucking it all up for someone who couldn't even take the time to say goodbye.

He worked on until everything he could do was done then washed his face and hands at the manifold, switched off all the lights, and lay in his hammock, staring up at the stars. He decided not to go looking for Anderson or Bea to tell them the news. It was time to stop latching onto others. Why should he go out of his way for anyone? All they ever did was let him down. He'd tell them when their paths crossed, not before.

He looked at the moon. It wasn't too late. Her boat might still be visible on the horizon. If he hurried to the dune, he could watch it pass by. Instead, after considering both options for far too long, he closed his eyes and went to sleep.

Honey swam through the turquoise sea without surfacing for air. The sun's rays penetrated the calm water, heavenly pillars guiding her path. With each stroke she grew younger and more radiant. The sunlight distorted as she neared a ship on the horizon. A storm had blown in. Lightning stabbed into the water like shards of glass. The clatter of unceasing thunder echoed. She kicked harder and thrust her arms forward in panic. Something made a splash in the white froth by the ship's hull. A lifebuoy. She shot up towards it as the shards pierced all around her. One sliced her calf. She screamed and reached into the blood clouding around the wound, then kept swimming. Just as she reached for the buoy, another shard came straight at her head. It was impossible to avoid. Bruno woke, breathless in the dark. He wiped the cold sweat from his hair, fluffed the rolled-up shirt he was using as a pillow and turned onto his side to sleep again.

By the end of the next day, the whole town knew that Honey had been found very much alive and well in the city. Some met the news with hostility. They'd welcomed her in all those years ago, only for her to take the money and leave without a word. She could have at least said thanks. Others were just glad that she was safe. Most knew she'd always wanted to move on and start a new life. They were happy that she was finally able to do it.

With everyone talking about it, there was no longer any need for Bruno to report the news to Anderson or Bea. Even if he *had* felt the need to tell them, Anderson's day-bar had been locked up like the others for the last few nights, and the only time Bruno saw Bea was when she was at the *carrinhos* with Carlos. And she didn't look anywhere near him. It had always been he who ran to them, but he wasn't going to do it this time.

Later that week, Bruno let Tiago go to fill jars at the well. Bruno watched him and the beekeepers at the opening of the path, wheeling barrows filled with transparent jars in amongst the trees and returning later with jars of red amber.

Around the table, the men told Bruno how difficult the job was: crouching in the mud around the well, spooning the sticky mess into the jars without spilling a drop. 'After a day your knees are gone,' said Riccardo.

'After that it's your back,' said Joao. 'Then your neck. And the heat is a nightmare.'

'There must have been a spoonful of my sweat in every jar when I did it,' Riccardo said, with a look of pride on his face. 'It's what gave it its sweetness.'

Sometimes Bruno saw Mac down there, sending the men all over the place, stacking the empties, gluing and sticking the labels, forming human chains to pass the jars up the slope and into a waiting 4×4. They worked non-stop, their clothes clinging to their sweat-drenched bodies.

A few days later, the first batches appeared in the shops: *Big Mac's Liquid Gold* handwritten on every label. Tourists all but fought over it, and the shelves emptied as soon as they were stocked.

It was served in the Horizon. Each morning Bruno dipped his fork into the jar and let it drip Pollock-like over his pancakes. It was like no honey he'd ever seen or tasted; golden-red like a robin's breast, it had a coppery aftertaste that offset the sweetness in just the right way. It was perfect.

A week after the job began, Bruno was tending to his seedlings by his fire when Tiago came to see him. He pulled another stool over from the brewery table. Tiago slumped into it, kicked his legs out straight and massaged his knees.

'Tiago,' Bruno said. 'The honey you're pulling out of that well is the best I've ever had. I'm serious.'

Tiago took a breath and stared at him.

Bruno waved a hand, and Tiago's vacant eyes came into focus.

'My knees will probably never recover,' Tiago said after a breath. 'My back neither. You've got no idea what I've had to go through. I can't wait to get back to this.'

'Near the bottom yet?'

'We're just over halfway. When Mac's there, we're working twice as fast, but most of the time he's at the beehives collecting for the next batch.' As he spoke, Tiago watched the forest over Bruno's shoulder. 'At least with his pushing we'll get it finished quicker.'

'How'd he even think to build a honey well?'

'He told us people have been harvesting honey here for thousands of years, long before the fishermen settled. He found a small well there when he was a boy. It was his mother who showed him how to make the beehives and take the honey from them. He built the well just before he built the temple. It's the same bricks.'

'Why a well, though? I thought honey never goes off.'

'Taste. Each batch has to be consistent. He said the honey these bees make has a lot of water in it, so it *can* go off. Keeping it cool in the well makes it last longer.'

'Tell me,' he looked over at Riccardo and leaned in, 'do any of the guys sweat in it?'

'That's the last thing you have to worry about. Anyway, Mac makes us put old T-shirts around our heads.'

'What do you mean, the last thing?'

'Nothing, Bruno. Look, the place is spotless. It's... It's pure honey.'

Despite Bruno's relief that Honey had been found unharmed, there was still the problem of what had happened to the horses to deal with. To ensure everyone's safety, and dispel any concerns the tourists might have, Mac ordered all who practised capoeira to show more of a presence in the street at night. Any more violence or strange acts could be disastrous for the town.

A rota was worked out. Once a fortnight, the *capoeiristas* would stand in pairs by the *carrinhos* to keep an eye on things. They were to stand watch until the town cleaners came on shift at four in the morning, despite having to work the next day. 'It's only once every two weeks,' Mac told them. 'Just until the next high season's over. Do your part for the town.'

Faka was the only one who served his shift alone, and he'd often turn up during others' rotations. As Bruno delivered the beer and took back the empties, he'd watch him linger by the carts. In his black outfit with his arms folded, Faka's lecherous eyes consumed the young women and stared with hostility at the men. His presence was more of a concern than a comfort for people. A half-thought began to form in Bruno's head that Faka was the reason Honey had run away so abruptly.

If a group stood close to Faka, instead of making space, he'd turn his back and stand his ground. Carlos was often in the crowd behind him, telling stories and impressing naive tourists with magic tricks any idiot should have seen through. His deep, sonorous voice carried through the air as if it were embedded in the music playing from Ivo's. Forever at his side, Bea sold her jewellery to the over-paying tourists without concern. The higher the price, the better. Bruno was glad to be away from it. His work now was being carried out at a just price and benefitted all involved equally.

Things were getting busier. Tourists, travellers and performers filed into town. High season wasn't even supposed to start for a few months. Bruno walked up Main Street and saw a musician at Zigzag tuning the strings of his guitar in front of the packed patio. He passed Papa Rouge at his grill, the shadow of a moustache like germinating mint seed above his lip. A group of contortionists dressed in red and black leotards performed a routine on stacks of painted-over powdered milk cans. 'You've moved on, Honey,' Bruno said to himself. 'I hope you're happy, wherever you are. You know I'm too reliant, I'm too soft. But if you're soft the world will eat you. I have to move on, too. I'll get this brewery going.' He looked around at the new faces in the crowded street, and deepened his voice: 'These people are thirsty, Vagaburro, let them drink!'

Bruno was more motivated than ever to get the job done. As the days passed, instead of idling around with thoughts of Honey or Bea or anyone else affecting him, he focused all his effort on his daily tasks. He pushed away any wandering ideas or concerns and dedicated his energy and time to himself. During breaks, he read and reread all the books he'd got from the city. At night, he frequented the restaurants and bars, his notepad tucked under his arm. While waiting for food or having a drink, he'd sketch diagrams and perform the calculations on brewing and construction he'd learned from the books.

He'd been so preoccupied with his own things that he hadn't thought much about Fatima. One morning, as if from nowhere, he woke with her image in his mind and decided to try to connect with her again. This would be his final attempt, and he knew what would give him the best chance of getting through to her. He'd make a necklace for her.

At work that day, he and the guys lifted a dairy tank, which had been modified into a two-thousand litre mash tun, onto the timber frame. It was difficult and dangerous work. At one point the tank almost came down on Selmo's head as he walked underneath it. Even Riccardo broke sweat, helping the others haul the rope through a rig of pulleys positioned all over the reinforced frame. After the guys went home that evening, Bruno set about tearing fibres from inside the upside-down tree and twisting them into fine cordage. All that remained of the makeshift prison was the marks on the outside of the tree left by the iron gate, and the prisoners' names scraped into the inside of the trunk.

Before breakfast the next morning, whilst the green-dressed cleaners combed the streets, Bruno trawled over the tideline for the best shells, sea glass and driftwood he could find. He did this after every high tide for a week, and gathered much more than he could ever use on a single necklace.

It took him over a fortnight to make. He worked on it during every spare minute, at lunchtime and in the evenings, whittling the driftwood, linking the strands of cordage and drilling the shells. He closed himself off from everything until it was done. No capoeira lessons, no yoga, no books. He was so focused that on many nights he forgot to eat and would fall asleep in his hammock, whittling knife and block in his hands.

On the nights he did make it back to his shelter, he had to tiptoe through the rubbish Carlos and Bea hadn't bothered to clean. The smell of meat and fish clung to the place, and the air was alive with flies. He'd often see Bea and Carlos sitting with the travellers at another camp, their faces red in the firelight, their eyes cast in shade. Sometimes they'd be laughing, sometimes serious, but Bruno tried not to pay any attention to them, and never responded to Carlos's taunts.

In his shelter, he pictured Fatima receiving the necklace, her smile, her gasp, loud enough to draw everyone's attention, but she'd be too interested in it to notice their stares. She'd throw her arms around him, and after resting his cheek against hers, he'd gently pull away, stand behind her and tie the necklace on the nape of her neck. Maybe he'd even chance a kiss just below the hairline, to show everyone present, if they couldn't already tell, that he and Fatima were now a couple. Part of him, indulging in childish spite, hoped Bea would be one of those to witness it.

The finished necklace was webbed, multi-stranded and multilayered. Cowrie shells sealed every joint, stones of

303

coloured glass shimmered like a breaking wave. Fishes, frogs, flowers and leaves carved from driftwood hung from every cord. He held it in a circle and gave it a knock. The wooden charms clicked together like the chime in her shop and the sea glass sparkled in the sun like a kaleidoscope. He knew it was the best piece he had ever or would ever make.

Instead of bringing it straight to her, he decided to carry it in his shirt pocket until he saw her again, hoping that some of his essence would be absorbed by it, and in that way his energy would always be with her. The bookshop was where it had to be given, in the presence of their mutual friends, the characters in the books on the shelves, who'd never hurt or leave them.

Now that it was finished, he once again jumped into his routine of exercise and work, but spent more time than usual in *A Gata Preta*, hoping she'd walk in through the door.

*

Tiago returned to work at the brewery that week.

'Back when all the hard work's done!' Riccardo shouted from the card table. He was playing blackjack with Rudi, as Joao helped Selmo weld another tank.

Tiago shook his head and spoke to the decking. 'I should get retirement on full pension. It's been hell.'

'Want to play?' Rudi asked, but Bruno was calling out to him.

'Come help me with these bottles,' he shouted from across the deck. Tiago came over and tipped the fermenter keg as Bruno held another bottle under it. 'Happy to be back?'

'No more crouching. No more backache. Finished. Bloody, sticky mess. You know how nice it is to stretch out your fingers without them sticking together? I've had nightmares about it. I try to pull them apart but they're stuck like glue. I really hope my knees are going to be okay. Everything cracks, my spine, my knees, my hips, my neck.'

He rolled his head around. 'Anyway, let's not talk about that, any more. I'm done with it. What's the latest here?' He spoke in an even tone, without looking at Bruno. It was only when Bruno spoke that he made eye contact.

'We're ready for the wind turbine. I still have to cut down three palm trees for the blades. I need you to take Riccardo and Rudi to the city to get the stuff. It's quite a lot. I don't want to know how you get it, but do your best and be careful.' He handed over a list.

'Truck axel × 2,' Tiago read, 'semi-traction batteries and load controllers… I don't even know what these are. Where are we supposed to get them?'

'Shipyard, I think. They use them on yachts. Riccardo should know.'

'100 × 100 angle iron. 1" thick metal sheeting, 6" × 20' pipe! What does the two lines above the numbers mean?'

'It's imperial measurement. Twenty feet is only a little longer than the truck bed. It might stick out the back a bit. Wrap a hi-vis vest on the end.'

'Assorted electrical motors… Okay, Bruno, I'll see what I can do.' He looked at his watch. 'Missed the tide. Tomorrow okay?'

'Tomorrow's fine. And, Tiago, keep your eyes open for Honey.' Tiago's shoulders dropped. 'I know,' Bruno said, holding his palms out. 'I know she was supposed to take the boat, but just go past the *Alencar* once. If you see her, you see her, if you don't, that's fine. But let me know. I'll go to the city with you next time if she's still there.'

'No problem.'

'I just want to find out what's going on with her.'

'Bruno…'

Bruno lowered his eyes. It was mostly anger that drove him, instead of concern for her, 'I know.'

Tiago pointed at a three-barrel Savonius spinning within a cylindrical frame. Milled barley poured into a bucket from a notch in the mortar bowl. 'How's Barrel Boy working?'

'Let me show you, come on.' He led him over to it. 'This thing is amazing.' He pulled on a rope and a heavy canvas sheet closed around the frame, like a giant shower curtain. It blocked out the wind. He slipped in behind the curtain. 'It does the job perfectly,' he said, before coming back out with the bucket. 'Take a handful.'

Tiago hesitated then dipped a hand in and held up the sand-coloured husks and white endosperm.

'See that? Husks still intact, perfect for lautering.'

Tiago nodded. 'Looks great.' He let the grain fall through his fingers. 'By the way, did you hear about the drummer women?'

'I saw the poster in the bookshop. Big Mac's Extravaganza.'

'Should be a great show. It'll be good for morale. Have you noticed how restless people are? A lot more tourists here than there should be. You'd think everyone would be happy, but they're not. They haven't rested enough. Uncle Ivo told me that even Mac said there's a bad energy. Don't tell anybody I told you that.'

'You know, somebody said that to me about Faka… That he had a bad energy.'

Tiago looked over his shoulder at the others. 'He's aggressive,' he said in a hushed voice. 'Everyone knows that. What have you heard?'

'Nothing,' Bruno said, 'but maybe he had something to do with Honey leaving.'

Tiago ran a hand over his face. 'He beat his wife a few months back. She left with the daughter. He thinks people are stealing meat from his shop entrance. You noticed he only wears black now?'

'I was in the shop when he ordered it. Black this, black that.'

'That's not how we do things here, Bruno. We all have colours assigned to us in line with *Os Orishas*. It's about our religion. Only the non-practitioners wear whatever they want. I'm not sure what's going on. Anyway, Mac will figure it out. Nothing gets by him, even if it involves his best friend.'

An engine screamed from the direction of Main Street. Someone was shouting for help. Bruno shot off towards the sound, Tiago at his heels. Riccardo and Rudi followed on after them.

The buggy was outside the salon. Hermes stood at the passenger door with one kite-surfing instructor. Another hunched over a man in the passenger seat, arms straight, palms bouncing on the man's chest. He stopped the compressions, pinched the passenger's nose and forced a breath into his lungs. Desperate to help, Bruno was about to ask what to do when Hermes looked him full in the face. 'Get him out of there!' With the help of the instructor, Bruno and Tiago lifted the unconscious man from the buggy. They lowered him onto the sand, and Hermes took over the CPR.

'Stop people crowding around,' Hermes commanded the instructors. They sprang at the onlookers and forced them away. 'Get Mac,' he told Tiago. 'We need a 4×4 to the city. Now!' Tiago ran for *A Gata Preta*. 'You lot.' He eyed Bruno, Riccardo and Rudi. 'There's nothing for you here. Back to work.'

They obeyed without a word. Bruno took a last look at the man's clean-shaven face, his slim adolescent body. He wasn't a man. He was a boy.

Adrenaline still coursed through him when he got back to the brewery. He wanted to do something, but it was as Hermes had said, there was nothing he could do. He was powerless. As Riccardo and Rudi sat back down to their card game, with Selmo and Joao lifting their welding masks and joining them, Bruno changed into his *abadas* and slid down towards the mangroves.

After squats, push-ups and sit-ups, he performed Carlos's yoga and breathing techniques, and although his thighs were burning, he ran through the capoeira moves, the *ginga*, *esquiva baixa lateral*, *queixada*, *esquiva meia alta*.

As he performed the manoeuvres, he played out Hermes's impressive handling of the situation in his mind. A few simple commands spoken with assertion and everyone had immediately done what was asked. A feeling of inadequacy swept over him. He'd never be able to command people in that way. Anderson was right; he didn't have the confidence and couldn't stomach conflict. He'd tried to drive the men on but hadn't been able to get the level of commitment or motivation he wanted. He wondered what Mac would think if he came by and saw him sweating over the fermenters while Riccardo and Rudi played cards. *He'd* be the one in trouble, not them. Like Ivo had said, he was supposed to be in charge. Selmo and Joao only worked well because it was in their nature, not because he had any influence over them. They took his instruction but didn't work for him. They worked in spite of him. He wasn't a leader at all because he wasn't brave enough to be one. This kind of thinking wouldn't get him anywhere, though. He was sick of telling himself, and being told, what he wasn't. What could he be if he really tried? His only barrier was of his own making. Success in anything would only come through breaking down his self-made walls and becoming something more than he was.

As he performed the capoeira moves, he ran through all the negative episodes in his life where he'd felt fear, injustice, or defeat, and pushed himself on. Sweat sprayed from his hair, his teeth clenched and he forced himself through the pain. His legs buckled and he crumpled to the ground, gripping his burning thighs. He rose to a crouch and pushed himself further. He fell again but was back on his feet in seconds. When his legs were too heavy and slow to do the *ginga*, he performed squats until he fell and couldn't get up.

On his hands and knees, trembling from the exertion, he crawled up the slope and sat on the edge of the decking. When the trembling stopped, he slipped off his *abadas*, walked over to the manifold and held the hose over his head.

He towelled off and dressed. At the beer store, he grabbed a few bottles and joined the men at the card table. Now wasn't the time to talk about work; not when a boy was fighting for his life. He'd get some more books on leadership tomorrow. Maybe he'd even ask Mac for advice.

Tiago returned an hour later and drew a thumb across his neck. The noise at the table hushed.

'A young life,' said Bruno, 'gone just like that, drowned in a sea thousands of miles from home. Was he alone?'

Tiago shook his head. 'Girlfriend. Hermes is comforting her now. She wants to go to the city but they've missed the tide. She said he'd been talking about this place for over a year. He was desperate to try kite surfing.'

'Maybe dying to try kite surfing?' Rudi smiled at the others, his face red from drinking.

'Come on, Rudi,' said Bruno. 'Some respect, please.'

'What?' persisted Rudi with the same grin. 'They attacked our horses. *Yemanjá* paid them back.'

'Fuck the horses!' Bruno laid his cup down. Rudi's grin disappeared. 'How old was he?'

'Don't know,' said Tiago. 'Looked about eighteen.'

'Too young to die, that,' said Joao.

'Young, old, middle-aged... Never a good time to die,' Riccardo said.

'I didn't mean to be so abrupt, Rudi. I'm sorry.' Bruno sipped his beer and looked around at the sombre faces. The alcohol had gone to his head. 'Use it for your own motivation, lads,' he said, trying to sound inspiring. 'Those who fear death haven't achieved what they set out to achieve, haven't lived how they wanted to live... Or at least haven't tried hard enough. Let's not make that mistake.'

After a brief silence, Riccardo took his glasses off. 'I don't know,' he said, wiping them on his shirt. 'I'm satisfied.'

'And the rest of you?' asked Bruno.

They murmured in agreement.

'Really? This is your lot? You're all happy?'

'What more do we need?' Joao asked, tearing a bloody hangnail from his thumb. Selmo pushed Joao's hand away from his mouth. 'We have family, community,' Joao said, chewing. He swallowed. 'Religion.'

'How about ambition?' asked Bruno. He filled everyone's glasses again, capped the bottle and set it aside. 'Rudi, what's yours?'

Rudi raised his eyebrows and smiled awkwardly. 'My what? Why me?'

'Your ambition. It's not a test. I just want to know. What do you want out of life?'

'Okay… Okay.' Rudi breathed in, bit his lip and looked up in thought. The others giggled, awaiting his answer. His palm slammed on the table and he grinned. 'To beat Mac in the *roda!*'

Laughter erupted. Selmo almost fell from his chair. Joao stood.

'Beat Mac! Nobody will ever beat Mac!' said Tiago.

'That's a dream,' said Joao, holding his arms out and looking around, 'not an ambition.'

'Faka would give him a go,' said Riccardo, before Bruno could speak again.

'Fucking never!' said Selmo. 'Mac would crush him.' He grabbed one of the empty bottles and beat it on the table, accidentally hitting the ashtray and sending the ash flying. Joao sat back down as Bruno wiped the ash from his face and short beard.

Their voices rose as the debate continued. Bruno leaned back and sipped at his beer. He almost fell asleep. When Rudi and Tiago got up to act out a possible fight between Mac and Faka, he slipped away to the campsite.

Under the gibbous moon, surrounded by camp fires burning, Bruno noticed how many more travellers had arrived. Guitars were strumming from every circle of tents. All around there was singing and laughter. The smell of *maconha* filled the night air along with the scents of frankincense, patchouli and myrrh. Silhouettes walked from fire to fire, glowing red ends of their cigarettes waving in the night like fireflies.

Bruno heard Carlos's laugh as he stepped into his shelter. He saw him amongst the people at Fortunato's camp, hair up in a samurai knot, pipe in hand, Bea at his side. The reflection of the fire in Carlos's eyes burned brighter than the fire itself. Bruno imagined pulling on either end of the coil of wire around his neck until he choked him dead. Carlos threw his drink in the fire and the flames rose up. The metal coils in his beard flashed. He put the pipe in his mouth, brought two fingers to his eyes and pointed them at Bruno. 'I see you, *boludo mio!*' he shouted. Bea craned her neck to look.

Bruno ignored him, stepped inside and let the flap close behind him. Something had changed in the travellers. When he first arrived they'd been cliquish, rarely straying from their immediate groups, but now they moved freely from one camp to the next. Like one big, happy family, they shared food, beer and yerba mate, and talked like lifelong friends.

As he lay down to sleep, he thought not of Fatima but about Bea. He had an overwhelming fear that something bad was going to happen to her, and that he was failing her somehow. Had he tried hard enough to reconcile things with her, or had he been so preoccupied with the brewery and fitting in with the locals that he'd neglected her when she needed him most? All his attempts to talk had been met with an insouciance he hadn't thought she was capable of; was it was out of character? What else could he do? Months had passed. All she felt for him was hostility and resentment, while for Carlos she acted like a doting child, like an empty vessel begging to be filled. He had no choice but to accept it for what it was.

There was something about her eyes tonight that troubled

him. While Carlos's were alive and glowing, hers were empty hollows. As she laughed with Carlos and those around her, it wasn't her laugh. It was the laugh of a ventriloquist's dummy. Maybe she actually wanted to cross over to this way of life, and him trying to go in the other direction had been too much for her to bear. Maybe she had to block him out because he was the last link to a life she thought she could never return to and needed to forget.

As much as he still loved her and would have done anything for her, he hated her idolisation of Carlos, the barrier she'd built between them, and the stinking mess she'd turned the camp into. He was still clinging too tightly to her. She was an adult. She'd been clear in what she'd said. If she wanted him in her life again it was up to her now, not him. He had to let her go, had to put more distance between them. This was all transitory, these mats, the tarpaulin roof and palm frond flooring. It was the shelter of a nomad, at odds with what he was becoming. He'd been trying to exist in both worlds for too long. It was time to ask Mac for a house.

*

The next morning in *A Gata Preta*, unable to find a book on leadership skills, Bruno picked up a biography of a communist leader from the shelf. With Rosy's face fixed straight ahead, but her eyes following him as far as their sockets would permit, he edged his way along the shelves to the back of the shop.

He pulled out another book, leaned against the wall and pretended to read. The office was a narrow, white room with a row of filing cabinets along one side. Pots of mint, basil and rosemary lined the windowsill. The twins sat with cash boxes on their desks. They were counting bank notes, slipping them into envelopes and sliding the envelopes into pigeon-holes marked out with letters and numbers: the pay grade scale.

Mac sat at a desk with his back to the far wall. He looked like a giant in a doll's house. On his desk sat a basic computer and an overflowing, multi-tiered filing tray.

One of the twins caught Bruno looking and muttered something to Mac.

'Vaga-B.' Mac stood from his desk. He came forward. 'You spend far too much time here and not enough at your construction site. I want to see wind turbines spinning and hot liquor bubbling.'

'The guys are off to the city for materials today,' he said, noticing a gold watch on Mac's wrist. 'I wanted to ask you for advice.'

'Advice.' Mac's lips parted into an ivory-toothed smile. 'Let's take a seat on the couch.'

Bruno returned the second book to its slot and walked through the empty shop, Mac like a moving wall behind him. He laid the book on the table and took a seat on one side of the couch. Mac remained standing.

'Now,' Mac said. 'What advice would you like?'

'I saw how Hermes handled the situation with the drowned boy yesterday... His authority... His leadership... And I—'

'You don't think you're cut out for it.'

Bruno pursed his lips. 'I know you took a chance and put a lot of faith in me. I want to do everything I can to live up to it.'

'Bruno, I don't want to call you a coward but I will say that you're afraid of confrontation.'

The vein at Bruno's temple began to pulse. He felt instant regret at having come.

'I see it all,' Mac said. 'Don't be embarrassed. I saw it the first time... But, let's not talk about that first encounter. That's behind us now. Bruno, there are ways to lead people without letting them know you're the leader.

'I noticed you looking at my new watch. We'll use it as an example. A well-run town is not unlike an automatic

313

watch.' He tapped the casing. He hiked his *abadas* at the knees, sat down, and held the watch under Bruno's nose. 'There are hundreds of parts in this contraption. You have the mainspring, the gears, the balance wheel, the arms, the escapement... Now, I know what you're thinking. Some parts are smaller and less important than the others... But Bruno, that just isn't the case. Every part, big,' he motioned to himself, 'and small,' he motioned to Bruno, 'has to work in unison for the thing to function as a whole. You see?' He touched a finger to his lips the way Anderson did on occasion. 'The town cleaner is just as important as the hotelier; the plumber is needed as much as the barista or the waiter. My job is not to tell people what to do, exactly, but to set the timing and keep the rhythm, you see?'

'I think so... But the only thing stopping the cleaners from one day becoming hoteliers is themselves, no?'

Mac smiled and wagged his finger. 'You're a thinker, Bruno, I always knew it... I know you only take the books from my mother's collection. I've read them all, too... I know what path you're on, but no. Bruno, the mainspring is always a mainspring, you see? The arms, these little ticking things that go round and round can't suddenly morph into gears. A flower could never sprout legs and become a rabbit. That's not in its nature, you see? No, not here.'

Bruno nodded.

'Back to your original question. Everyone is motivated by something different. Some people need to be shouted at, others respond to flattery, others still value honesty and need to know they're doing their part for the whole and that it's appreciated – you, Bruno, fall into this category – and one thing I will say is that I pride this town on its transparency. We pay everyone a wage that makes sense and is defendable in front of everyone else.' He stood.

'I know you're trying your best, Bruno. Keep trying. Find what motivates the guys. Learn their natures, and they'll sweat for you as they would for me.' He turned towards his office.

'Mac... excuse me.' Bruno started from the sofa. 'I'd like a house.'

'Ah... I wondered when you were going to ask. Finally had enough of those parasites? Decided to come completely over to our side? Let me ask you something, Bruno.' Mac looked at the door and lowered his voice. 'How would I go about getting rid of them without seeming to be unfair in the tourists' eyes? You see how many there are? They're like maggots on rotten flesh. It's not even high season.'

'The tourists like them, Mac. They're doing no harm. They...' He couldn't bring himself to say they were good for the town. He had to take the town's side. He remembered how Mac had taken Carlos's model. 'You could tax them or put your own people on the street to undercut the prices.'

'Not cost-effective. I need an event, Bruno. I need something to happen that reduces their value to the tourists; that shows them for what they really are.'

'Mac.' Bruno cleared his throat. ' "We were born for cooperation, like feet, like hands, like eyelids, like rows of upper and lower teeth. So to work in opposition to one another is against nature: and anger or rejection is opposition." '[7]

Mac patted his finger to his lips and raised his eyebrows. 'You didn't get that one from my mother's collection, but Bruno, it misses the full picture. A rotten tooth needs to be pulled, does it not? A gangrenous foot must be chopped. For are they not also working in opposition? Leave everything with me.' He walked away. 'I'll look into it.'

Bruno sat back down on the couch, unsure as to whether it was his request for a house or getting rid of the travellers that Mac would look into. He picked up the biography and began to read. The metallic chime rang out as the door

7   Meditations – Marcus Aurelius

opened. He listened to the footsteps approach the nearest bookshelf, looked out over the book and caught his breath. It was Fatima.

'Fatima,' he said, forgetting himself. Rosy scowled. He reached for the bulge in his shirt pocket, took an even breath and approached her. He touched her elbow. 'Hello,' he said as she turned to face him.

'Hello, Bruno.'

Act confident, he told himself as she turned back to the bookshelf. He watched her eyes scan the spines of the books. It was now or never. He had to make everything obvious.

She reached for a book, and he laid his hand on hers and eased it back into its slot. She turned to face him. The fear in her eyes shocked him. He'd gone too far, way too far, but there could be no back-stepping. *Courage*, the voice in his head said. *Have courage.*

'Try this one instead.' He grabbed the first book his hand landed on and handed it over. She took it without a word or glance and went to pay for it. As she passed her banknotes to Rosy, Bruno winced at the sight of her trembling hands.

'Fuck-fuck-fuck,' he said, moving towards the door. He had to see this through. Rosy's eyes were on him again, swivelling chameleon-like in their sockets. Even as part of him was saying, *give up and leave*, another part – the part that told him to stare life full in the face no matter what the consequences – was forcing his hand into his pocket and pulling the necklace out. He held it up to her as he opened the door, but she hurried past without noticing.

'Leave that young girl alone!' Rosy said. The words hit him like a fist, but he couldn't stop. With sweat running freely down his face, he bolted through the doorway, and followed Fatima down the street. He caught up, got around in front and held his hands up. She stopped and walked backwards, about to turn in the opposite direction.

'Fatima,' he said. 'Don't be afraid. I'm not here to harm you! Look!' He wiped the sweat from his brow and around his eyes. 'I didn't mean to scare you, I know you're shy, but please.' He held up the necklace. 'I put my soul into this. I made it especially for you. I like you, Fatima. It's been so long since I've said that to anyone. We could be happy together, if you just give me a chance. I want to take you out, I want to talk about books, walk the streets and watch the performers. Let's have dinner in every restaurant, let's drink wine and chat with tourists at the *carrinhos*. Life's too short to waste it on your terrace. You're far too beautiful for that. Here...' He grabbed her hand and tried to fold her fingers around the necklace.

'No!' she said, pulling away from him. Tourists walking by stared.

'Bruno, I can't accept this. My life. My life only foh one. I don't need no one else. I'm happy alone.'

He stared at the ground.

'Bruno, I know you good person. I know you have lot to offer a woman. But I don't want a relationship. I'm happy alone.'

'Okay,' he said. He couldn't look her in the eye. 'I understand. I... I'm really sorry.'

She tilted his chin up so she could read his lips.

'I understand,' he said again, his body heavy as he looked at her golden-brown face. 'But still. Please take it. I don't know you well, and you don't know me, but I felt something when we met. I feel something now, you know? I made this for you, only you, and if you don't take it, it's going straight in that bin over there.'

'Bruno, don you see? We do this to ourselves. Love is not something between two people. Is something only in our own heads... Give it to me.' He held it out. 'Help put it on.'

He moved behind her, brushed her hair over one shoulder, and with trembling fingers, got the necklace tied. He touched his lips to her neck.

She turned and smiled at him. 'Thank you,' she said.

'Fatima.' He smiled despite the hurt of rejection. 'You're

not out a lot, so I don't know when I'll see you again, but let me just tell you that you're special. I wish you everything in this world… I really mean it. I'd like to be part of it, but I understand.'

She touched his cheek. 'I'm happy. And I'm around. You'll see me. Don't worry. You'll be fine. We both will be.'

After that, Bruno's thoughts often returned to Fatima but he no longer fantasised over a possible future together. Every time he thought of her, her same two words resonated in his mind: *Happy alone.* It echoed what he'd told Honey. Maybe that really *was* the key to a good life. He wondered where in the world Honey could be. Tiago hadn't seen her in the city again. Maybe she *had* been able to track down her first love; or had she accepted her life as it was and found peace in her retirement? Bea constantly came to his mind as well, but the way she'd ended their relationship prevented him from reminiscing about the good times they'd shared. He resented himself for wasting any more time on her, and made an effort not to.

He woke early every day and worked hard on the wind turbine. He planed the blades down, cut the alternator casing, welded the yaw bearing and the tail hinge. It was progressing better than he could have expected. To minimise distraction, he sent three of the guys to the city every other day to look for anything they thought might be useful, keeping only whoever had the skills he might need. He made sure Tiago and Rudi never went to the city together so he'd always have one of them to guide his capoeira training. Every lunchtime and evening he practised. He was pushing himself harder than at any time in his life and was beginning to feel good about himself. His body was filling out so much that even the men commented on it.

Despite the shame he felt about Rosy's words, words that only months ago would have been enough to stop him from ever going back to the shop, he composed himself and returned.

Instead of locking it all inside, or drowning it in a bottle of whisky, he explained everything to her. He told her about Flora, and Bea, without naming her, and let her know he'd chased Fatima because he thought they were well matched, and knew he'd have regretted it for the rest of his life if he didn't at least try.

After that, Rosy completely changed towards him. She never failed to greet him with a smile, and always took an interest in what he was reading. He came to speak with her as a friend, and at break times, when the others were playing cards or dominoes, he'd be sitting on the perished leather couch in *A Gata Preta* drinking the paint-thick coffee and talking to Rosy, tourists or just reading a book.

Tiago brought a new watch back from the city one evening and sold Bruno his old one. For the first time since clocking in at the machine shop, or lining up at the food banks, Bruno's life became ruled by the clock. Where once he'd worked, trained and read until he fell asleep or missed a meal, with the watch on his wrist he organised his life by the minute. Everything was given an allotted amount of time. There was no point in working until he fell. No point in training his body without developing his brain. Reading was as important as physical exercise, physical exercise as important as work. Work, a structured diet, breathing, meditation and yoga; each activity complemented the next. He was taking as much control as he could.

'You're getting so good, so fast,' Tiago said, picking himself up off the ground one afternoon. Bruno had tripped him with a *negativa derrubando*. 'You should come and watch at the *roda*, pick up more moves.'

Bruno often watched from the back of the crowd without Tiago's knowledge, but after this suggestion, and with a mind to embrace local life a bit more, he went along every night, taking a position between the tourists and locals, where Tiago could see him.

After Honey's disappearance, the atmosphere amongst the *capoeiristas* had been tense. They hadn't been playing capoeira any more but actually fighting. Stern faces, pounding drums, spraying sand, it was faster paced and more violent. It was a dance of war, not unlike the dances in the temple, but instead of the rhythms used to evoke a god or goddess, it was as if they were trying to cast something out. The bad energy about the place had been lingering, but things were calming as the weeks crawled by, and as Bruno watched the action, he saw smiles, and heard more benevolent rhythms in the drumming. Tourists were arriving in higher numbers than ever. Shops were selling well and restaurants and bars were filling up. Locals were getting over their lack of rest and were now fully occupied and constantly working. The bad energy was disappearing, and it showed in the *roda*.

Over the weeks, Bruno learned the songs, and as the tourists and locals clapped around him, he clapped along, sometimes singing the words in quiet undertones as the zealous locals shouted over him.

Tonight, Rudi was in the *roda* with a woman called Lucia. Their lithe, sweating bodies glistened under the reddening sun. They performed manoeuvres with a technical ability and style that Bruno could still only dream of. He knew the basics, and was proud of that, but they said that it was only after mastery of the basics that capoeira really began.

As Rudi walked out of the *roda*, Bruno watched him sidle up to Mac and stand on his tiptoes. His lips moved next to Mac's downturned ear. Mac looked at Bruno, raised the *baqueta* of his *berimbau* and pointed it at him. Bruno's eyes fixed on the polished wooden rod. It turned upwards and beckoned him forward.

*

Amid the clatter of applause and the voices of everyone

cheering him on, Bruno wished he'd never been near the *roda* even once since he'd arrived. With everyone's eyes on him, he stepped through the crowd, muttering every swear word he knew in every language he spoke. He felt like a fly heading for Anderson's blue zapper.

He stood in the wide open space of the *roda* and looked at a wall of faces, but the only one that registered was Mac's. He tried to control his breathing and slow his heart.

Mac's *baqueta* pointed over Bruno's shoulder, and Bruno turned to see a boy of no more than twelve enter the *roda* behind him. With a swagger that even the laughter of the tourists couldn't dent, the boy walked straight up to Bruno and crouched into the *ginga*.

The music started. Bruno followed the boy's lead, copying the *ginga*, trying not to lose balance or rhythm. The cheering of the crowd mixed with the music, turning it all into static noise that rose in pitch as the boy threw an *au batido* kick and immediately dipped into an *s-dobrado* that almost put Bruno on his back. As the boy back-flipped to his feet, Faka, in his black *abadas*, marched in and put a hand on the boy's shoulder.

Bruno looked at Mac as the boy hesitated, bowed and blended in with the crowd. Mac didn't mirror his concern. He brought the band to life with a pluck of his *berimbau*, and Faka crouched into the *ginga*. Bruno held his hands up and looked for Rudi. 'It's okay,' he heard Rudi shout. 'It's just playing.'

Bruno's peripheral vision closed in along with his hearing. All he saw was Faka's unblinking eyes, sneering lips and writhing body. Even in the street, he didn't want to be near this guy, yet here he was in the *roda* with him. His head became light and his body tensed. He watched Faka's movements, tried to get the timing, then fell into step. Faka threw a slow body kick to Bruno's left side that had him jumping to the right. They moved into the *ginga* again, back and forth, back and forth, Bruno was loosening up a little, finding the rhythm. Faka threw the same body kick, sending Bruno in a jump to the right.

It is *just playing*, Bruno thought. Faka was taking it easy on him. He gave him a smile. Maybe he'd been wrong. Maybe the hate he'd perceived wasn't personal but a warped reflection of his own paranoia. Nothing bad would happen in front of the tourists. Once again Faka made to throw the same slow body kick, and Bruno jumped to the right, but this time Faka's hands planted on the sand and his right foot snapped up like the tail of a scorpion. His heel struck Bruno's skull. Bruno heard the crack of a distant whip. It seemed to pop inside his brain. A strange smell and taste filled his senses as the ground flew up between him and the wall of faces. The last thing he felt was the cool sand on his cheek.

They surrounded Faka,
pleading for him to drop the club

14

Bruno woke in a double bed wrapped in white cotton sheets. The springs of the mattress dug into his back while a soft pillow cushioned his head. He looked up and reached for his right eye in a panic. He couldn't see out of it. The eye and half his head were bandaged. Every part of him was in pain. The ache up his neck and along his jaw stopped him when he tried to raise his head. He got hold of another pillow, so weak he was barely able to grip it, and propped his head up. Hermes was asleep on a sofa across the room. Behind him was a small kitchenette; in front was a wooden coffee table with an empty ashtray. Bruno's eye and brain hurt taking everything in. Through a door by the bed was a bathroom. The place reeked of disinfectant, but a familiar scent of stale tobacco and musk lingered.

'Hermes,' Bruno tried to say, but his voice was thinner than a whisper. He cleared his throat and swallowed against the pain. 'Hermes.' A glass of water stood next to a bottle on the bedside table. He brought it to his lips and tried to drink, but spilled most down either side of his mouth.

'Hermes,' he said again. Hermes's eyes opened. 'Where am I?'

Hermes licked his thumb and ran it over each eyebrow. He got up and opened a slit in the curtains. A beam of light split the room like a guillotine. 'Morning,' he said, closing them again.

'Can you leave them open a bit?'

Hermes took a seat on the edge of the bed and poured Bruno another glass of water. 'How are you feeling?' He placed the back of his hand on the un-bandaged part of Bruno's forehead.

'Is my eye okay?'

'Your vision will be fine. Don't worry.'

'My neck,' Bruno said. 'It's too sore to lift my head.'

Hermes prodded both sides of his jaw and neck and massaged the vertebrae at the back.

'My head... My voice...'

'I'll get you a brace. Your voice will come back. Do you remember anything?'

Bruno thought back to the brewery, the mangroves, training with Rudi. 'The *roda*,' he finally said. 'Faka! That fucking bastard.'

Hermes nodded. '*Escorpião*. I had to stitch you up.'

'Will I see again?'

'The eye is fine, Bruno. It's just swollen and bruised. He caught you on the side of the head. Six stitches. You need to rest. Don't move from the bed.'

'Whose bed is this?'

'Mac said he was going to give it to you later in the week. It was Honey's. Now is yours.'

'Honey's! But can't I get a place of my own?'

'Rest, Bruno!' Hermes cupped Bruno's forehead and pressed him back down to the pillow. 'Try not to talk. Try not to think. Just lie here and drink plenty of water. C'mon, drink up.' He filled the glass and held it to Bruno's mouth. 'Your *abadas* are drying.' He glanced out the window.

'What?'

'Sometimes a bad knockout can cause the body to lose control of—'

'I pissed myself?'

'—its bowels.'

'Oh Jesus, no!' Bruno closed his eyes. 'I shat myself? In front of everyone?'

'Could have been any of us,' said Hermes.

Bruno lifted the covers and a smell of herbs and rosewater wafted up. 'You... You cleaned me?'

Hermes smiled gently and brushed Bruno's hair back. 'I'm going to get you some breakfast. Fruit only. I want your strength saved for healing, not digestion.' He made for the door. 'I'll bring that neck brace too... I hope you don't mind me saying, but Bruno,' he gripped the door handle, 'it would be an injustice to mankind if you don't pass that blessing on.'

'What are you talking about?'

Hermes raised his eyebrows, and Bruno followed his gaze to the bulge in the sheets where his thighs met.

Bruno raised his hand to cover his good eye and turned away.

'Rest up, *Brunão*.' The door opened in a searing flash of daylight and then closed.

Bruno didn't leave the bedsit that day or the next. Hermes brought him a plug-in fan and some simple food from the supermarket, telling him that Luis sent his regards. For the first time since he'd left his city Bruno had his own room. Walls of brick and a solid roof; there was modern furniture, ceramic plates, steel utensils and electrical appliances. Unlike the mirror in the campsite toilets, the one here was clean and in one piece. He stared at himself in it every day, at the lines Niki had made, and at the blue-grey of the old one where it seemed to leak through. He pulled facial expressions and could just see the natural lines of his eyes and mouth, deepening with age. He was almost able to imagine himself without it. He'd never seen a photo of himself as a child, and tried to remember how he'd looked then. What would he say to that boy now? What would that boy say to him?

Everything was so different. He'd been living in forests

of every shade of green and brown, picking wild fruit and berries, swimming in the streams and ponds. Now, here he was in a cube, everything square, synthetic: paint, plastic, chrome-plated steel. As he went to sleep at night on his factory-made bed, he thought about everyone else in the town lying on theirs in their cubic rooms, all stacked one above the other. He'd never considered any of these things when he was in the campsite. There was something unsettling about the order of it all.

The ache in his head didn't go away as quickly as he expected. His actions were delayed; his arms and legs moving a fraction later than his brain told them to. His eyes were sluggish in their sockets; it was easier to move his head to see things, even with the brace on. His body had lost its coordination and balance. There was no strength in his fingers. He could barely find a reason to get out of bed, and only got up when hunger or thirst became painful. Once, as he was preparing something to eat, he burst into tears without reason. That night, Tiago and Rudi came over to see how he was doing.

They greeted him as if he'd won the fight, placed beers and dominoes on the table, and made him join them in a game. They were quick to rebuke him when he said he'd never practise again, and criticised how he was dealing with things. It wasn't healthy to lock himself away like this, they said. He had a concussion, nothing more. He had to get back to work and get on with life. Everything would be alright. Too tired and unable to think straight, he gave up on the dominoes and watched them play.

'I don't think I'll recover from this,' he said.

'It's just a concussion, Bruno.' Rudi sipped his beer. 'I felt the same. Can take weeks, even months to get better. You just have to stay positive.'

Tiago got up and filled Bruno's glass of water again.

'Thanks for coming over, guys,' said Bruno. 'You didn't have to.'

'You're part of the team.' Tiago laid another domino. 'We look after each other.'

Bruno thought about how different their lives had been to his own. These were young and enthusiastic men, brought up in loving families, the kind of family he'd like to have. But this was their home, their life. They were content. Was this *really* what he wanted from his life? He was so close to the forest.

The next day, although he wanted to keep away from everyone, he took Rudi's advice and returned to work. He avoided all but light conversation, and carried out simple tasks, alone, at the slow pace his body permitted. He stayed away from the bookshop, despite Riccardo – whose back pocket was threadbare and always bulging with one of the crime novels he'd kept pushing him to read – telling him how concerned Rosy was. He avoided the restaurants and bars, and cooked, a little uneasily, under the extractor fan of his electric cooker.

As the days passed, the humiliation Bruno felt turned to anger. Despite going out of his way to avoid him, Faka's bestial face and beady eyes forced their way into Bruno's head and dreams.

It wasn't out of fear of Faka that Bruno avoided him. It was because he wished him dead. He had learned something a long time ago that he knew Faka would never realise: it's not how tough you are but how far you're willing to go. Bruno knew that if he really wanted to, he'd find a way to harm or kill Faka, whether through poison or setting a trap or some other means. Nothing was stopping him but his own sense of right and wrong.

Just as Rudi had told him, after a few more days, the fog in his head began to drift off. He read his philosophy books again. Every one of them came to the same conclusion. It was wrong to take revenge on someone, no matter how severe the altercation. He couldn't understand it. It was easy for these thinkers to say that an eye for an eye would make everyone blind, but would they be repeating it as their torturer cranked the rack? Would they wish leniency on their wife's murderer or their child's abductor? Surely not, but Bruno knew his limitations. These books were written by smarter men, and although he didn't agree with what they were telling him today, maybe one day he would come to understand it.

He knew the books were right about one thing, that every time his anger brought thoughts of ill will towards Faka, every plan of revenge he dreamt up, every time Faka's beady eyes entered his mind, was time lost for himself. He couldn't allow this hate to fester. The only way forward within his means was not revenge but complete mastery of himself. Once again, he took to routine, and concentrated on becoming something greater than he was.

He punished himself through physical exercise every time a thought of Faka entered his mind. Even if he was in the presence of others, he'd drop to the ground and do push-ups, sit-ups or squats. Soon, he was up to fifty push-ups in a row. Something he'd only managed to do once as a teen. Not long after, he was up to a hundred. Time passed, and as his body grew stronger, the thoughts of Faka eroded. He began to feel as good as he had before entering the *roda*, better, even. He'd been able to turn a completely negative situation into a positive one. He'd rebuilt himself again. It hadn't even been that much of a challenge. He smiled at himself in the mirror. Whatever was going to happen was inevitable. He couldn't control life, nor the actions or reactions of those around him, but he could control how he dealt with things. He knew now just to get on with living.

After the kick, the locals took to him more. Instead of the pitying looks, the pointing and laughter he'd expected, people he'd never spoken to went out of their way to ask how he was. It was as if the respect and dignity he now granted himself reflected in those around him. Bea had been right all those months ago. 'The world's a mirror,' she'd said. 'It only sees what you do.' His self-loathing had been contagious.

With his head completely clear and his confidence higher than it had ever been, Bruno returned to the campsite to collect his things. A ceramic bowl, porridge oozing down its side, sat on the sand at Bea's hip. She didn't look up from her pen and paper. Carlos had latched open the front of Bruno's old storage compartment, and was standing inside.

All the materials Bruno had accumulated over many months were gone, replaced by a big enough pile of wire coat hangers to fill the wardrobes of half the houses in town.

'Making coat hangers now, Carlos?' Bruno didn't care about the missing junk. 'Maybe I can buy some from you?'

Carlos cocked his head and eyed him with a smile. 'Aye, Bruno, my boy.' He held up a finger. 'Nothing gets by you... Isn't that right, Bea, my little jack-o'-lantern?' He looked at her over Bruno's shoulder and lowered his voice, the crackle in his throat like a layer of white noise. 'I haven't seen you around, Bruno. We thought you and Honey had eloped. Secret rendezvous, aye?'

'Carlos, look, I'm here for my things.'

'Moving on?'

Bruno nodded. 'They've given me a house.'

'Oh, may I offer my sincere felicitations.' He extended his hand.

It was the second time Bruno had felt the power of Carlos's grip. He was completely at this man's mercy. If Carlos wanted to, he could squeeze until every bone in Bruno's hand was crushed. Bruno made an effort to hide his relief when the grip was withdrawn but the flicker of a smile under Carlos's moustache showed it hadn't been enough.

'Has it a number?'

'Excuse me?'

'Your cell.'

'Six.'

'Ahhh…' Carlos pushed his bottom lip up over the top one, fanning out his moustache like the tips of a vulture's wings. 'A good number. A perfect number. Six-six-six.'

'Carlos, I don't understand why you can't ever be serious.'

'Is that so?' Carlos flicked his moustache. He chopped his hand down from forehead to chin and looked at Bruno with sad eyes and a quivering lip. 'I… I…' His voice trembled. He bit his fist and held up the other palm, inhaling theatrically. He composed himself and spoke in an even voice. 'I show people the person they want to see, Bruno. You want to see a fool, do you not? Here you have the fool.'

Bruno left him standing by the pile of coat hangers, slipped into the sleeping compartment and gathered up his things. He was relieved to find the camera still in the hole he'd dug under the mats.

With the camera tethered to his neck, and his bag clanging with the machetes and bush-tools that hung from every web he'd woven into it, he walked over to Bea.

'Bea,' he said. As soon as he spoke his mouth clammed up. She looked at him with her empty eyes, her lip puffing and her nostrils flaring as she breathed. 'I don't know what's gone wrong here. I have some ideas but can't know anything for certain. It just feels like the right thing to do,' he nodded to himself, 'is to give you more space. That's what I think you want.' He cleared his throat so the emotion wouldn't stop him from saying what he needed to say. She kept silent, and he continued. 'I just want to let you know that I don't blame you for anything. You've done so much for me and I appreciate it. I owe you everything, I really do. If you won't speak, will you at least stand so I can give you a hug, please?'

Pen in one hand, notepad in the other, she got to her feet.

Encumbered by all the gear, he wrapped his arms around her and pressed his cheek into hers, ignoring her flinch and groan. 'You might seem small to some people,' he whispered, tears escaping from his eyes, 'but I know how big you are.

330

You're a giant to me, Bea. I love you. You're my best friend and my biggest inspiration. I wish you the world, no matter what happens, or what you think of me. Your happiness is so much more important than mine. It's only because of that that I'll let you go, okay? Okay, my dear? If you ever need anything, I'm here. I'm right fucking here for you.' He stood back. A single tear spilled from her eyelid to her cheek. 'You're family, Bea. Family.' Even with all the pain in his heart, he managed to smile at her. He'd said all he could say, and would no longer be a burden.

He approached Carlos. 'Carlos.' He wiped the dew from his eyes and took a breath to steady his voice. 'Take my shelter. With all the mats cushioning the sand, and the height of it, it has to be more comfortable than your tent. He hesitated and lowered his voice so Bea couldn't hear. 'I'll be honest, Carlos. I've hated you for taking Bea. I've been jealous, angry. I… I don't know what. I never felt like myself around you. Everything was a struggle. But I've realised that we all have to be ourselves and accept that. I don't have to live up to anyone's expectations, and neither do you. As long as we try to live up to our own, isn't that how it should be? I wish you all the best, too.'

'Thank you, Bruno,' said Carlos, in such a natural tone, and with such a sincere demeanour, that Bruno took a step back and stared. 'A truer word I never heard. For that I'll go easy on you when I take over.'

Bruno forced a laugh. Even after all this he wasn't going to be serious. 'You're a crazy guy, Carlos. I've never met anyone like you, but the world would be a boring place if we were all the same, wouldn't it?'

'I'll take that as a compliment.'

'Look after her. Don't you ever let her down.' Bruno walked through the campsite and on to his house.

That night, while re-stocking the *carrinhos*, Bruno noticed the light was on at Anderson's. He decided to go over and say

331

hello. It felt strange approaching him after so long without having spoken. Behind the counter, Anderson watched him as he approached.

'They found her,' Anderson said. 'Off to find that Pavel guy. Has she gone senile? Even if he's alive, how does she expect to find him?'

'It's kind of romantic when you think about it.' Bruno slid onto a bar stool.

'Stupid's what it is. Let's go out back.'

Bruno hopped off the bar stool as Anderson turned for the back door. 'It was a lot to take in,' Bruno said, walking around the kiosk. 'I thought things had ended much differently.' He sat down on the scrub grass. 'I thought the tourists had killed her.' Anderson closed the door and took a seat on the step. He passed Bruno one of the two beers in his hand.

'Ditto.' Beer hissed from the can as Anderson opened it. 'In hindsight, it's obvious Mac would've got it out of them if they did. Three days they were locked up in that tree. They'd have been singing just to be able to stretch their legs out.'

'I'm not so sure, Anderson. Guilty in a city is prison. What's guilty here? Rocks tied to your feet and thrown into the sea?'

'Something would've turned up eventually: her body, her clothes. Anyway, she's on the road now. She's fine.'

'I just hope she finds what she's looking for.'

'I hope that for us all.'

'You haven't been around, Anderson. I was surprised to see your light on. I thought I'd done something wrong.'

'I've been in the same routine for so long, Bruno. I needed a change. It's nothing to do with you. Things have just got a bit tiresome.'

'Still reading that book?'

'The Bible? Sometimes. You might not agree with it, but for me, it gives more than it takes, so I'm sticking with it.'

'I have a house now, you know? Honey's. You should come by, have a beer with me.'

'I'm not drinking that much any more to be honest. Maybe someday.'

Bruno nodded. 'You seen much of Bea or Carlos? I saw them over at the *carrinhos* just now. Faka's on shift.'

'I heard what he did to you. That guy's just bad news. He'll get what's coming. Don't you worry.'

'I'm over all that,' Bruno said.

Anderson swigged from the can then swilled the beer around in it. 'Bea and Carlos pass by now and again, never for long, though.'

'She mentions me?'

'You know how women are, Bruno. Don't worry yourself about Bea. She's fine. I see that brewery of yours is coming along.'

Bruno exhaled and looked at the ground. 'The turbine will be spinning soon.'

'You've come a long way, Bruno.' Anderson smiled. 'Remember that first night? Did you ever develop that photo you took?'

'Still in the camera. If I do I'll bring it to you. Maybe I should get the guys to develop it in the city. Hey, you want to go and see the drummers? The guys won't shut up about them.'

'I'm keeping to myself a lot more nowadays, Bruno. The crowd will be too big.' Anderson took a heavy drink from the can.

They sat in silence for a while. 'Am I keeping you from something?' Bruno asked.

'No, of course not. I just need to clean the place up a little bit more then I'm done for the night.'

'You cleaned the place up last time we spoke. Need help?'
'No, it's fine.'

'Getting all your news on the campsite from Bea now? Abilio and his lot been making a nuisance of themselves?'

Anderson shrugged. 'They're not that bad, I suppose.' He stared out over the rocks into the night. Where once he'd talked openly and without effort, Anderson now seemed guarded and hesitant to speak.

'There's nothing bothering you?'

'Not a thing.'

'I'll go, then. You know where I am. Come by anytime. Don't get too much into that book, Anderson. Remember, that's all it is. A book.'

'Sure thing.' Anderson got up. 'Come here,' he said and embraced Bruno. 'You take care of yourself.'

Bruno pulled away and looked at him. 'You better not run off too, Anderson. If you need anything, you know where I am, okay? Don't hesitate.'

Anderson nodded, opened the door and slipped inside.

On Saturday, the day of Mac's drumming extravaganza, Lagarto commandeered all of Bruno's men to prepare the area in front of the temple for the event. Tiago stayed with Bruno to help with the bottling.

From the decking, Bruno and Tiago watched the work commence. White bulbs on the *caju* trees were changed for ones of all spectral colours. Steel rods were staked into the sand around the site, then ringed out with red and white plastic ribbon. A low wooden stage was constructed, and metal poles, which Bruno recognised as stripped city street lights, were driven into the sand at each corner. Spotlights taken from Ivo's were mounted to the top of each pole, and the cables taped down the sides.

The women arrived in three 4×4s, with Mac at the wheel of the first. There were nine of them, dark-skinned beauties with ivory eyes and full lips the shade of the leaves on a black cherry-plum tree. Townsmen helped them haul their bags and conga drums into the temple. The dark-wood drums were carved in the same style as the temple doors, the stretched drum-skins held taut by frayed twine.

In the late afternoon, the *carrinhos* were wheeled into position, and a pair of buckets with *1 CONTO ENTRY* painted on them, were placed at either side of the opening. As the sun dipped toward the dune, Mac came out of the temple and inspected the site with Lagarto, who then released the men.

Bruno went back home, cooked a small meal and rested. He fell asleep and dreamt of Honey again. It was the same dream as the one he'd had in the hammock.

She was swimming through the turquoise sea, never surfacing for air. The sun's rays penetrated the water like heavenly pillars, and with each stroke she grew younger and more radiant, but as she neared the boat on the horizon, the sunlight distorted and the storm took hold. Bolts of lightning shot towards her. Thunder crashed. As she reached for the lifebuoy, the final bolt came at her. He woke.

*

It was night when he returned for the performance. The space was already full. Tourists and townsfolk crushed together. The heat from their bodies rose above the tree lights in an effervescent stew.

A pair of townsmen rattled the *1 CONTO ENTRY* buckets as the people streamed through the entrance. Next to them, a group of cool-box-men shouted: 'Burro Beer! Five *contos* a pop… Ice water three *contos*… Don't be shy…' They all smiled at Bruno as he tossed a note into one of the buckets and joined the crowd.

Over people's heads he could just make out the tips of the *berimbaus* on the stage. He heard the melody but couldn't see the musicians or the *capoeiristas* performing. He squeezed through the throng of T-shirted and bare-shouldered men, women in bikini tops, and trampled over empty plastic cups and cigarette butts to the nearest cocktail cart.

'Two *caipirinhas*, Luc,' he shouted above the competing

voices. He slugged them and ordered two more so he wouldn't have to return during the performance.

'Go down to the stage,' Lucio said. 'You'll get the best acoustics.'

Bruno drank his third cocktail and edged towards the front, apologising for every bump and shove he caused. Hundreds of warbling voices amplified together, adding to the electrolyte charge that buzzed through the humid air.

The capoeira performance had finished and the stage was empty by the time he reached the plastic ribbon in front of it. The cocktails were already having an effect. He'd barely drunk since his concussion and his tolerance had diminished. He felt the alcohol lingering behind his eyes like a co-pilot ready to take the controls. He sank the final drink, dropped the cup to the sand and bit down on the melting shards of ice. The grassy scent of *maconha* seeped through the odour of musky sweat and beer. It brought a smile to his face. He looked around for its source.

A male tourist noticed him looking, reached over the people between them, and passed Bruno the joint. He pinched it between his fingers and held the tip to his nose. He'd only smoked once before, as a teenager with Flora, but hadn't forgotten how. He brought the roach end to his lips and inhaled, hearing the crackle of the flame, watching the embers flare. This was his rebirth; not the tattoo, not getting the job. It was a rebirth brought on by mastery of his mind and body, achieved by, and accountable to, himself alone. For the first time in his life, he realised he was a full person. He held the smoke in his lungs, struggling against the need to cough, and passed the joint back to its owner.

'*Hold it as long as you can*,' he heard Flora say. He closed his eyes and nodded to her. Wherever she was, he hoped she was happy. Face to the stars, he opened his mouth and let the smoke rise up into the night.

Mac appeared on stage, bare-chested as usual and in his red *abadas*. His gold watch glinted under the spotlights as he rubbed his hands together. With wide eyes and an arrogant smile, he nodded at the crowd. *He's done well for himself*, thought Bruno. *Who can blame him?*

'Brothers and sisters, friends, thank you for your patience.' He flung his arms out as if to embrace every one of them. 'I'd like one more cheer for the child *capoeiristas* and *berimbau* band!

'This is not my night,' he continued, ushering the crowd to settle down. 'It's yours, and it's with great pleasure and pride that I present to you *Os Percussionistas do Mundo Antigo!*'

In an eruption of applause, the women hobbled onto the stage, straddling the great drums slung from ropes digging into their hips.

They wore skirts woven from bush grass, and earthen clay brassieres. Wooden beads draped their necks, wrists and ankles. Their hair was separated into strands like tree branches, each strand wound in colourful thread. Their faces were painted with white lines and dots that followed the contours of their eyes, cheeks and mouths in the same way as the black lines did on Bruno's face. He cheered without restraint and smiled up at them as they took their position on the stage.

Without a word to each other or the audience, the woman in the middle brought her heel down like a hammer. They began to chant. Strange harmonies that were almost visible escaped their throats and flowed through the air, leaching into the crowd like conscious entities.

In the grip of the *maconha* and alcohol, Bruno watched as well as listened to the music. It saturated his consciousness, at some moments threatening to whisk him out of his body, at others pulling him back and letting him settle in and breathe.

The drums crashed in fast and heavy, like cattle traversing a plain; the wooden *chocalhos* on the women's wrists and ankles shook like the flapping of wings. He looked up to the sky for migrating birds, but it was empty. With the music pulsing through him like a second heartbeat, he closed his eyes and released his grip on his mind.

He forgot about the crowd but could feel the great collective energy flowing from it. He felt the movement of every muscle, every fibre of his being. The sound of the drums and chanting drove on, carrying him with it. Neither asleep nor awake, he felt himself separate from his body then reconnect to it. One rhythm had a cold sweat running down his face, another had him taking his shirt off to cool down. At one point he was near tears, at another he experienced euphoria.

He saw his past, remembered the glorious days he'd spent with Flora, and later, the drinking in harbour bars with seafarers, prostitutes and down-and-outs. He'd gone there to take their photographs, trying to show that even in the darkest of corners of life there was colour and beauty, but after time he'd forgotten his purpose. Flora's disappearance had been the catalyst of his descent, but it was in those bars that his hatred really took hold. It was there that the depression and alcoholism began.

Another rhythm struck up. He clenched his jaw. There came no thoughts, no memories, only the drums, the chanting. The atmosphere filled with the smell of leaves, tree bark and soil. He was in a forest. A fire was burning. He smiled at the sound of the women's voices. The noises they made were familiar. They were singing in the same language Mac had used to wake the tourists at the corral.

Bruno opened an eye and looked at the nearest drummer. She was shorter than the others and well padded, with thick, strong legs and arms. The rope of her drum dug deep into her fleshy curves. He watched the creamy palms of her hands beat on the bleached drum-skin then looked up into her face.

Her eyes were on him, and when he looked away then looked back again, her cherry-plum lips spread into a milk-white smile. She winked. He nodded at her and smiled back.

Another change in the drumbeat brought him back to the crowd. He wanted everyone to huddle tighter to him, to feel the heat of their bodies, feel their movement. They were all in this together, were they not? An organic, throbbing, united mass. He raised his face to the night sky, overcome by its vastness. He wished his eyes could take it all in, millions upon millions of stars, planets, solar systems; the whole universe right there. He reached up to grab it, then remembered the *maconha*. He wanted more. He looked for the man who'd passed it to him, but he was gone.

'You know?' he said in the ear of the person next to him. 'You know... there's more space in your body than... than anything else?'

'Excuse me?' the voice replied.

'Space,' Bruno repeated, holding his hands out above his head. 'More space... in your body.'

A pair of eyebrows rose into a wrinkled forehead, then the whole face disappeared.

Bruno turned his attention back to the woman on the stage. She understood him. He winked at her and she smiled.

The music stopped so abruptly he almost fell. For a moment nobody in the audience seemed to know what to do. The women stood motionless on the stage, the sweat on their bodies sparkling under the spotlights. Bruno stared at them with an empty mind. A whistle sounded from far away. Applause erupted all around him. The women bowed and waved, all smiling and happy. They shuffled off the stage towards the temple doors. He bounded forward and reached out for the woman. The others laughed and waited for her. She looked from him to them and laughed. She held five outstretched fingers to him, telling him to wait, and followed the others inside.

He sat on the edge of the stage and watched the crowd disperse. The locals followed the drummers into the temple while the tourists headed back into town. A few tourists lingered at the *carrinhos*, where the exhausted cart-boys served them without enthusiasm. Valter waved a group on from his kart to the next and hauled it away.

Plastic cups, straws and cigarette ends were strewn on the sand. A few cups stood upright, filled with either flat beer or urine. A pair of black lace knickers lay twisted not far from the stage. There was still a trace of sweat and beer in the air, a warmth to the sand underfoot.

With trembling hands, Bruno lifted the front of his shirt and wiped the sweat from his face. The hairs on his arms were dry and standing. His legs twitched with nervous energy. The withdrawal of the music had left him blank and anxious.

The door of the temple opened, and the drummer woman, now dressed in black shorts and a white T-shirt, emerged. She was carrying a hemp shoulder bag. Her face was still painted with white lines and dots, but the change of dress had transported her from a primal world to the modern age. He wished she'd kept the dress on, but the smile on her face and the welcoming look in her eyes put it out of his mind.

Before he could say anything, she hugged him.

'What's your name?' he asked.

She stared at him and was silent.

He touched his chest. 'Bruno.'

She patted the skin above the neck of her T-shirt. 'Mimosa.'

'Mee-moh-sah,' Bruno repeated.

'*Hewa.*' She touched her chest again. 'Mimosa.'

'*Habla Español? Português?* English?'

She smiled.

He realised the eyes of the remaining cart-boys and tourists were on them. He had no idea what to say or do. Almost automatically, his palm extended towards the opening between the steel rods. 'Shall we go?' he asked.

As they walked past the carts, he tried to keep her attention away from Lucio, who was pumping his hand, and tonguing his cheek. Bruno held up a fist at him behind her back.

He mimed beating a drum as they crossed Main Street. 'Very good,' he said, nodding at her and raising a thumb. '*Muito bom, muy bien, khoroso.*'

She replied by smiling. Her pleasant eyes were at once terrifying and thrilling. Here he was, in the company of a real woman. He couldn't believe it. 'I guess we'll go to my house,' he said, wiping fresh sweat from his brow.

He dropped the key twice as she waited, but finally slid it into the lock and got the door open. He closed the door and guided her to the couch. 'Sit. I'll bring us some beer.'

He grabbed a bottle from the fridge and snapped two glasses together. His temples throbbed in rhythm with his heart as he looked at the back of her head. This was really happening. He sat down next to her, hoping she didn't notice how nervous he was, placed the glasses on the coffee table and filled them.

'Hot,' he said, passing her a glass before drawing his own across his forehead. She raised the glass and sniffed at the beer. 'You don't understand a thing I'm saying, do you?'

Side by side, with her staring straight ahead, he tried to think. 'I make this.' He pointed at the glass. 'Not the glass, of course, but the beer. I make the beer.' He drained half the glass. From the corner of his eye he watched her take a tentative sip.

'*Tchivê.*' She spat it back in the glass and put it down.

'You don't like it?' He laughed. 'I'm sorry. Something else maybe? Vodka? Whisky? Water?' He rushed to the kitchenette and brought her some water. Despite his nerves, he laughed again. It was one of the strangest situations he'd ever got himself into. They didn't even share a common language. What could they do?

'*Nhê wa ndinenela kulo?*'

He tried to interpret what she was saying through her tone of voice and her body language, but had no idea. She shrugged and looked at the wall. He glanced at his watch. It was almost one in the morning. *She's in your house*, he thought. *It's* obvious *what she's here for. Don't waste any more time.* With a jolt of courage, he leaned in and pressed his lips into hers. Her hands landed on his shoulders and she pushed him away.

'*Ove nhê okassi lo kupanga?*' She stood.

'I'm sorry,' he said, holding his palms up. He'd offended her. He got to his feet. 'I'm really sorry. I thought that's what you wanted.'

'*Ove kwandi kulinhê! Ove kwa kulinhile oko nda tundilila!*'

'Here,' he said, holding up her water. 'Drink. I didn't mean to disrespect you. Sit down, please.' He held his hand out to the sofa again, but she wouldn't sit. Her eyes were on the jar of marker pens, pencils and chalk on the table. 'You want to write?' He reached for the jar and the notepad and held them up to her.

She pulled out a marker and motioned to the empty wall.

'Use it.' He threw the notepad on the sofa, strode to the wall and spread his arms out across it. 'Use all of it, as much as you want.'

'*Etu ka tulievite tchiwa,*' she said, '*pamwe wiya olimbika oviluyaluya vyangue. Ame ndiya ndu kulekissa tchossi, nde kefetikilo.*' She drew a jagged, vertical line, then turned to look at him.

'What?' He almost laughed. 'It's a line. What am I supposed to take from that?'

She exhaled and threw a hand up. '*Ove kunshê?*' She turned back to the wall and extended the line down. It curved round and came back up ragged and uneven, then cut across horizontally.

'Africa,' he said. 'You're drawing Africa.'

She giggled, continuing the line around Morocco and the

Sahara, then brought it in and down to where she'd started. She circled a dot in the centre of the first line she'd drawn.

'Namibia?' he asked. 'Angola?'

'*Ngola*,' she said without turning to him. '*Hewa*.'

She began talking as she drew. He came up to her shoulder and watched as she drew a woman wrapped in cloth. She gave her a spear, a shield.

'A warrior,' Bruno said, but she added a crown. 'A queen.'

'*Nzinga*,' she said, tapping the end of the marker on the crown. '*Nzinga Mbande*.'

She drew galleons sailing in from the north. On their sails was the cross of the Order of Christ. He realised she was drawing the beginning of the Portuguese occupation of Angola and its slave trade. Europeans appeared with Africans in chains. There were battles where the queen led her army against the invaders. She sketched her in a meeting, sitting on the back of one of her servants after the Portuguese official didn't provide a chair.

He watched the flutter of Mimosa's hand as it led the pen across the wall. The black, glossy illustrations left behind it jumped off the once white surface, now stained a shade of yellow by Honey's cigarette smoke. She spoke without pause in her impenetrable language that somehow suited her style of drawing perfectly. It was as if the *maconha* kicked in again. The cadence of her voice, the poetry of her words, the scratching of the nib on the wall transported him into her world, full of colour, sound and smell. He saw kings, queens and warriors, vicious battles, glorious victories, agonising defeats. He learned about Nzinga's sister Bantu. How the Portuguese had tried to drown her in a river, but she'd escaped only to be recaptured by slavers and, unrecognised, shipped over the Atlantic. It was in Bahia that she'd met Yoruba and Fon, a pair of men who were young in years, but wise and strong. Like herself, they stood out from the others. Natural leaders, the three were idolised and followed by everyone. Yoruba and Fon taught her about *Os Orishas*, about how to live in balance with both nature and the unseen world. In return, she taught them the dance of the zebra, which kept them strong and supple, ready for any uprising. Seeing it as harmless, the slavers ignored the dance, no matter how many of the slaves practised it. It evolved without obstruction into the martial art of capoeira. Inspired by her sister's veil of Christianity, Bantu convinced Yoruba and Fon to disguise *Os Orishas* as Christian saints. In doing so, the religion still practised by Mac was born.

By the time the nib came to a final stop the whole wall was covered. She'd drawn the entire history of a civilisation right through to the present day, where she, the other women and a multitude of practitioners across the continent, were spreading their way of life all over the vast lands of rural Africa.

From her drawing alone, he'd understood everything she'd told him. He looked in her intelligent eyes and could see that she knew he'd understood. She smiled.

He went to fill her glass again and was shocked to see the light of day shining through the gap in the curtains. Panic shot through him. He wanted more time with her, wanted her to help him learn about himself and his world. He could learn her language, get to know her as a person, see what her everyday life was like. Before he even got the tap running, she was at the door. 'Wait,' he shouted. 'Stay. Stay here. I can look after you.'

He took her hand from the handle.

'*Ove kuyongola otcho ndende?* (You don't want me to leave?)' She combed his hair back from his forehead with her free hand. 'Bruno, *ukayocoke. Lô muenho. Tchitchapo, ho muenho ulivale látcho* (Don't worry about life, life will take care of itself).' She smiled. '*Ove umonlà wa ñgo*, Bruno, *ove umonlà wa ñgo nda* Mac, *ove halopo umonlà* (You're a boy, Bruno. Just like Mac, you're still only a boy).'

She walked back to the wall, touched the first dot she'd drawn on the map, then held her hand to her chest.

He took a breath, unlocked the door and held it open for her. 'At least let me walk with you,' he said. 'I'll take you back to the temple.'

She opened the door and both of them squinted into the sunlight. She stepped outside, and as he went to follow her, her hand landed on his chest. She pointed to the bed and clasped her palms together at the side of her face. When his shoulders fell, she pulled him to her and kissed him on the forehead. He pressed his cheek to hers and held her. 'Thank you,' he said.

She stroked his hair again, nodded, and walked away.

*

That night, Bruno found the men playing cards around the table at the brewery. He looked at the wind turbine looming over the whole construction and imagined the blades turning. He smiled. Very soon, they would be. This was all his doing, an idea made tangible. He'd created something from nothing.

'Here he is!' said Riccardo, cutting off Tiago, who was leaning in amongst the glasses and beer bottles talking about something. 'Top shagger! How was she? I bet she went some.'

'Wasn't anything like that,' said Bruno. He took a seat next to Tiago and pulled over a glass. Rudi passed him the bottle. 'I mean, I tried, obviously, but she wasn't interested. I'm kind of glad about it, actually. It was perfect as it was.'

'But you don't even speak the same language,' said Selmo. 'What did you do, cuddle?'

'Lagarto said they were already in the 4×4s by the time she appeared, said she had a huge grin on her face and the other girls were teasing her about it.' Riccardo's forehead creased as he looked at Bruno.

'Nothing sexual happened, I'm serious.'

'You're telling me,' Riccardo tilted his head and eyed him over the frames of his glasses, 'that she stayed the _whole_ night, you couldn't speak to each other, and you didn't even have a feel?' He fondled an imaginary breast.

'Didn't have to speak. She's an artist. She showed me everything.'

'Showed you what? How?'

'History. She drew. She drew everything right from the start.'

Riccardo took off his glasses and rubbed his eyes. He pulled a cloth from his pocket and wiped the lenses, all the while shaking his head in disappointment at Bruno. 'Anyway,' he said, turning his attention to Tiago. 'Where were we?'

'Maybe it's lack of sleep,' said Tiago.

'Ego,' said Rudi. Selmo patted the table in agreement.

'Talking about Faka.' Tiago passed a note to Bruno.

Bruno read aloud: '*THEEFS WILL BE PROSICUTED.* What's this?'

'He told me to give it to you. It's painted on the front of his shop, too. He's sure someone's stealing from him.'

Faka's presence at the *carrinhos*, which had long been affecting the tourists, was now making the cart-boys uneasy. Throughout the night, he'd push through the crowd, beat his fist on the cart counters and demand free drinks. His leering at the young tourist girls had intensified and he almost got into fights with the men. His actions at the *carrinhos* were not the only cause for concern. His *bermibau* playing at the capoeira sessions was out of sync. Rumours had begun circulating that in the back of the butcher shop he took pleasure in killing the animals as slowly and painfully as possible. There were even whispers that during the *Festa De Yemanjá*, when the men were in the water, he'd let the sedan chair handle slip – a great insult to the goddess. Many of the townsfolk, although careful in their wording of it, were now blaming him for the bad energy that seemed to have reappeared after his assault on Bruno in the *roda*.

Bruno touched the corner of the note to a glowing

cigarette in the ashtray. He held it aflame until the heat nearly burned his fingertips then dropped it to the decking and stamped on it. He reclined in his chair and smiled. He'd come so far with the men. They were opening up more and speaking to him as if he'd always been a townsman, instead of one of the travellers they quietly resented. Religion was discussed freely in his presence. They spoke of *Os Orishas*, their colours, favourite foods and drinks, and even about sacrifice and possession, unaware that Bruno already knew much about it from his spying days. They even suggested he convert, telling him it was more of a lifestyle than a selfish and cruel monotheistic religion like those he'd more than likely been exposed to. When he questioned them about such religions, he realised they knew almost nothing about them.

For as long as Bruno could remember, he'd never been able to turn to religion. He always entertained the idea with enthusiasm after a few beers when they asked him to join, but his mind had been set long ago. '*Dust, bone and the abyss,*' he wanted to tell them. '*That's all that waits for us.*' Nothing good could come from saying it, he knew, so he kept it to himself.

One night, when Selmo joked about donkey and horse burgers, Bruno held his breath. Were they capable of such a thing? He wondered how Bea would react if she knew the possible origin of the meat she'd been eating. While Bea had gone back to consuming meat, he'd been enjoying the discipline of following a vegetarian diet and had decided to continue it.

The more the men talked of their religion, the more Bruno tried to influence them to come round to his way of thinking. He quoted the words of great leaders and philosophers from books he'd read, and tried to engage them in philosophical debates, but they were never interested. Whenever he paused for breath, they'd change the subject to capoeira, the temple, or local gossip.

One thing that Bruno admired in the guys was that they never spoke of money. Here he was, an outsider, a man who'd lived off the land and wandered alone with nobody and nothing, arriving in their town and walking straight into a higher position than any of them. There wasn't even a hint of animosity. Sure, he'd struggled to motivate them, to keep their interest, but that was through his own incompetence. He was now at work on all his weaknesses, and making real improvements. Their lack of output had nothing to do with money. Mac had been sincere when he mentioned a defendable wage. This really was a town built on respect instead of exploitation. Everyone was happy from top to bottom.

'Faka will break soon,' said Joao. 'I'm telling you. Mac's been too slow.' Selmo stopped shuffling the cards. The men's eyes fixed on Joao. He cleared his throat. 'Mac's been extra cautious about this, that's all I'm saying. Something'll happen. I can feel it.'

'Mac will sort it out,' said Riccardo. 'He always does.'

'You guys felt the atmosphere at the drumming, didn't you?' said Tiago. 'Bruno, did you?'

'I'm not sure what was happening that night,' said Bruno. 'I think I drank too much.'

'Was it a good energy or a bad energy?' asked Rudi.

'Good.'

Tiago raised a hand to the others. 'See! Even Bruno felt it. Faka wasn't there. You go to the *carrinhos* and it's a different atmosphere altogether, I'm telling you. It's suffocating.'

'It's obvious Mac brought those women here to help fix the problem,' said Riccardo. 'Mac will sort Faka out, if he hasn't already.' He pushed his glasses back from the tip of his nose and looked at the men. 'You wait and see.'

It wasn't Riccardo's prediction that proved correct, though. It was Joao's. It happened a few days later, on Main Street, in front of the packed restaurants, bars and shops.

Adelina came sprinting down the street, the infant squeezed under one arm and a trimming of red meat, marbled with fat, gripped in her other hand.

She slowed just long enough to stand the hysterical infant on the hot sand and point which direction for it to go, then ran on. Despite the strangeness of the spectacle, the crowd watched without concern. Adelina wasn't screaming or crying for help. The only noise came from the chafing of her clothes, her gasping breaths, and the whipping of the meat in her hand.

The calm of the crowd was broken, however, and a collective gasp of alarm rang out as Faka charged into view. He pursued her with a club made from a long-spined cactus limb. He knocked the infant out of his path with the side of his foot, caught up with Adelina and sent her tumbling with a kick to her trailing leg.

She cowered in the foetal position as Faka strode up to her. Tourists rose from their chairs. Workers halted their service. They all stood unblinking, silent. The infant wailed.

'Won't steal from me again, will you?' Faka roared. He raised the club.

'No!' she cried from the crook of her arm. 'Please don't.'

He brought the cactus limb down hard towards her head. She shielded herself, and caught the blow on her forearm. A scream rose from the pit of her stomach. She rolled onto her front. Again the club came down, its spikes snagging on her clothes, her hair. It crashed onto her hip, then her back.

'Stop!' a tourist yelled. His cry was echoed a hundred times as others around the street joined him, calling for mercy. Waiters and baristas ran into the street. They surrounded Faka, pleading for him to drop the club. The tourists rushed over behind them.

'Won't steal from nobody!' The club bounced off her, sending fibres of clothing, clumps of hair and spots of blood flying.

'Steal from me?' His voice sounded above the cries of the tourists and locals.

She couldn't catch her breath to speak. The club came down and a chunk flew off, exposing the metal bar in its centre. Oozing puncture holes mottled her flesh. Locals tried to time the movement of the club and grabbed at Faka, but he tossed them aside. He pounded her again and again, swinging the club at anyone who tried to drag her into the crowd. His chest heaved from the exertion. The club was now no more than a metal bar with a mash of green and red pulp bleeding down it.

Adelina's back and hip were completely exposed. Her skin looked more like the meat still gripped in her fist than human flesh.

Mac forced his way through the crowd as Faka threw the weapon aside.

'She's still clutching the meat,' Faka said to Mac, brushing the pulp from his hands. He pointed at her white-nailed fingers. 'Told you I'd get 'em.' Adelina tried to speak. 'She wants more.' Faka wiped the sweat from his cheeks, took half a step forward and pulled back his fist. Mac's heel connected just behind Faka's ear. He collapsed to the ground, rigid as a corpse.

'Get Hermes!' Mac shouted at the first local he saw. 'Ivo, Lagarto and Neves to the temple, now!' he shouted at the next.

He held his hands up to all present. 'I stand in front of you all and take full responsibility for this freak event. Please accept my sincere and humble apology.' Adelina writhed on the sand muttering unintelligible words: 'Bab... Bab...'

'Don't just stand there!' Mac eyed a pair of baristas. 'Help the woman.'

'This lady is going to receive the best medical attention money can buy,' he said to the crowd. 'It's only superficial. Looks much worse than it is. She'll heal up very well.'

A crying tourist brought the infant over, and Adelina

reached out for it with her free hand. 'Thank you,' she said, gripping the infant to her chest. 'Thank you so much.'

'This man will be removed from the town.' Mac glanced at Faka, whose feet were twitching. 'You'll never see him again. I promise you that nothing like this has ever happened or will ever happen again. Brisas is a safe town. The safest town you can visit, and it will always remain so.'

Hermes sprinted down the street with his first aid kit. He crouched beside Adelina and dabbed at the blood, and began picking the broken spines from her head and back.

'See,' said Mac. 'Nothing serious. Hermes, we'll send her to the best hospital in the city. No expense spared.'

Tourists consoled each other while Mac spoke. Some wiped at tears. There were mutterings about cruelty and injustice.

'If any of you,' Mac said, 'are too traumatised by this, then please come to my office in *A Gata Preta*. We can talk there. I promise you she'll make a full recovery.'

With the help of two kitchen staff, he dragged Faka to the back of a 4×4 and drove up the street.

For the first time in his life, he'd been presented with a problem he didn't understand

15

The relief the townsfolk felt at Faka's expulsion was visible all over town. Bruno saw it in the faces of the waiters and baristas. He saw it in the shop workers, and he saw it in the way the men acted at work. This bad energy, that they once thought had been taken care of, had now been routed out and was gone forever. Things were back to normal, and tourists were still flooding into town. It would be a record-breaking year.

At work, the men talked non-stop about the kick Mac had delivered. A *meia lua de compasso dupla*.

'He isn't human,' Rudi said at the card table. 'Nobody will ever beat him.'

'Faka's lucky he's alive,' Tiago said. 'Maybe you'll be getting back in the *roda* now, Bruno. How about tonight?'

'Let's see,' said Bruno. He leaned in and lowered his voice. 'You're sure he's alive?'

'Of course he is.' Tiago sat upright.

'They left him at the city hospital,' Joao said.

'At the entrance.' Selmo flicked the deck of cards from one hand to the other. 'Mumbling nonsense, with nothing moving below his neck.'

'Paralysed?' Bruno ran a hand down his nose and mouth. Selmo nodded.

'Now, Selmo, we don't know that for sure,' said Riccardo. 'If you don't start dealing, I'll have to go.'

'Deal the cards, Selmo,' said Joao.

The capoeira sessions were busier than ever. Even Riccardo and Joao turned up at the *roda*, playing and singing along with the rest of them. The *capoeiristas* no longer had to take turns at the *carrinhos* or keep watch outside the busy bars. Everything was to be focused on the balanced running of the town, and ensuring the tourists' every whim was catered for.

Mac's popularity amongst the tourists grew. He gave every one of them who was in the town on the day of Faka's attack half their money back, and let whoever asked about Adelina know that he'd been monitoring the situation personally, and it wasn't as serious as it had looked. She'd be back very soon.

'Brisas will do the right thing,' he told the tourists. The phrase caught on, and every time a tourist complained or commented to a local, they were met with the same words: 'Brisas will do the right thing.'

Bruno noticed a difference in Mac from that day on. White stubble could often be seen on his chin. A slight sag under the eyes betrayed troubled sleep. Faka had been his second-in-command, his best friend and biggest ally. He'd been with him from the start. Everything had been so normal until only a few months ago. How could it have changed so quickly?

If Mac wasn't behind his desk, he was at the *roda*, the church or the temple. He no longer wandered the streets talking to tourists and micro-managing the workers. His time was dedicated to *Os Orishas*. The cross outside the church received a fresh offering every day. The cleansing scent of sandalwood saturated the air around town like never before. A hose was rigged up over the doorway of the temple to spray anyone who entered with a fine mist, ensuring purity was maintained within. Tiago said that, inside, the temple had never been so well-kept. The herbs and plants were pruned, and the soil weeded with extra care. The walls were washed and repainted. Wax dripping from the candles was cleaned and the candle wicks trimmed back.

Despite Mac's piety, and his new show of tolerance towards the travellers, Bruno knew an undercurrent of regret ran through him. He'd missed an opportunity. Had he caught on sooner to Faka's state of mind, he'd have been able to prevent the violence in front of all the tourists, and could have used the stealing of the meat as an excuse to throw all the travellers out. Faka's stupidity, and his own lack of foresight, had ruined the chance he'd been looking for. He wouldn't let the next one slip.

Adelina returned from the city a few days later. She had a slight limp and was a little hunched, but went about her daily life as usual. When Bruno passed her one night as she sat peddling sandals to the hordes of tourists, he saw the same old hostility in her eyes, but now they held a glimmer of mocking. Instead of playing the victim to gain sympathy and reap its advantages, as he thought she would, she bore her wounds like a trophy, as if she'd caused them herself through an act of self-flagellation.

*

At the bookshop one break time, Bruno heard Mac yelling in the back room: '...and I want it done! Is that clear?'

Bruno pretended not to listen, but lingered at the South American section, beside Rosy's desk. A book with the word *Huaorani* in the title caught his eye. Lagarto marched past and slammed the door.

'Problems,' whispered Rosy, as he paid for the book.

Bruno nodded. The sight of Lagarto confirmed his suspicion that it was about the brewery.

'Bruno.' Mac's voice was firm and even. Bruno turned

to see him leaning against the shelves. 'When will it be fully operational?'

'In just over a month, I think,' said Bruno.

'I gave you a chance here, Bruno. You know what's happened. I want everything in this town to be perfect. You need to get it done. Did you find a way to motivate the men?' He walked up to him.

'Yes I did. Don't worry. Everyone's completely committed to it now.'

'I don't worry. The weak worry. The strong get the job done, do you hear me?' He shouted in his ancient language to the back office. One of the twins came through with a bundle of pay packets and Mac pushed them so hard into Bruno's chest it knocked him back against Rosy's counter. 'Give the men their pay and get them working. If I see them playing cards at that table again in daylight I'll string you up.'

'They only do that at breaks.'

'Breaks are for eating and drinking, not for cards! They can do that at night.' Where once Mac had been able to control his voice and facial expressions to dampen any sign of emotion, his voice now rose and his eye twitched. 'Now, get on with it!'

Bruno walked out into the sunlight with the padded, weighty envelopes in his hand. He flicked through the pile until he found his own. It wasn't half as thick as the others. *Higher denominations*, he thought, but slipped into his bedsit to find out for certain. He pulled Tiago's from the stack, held the gummed flap over the steaming kettle and opened it. It contained exactly twice as much money as his own did. So there it was, the truth. He'd been getting fucked over from day one. In spite of himself, he laughed. He crumpled the notes up in his hands but resisted shredding them.

'This fucking place,' he said, leaning against the worktop. He hesitated, then headed back to *A Gata Preta*.

'Mac,' he called, walking straight past Rosy and the

tourists on the sofa. 'This is what I'm worth? Half of what my apprentice gets! I designed the whole fucking thing!'

'Don't you ever—' Mac came forward and dug his fingers into Bruno's shoulder. He noticed the tourists on the couch and turned his grip into a rub. 'Let's walk.' They left the shop and, in silence, headed down Beekeeper Close, past all the tourists, many of them stopping Mac for photos.

'You opened someone else's pay packet?' Mac said, as they skirted the corral.

'Only because it was twice as thick as mine. I'm the boss. Without me this thing dies.'

'You're the coordinator.'

'I'm saving this town a fortune. I've designed every part of it. I've studied every book, bled over every bolt. I've lost sleep checking the calculations and planning jobs for the guys. Mac, I've turned a blind eye to the bullshit and stealing from the city, and poured everything into this, and I'm only worth *half* of what Tiago gets? He's my fucking apprentice!' Bruno tried to keep up with him as he marched up the dune.

'Bruno,' Mac said at the top, 'you were nothing when you came here. You were a homeless drunk! I took you in. I gave you a chance. This town,' Mac swept his arm out above the rooftops, 'took you as one of their own. You've seen how the travellers are. Leeches! Sucking the blood from our veins and running off, leaving all their shit behind for us to deal with. Can you see how difficult it was to get you in? But I did it! Have you not been accepted by the guys? Have you not been welcomed in every restaurant and bar? You've been allowed to dress like us. You've even been in our *roda*. That's sacred space.'

'I was nearly killed in that *roda* because you didn't see the danger! A woman was mauled because some maniac caught her stealing a couple of pieces of meat. You blame the travellers for putting everything at risk but it was your second-in-command who nearly cost you it all.'

Mac's thumb dug in under Bruno's collar bone. The pain crumpled him to his knees. 'Shut your mouth and listen. We're heading forward, not back. This will be a record-breaking year with or without you. Yes, you're on half the pay of your *fucking* apprentice. He's Ivo's nephew, he's devoted to our way of life, and he's got potential. You can see that as well as I can. I'm not going to argue with you over money. I told you this town pays a defendable wage. I was sincere. You go talk to the guys about it. Ask them what they think.'

'But it's—'

'Silence!' Mac released his grip. 'Look, Bruno, I once told you a flower couldn't sprout legs and become a rabbit. I've thought about it and realised that it wasn't entirely true. Here in Brisas things can change. You've changed, Bruno. A plant can become a hare, and if a hare runs fast enough it can become a panther. Embrace our culture, Bruno, embrace our beliefs, and you can climb to the highest rung, I promise you. Here, give me the pay packets. As of today, you're on the same salary as Tiago. Collect them after work.'

Bruno didn't mention his meeting with Mac to the guys, but was sure they'd hear about it soon enough, if they hadn't already. That night, he sat thinking in the bedsit. He couldn't figure out if Mac really believed what he was saying or was just trying to manipulate him. He thought of how he'd admired the men for the way they'd handled themselves when he thought he was on a higher wage, only to realise they'd probably known all along that he was making much less. Did they, like Mac, think this was his worth, or could this have been why they didn't work as hard as they could have done, their way of protesting the injustice of his low pay? It didn't matter.

He resisted reaching for his philosophy books, or the bottle, and tried to let the anger dissipate. He sat cross-legged on the floor and thought things over. Was he not enjoying the project, feeling the thrill of creating something from scratch, even if much of it was from stolen materials? Could he not eat a meal in a restaurant every day with his earnings? Was it not worth it just to test himself? Bea aside, that was why he stayed in the first place.

It had never been about the money. If it had been, he would have checked right at the start. The reality was that he'd accepted the price he was offered and had been well aware of the risk of Mac exploiting him. Now he was so close to completing it that his old self was probably looking for a way to prevent what would be the first real achievement of his life. A self-saboteur, as always. He wasn't going to let it happen this time. He'd see this project through then take things from there.

In bed that night, he had barely closed his eyes when he felt his bed sheet billowing up above him, cocooning him in a great white tunnel. It fell back to his body and began to twist like a giant dishcloth being wrung out. His arms were pinned to his chest and his crossed legs were binding together, bone upon bone. Honey's voice came to him. '*Entropy,*' she said. '*Bruno, entropy.*' His ribs were compressed so much it stopped his breath. The pressure built and Honey's voice was replaced by a soft ringing that amplified as the dishcloth tightened. It was the ringing of a huge chime that jarred in the depths of his unconscious. All the air was forced from his lungs as the noise resonated, hollow and low, loud and clear like a large brass bell.

He woke with a start and almost fell out of bed. The continued ringing confused him. It was the church bell. He grabbed the buckets and desert scarf from the corner, threw open the door and bounded for the church.

He found Mac standing next to an unconscious tourist, whose hands gripped the bell-cord. A vision of the pair at the corral on the day of Honey's disappearance flashed in Bruno's mind. Mac's eyes were full of pain and confusion. Whatever was causing these things to happen hadn't been

Faka. Whatever it was, it was still here. Bruno scanned for Bea's face amongst a growing crowd of travellers by the campsite toilets.

'Just like the others?' he asked, relieved to have spotted her in the crowd. Carlos was behind her with his hands on her shoulders. He pointed Bruno out to her, and with a stupid smile on his face, raised her hand like a puppet's and made it wave. Bea pulled her hand back to her side and slipped into the crowd.

Mac hadn't seemed to hear him, but his eyes blinked and he cleared his throat. 'Exactly like them.'

Others started arriving, Anderson, some fishermen, dayshift workers and allotment farmers. Only a few were prepared to fight a fire. Drunk tourists had followed and watched from the street.

'What took you so long?' Mac asked, walking right up to Anderson. 'Anderson, how will you put out a fire with no bucket?' He marched down the line of them. 'Alberto, Clementina.' He cleared his throat again. 'Eduardo, will you cup your hands and throw water, like this?'

Nobody spoke. They looked on with sleep-glazed eyes and solemn faces. Bruno realised he'd never heard Mac clear his throat before. Anderson looked over at him. He'd told Bruno that the bell hadn't rung in all the years he'd been resident. Now here it was, ringing again.

'Look at this man,' Mac said, pointing at Bruno. 'Two buckets and a cloth to guard against smoke. And he's not even local! He has the least to lose! How can I get the message across to you fools? This is the level of professionalism I expect. You've given me no choice. I'm setting up regular fire drills to make you doddering idiots treat this with the seriousness it needs.'

'We'll be quicker next time,' shouted a voice from the expanding crowd. 'With buckets,' said another. 'We'll get it right. No need for drills!' All eyes were fixed on the tourist. How could he possibly be sleeping with his hands gripped so tight on the cord and with Mac's voice echoing around him?

'When this bell rings,' Mac said, grabbing the cord and ringing it again, the tourist's hands bouncing up and down with it, 'you come right here. Understood? Now go! Clementina, wake Hermes. Tell him to bring the medical kit.'

Bruno filed away behind the others, watching Anderson disappear down his street. His light was hardly ever on, and he'd never come to the bedsit, or to see the brewery; another friendship that had evaporated, lost to the words on a few thousand-year-old pages. He pictured Carlos's thick fingers wrapped around Bea's shoulders. 'How many times do you fuck her each night?' he whispered. *It's none of your business,* the voice within him said. 'Sort your own shit out and forget about her.' *Why can't you just let go of these people?*

*

The same multilingual notice appeared all over town again:

The church bell shall only be rung in the event of a fire or other emergency.

Anyone can and has a responsibility to ring it if required.

However, misuse of the bell will result in immediate expulsion from the town.

It did nothing to settle the townsfolk. The comfort they'd known their whole lives through the certainty that Mac could solve all problems had vanished, and fear had set in. Bruno noticed it in his workers. No more card games, no more joking around. Riccardo didn't sneak to the back of the upside-down tree for a cigarette any more. They were actively seeking work instead of hiding from it. Lagarto and Ivo appeared constantly to check on the brewery's progress. Bruno watched their hushed conversations with the guys. They all shared the same look of fear and doubt.

Bruno didn't need to hear anything they said for him to know what was going on, what they were asking each other.

This leader of theirs, their prophet and saviour, their god-shaped man of blood and bone, had made a mistake. He'd paralysed Faka and ditched him on the doorstep of a city hospital, but Faka hadn't been the cause, he'd been another victim.

Bruno visualised Mac's eyes that night at the church, and knew he had the same questions and concerns about himself as the men had. A crack was opening in his previously unbreakable confidence. Up to that point, his life had been one direct path, never once deviating. Every word he'd spoken had flowed from his mouth as if read from a script. Everything he'd done had been instinctual and flawlessly executed, with the certainty of a man who never had been, nor ever could be, challenged. For the first time in his life he'd been presented with a problem he didn't understand. There was now a tremble in his voice, a barely perceptible hesitation in his actions. He'd forget the words at the capoeira sessions and ignore the tourists when they called out to him. It was said that late into the night he sat at his desk staring at the empty computer screen until he fell asleep. His anger and confusion manifested in bouts of aggression towards the travellers on the streets. But the more worked-up he got, the bolder the travellers seemed to become. Where once they'd been afraid and timid in his presence, they now seemed to draw power from him and goad him.

With the men motivated, Bruno worked as hard as ever. He turned the bedsit into a workshop, where he stripped motors and experimented with magnets to optimise them for the low speeds the turbines would run at. The room was so cluttered with tooling and materials that he had to climb over to the bed instead of walk to it.

So close to completion, the brewery attracted the attention of the tourists. Despite taking great pleasure in showing them around and explaining how it all worked, Bruno decided to let Tiago take the lead. Up to six times a day he tagged along during these impromptu tours, ensuring

361

Tiago explained everything correctly and knew exactly how it operated.

With the *capoeiristas* back to working shifts at the *carrinhos* and outside the bars, and the townsfolk's hostility towards the travellers increasing, there was a tension in town that Bruno hadn't experienced before. He couldn't stop fearing for Bea. Trying to push her out of his mind hadn't worked. He wanted to talk and make up with her. Surely by now she'd had enough time to think, and if he could only get her alone for a while, she'd forgive him and let him be there for her in case something happened. He had another reason for speaking to her. He felt like whatever was going on in town was just beyond the limits of his comprehension. He was sure that with her sense of perception and help, they'd be able to figure out the whole thing together.

He watched her at the *carrinhos*, hoping for an opportunity to speak, but every time their eyes met, although her gaze seemed to linger on him for longer than past weeks, she turned away. She had changed physically since he'd left the campsite. Her hair had lost its sheen, her eyes were dark and lined, and even her strong, compact body seemed to have lost a bit of its vitality.

Bea still gained the attention of admirers, but where once she turned them away with a subtlety that embodied kindness, and allowed them to keep their dignity, now, in the presence of Carlos, she toyed with them, leading them on before discarding them with a callousness that caused resentment of her and ridicule of them.

As Bruno distributed the Burro Beer to the carts, he watched Bea flirt with another tourist. He had curly black hair, olive skin and was handsome despite his bulbous, sunburned nose. There was an arrogance about him, a sleazy look in his eyes. The repulsive way he nibbled his bottom lip while gazing at her, had Bruno turning away in disgust. He didn't want to look, but couldn't stop himself. She was standing cheek to cheek with the man, whispering in his ear, continually glancing at Carlos, who was entertaining a group of couples with another silly magic trick. Bruno wanted to go to her, to pull her away and say, '*Bea! You're worth a million of those guys. This isn't you! You're better than this.*' But it was none of his business. All the empties were in his bag. He realised he was staring, and people were looking from him to her and the man. He threw the bag over his shoulder and walked back to the brewery.

*

A few mornings later, Bruno was at Horizon enjoying his breakfast pancakes. His sleep had been dreamless, and he'd woken refreshed and ready to put in another good shift. His saplings were growing nicely in their pots. He'd have to transfer them soon. Maybe he'd take some soil from the forest and make a real garden. The brewery would be done within the month. He'd take his camera out and get a photo of himself and the men in front of it. Maybe he'd go to the city and have enough copies made for each of them, a thank you present for the work they'd put in. The problems in town would sort themselves out, he knew. Crises came and went. This one would be no different. With his mouth stuffed with as much pancake as he could chew, he twisted the fork in the honey jar again and let the golden-red elixir pour over the remainder of his stack. He drew eights on the pancakes that disappeared the instant they formed, absorbed into the sponge and pooling around the plate.

He watched Gina refill the coffee mugs of some tourists at the table across from him, and looked into his own nearly empty one. She walked straight past, ignoring his smile. Her shoulders dropped as he called out to her. He held his mug up and wagged it when she turned.

'Beautiful morning,' he said as she sloshed the coffee into his mug.

'If you say so, Bruno.' She walked away.

Well, that's progress, he thought as he took a sip. *At least she's using my name now.* He wrapped both hands around the mug and watched her disappear into the kitchen. He'd be coming here in twenty years and she'd still be the same lazy, pessimistic person. As long as she was happy, he didn't mind. He smiled again at the memory of his confrontation with Mac. He'd run it through his head many times since it had happened. It was only a small thing, but it was good that he'd done it. Nothing good ever came from suppressing himself. He should always be prepared to stand up to people when he knew he was right.

There was no way Bruno could join their religion just to progress through the town's ranks. The men at work were pressing him to convert, no doubt at Mac's insistence, but it wasn't going to happen. All he could hope for here was peace. Thoughts of the forest had slowly been retreating in his head, and he was beginning to believe there was a real possibility of a permanent future here.

With nothing to read and not many people to watch, Bruno became conscious of his gaze always returning to the nearly empty jar of honey. It wasn't the beauty of its rust-red colour, glowing in the soft morning sunlight, that caught his eye, nor the unusual way in which the crimson seemed almost separate from the gold, as if it were an addition of some other liquid entirely. Something else had caught his attention, and now he couldn't peel his eyes away. He set his coffee on the table and picked up the jar for a closer look.

He removed the lid and tried to hook the thing with his fork, but lost patience. Panic was seeping in from the periphery of his mind. He threw the fork down, tipped the pancakes from his plate and emptied the jar into it. He pinned the thing to the bottom of the plate and dragged it to the edge where he was able to pinch it between his now trembling fingers. He inspected it in the sunlight, unconsciously rising to his feet. His brain seemed to pop and his legs almost fell out from under him. He had to grip the table to keep upright.

He balled his fists and screamed, sat down but was up again in an instant. He'd been a complete fool. It had all been so convenient, too convenient. The talk with Ivo, the sighting. It had been a lie! A fucking child's fable! How had he not seen through it? He looked at the blank, unrecognisable faces watching him, his thoughts whirring incoherently. He gripped his head to stop the rage from spilling out. He looked again at the plate, filled with the unnaturally red honey, and tasted the copper in his mouth. He found the thing on the table where it had dropped from his hands, a single strand of peroxide blonde hair, grey at the root. He visualised his dreams, the languid way Honey's hair had moved in the water; it hadn't been water at all. He forced his fingers down his throat and vomited, threw the table out of his way and ran.

Tiago was leaning against the frame of the cooling loop as the rest of the men helped themselves to tea and coffee. He smiled as Bruno walked up to him, but the crash of Bruno's fist in to his face sent him to the ground. Bruno pounced on him and landed another punch before the men got him off.

'Let go of me, you bastards! You animals!'

Tiago rolled onto his side and covered his face. Blood tricked through his fingers.

'What the fuck are you thinking?' Joao shouted.

'I've treated you like a brother.' Bruno fought to get free.

'Calm yourself,' said Riccardo. 'What's wrong?'

Selmo and Rudi were at Tiago's side. They helped him to his knees. Rudi gave him a handkerchief, and he held it to his bleeding mouth. He got to his feet.

'Catching a boat. You lying little fucker.'

'Now, Bruno,' said Riccardo, realising what was going on. 'That's what this is about? It's no reason to lash out. We were following orders. You weren't doing your job, we needed to motivate you. For all we know she *did* catch a boat. Nobody knows where she is, or what happened.'

'Tiago knows. Don't you? You know what I have for breakfast every morning, too.'

The whites of Tiago's eyes flashed. 'But how did you—'

'I found a hair in it! *Her* hair!'

Riccardo and Joao glared at Tiago. 'What's he talking about?' asked Joao.

'Pure honey. How could you?'

'Mac made me do it. When I told you we found her, we didn't know what had happened, I swear. If I'd known she was in the well I'd never have lied to you. I had no choice.'

Selmo and Rudi stepped away from Tiago.

'They found her in the well?' Joao's grip on Bruno's shirt loosened. Bruno started forward again, but Riccardo got hold of him.

Tiago spoke with downcast eyes. 'You know Mac has the keys for the thing. He opened the locks. It took five of us to lift the lid off. How could she possibly be in there?' He shrugged. 'Mac gave the orders. I can't say more than that.'

Tears fell from Bruno's eyes. 'I'm done with this,' he said. 'Let me go. I'm fucking done. Let me go, I said!' He shrugged Joao and Riccardo off and walked to the bedsit.

In the bedsit, he threw over the coffee table, sending plates and cups smashing on the tiles. He punched the plasterboard wall until it broke through, each punch shooting pain further up his arm. He picked up a motor he'd been stripping and hurled it against the wall. It clattered to the floor, bouncing off the wooden facing and peeling it from the wall's base. Bank notes spilled out from behind the facing. He knelt and pulled them out. There were hundreds of them, thousands of *contos*, all jammed in behind the plasterboard. A life's work left rotting between the walls of a house she didn't even own.

He sat down against the wall, cushioned from the hard

floor by the bills. *How could I not have known?* he asked himself. *Why didn't I look harder?* He'd accepted it all so easily. One less problem to worry about, one less distraction. All the time he'd believed them, wanted to trust them, but his subconscious was telling him the truth, and he hadn't listened.

He left the door open and walked out, not knowing where to go. He passed through the campsite, over the hill and went down amongst the coconut palms. He turned and walked to the bay, around the dune and into the mangroves.

From the cover of the trees, he watched the beekeepers at the well. Mac was there pushing them on, trying to get it filled, trying to wash away the crime. He spent the rest of the day in the mangroves thinking, working himself up into a mess of confusion, blame and anger, ready to leave right from that spot, never to return again. His head and body ached as he thought everything through, but each time he reached the decision to leave, the same thing prevented him from taking that first step. As long as Bea was in town he'd stay. He'd never leave her; even though she wanted absolutely nothing to do with him, he'd be right here waiting just in case she ever needed him.

That night, after drinking from one of Honey's cups, washing in Honey's shower, and lying in Honey's bed, he finally managed to fall asleep.

The same recurring dream materialised. Honey was swimming out for a distant boat through the turquoise water. This time the sun didn't penetrate in pillars of light, but refracted within it, turning the whole sea golden. The storm came. Bolts of lightning shot through the water amid the clatter of the thunder. The water became more viscous as she struggled, as she fought to get away from whatever gripped her. Fine white blades like bush grass shot from her wrists. The horses' tails. A wire spooled around each wrist, binding the tails to her, the duct tape securing it. The bolts

367

of lightning were the strikes of the horses' hooves on her body and head. The thunder was their galloping on the muddy ground. The lifebuoy splashed on the golden surface and the horses disappeared. The storm was over. '*No!*' she cried, air bubbles escaping her mouth. '*Please no!*' A crimson arc spread from her eyebrow to her crown, bathing her face in blood. The lifebuoy grew solid and grey. It blocked the light from above like a solar eclipse. The lid of the well. As she sank, the air leaving her lungs and the blood spiralling from her wounds left a trail of bubbles and red vortexes in the golden dark.

The next morning, Bruno went to work at his normal hour but couldn't bring himself to do anything. He had no interest and wouldn't give the men any orders. They could do what they wanted. To hell with them. To hell with the town.

Without his guidance, the men tried to keep busy. They made every effort to contain the problem and sort it out by themselves, but their attempts at reasoning with him got nowhere. Lagarto had to be informed.

Early that evening, Lagarto appeared and sent the men home. He sat at the table and pulled out a chair for Bruno. When Bruno remained standing, he got back to his feet.

'Bruno, I know you got some news you didn't want to receive, and I apologise for that. It may have been bad judgement on my part not telling you exactly what happened, but as much as we try to be fair to each individual, we have to make the best decisions for the town as a whole.'

'One of my true friends was killed, Lagarto, trampled by horses and left to die in a well.' Bruno couldn't look him in the face. 'What did you… No. I don't want to know.'

'Bruno, we gave her a proper burial. It was as close to a Christian burial as we could manage.'

'Where?'

'Beside the well. I can take you there.'

'It won't change anything.'

'Tell me how we can make this right, Bruno.'

'Give me time to think and get Tiago away from here. I don't want to be near him, or Riccardo, or Selmo.'

'Bruno, they're our team. They're who we have. I'll have to ask Ivo. How long will you take to complete it without them?'

'I don't know.'

'It's nearly done. Surely it won't take much longer.'

'I don't fucking know! Look, I don't know what to do. Give me some peace for a while, okay? Let me clear my head.'

'I see you're not interested in talking, Bruno. I went to Mac before coming here. I told him to let me try before he got involved. Give me something positive to report back to him with. Something concrete.'

'I can't give you anything, Lagarto. I just can't.'

Lagarto tapped a hand on his thigh. 'Be at the allotments at six o'clock tomorrow morning. Don't be late, and stay out of his reach. Mac's not as patient as he used to be.'

*She stood with her hands at her sides,
her red-lidded eyes wide open and
filled with tears*

16

Bruno woke without appetite. He had slept in his hammock at the brewery, having decided not to spend another night in the bedsit. He washed at the manifold and made the walk out of town towards the interior.

Sparse tufts of scrub grass on the dunes became thicker and greener the further inland he walked. The green hills and mountain range came into view. He shielded his eyes against the morning sun and saw the flashes of the streams through the foliage, snaking down the mountain faces and over the hills. There were huge elevated lakes in the mountains, continually filled by rains that never reached the town. They provided Brisas with all the water it could ever need.

Bruno knew that the farmers controlled the water to the allotments via a series of dams: small boulders, rocks and wooden paddles they manipulated to route it where it was needed most.

The allotments, hacked into the forest on the flats and up the hillsides, were each about the size of a tennis court. There were hundreds of them. Some were as flat as bowling lawns, some crowded with knolls and hillocks, others were set on steep inclines or sunken in troughs. The highest of them held the pigs, cows, sheep and goats. The vegetable plots were below them, and on the flats were fruit trees and the corn. Earthen footpaths crossed between them like a lattice.

This farming area was a testament to the hard work of the people, who had been a source of inspiration for Bruno when he started on the brewery. He watched them on their knees tilling the soil of the vegetable patches, swinging their scythes through the corn in pendulous synchronisation, walking the trails shouldering crucifix-style balance beams with produce-filled baskets.

These people were a completely different breed to those who attended the temple and worked with the tourists. They were robustly built, with strong, rounded shoulders and short, stubby legs. They wore hats made from the broad-leaved scrub grass growing on the dunes, wide, simple trousers and washed-out shirts. Their brows were creased and their hands calloused from years of working the land. There was no machinery out here, and the animals were bred for meat and milk alone, never utilised for sowing seed or ploughing.

The average age out here was around fifty, and like the fishing, the trade was passed from generation to generation. What youth there was worked alongside the elders, younger castings from the same mould. Young wives carried children on their backs within folded and knotted sheets. Little feet stuck out at either hip. These infants rested their heads between their mothers' shoulder blades and slept with ease as their mothers went about their work.

As with the fisher-folk, these were strong and able people who worked without complaint. Although at times they wandered around town, they kept mostly to themselves, tending their gardens while listening to their radios, or playing dominoes outside their gates, rarely frequenting the bars or restaurants.

Bruno always felt a great admiration for them when he saw them about. They were like relics from another time, always taking their hats off when talking to someone, never passing a peer without greeting him. They held themselves in a self-respecting, humble way that those of the temple and tourism never could. If Mac's tribe was the town's lifeblood, these farming and fisher-folk were its lungs and heart. Brisas couldn't exist if either failed to serve its function.

With no sign of Mac, Bruno wandered around on the footpaths. A farmer led a pair of cows past him held by a rope tied through their noses. He watched them over his shoulder as he ascended and walked straight into an old woman. Her hat fell to one side of the path and her ledger to the other. He crouched to pick up the hat as she gathered the spilled pages.

'I'm sorry,' he said, handing her the hat. 'I should have been looking.'

He noticed a thumbprint-sized scrap of paper with what looked like Bea's writing on it, but the ink was blue instead of the crimson that Carlos had her using. The woman picked it up, and he was sure she popped it into her mouth.

'Why are you out here?' she asked.

He watched her jaw for any sign of chewing, wondering if he'd seen properly. *This paper is my body*, he thought. *The ink is my blood.* 'Meeting Mac,' he said. 'I don't know why he wants to drag me all the way out here, though. We could just as easily have met in town.' He looked back down at the distant dunes, and there he was. Mac, bare-footed in his red *abadas*, strode over the scrub grass with no sign of urgency in his step, despite being half an hour late. Bruno turned again to the woman, but she was scuttling back up the path. He headed down to the lower allotments, trying to guess at what Mac would say.

'Do you know why we keep the swine and kine up at the top, Bruno?' Mac asked in a pompous tone, trying to hide the frailty that Bruno knew gripped him.

'Why?' Bruno didn't try to hide his disinterest.

'Manure.' Mac cleared his throat. 'It's more efficient to carry a tonne of cow shit downhill than it is to carry it up.

372

You can see these people do everything by hand. They don't have the luxury of your engineering, your pulley system, of having every part of the operation built in one place to suit their own individual preference with no interference whatsoever. No, not at all. They had to make do with what was there. They've tilled and toiled on this land for decades now. They've reshaped a mountain to fit their needs.' He cleared his throat again. 'Our needs!'

'You're a smart man, Bruno, so I'm not going to explain why I had you walk all the way out here, but Brisas is bigger than you or me. It's bigger than Honey as well. Have you been out here before?'

'Once or twice.'

'I mean as a townsman, not as you were in the past.'

'Mac, I respect what you've done with this town but I've got no energy. Can you please tell me what it is you've come to say?'

Mac nodded and looked around. He cleared his throat a third time. It had got worse since the night the tourist rang the bell. Now he couldn't string a sentence together without clearing it. 'I wanted you to see how hard these people work. Have you ever touched one of their hands?'

Mac's eyes fixed on a man in the nearest allotment. He was pulling potatoes from their roots and throwing them in sacks. 'Yes,' Bruno said, guessing at Mac's intentions. 'Many times.'

'No you haven't.' Mac whistled to the man, who came over and held his hat against his chest. Without saying a word, Mac took hold of one of the man's hands and held it up in front of Bruno. 'Touch it,' he said.

'I'd rather not.' Bruno was more interested in the state of Mac's own hands. They were covered in tiny sores, some of which seemed to be oozing. Bites from the bees, he realised. In Mac's hurry to refill the well, he'd been aggravating them. They'd bitten him so much, his skin was like the scales of a tortoise.

'Don't anger me, Bruno. Touch the man's hand.'

'I'm sorry,' Bruno said to the man and ran a finger down the hard leather of the palm.

Mac noticed Bruno's eyes on his own hands. 'Back to work,' he said, releasing the man and folding his arms behind his back.

'You felt that toughness of the skin? That's hard work, Bruno. We work with our heads, you and I, our bodies are kept in shape by choice, and serve us for many a year, and our active minds remain sharp through complex problem solving, but these workers,' he looked across the hills, 'wear their bodies down through labour, and their minds waste away, just like a muscle, through lack of use. Bruno,' he cleared his throat, 'these people sacrifice their health for the benefit of the town and future generations. They know we're stronger together.

'I'm here to apologise for what happened. We had too much at stake. Everybody knew the well was full. The jars had already been bought, as were the labels. If we didn't go ahead with it, you know as well as I do that questions would've been asked and rumours would've spread. Inertia, Bruno. That's all. Inertia. A process was in motion and I couldn't stop it. What if I *had* stopped it and told everyone that she was in there, the victim of a brutal murder? It would've finished us, that's what would have happened. The town would be gone. I know you don't want that. Otherwise you wouldn't be standing here. You saw something in this place, don't deny it. My mother saw it too. Just like you, she was on her way elsewhere but looked ashore and knew this was where she had to be.'

'It would have been better if I had just kept moving.'

'Nonsense, Bruno. Don't be like that. You're richer for every minute you've spent here, good and bad. You know… I saw you that very first day with your bag and your knives. I knew you were different from the others. And that shelter you built… I have to say I was interested in you. I kept an eye out... But about Brisas, there's something special here, isn't there? I don't know if it's the remoteness, or the lie of the land or sea and the direction of the winds, but people are drawn here. You would have loved my mother, Bruno. A just woman. Wise beyond her caste. I see your eyes there, but yes, there was a caste system in those days, still is one down south. You know it's true. It's only more hidden. But my mother surpassed the limitations imposed upon her. She did what she had to do to find what she desired, and she didn't find it in those books, Bruno. No. All those books that you and I have *both* read.' He cleared his throat. 'They were the starting point, but it was her *actions* that led her here. She too came from those cities in the south with their crime and corruption, their greed, their prejudice. But you don't find any of that here, do you? That's not what we're about. You compare this place to the greatest city you can think of and you'll see that our way of doing things is the right way. We look after our own, and we follow the one true religion, straight from the source of man, straight from the Great Rift Valley.

'I'm here to apologise for one unfortunate incident that spiralled out of control. It's my fault, Bruno.' He put a hand on his chest. 'I'm to blame and I am here to say sorry. What heads of state, what corporate leader would show such humility and stand up in front of you as I'm doing now? None. Not one of them.'

'Mac,' Bruno closed his eyes and drew a hand through his hair. 'I ate that stuff every day. She was murdered, and her killers are still out there enjoying their lives while I sleep in her fucking bed. What kind of person does that make me? You could have told me. Tiago could have told me instead of some fucking lie. I would've kept it secret. I would've helped bring justice.'

'The fact that neither Tiago nor anyone else told you is why our way of doing things works. Who wants to live in a place where your friends and colleagues betray you as soon as your back's turned? I ask you not to hold anything against them. They remained silent, on my command, for the greater good. I truly am sorry, Bruno.'

Bruno looked at his feet. He knew Mac was being sincere, but he wanted to walk away. He was done.

'I know you want to make a difference in life, Bruno. That's why you're still here. You know how much I, the temple, these farmers, these fishermen, need the brewery to be a success. You're in a rut and lingering in the past. There is no justice in life, Bruno. Justice can't bring her back. Justice can't change the past. Only acceptance, forgiveness and taking action towards a better future can be of any benefit. You need more motivation to live this life that you've chosen, so I made a decision. I cut the supply of beer from our providers. When the quantity we have runs out, it's done.'

'You think I care?'

'You have two weeks to get that brewery up and running. The survival of this town is in your hands, Bruno. I know you won't fail us.' He walked down the path.

Back in the bedsit, Bruno skimmed through his philosophy books, but he already knew them all by heart. There was nothing left to take from them. He stayed there the whole day and ran all the events that had happened since his arrival in Brisas through his mind, tried to keep calm and watched the daylight fade outside the window. The window was like a camera lens. If he tried hard enough he could stay behind it, pretend that everything outside was fictional. It was all happening out there, and in here behind the glass, he could allow himself a sense of detachment, an escape. But he'd locked himself away before, and that didn't do him any good. Ignoring the problem would never solve it.

He knew that Mac really believed everything he was saying, and that the men were content with life here. The more he thought about it, he realised that he didn't hold any resentment or anger towards the townsfolk, or the travellers for taking his beer, or himself for his own past actions, faults and failures. He had to accept, forgive and let it all go just as Mac had said, or it would fester and grow into another obstacle he'd be unable pass. This just wasn't him any more. This was a chapter of his life that had to end now.

Anderson, Honey, Bea and everyone else he'd spoken to had said that Brisas wasn't a place to find yourself but a place to get lost. But Bruno *had* found himself here. Maybe he hadn't found exactly what he was looking for, but he'd found himself, and that was enough to be thankful for. All the feelings of guilt, shame, and cowardice that he'd been carrying around since he left the south were now gone. Everyone had their own life to lead, their own path to walk on, and he was no different. 'I'm sorry, Honey,' he said. 'I'm sorry, Bea.'

He pushed all thoughts from his head, closed his eyes and visualised the green forest and the gentle flow of the great river. Despite the weight of the melancholy that came with his acceptance of how things had to be, a smile came to his face. He was ready to move on again.

A few hours later, after he'd packed all his things, he was just finishing the book on the Huaorani people when a frantic knocking rattled the door against its frame.

He laid the book on the bed and crept to the window to see who it was but couldn't see a thing in the darkness. The knocking changed from the rapping of knuckles to the thudding of the base of a fist. It stopped. He put his ear to the door and listened for any voices. Silence. He twisted the handle, his breath held, and eased the door open just enough to look out. She stood with her hands at her sides, her red eyes were filled with tears, her black hair hung at either side of a face filled with heartache and desperation. It was Bea.

*

'I'm sorry for everything, Bruno.' Her voice broke. 'I really mean it.' She threw herself against him and cried into his chest. He put his arms around her and hoped she hadn't noticed him flinch in shock. It felt like he was embracing a frail, elderly woman. Her once strong and compact body had withered away. There was no padding on her shoulder blades, each vertebrae was a jagged edge, all but snagging on her baggy shirt. There was only bone above where her biceps should be. He led her to the sofa, sat her down and let her cry. It was painful to see her in such a state, but warmth welled up from his stomach to his eyes. She'd come back. Just as he was leaving, she'd come back.

He stroked her hair to calm her down like he'd seen her do so many times with her tortoise-shell brush: long, slow downward strokes, careful not to get his fingers caught in the knotted clumps. This close, he saw how hollow her cheeks were, how sunken her eyes had become.

'I feel numb,' she managed to say. 'I don't know who I am… What I am.' She looked up into his face, her eyes bloodshot. 'I thought I was going to die in my sleep last night.'

'What happened?' he asked, still stroking her hair and holding her to his chest.

'I don't know. I've felt like this for so long. I haven't been able to get my head straight, but last night, for the shortest time, my mind kind of switched and I had clarity. I could think a little bit…'

'And what came to your mind?'

'Nothing, really. Everything, I mean. But it got too heavy and clouded and—' She pressed against him and cried again.

'It's okay,' he whispered. 'It's okay. It sounds like an anxiety attack. I've had them before.'

'I haven't felt right for months, Bruno. I was so scared last night, but I woke today. I'm still here. I don't know what to do. I'm sorry for how I've treated you. I should have been more forgiving. I should have listened. I held everything against you. Everything.'

'Don't worry,' he said. 'You're here now. You're going to be fine, but you need to drink, you need to eat!' He got up and brought her a glass of water. 'Drink and calm down.' He took a pair of avocados out of a pouch slung from his bag and got his knife.

'I'm so glad you're here, Bruno. I was knocking so long.'

He cut the fruits in half, hacked out the seeds and passed small sections to her. She washed them down with the water.

'Bea, there was nothing I could have done that night, I promise you. If I could have stopped it, I would have. They had Tonino right there against the tree. Any move I made would have been spotted. I would never have got to her.'

She nodded. 'I don't know why I took it out on you so much.'

'It's been hard for me, you know? I've been desperate to make things right. I've never passed you without trying to get your attention. Why was it me? Why not Mac or Faka?'

'But you should have told me straight away instead of hiding in your tent. You know how much she meant to me. The first thing you should have done was tell me.'

'Bea, all this time I've been trying to get your attention, trying to apologise, but you wouldn't even look at me. And with all this shit that's been going on. Whenever anything happens I've been terrified for you. That night at the church I was going out of my mind until I saw you. If you hadn't been there I don't know what I would have done. But you haven't once thought about me.'

'That's not true, Bruno. I wanted to talk. I wanted to ask how you were, but something always stopped me. It was like a blockage. I—'

'Faka could have killed me in that *roda*. I'm sure you heard what Mac did to him. That could have just as easily been me.'

'I knew you were okay. Anderson told me.'

'And he's another one who's changed. I haven't spoken to him in ages. All he's interested in is that fucking Bible.'

'Bruno, we all have our own personalities, our way of dealing with things.' She edged away from him. 'I knew this would end up being about you. You never thought that any of our actions might have nothing to do with you at all?' She swallowed more water. 'Something that's important to one person might not be important to another.'

'Family is important, Bea. Friends are important.'

'Just because you react one way doesn't give you the right to criticise people for acting differently. There's a lot going on you don't know about.'

'People should have the emotional intelligence to know what's important to those they supposedly care about. To know what they need. All I needed was a wave from you, a sign to let me know you were okay, but you wouldn't even do that. You have no empathy, Bea. Anyway, I never gave up on you, even though you left me as soon as someone else came along.'

'I'm here now, aren't I? I came to you. Does that not count for anything? Anyway, he doesn't care. He's been using me all this time. I've been a fool, Bruno. All this time I've been trying to get him to love me, I've been throwing myself at him, but he doesn't want me. It's impossible.'

'So that's why you're here. You've exhausted that option and came back. You're smart, Bea. You make the right choice when it needs to be made, I'll give you that. You'll never be stuck anywhere, because you know exactly what to do when things get tough.'

'I see I'm not welcome here.' She stood. 'I'll go.'

'Of course I want you here! It's all I've wanted. I'm just fucking angry with it all. It had nothing to do with Iansa. Admit it.'

'What *was* it about then?'

'You didn't want me around while you latched onto Carlos.'

'That's what you think of me? Why are you making me feel guilty about all this? You know how heartbroken I was over Sean. You had no interest, and Carlos was—'

'Bea, I've told you already, you're family. That's never going to change. But you should judge yourself, too. Not just other people.'

'Iansa *was* a huge part of it. Don't say she wasn't; and you told me to do whatever I had to do to get over Sean. To start with I just wanted someone to take my mind off things. Carlos was there, and I'm not proud, but I settled for him. I don't know how, but the more time I spent with him, the more I started to feel different towards him. I can't explain it. I'd give my... I mean, I'd have given my soul.' She looked at her palms. 'But look at me. I'm a mess. I've become something else. I've become rotten. I'm ugly.'

'Nobody can help their feelings.'

'But I can help my actions. I know right from wrong. I've done so much, Bruno. I didn't mean for it to get so out of control. I don't know what else to do. There's something going on. I can't do this any more. Help me. Can I work at the brewery?'

'You know what you should do.'

'Home,' she said, lowering her eyes. 'Bruno, I can't.'

'I don't know what you've been up to, but that's where you need to go.'

'It's Carlos.' She stared at him. 'He's been controlling me. I can feel him prying around in my head. He's the reason I haven't been able to think about what I'm doing.'

'What's been going on, Bea? Tell me.'

'I don't know. I can't say. It's just... You have to help me. Sometimes I want to just rip open my skull and wash my brain out. I'm not normal, Bruno.'

'I'm not a psychiatrist, Bea.'

'I'm not asking for a psychiatrist! You helped me when I arrived. There's got to be something you can do.'

He looked at the book on the bed. He knew what he was

going to tell her would sound ridiculous, but it's all he could think of. 'Have you ever heard of *ayahuasca?*'

She shook her head.

'I met a *gringo* once who told me about it. I haven't thought of what he said until I found that book over there. He spent time with the Huaorani people. They use *ayahuasca* for healing. It can dissolve all your barriers and leave a new starting point to rebuild from. The guy said you're thrown into a blast-furnace of self-reflection at the same time.'

'It's a drug?'

He brought the book over and flicked through the pages. 'Look at these drawings. It's a mixture of two plants. *Jurema* root bark and the *caapi* vine. You brew them together and drink it. It gives you visions.'

She looked away. 'I can't take drugs, Bruno, even like this.'

'Just give it a try, Bea. It's all I can offer you. You came to me for help, this is it.'

'You really think this will work? Do you even know where to find it?'

'I've seen *jurema* in some of the gardens. The *caapi* grows out near the allotments.'

'But what if I overdose on it? What if it goes wrong?'

'There's nothing in *ayahuasca* that doesn't already occur in your own head. The main ingredient is dimethyltryptamine. That's what your pineal gland holds, right between your ears. It's your own brain chemistry, just on a bigger scale. Nothing bad can come of it, I'm sure. And I'll be right there watching over you. There's nothing to be afraid of.'

'When can you have it ready?'

'I'll get the stuff tonight and brew it tomorrow morning.'

'Okay, let me think about it.' She got up and made for the door.

'What are you doing?' he said, following after her. 'You're not going back to that campsite.'

'I have to go back.'

'It's not safe. I don't trust him. I never have.'

She opened the door, but he put his arm across the frame.

'Bea, I have something important to tell you.' He was going to tell her about Honey's murder, but changed his mind. He didn't want to get her any more worked up than she was. 'I'm not going to stay here any more,' he said. 'I want you to come with me. We can make the *ayahuasca* on the way.'

She shook her head. 'Tomorrow,' she said. 'Let's do it tomorrow.' She dipped under his arm and hurried away. 'I'll come here at the same time.'

'Bea, wait! Tell me what's going on.'

'Tomorrow,' she said.

'Now!' he shouted, but she ignored him. 'Don't eat after breakfast, or it won't work. Six o'clock tomorrow night. You better come, Bea!'

*

That night, Bruno sneaked into a garden, dug up a *jurema* shrub and brought it back to the bedsit. He made the trek over the dunes towards the forest, shining his headlamp on the ground at his feet to avoid stepping on any scorpions. He found a *caapi* vine and hacked it into small pieces. He wrapped the pieces in a muslin cloth and carried them to town.

After a restless sleep in his hammock, he woke early and sat at his fire behind the brewery, where he ate a simple breakfast of porridge oats and coconut milk. When the men arrived, he set them to work with the minimal amount of words, then went to the bedsit.

He washed the dirt and sand off the *caapi* vine sections, wrapped them in a towel and beat them with a hammer until they shredded. He added the shreds to a pot of water and let it simmer while he repeated the process for the *jurema* root, after discarding its fern-like leaves and fibrous stems.

The pots simmered for three hours then he strained each through muslins and re-boiled the brews with fresh water before straining them again. Once each pot cooled, he combined the contents into one bowl, stirred it and poured the *ayahuasca* into a plastic bottle, ready for use.

After resting for a while, he sat with his eyes on the door, waiting for Bea. The seconds on his digital watch ran on repeat from one to sixty in the corner if his eye. He saw every minute from half past five to six, to five past six, to quarter past. He should never have let her leave. Something had happened, he was certain. He threw the door open and ran to the campsite. It was empty. He shouted her name over and over.

'She ain't here,' said a voice from one of the tents.

'Where is she, then?' He looked around for the source of the voice.

'Makin' sales, I'd say. Main Street.'

He ran to Main Street and weaved through the crowds, scanning the vendors under the trees. He looked for her at the *carrinhos* and on the beach in the gathering around the *roda*. She wasn't there. He ran up the dune and looked for her amongst the people watching the sunset. He began to panic and struggled to hold it together in front of everyone. She wasn't here. If anything had happened to her he'd never be able to live with himself. He turned and was about to scream her name when he saw a dark-haired figure at the fence of the corral. It was her.

'Damn it, Bea.' He pulled her to him. 'I've been looking everywhere.'

'I had to come here.' She seemed much calmer than the night before.

He shook his head and sighed. 'Bea, you had me so worried. Can't you understand that?' She didn't speak. 'Are you ready? Have you eaten?'

'Not since breakfast, like you told me.'

'Come then. Let's go and get it.'

'Bruno, I don't want to do this alone,' she said, as they walked up Beekeeper Close.

'I don't need it any more, Bea. I know what I want already.'

'Well I won't take it then. Maybe you can get prescription stuff from Hermes. Maybe that's all I need. I'm already feeling better.'

'No. No prescriptions. Where's Carlos now? Why's the campsite empty?'

'He's busy. They must be selling. Why?'

'They're not *all* selling. He's not in the tent?'

She stopped. 'No, he's not in the tent. Look, is this an interrogation? Are you going to help me or not?'

'I just wish you'd tell me what the hell's going on. Okay, I'll take it with you, but let's do it in the campsite, not in some concrete cube.'

At the bedsit, he grabbed a few candles from a drawer and handed them to her. He picked up the brew and a pair of coconut shell cups and led her back out into the street. Adrenaline was already coursing through his body. He looked at her and smiled in spite of his fear. 'Are you nervous?'

'A little,' she said without emotion, 'but I just want to get it over with and see what happens.'

'We'll do it in here,' he said, throwing open his shelter in the dark silence of the camp. He slipped into the storage room; it was cool and damp inside. The air held a trace of sweat. 'Let's clean the whole place up first. I don't want any flies. I can't believe the state of the place.'

He led her back outside and across the campsite, pulled the liner from the nearest bin and got Bea to hold it open for him. He picked all the rubbish from the sand and cleaned the fire pit.

'Where's the rake?' he asked.

'Carlos must've got rid of it, along with everything else.' There was something in her voice, but he wasn't going to judge. Even if she was lying, there was nothing to do about it now.

With the camp tidied, they went back into the shelter. He held the candles for her to light, then placed them around the compartment, dripping wax onto the mats and standing them in it as it hardened.

'What's this?' he asked, noticing a black curtain running across the back wall.

Bea took a seat on the matting. 'Ignore it. Come sit down.'

He lifted the bottom corner of the curtain and held up a candle inside. 'My God,' he said, and pulled the whole thing to the floor. 'You knew about this fucking thing?'

'It's his masterpiece.' She didn't look at him.

A life-sized wire statue of Jesus, bearing more than a passing resemblance to Carlos, stood with nails through the feet and hands but attached to no cross. The face was contorted, and every muscle in the body so tense that Bruno could feel the agony, could almost hear its screams. All over the thing wire stuck out like cactus spines, each a needle of excruciating pain. Bruno took a closer look. 'Why?' he asked. He held the candle to the joints. 'It's the coat hangers, isn't it? He made it from those coat hangers.'

She nodded. 'The spikes represent the pain and suffering he went through for us.'

'*Us?* Bea, no tourist can take this home. Why would he build something so big?'

'It's just a statue! Can we please do this now?'

Her top lip swelled in anger. He went to speak again, but knew she wouldn't say a thing. 'Damn it, Bea!' He crouched in front of her, placed a cup at her feet and filled it. He sat at her side and sloshed the *ayahuasca* into his own cup. '*Saúde,*' he said, raising it to his mouth. He skulled it. As soon as the liquid passed his gullet he began to shake and drool. He

386

watched her touch her cup to her lips and gag as she tipped the contents into her mouth and swallowed.

'I think it'll be better with the candles out, actually,' he said, and snuffed those around the room before blowing out the one in his hand. Bea licked her fingers and pinched the wick of the candle at her feet. Its hiss shrouded them in darkness.

He tried to be brave for her, and concentrated on his breathing to keep calm. Breath after breath he calmed his mind, but his body went beyond the feeling of relaxation to a point where it felt heavy and burdensome, like a skin that had to be shed. Nausea hit him again, and the effort to keep his eyes open was so wearing that he had no choice but to let them close. He became aware of the music from the bars and the drums of the *capoeiristas*. Upon these sounds and their vibrations the *ayahuasca* seemed to seep in from outside of his body but also grew within it, pulsing like an echo from each stage of his growth.

It was as if the spirits of the plants and animals all around were calling to him, as if the great forest was reaching out. Colourful, geometric patterns materialised in the darkness, flowing in the most impossible yet natural of ways.

He lost track of time but could hear Bea retching. It was then that he felt an entity above him, a feminine force with an order of intelligence much greater than his own. He tried to sit straight, and in doing so felt every vertebrae in his spine slot perfectly into place. An overwhelming feeling of responsibility bore in on him. It was too much to bear. He slumped to his side and curled up like a foetus. Another vision entered his mind. He was confronted with each of his imperfections, how he thought too much, feared too much, how he tried to control too many things, the burden of practising humility in every aspect of life. He felt the physical weight of it all and curled further and further into himself until his shape, his humanity, was lost. His body was gone. Without form, he moved through a labyrinth of thought, a kaleidoscope of colour and energy. Hours or maybe even days passed. At first it was almost pleasurable. He was part of the energy, part of the colour, the sound. Everything was as it should be, but he began to panic. He was in too much of a hurry. It was too quick, there was so much to take in. He had to find something, a single point of reference to grip onto. The panic became his reference, and by acknowledging it and accepting it he found himself again and realised he was a breathing organism with a beating heart. He remembered after a time that he had a body somewhere, and tried to focus on its shape, its size, its weight. He concentrated on its breaths, its warmth, its subtle twitches and movements. He latched his mind and memory to them and travelled back from distant space and time until he found it and settled into its physical form. He felt his body shaking, felt the floor mats on his arm, hip and side. He heard a man crying and felt a hot, tickling wetness. It was he who was crying. The tears dripped from his face. He made the crying stop, opened his eyes and breathed his consciousness awake in the darkness.

He remained still until he felt completely within himself, got to his knees and called out: 'Bea, are you there?' His voice sounded fake. It came from him but not of him, like a mixture of energies thrown temporarily together. 'Shall I light the candles?'

'Light them,' she said, and he did. In the candlelight he saw that she'd been crying too, but was now smiling. Despite the puffy redness around her eyes, they were as alive and full as he'd ever seen them. 'You're smiling,' she said.

'You too.' His smile became a laugh. Although there was joy and warmth, his body felt tender and his mind balanced on a fine edge. It could just as easily rise up or fall. 'I think I should go sleep now,' he said.

'I understand. I don't want to talk too much, either. I have a lot to process. God, my voice sounds weird.' They both laughed. 'I feel light, Bruno. I think this is what I

needed. You were right. I'm going to be okay.' Fresh tears
came to her eyes and she stood.

He followed her outside and hugged her by her tent,
stroking her hair, down and down. He whispered her name
in her ear. 'Bea, I'm glad you feel better. I'm glad I'm with
you.'

'Everything's clear now,' she said. 'Let's talk tomorrow.'

'Sleep in the bedsit.'

'Bruno.' She squeezed his arm. 'It's okay. There's nothing
to fear.'

Bruno accepted her response and walked away. He
took in all the sights on his short journey to the brewery:
the travellers returning from Main Street, the houses and
gardens, the church with its cross and the fresh sacrificial
offerings. Music blared from the bars. The frailty of his
mind was passing. He felt unburdened yet humbled. He
knew what he wanted. All the feelings he'd experienced
in the bedsit the day before had been amplified, and for
the first time since his early days with Flora an unbridled
excitement, verging on euphoria, possessed him. There was
no guilt or fear that he couldn't handle. He was self-aware
and becoming stronger. The only thing blocking him in
life had been himself, but that block was gone and he was
bounding forward. He crouched to lift a handful of sand,
rubbed each grain through his fingers and looked up at the
multitude of stars.

17

Bruno walked around the brewery with Tiago listening to him talk, making sure he knew, with absolute certainty, the whole process and the function of each part. '...and we seal off this fermenter tank and roll it over with the others in the plus-three-week section,' said Tiago.

'As well as the tours, I want you to lead the guys now. There's not much left to do, is there? Fix up the cooling loops, what else?' Bruno scratched his coarse beard.

'Barriers to go around the conduction heaters.'

'Get Selmo working on that today. Joao on the cooling loops, and get Riccardo to check all his wiring. I tidied a lot of it, but it's better if he learns to do it himself.'

'Is everything cool now? Between us, I mean.'

'Everything's how it should be. I'm not going to preach to you, but just know that people should stand alone sometimes, consider what's at stake and make the right decision, even if it's not ideal for themselves or those they're loyal to. Anyway, let's just get this thing running as soon as we can, shall we? Shouldn't take more than a few more days.'

'Okay.'

'I'm going to write procedures. That way, if you can't find me, you'll have everything you need on paper.'

Bruno left Tiago standing by the fermenter tank. He walked past the rest of the men at the card table. 'Tiago will sort you out today,' he said, without breaking his stride. He stepped off the decking and crossed the street.

At the bedsit, he set all his books out on the bed and sorted them into stacks, his three philosophy books in one pile, and the brewing and engineering books in another. He took the rest to *A Gata Preta*, where Rosy let him swap them for a couple of blank jotters.

'Have a great day,' she said.

'Take care of yourself, Rosy,' he replied, and walked out the door.

The clutter in the bedsit was distracting. Junk that would sit for years without being used. It was unnecessary weight, a burden. He'd known once that it wasn't healthy to hoard, but only re-learned it through the *ayahuasca* the night before, along with many other things he'd known once but had forgotten.

To concentrate better, he made his way to the coconut palms and sat in the shade. He wrote everything he could think of that was relevant to the operation of the brewery: how the equipment worked, different recipes, and calculations for getting the ratios right. He even added a troubleshooting guide. They were bound to have problems with the turbine and most of the electrics. He'd seen better wiring than Riccardo's when he worked as a day-hire bilge-rat in the harbour all those years ago. On the final pages, he referenced all the engineering and brewing books, and was confident that Tiago had the ability to turn the project into a decent operation. In spite of everything, he was a good kid, and those wind power books by Hugh Piggot would get him through any possible problem with the turbine.

He worked on the book from morning until late afternoon, then handed it over to Tiago, together with all the brewing and engineering books. He took a seat with the guys at the table and listened to the same old gossip, the capoeira talk, Selmo's deadpan jokes, Riccardo speaking as if he knew everything. As Joao nipped another hangnail between his teeth and tore it from his bloody finger, Bruno left and went to find Bea.

She was sitting alone amongst the tourists on the dune, waiting for the sun to go down. As he passed the cliques, he spotted the guy she'd been flirting with a few nights before; a time that seemed so far in the distant past it was irrelevant. The man's bulbous nose had been burned a shade of purple by the sun. It looked like an overripe cherry ready to burst. He grabbed two bottles of water from a cool-box-man and sat down beside her.

'I'm still trying to take it all in,' she said, reaching for the bottle he offered. She wore a long skirt and a striped shirt. Her hair was unknotted and its lustre was already returning.

'I think we'll both be processing it for a while yet. We've come a long way.' He uncapped his bottle and took a sip.

'I know it sounds crazy, but for a long time a jaguar was sitting next to me. I was scared to begin with, but it was just sitting there. I didn't know what to do. I couldn't look away, and it didn't seem like it meant any harm, so eventually I reached over and took a handful of its fur. It was as real as you or me. I could feel its warmth, its fur bristling between my fingers.'

'You think it had any relevance?'

'I don't know. It was facing north, maybe pointing out the direction I need to go.'

'I wasn't sure what to expect from it, but it wasn't that. All those colours, the speed, the noise, it's like I had all these lost thoughts, ideas and memories scattered around in my head, and I travelled great distances just to visit each one, pluck it out and set it in the right order with the rest of them.'

They watched the sunset, sipping their water in silence and applauded with the tourists as the sun dipped under the horizon.

'Let's sit for a while,' said Bea, 'let the night close in. Did I tell you I was afraid of the dark when I first came here?' He shook his head. 'I'm not afraid any more.'

She lay back on the sand and stretched her hands above

her head. Bruno looked past the descending tourists to the capoeira session that had just ended. He watched the *capoeiristas* turn up Main Street with the tourists following on behind.

In the last remaining light a horse tour returned, skirting the foot of the dune in single file, with Silvia out in front. So much had changed but somehow stayed the same, repeated roles being played out by new characters.

The town lights came on, the music in Ivo's amplified and the cart-boys started their shift. Bruno looked towards Anderson's bar. The light was out. He'd have liked to speak to him, let him know how much he'd appreciated his friendship, but he wasn't going to have the chance.

He lay back beside Bea in the darkness and felt at ease. Stars peered down from the vast night. Each a twinkling, beautiful eye that had seen the birth and death of millennia, the rise and fall of civilisations, cultures and individuals, none more or less important than the other, the evolution of man and planet. 'Respect and tolerance,' Bruno said. 'That's the starting point. People have to open their eyes and think. We need compassion, education, novelty. There's so much to be done, Bea.'

'But there's only so much you can do,' she said. 'Live your life on instinct and be as true to your nature as you can.'

'I'm ready now,' he said. 'It's taken me long enough, but now I know how to deal with everything.'

'I sent a letter to my parents today for the first time in months. I told them I'm coming home. It's been so long, Bruno. I hope they're okay. I'm terrified by what I'll find there.'

'But you're always writing letters, surely it hasn't been that long? All will be fine. You'll see.'

'Those weren't for my parents. Everything I've written since I met Carlos has been for him.' She took a deep breath as Bruno turned to face her. 'You know what he told us?

He said he's the final messenger of God. Calls himself the Übermensch. Even I believed him.'

'Us? You used that same word about the statue. You ready to tell me now?'

A tear fell and she stared straight ahead. 'I didn't mean for anything to happen. I was so angry and hurt and—'

'I'm not judging you, Bea. Just tell me.'

'You know already. You saw the statue. The coat hangers are from all the farmers and fishermen, all his followers. He wanted everyone to have a hand in it. I thought I loved him; I mean, I got butterflies in my stomach every time he looked at me. All I could think about when I was alone was his face. Even while I slept all I could hear was his voice running over and over in my head. I thought I could make him love me back, but he never held the slightest bit of affection for me. I don't think he's capable of love.'

Bruno smoothed his hair back. 'You didn't sleep with him?'

'Never. He used me, Bruno. He figured me out and everyone else too. You heard what he was dictating that time you said goodbye to me. I think that was when I started to break away. Don't you remember any of the words he used?'

'He was always joking around, talking nonsense. How could I take anything he said serious? He said something like the letter was his body and blood.'

' "This paper is my body, the ink is my blood." Bruno, I had a look at my ink again last night. It's blue. Same as always. It never was red. Remember that wine he first gave us on the first night. It was water, I'm sure of it. You know there's a saying, you can't be all things to all people? Well he says you can be. You only have to show them who they want you to be. You saw your version of him, I saw mine, and all the farmers, fishermen, the Jingubans, saw him as—'

'You're saying they're following him?'

'He got me to go around and talk to them while he watched over the temple. He knew they'd be more open to me than to him. He taught me what to say from his *Book of Verses*. It took a long time but I...' She shrugged. 'I did it. I gained their trust. One by one, then in small groups, he preached to them at the boats, by the allotments, in the forest, even at the dominoes tables. You know how good a talker he is, how unique a voice he has. He'd say things with a beauty I'd never heard before. Think how it must've sounded to these people. His words were a revelation to them. He told them that all these bad events that have been happening, all this bad energy is a result of Mac's religion. Only by following the one true religion – His religion – could we save this place.'

'So, when I bumped into that woman at the allotments it *was* your writing on the paper. She really did put it into her mouth.'

Bea looked him in the eye. 'She came back and told us Mac was on his way. We were at the cemetery one time when you were there, too. One of the elders signalled to us.'

'How's it been kept secret for so long? There are no secrets here. There's too much gossip.' As he was saying it, he thought of Honey. He wondered when that news would surface.

'There are secrets everywhere, even in small towns like this. It's like Carlos said, you can unravel something from the bottom without the top knowing a thing about it. If you do it right, the last link will hold until you're ready to break it. Then it's easy. It just goes pop and it's done. Nothing anyone can do.'

'But Bea, what's he got planned?'

'He says he'll reduce gods to men. He told everyone this week that the next time the bell rings we have to go straight to the church.'

'And you're just telling me this now, Bea? We have to do something. People will get hurt.'

'No. He promised no one will get hurt. He'd never hurt anyone. He's not like that.'

'Why the hell's he doing it, then?'

'It's his beliefs, Bruno. He has to stay true to his religion.'

'That's bullshit. He must want power or money.'

'You have to believe in something, Bruno. He's liberating people. You've seen yourself how much the place has fallen apart under that religion of theirs. It's a cult. He's going to get rid of it. It's for the greater good.'

'It's not for the greater good, Bea! It's not safe for anyone here now. We have to do something.'

'Carlos isn't dangerous, Bruno. He's smart.'

'How could you get involved with that guy? You should have come with me, helped me build the brewery.'

'After what they did to Iansa? Never.'

'Let's not get into this. It's done. Just don't leave my side again.'

'He'd never hurt me or anyone else, I'm serious. Let's go to the *carrinhos* and relax. It's going to be fine.'

He followed her down the dune and waited as she bought a couple of beers from Kart de la Revolución.

They watched the mingling tourists, as they sipped their drinks: strangers talking, drinking, fighting and fucking. The guy with the sunburned nose was amongst them, as was Carlos, who was performing his usual old magic tricks. He waved his empty hands in front of the guy's face then reached out and produced a coin from behind his ear. Bruno turned away from them so he could enjoy this time with Bea. He didn't want to leave her but knew that the time when he'd have to was coming fast. He watched her face and tried to commit it to the depths of his mind, where it would always be safe.

They sat talking long after midnight. Bruno was happy that while Carlos was there, he didn't come near them, nor give a sign he'd even seen them, but after he'd left, Bruno couldn't get him out of his head. The crowd got bigger, the music louder and Bruno watched Bea's eyes grow heavier with every sip.

He was sure he could smell a trace of frankincense in the air, and remembered when Carlos had burned a stone of it on the hot coal, how gripping it had been on him, just like the strange harmonies and rhythms of the drummer women.

'You're getting tired,' he said.

She smiled. 'I won't deny it. Maybe I should get some sleep.'

'Go to the bedsit, Bea. I'll sleep on the floor or in the hammock at the brewery if you want privacy.'

She put a hand on his arm. 'I'm a big girl, Bruno. I might not look like it or act it sometimes, but I am. You're going to have to realise that and let me go. Stop being afraid for me.'

'I can't help it.'

'You can,' she said, kissing him on the cheek as she stood. 'You will.' She slipped into the crowd.

*

Bruno caught glimpses of Bea as she eased through the tourists, heading towards the day-bars. He bought another beer, leaned against the outside wall of Ivo's, and watched the people. Generation after generation, they'd all do exactly the same thing, make the same mistakes, share the same highs, think the same thoughts. There was nothing that could be experienced now that hadn't been lived through before. He visualised following the beach northwards, finding the river and skirting it all the way inland. It had always thrilled yet terrified him because he had been looking at every decision as a permanent choice. Now he understood that nothing was permanent. He was free to go wherever he wanted, and if what he found there didn't suit him, he could go elsewhere and do something new.

Above the conversation and the music came a scream unlike any he'd ever heard before. It drilled into his bones rather than sounded in his ears. He threw his cup aside, pushed through the crowd and sprinted past the day-bars. 'Bea!' he shouted, rounding the corner and running up the path. Lights in the neighbouring houses flicked on. People were out in their gardens calling into the darkness.

In the dim light from the windows, Bea stood over a man on his knees screaming into his hands. Her eyes were wide and unblinking. Blood tracked from her mouth and down her naked torso to the waistband of her skirt. 'Bea,' Bruno said. 'You're bleeding. What's he done?' He took off his shirt and pressed it to her mouth.

'It's not mine.' She stared past him in a daze. Her hair was tangled and covered in sand.

Bruno looked at her lips, then down at the tourist. Though his blood-caked hands were covering his face, Bruno could tell it was the man with the bulbous nose he'd seen on the dune and then with Carlos at the *carrinhos*.

'He tried to rape me,' she said, emotion rising in her voice.

'I didn't!' the man screamed. 'She's lying. She attacked me!'

'Put this on.' Bruno helped slip the shirt over her head.

Others from the *carrinhos* appeared. A local and two tourists knelt by the man and tried to calm him.

'She bit me,' he shouted. 'My nose. It's hanging off!'

The faces of all present turned towards Bea.

'He's a rapist!' she said. 'Look at my shirt! My underwear!' She pointed them out on the path.

By the torn clothes Bruno noticed the whistle he'd given her months ago. He stiffened as the need to protect and defend her surged through him. 'That's all the evidence right there,' he said.

'He pinned me down by my face. Look, his fly's still open.'

'She's a liar! I was taking a piss. She attacked me.'

The people assisting the man managed to get his hands

lowered to see his wounds. There was a silence then a girl vomited. His nose had been completely torn off. A red bubble of snot blew from one of the black craters within the triangle of blood and gore.

The local tending to the man came up to Bea. 'Where is it?' he whispered.

'I don't know where it is!' She threw her arms out. 'I had no choice. It's all I could do to defend myself.'

'A torch!' the local shouted at the people in their gardens. 'Bring a fucking torch, quick.'

'She's been flirting with him every night!' called a voice from the crowd. 'Whore,' shouted another. 'She's been asking for it. Flirts with everybody!'

'Fuck you!' she screamed. Tears fell from her eyes. 'It was rape. What could I do?' She turned to the tourist, who cupped his face again. 'You know the truth! You know what you are. Tell them!' She raised a foot to kick sand at him, but Bruno got hold of her.

'Come,' he said, dragging her away. 'Forget them. Let's take care of you.' He shouted over his shoulder at the crowd: 'You all know what happened here. She's the real victim. It was all in self-defence.' Nobody followed as he led her up the trail.

'Hold on,' she said at the opening of the campsite. 'Something's stuck.'

By the wall of a lit-up garden, Bruno got her to raise her face and bare her gums. He pulled a string of gristle from between her teeth and flicked it to the ground.

Carlos was sitting in the red glow of the fire when they approached the camp. Bruno shouted for him to bring some water. He didn't move. A smile came to his face.

'Some water, Carlos,' Bruno said again. 'She's been attacked.'

Carlos stayed put.

'Get some clothes,' Bruno said to Bea. He opened the tent for her. As she slipped inside, he whispered to Carlos

'They'll come for her, you know that. She defended herself.'
He lowered his voice further. 'The guy's nose is off. They'll
empty this whole campsite.'

'I suppose she's told you all about me, hasn't she?' Carlos's
voice boomed as he got to his feet. 'At least she served her
purpose. No point in playing the fool any more, aye?' He
stepped over to the storage compartment, flung it open and
carried the statue out. 'Chaos from control,' he said, 'feigned
weakness from strength, illusion of fear from courage. You
really thought I was scared of him?' He carried the statue
towards the church.

There was nothing Bruno could say. He watched him set
the statue against the cross. It had been made to measure.
He turned to see Bea with her head lowered, crying into
a bundle of clothes hugged to her chest. 'Come,' he said.
'You're safe now. We'll get you all cleaned up.'

'I don't want to be alone.' Her voice broke into sobs.

'I'll be right outside the door. You did good, Bea. I'm
proud of you. Don't be afraid.'

He led her into the cubicle and turned the water on for
her.

From Main Street, a few travellers walked up to Carlos
and stood admiring the statue.

'Hear about what happened?' one of them asked him.

Carlos nodded. 'Nose gone clean off. Stand by the
toilets,' he told them and approached the church doors.
With one heavy tug of the cord, the church bell rang out
and he marched into town.

Travellers came from around their fires and out of their
tents. They stood at the toilets beside Bruno. Abilio, holding
the infant, pointed him out to Adelina. 'Got some nerve
standing here. Go be with your townsfolk.'

'It's about Bea,' Bruno said. 'Someone attacked her. She's
in the toilets.'

'Luna,' Adelina said to a woman with dreadlocks standing
next to a tall man, 'come with me.' They entered the toilets.

Bruno went in behind them. 'Beatriz dear, it's Adelina and Luna. Let us in, dear.'

The door unlatched and they slipped inside. 'Oh you poor thing,' Luna said. Bruno went back outside and waited. They emerged a few minutes later with Bea, fully dressed, her eyes cast downwards, her lip swollen and her chin red from the man's hand. She was trembling.

They took her to stand with the rest of the travellers. Bruno followed them. The fire-fighting team began to congregate. There were more farmers and fisher-folk than Bruno had ever seen. They gathered around watching the church, looking from each other to the travellers.

With flaming torches held high, Mac led the locals into the opening. He staked his torch a few steps back from the driftwood cross, before Ivo and Lagarto did the same. The others formed a semicircle at their heels, staking their torches in the sand at their sides. Mac looked at the large crowd of elders, and then the statue. Bruno noticed a slight squinting of his eyes, a twitch of his head. It was as if he'd put it all together but didn't quite believe it and cast the thought aside. He fixed his attention on the campsite.

'Come forward where I can see you,' Mac roared at the travellers. 'Come out before I drag you from your squalor.'

Travellers were still returning from town. Some drunken tourists who must have heard the bell ringing had arrived to investigate. They stood off near the houses and watched with belittling smiles on their faces. Bruno could hear more tent zips being undone. The crowd around him swelled. He looked down at Bea, then smiled at Adelina, who held her close, with Luna at her other side. They'd had their disagreements, but he was glad she was here tonight to provide a motherly touch when Bea needed it most.

'This tramp,' said Mac, singling Bea out to everyone there, 'has attacked a tourist. Unprovoked! Vicious! Dangerous woman!'

'It's lies,' Bea cried. 'It's all lies!'

Mac continued as murmuring undertones spread through the crowds. 'The attack has left him completely disfigured. His nose has been bitten off!'

Bruno hated to see the way people were looking at Bea. 'He tried to rape her!' he shouted. 'She did what she had to!'

Mac ignored him and addressed the growing crowd of tourists. 'The victim is receiving medical treatment. We're arranging a 4×4 to take him to the best hospital in the city. We found the detached part, and have it on ice, but it'll be a miracle if they can reattach it.'

The tourists glared at Bea. 'Throw her out!' one shouted. 'Lock her up!' said another. A camera flashed.

'You tourists mean everything to us. Your safety,' Mac looked into their faces, 'is our primary concern, and for that,' he turned again to the travellers, 'I'm clearing the campsite tonight. All you travellers will leave at once and you're never coming back.'

All around him, Bruno heard the groans of disapproval. Adelina and Luna backed away from Bea and joined the others. A space opened between the travellers and Bruno and Bea. 'Where's Carlos?' one of them asked.

Bruno stared at Adelina. He pulled Bea to him and hugged her. 'Don't mind them, Bea. Don't listen.'

'This isn't fair,' Adelina shouted. 'Was she who did it, not us! We've done nothing.'

'I didn't do anything either!' Bea screamed.

'Shh,' said Bruno. He put his hands on her ears but she shrugged them off.

'She's not with us,' Fortunato called out. 'Always worked alone, she did. Was never one of us.'

'That's right,' said a bald man in camouflage trousers. 'Throw her out. Can't punish us none for this!'

The travellers roused themselves up into a fury of protests to Mac, and anger at Bea. Their innocence and distance from her could not be questioned. 'Both of you,' Abilio said, looking at Bruno. 'Both of you get out of here.'

'Silence!' Mac ordered. 'Bruno! Come here.'

Bruno shook his head. 'No.'

Mac cleared his throat. 'There is no option! You stand with us, now.'

From Main Street, Carlos strode between the tourists and locals then stood by the farmers and fisher-folk. Mac understood it all then. '*Malandro*,' he uttered. He sniffed the air and looked back at the town. There was an orange glow behind the rooftops. 'Go and put out that fire!' he shouted at the elders.

'Stay where you are,' Carlos commanded. He smiled at Mac.

'Now!' Mac demanded of them. He eyed Carlos and walked to the statue. His leg swung in a low arc. The clatter of his shin on the wood echoed as the cross split at the base and the whole thing dropped to the sand.

A few elders began to move but Carlos stopped them. 'Stay!' he warned. 'Stay.'

'You're leaving with the rest of the scum,' Mac said to him.

'I'll be staying,' said Carlos.

Bruno noticed Anderson coming up the trail and waved to him. 'Anderson,' he shouted. 'Over here.'

Anderson came into the clearing and passed into everyone's view. His path didn't waver. 'Anderson,' Bruno shouted again, 'we need you. Bea needs you.' Anderson glanced at him and Bea, rubbed the back of his neck but walked straight ahead, passing Mac to join Carlos.

'You?' Bruno said. 'He got to you?'

'Anderson!' Mac called at the same instant. 'You of all people betray me?'

Bruno looked at Mac and back to Anderson, who slipped into the crowd behind Carlos. He realised what had been going on, and ran over. 'The whole time, Anderson! This whole fucking time you were spying and reporting back to him!' He pointed at Mac. 'Anderson, it was all an act?

Look me in the eye. And now you're standing now with this maniac? Bea was almost raped!'

'I tried to tell you!' Anderson said. 'I told you to look out for yourself and nobody else, but you wouldn't hear it.'

'What about us, Carlos?' Abilio shouted over. 'We're staying too, right?'

'You are,' Carlos confirmed, 'but a crime has been committed, and without a court, we have to send both away. That's fairness. That's balance. The girl will leave tonight, and the tourist also.'

'You know her name,' said Bruno. 'Use her name.' When Carlos didn't speak, he returned to Bea. He started to lead her away but stopped. 'Wait,' he told her, and stepped back into the space between the crowds.

'You've made a big enough spectacle of yourself,' Mac shouted to him. Go put that fire out!' He turned to the elders and cleared his throat. 'You old fools! You think you can make something of this town with him? It won't last a week. This rodent will take everything you have! I took you in! I looked after you when you had nothing! You came begging, and I gave you a salary! I gave you a house! And this is what you do?'

'Ignore him,' Carlos said. 'He's the source of his own failure, but he doesn't know it. He's too blind to see that *he's* the cause of this bad energy! He and no one else. The *hounfort* burns! The office burns! All your troubles are brought by him! I've answered the prayers you've been voicing for decades.' He spoke to the locals behind Mac. 'It's not too late, children. Cross over. Come to me, all of you, you're weary and burdened, you don't know what he's done. Come over now. Only with me is there hope!' The locals grew agitated. They whispered amongst themselves and looked from Carlos to Mac.

'Listen to you! Look at you all!' Bruno shouted. 'You're all using this for your own advantage! You know what went on here tonight. She's the victim! Not the tourist. Not you!

Can't we all stand up for what's right? Isn't that best for us all? She was attacked and defended herself the only way she could. You all know it! Adelina,' he said, approaching her. 'You know that's right, can't you stand up for her?'

'Got my baby to feed, do I not?' she said in a thin voice, shuffling behind Abilio.

'Anderson!' Bruno ran up to him again and put his hands on his shoulders. 'You love this girl, or was that an act too? Do the right thing, Anderson. You want to be judged on this?'

Anderson shrugged him off and stood back. He wouldn't look him in the eye. 'God's all I have to answer to. Don't bring guilt into this. I'm standing behind Carlos.'

'Behind him? Hear yourself! Not side by side but behind! Don't do this, Anderson. Don't be a coward. You,' he said, turning to Carlos. 'What have you got to say?'

'God's will,' said Carlos, with a shrug. 'We all saw how she flirted, how she walked around with those clothes, swinging her hips, showing her body. She was asking for something to happen, begging for it. This is her own doing. The good people of this town will not suffer for the error of her ways.'

'Yeah!' shouted one of the tourists. 'She didn't have to bite his bloody nose off!'

'This is entertainment for you!' Bruno shouted. 'You come here and laugh at the simple, little people, flash your cameras a few times before going home to your big, cosmopolitan lives thinking you're better than all this. You're far from better, believe me.

'Is there anybody here willing to stand up for her?' He looked at the faces behind Mac, caught Hermes's eye and ran to him. 'Hermes, please! Come stand with us.'

'I'm sorry, Bruno,' Hermes whispered. 'I really am.'

'Valter! Riccardo! Tiago! Come on, this is your chance.' He looked around at the faces in every group. 'Don't spend the rest of your lives wishing you made a stand… Luis!' He saw him in the crowd behind Carlos. 'Papa!' He noticed

Fatima and swallowed hard. 'Fatima! Fatima,' he sighed. 'Really? He got to you? Surely you have something to say?'

She shook her head. He looked into her eyes, pleading to them, but she turned away from him. The necklace he'd given her was still around her neck.

Everywhere he looked he saw blank, indifferent faces. All of them were standing, waiting for something to happen, waiting for someone else to tell them what to do. He saw a man amongst the elders, an apron folded at his waist, his T-shirt covered in flour. The secret baker. Bruno raised his palms to him and waited for a response. The baker dusted his trousers and stared back.

'She's a whore!' someone shouted from Mac's group.

'She's not a fucking whore!' Bruno shot back. 'She's a virgin! She's innocent. How can we expect anything if we can't even unite on this? Tiago, I just fucking told you that today! What will happen if we let selfishness, greed and fear rule us like it always has? If we let false prophets like this,' he held a hand out at Mac, 'and criminal manipulators like him,' he pointed the other at Carlos, 'control our actions and suppress our thoughts? It's not just them, we do it to ourselves. Stop it now or be ashamed. All of you, take action or forever hang your head.'

Before he could say any more, as everyone's eyes were on him, he noticed Carlos walk up to the row of torches in front of the locals, pick two up and rush at the church door.

'What the hell are you—' Mac didn't finish.

With one kick, the door burst open. Carlos tossed the torches inside, and the dried grass that matted the floor caught fire. He stood in front of the door and held his arms out in a cross as the flames rose behind him. Sparks flew from the building and caught the bushes around it. Flames erupted from them. The crowd on both sides gasped, elders and some travellers began crossing themselves. A coil of wire around Carlos's wrist flashed gold in the blaze. Bruno's final dream about Honey flooded his mind. He'd dreamt of wire

406

wrapping around her wrist, not twine like the tourists had been caught with. Wire.

'It was you!' he screamed at Carlos. 'You did it. You did everything!' The truth of all that had happened unravelled quicker than he could tell it. He walked towards him. Carlos, who had turned water into wine. Carlos, who could make you see red ink when it was blue, who'd been prying in Bea's head all this time, his little *jack-o'-lantern*. He'd been with the tourist just before she was attacked. Carlos had been the architect of it all. 'You set it all up. You framed the tourists and threw her in the well. You got Adelina to steal the meat. Always right next to Faka at the *carrinhos*, muttering your stupid chants and whatever else you do to control people… It was him!' Bruno said to all around. 'He planted the club in the butcher's shop. He messed with Faka's head. He made the tourist ring the bell and he murdered—' Before he could finish his sentence, a dark blur flew past him, knocking him off his feet. From the sand, he saw Carlos backing away as Mac stalked after him. The crowds closed in, goading each other, advancing and retreating, but always focusing on Mac and Carlos.

Mac leapt forward, pivoted and threw the same kick he'd delivered to Faka. Somehow, Carlos escaped under it, but he couldn't avoid Mac's fist. It drove into Carlos's ribs like the piston of a steam engine. It was a punch that would have laid most men flat, if not killed them. Carlos collapsed to a knee and gripped his flank. As Mac rushed in with another kick, something flashed in Carlos's fist. Mac winced and almost tripped as he retreated, trying to hide the limp the cut had given him. Carlos got to his feet and smiled. Mac smiled right back, but it was a forced one. He threw another kick that Carlos blocked with his hands. The knife flew from them. Mac swung a punch that caught Carlos on the forehead. As he wiped his skull and looked for blood, Bruno saw Mac shake his hand. It was broken. Carlos slipped in under another swing from Mac and got a hand around the back of his head. He drove punch after punch into Mac's face. Mac tried to pull away but Carlos got his other hand around his neck and was lifted off the ground as Mac arched his back trying to pull away. They fell over with Carlos landing on top. He drove punches, knees and elbows into Mac's face and body with a ferociousness that had both parties ignoring pleading for an end to it. Even the travellers called for it to stop. Mac curled up to protect his face, but the punches were still getting through. 'Arrogance is your downfall!' Carlos shouted as he struck him. 'Ignorance! Corruption! Exploitation! Murder!'

Ivo, Lagarto and some others moved forward to help, only to be met by Golias, Fortunato and newcomers that Bruno didn't recognise. They faced each other, ready to jump in if either group got involved.

A knee drove between Mac's arms, snapping his head back. He went limp.

In the silence, Carlos got to his feet, sweating and bloodied. He seemed taller and stronger. He stared at all present in the same way Faka had done after he butchered Iansa, mocking and defiant. Mac's eyes twitched. He rose to his knees. Blood dripped from his mouth and nose and pooled on the sand. He spat out a tooth. It glowed white in the crimson puddle. Ivo, Lagarto and the closest *capoeiristas* tended to him. Ivo took off his T-shirt and tied it around the cut on Mac's calf, Lagarto balled his vest and pressed it into Mac's mouth and nose. The travellers cheered and screamed at Mac and the locals, many of whom stood still, eyes fixed on their leader, broken, bleeding and defeated. Abilio and Fortunato took Carlos's hands and raised them above his head.

'You lot,' Carlos said to the *capoeiristas*, shaking Abilio and Fortunato off. 'Don't let the fire spread.' They didn't move. 'What's happened has happened. There's no time for shock. Do as you're told.' The elders had merged with the travellers during the fighting. He approached them all.

'Was I wrong? Is it not as I said it would be? God is smiling down upon us now, the true God, not this man lying before you. See his blood? See his bone? Gods will become men, did I not say that? I am the light, not he. I am the way, not he. Follow me from this moment forward and believe now, if you didn't believe before.' He led them into town, many of the elders trailing behind, shocked and afraid at what they had seen. 'There is still time to cross over,' he said as he passed the locals, their incomprehension at what had happened visible in their eyes. 'I will forgive you.'

Bruno went to Bea and took her in his arms. The night sky was aglow in red and orange. Everywhere was the smell of smoke, the noise of burning. He helped her pack her tent as those who'd remained in the campsite celebrated their victory. By the time they got to the top of the dune, the light blue of dawn was rising above the red flames and the grey smoke. He heard the frantic cries of the locals trying to put the fires out. It was pointless. They were all too late.

He thought back to what Flora had said about people not looking inside themselves, how they always looked to others for the solution. He pictured all those blank, indifferent faces tonight and realised there was more to them than that. They were not real faces but masks, worn to hide the embarrassment, the fear and the knowledge that what they were doing was wrong. They didn't have the courage to take the masks off. He couldn't hate them for it. In spite of it all he was filled with hope. Some of them were almost ready. Some nearly came over under his influence. It would come together eventually, he knew. Someday they'd get it right. He pictured the faces he'd come to know well over the time he'd been there. Regardless of whether they'd had a positive or a negative impact upon him, they'd all contributed to what he'd become. Their paths had led them to this town, just as his had, but theirs had ended here. His path was still open.

'I'm shaking.' Bea rubbed her eyes with the handkerchief he'd given her. 'I can't take it all in. I can't believe it happened. Did he really kill her?'

'Hush, Bea, don't think about it. You did so well tonight. Are you sure you don't want to wait until morning?'

'No. I don't want to spend another minute near this place. Let's start walking. It'll keep my mind occupied. Keep talking to me. I don't want to think. Why didn't you take your things?'

'I don't need them any more. I don't need anything. It's going to be a long hike to the city, Bea. You can help me build our shelters for the nights. I can teach you how to forage, how to purify water.' He didn't mention the time they could save by following the road, or the possibility of hitchhiking. If they took the coastal trail through the mangroves and the forest, he could prolong the few days he had left with her.

'Where will you go?' she asked.

He was already picturing his walk north from that last city, the trail opening up before him, the wind in his face, the noise of the sea in his ears and the heat of the sun on his body. He could see the expanse of the river. The ebb and flow, the landscape around it. The forest was waiting.

His eyes grew hot and his vision blurred so much that he could barely see her. He heard her sigh and felt the warmth of her body as she embraced him. He put his hand under her chin and tilted her face up so he could look into her eyes. He stroked the hair down either side of her face, touched his forehead to hers, and tried to speak to her straight from his heart. *I love you*, he said. *I love you, I love you, I love you.*

Dear Reader,

If you enjoyed this novel please consider helping it reach a wider audience by recommending it to a friend and leaving a review or a rating online.

Acknowledgements

A huge thank you to the writer Courttia Newland for his long-term belief, guidance, encouragement and support through every stage of this endeavour. Thanks to Professor A.C. Grayling for permitting the use of material from his book: *The Meaning of Things: Applying Philosophy to Life*. Thanks to Helen Baggott for proofreading, Adam French and the team at RefineCatch for typesetting, Isabel and the team at Clays for printing, Mike Coles for the cover, Stefeni Jung for the blurb and Juno for the copy edit. Thanks also to Lucy Chang, Anne Buchan, Debbie-Ann Noble and numerous others who gave feedback on earlier drafts and inspired me to keep going. Finally, thank you to my family.